XEELEE: ENDURANCE

OR BEFORE
LOW

XEELEE: ENDURANCE

STEPHEN BAXTER

GOLLANCZ

LONDON

The right of Stephen Baxter to be identified as the
author of this work has been asserted by him in accordance
with the Copyright, Designs and Patents Act 1988.

First published in Great Britain in 2015 by Gollancz
An imprint of the Orion Publishing Group
Carmelite House, 50 Victoria Embankment, London EC4Y 0DZ
An Hachette UK Company

A CIP catalogue record for this book is available
from the British Library

ISBN (Cased) 978 1 473 21270 1
ISBN (Export Trade Paperback) 978 1 473 201271 8

1 3 5 7 9 10 8 6 4 2

Typeset by Input Data Services Ltd, Bridgwater, Somerset

Printed and bound by CPI Group (UK) Ltd, Croydon CR0 4YY

The Orion Publishing Group's policy is to use papers
that are natural, renewable and recyclable products and
made from wood grown in sustainable forests. The logging
and manufacturing processes are expected to conform to
the environmental regulations of the country of origin.

www.stephen-baxter.com
www.orionbooks.co.uk
www.gollancz.co.uk

It was the fourth millennium.

Earth was restored. Great engineering projects had stabilised and preserved the planet's fragile ecosystem: Earth was the first planet to be terraformed.

Meanwhile, the Solar System was opened up. Based in the orbit of Jupiter, an engineer called Michael Poole industriously took microscopic wormholes – natural flaws in spacetime – and expanded them to make transit links big enough to pass spaceships, enabling the inner System to be traversed in a matter of hours rather than months.

Poole Interfaces were towed out of Jupiter's orbit and set up all over the System. The Jovian moons became hubs for interplanetary commerce.

And Poole and his colleagues pushed further out.

RETURN TO TITAN
AD 3685

PROLOGUE

The spacecraft from Earth sailed through rings of ice.

In its first week in orbit around Saturn it passed within a third of a million kilometres of Titan, Saturn's largest moon, sensors peering curiously down at unbroken haze. The craft had been too heavy to launch direct with the technology of the time, so its flight path, extending across seven years, had taken it on swingbys past Venus, Earth and Jupiter. Primitive it was, but it was prepared for Titan. An independent lander, a fat pie-dish three metres across, clung to the side of the main body.

Dormant for most of the interplanetary cruise, the probe was at last woken and released. And, two weeks later, it dropped into the thick atmosphere of Titan itself.

Much of the probe's interplanetary velocity was shed in ferocious heat, and then the main parachute inflated. Portals opened and booms unfolded, and, more than a billion kilometres from the nearest human engineer, instruments peered out at Titan. Some fifty kilometres up the surface slowly became visible. This first tantalising glimpse was like a high-altitude view of Earth, though rendered in sombre reds and browns.

The landing in gritty water-ice sand was slow, at less than twenty kilometres per hour.

After a journey of so many years the surface mission lasted mere minutes before the probe's internal batteries were exhausted, and the chatter of telemetry fell silent. It would take two more hours for news of the adventure to crawl at light-speed to Earth – by which time a thin organic rain was already settling on the probe's upper casing, as the last of its internal heat leaked away.

And then, all unknown to the probe's human controllers back on Earth, a manipulator not unlike a lobster's claw closed around *Huygens'* pie-dish hull and dragged the crushed probe down beneath the water-ice sand.

1

'There's always been something wrong with Titan.'

These were the first words I ever heard Harry Poole speak – though I didn't know the man at the time – words that cut through my hangover like a drill.

'It's been obvious since the first primitive probes got there seventeen hundred years ago.' He had the voice of an old man, eighty, maybe even ninety, a scratchy texture. 'A moon with a blanket of air, a moon that cradles a whole menagerie of life under its thick atmosphere. But that atmosphere's not sustainable.'

'Well, the mechanism is clear enough. Greenhouse effects from the methane component keep the air from cooling and freezing out.' This was another man's voice, gravelly, sombre, the voice of a man who took himself too seriously. A voice that sounded familiar. 'Sunlight drives methane reactions that dump complex hydrocarbons in the stratosphere—'

'But, son, where does the methane come from?' Harry Poole pressed. 'It's destroyed by the very reactions that manufacture all those stratospheric hydrocarbons. Should all be gone in a few million years, ten million tops. So what replenishes it?'

At that moment I could not have cared less about the problem of methane on Saturn's largest moon, even though, I suppose, it was a central facet of my own career. The fog in my head, thicker than Titan's tholin haze, was lifting slowly, and I became aware of my body, aching in unfamiliar ways, stretched out on some kind of couch.

'Maybe some geological process.' This was a woman's voice, brisk. 'That or an ecology, a Gaia process that keeps the methane levels up. Those are the obvious options.'

'Surely, Miriam,' Harry Poole said. 'One or the other. That's been obvious since the methane on Titan was first spotted from Earth. But *nobody knows*. Oh, there have been a handful of probes over the centuries, but nobody's taken Titan seriously enough to nail it. Always too many other easy targets for exploration and colonisation – Mars, the ice moons. Nobody's even walked on Titan!'

Another man, a third, said, 'But the practical problems – the heat loss in that cold air – it was always too expensive to bother, Harry. And too risky . . .'

'No. Nobody had the vision to see the potential of the place. That's the real problem. And now we're hamstrung by these damn sentience laws.'

'But you think we need to go explore.' That gravel voice.

'We need Titan, son,' Harry Poole said. 'It's the only hope I see of making our wormhole link at Saturn pay for itself. Titan is, ought to be, the key to opening up Saturn and the whole outer System. We need to prove the sentience laws don't apply there, and move in and start opening it up. That's what this is all about.'

The woman spoke again. 'And you think this wretched creature is the key.'

'Given he's a sentience curator, and a crooked one at that, yes . . .'

When words like 'wretched' or 'crooked' are bandied about in my company it's generally Jovik Emry, my good self, that's being discussed. I took this as a cue to open my eyes. Some kind of glassy dome stretched over my head, and beyond that a slice of sky-blue. I recognised the Earth as seen from space. And there was something else, a sculpture of electric-blue thread that drifted over a rumpled cloud layer.

'Oh, look,' said the woman. 'It's alive.'

I stretched, swivelled and sat up. I was stiff and sore, and had a peculiar ache at the back of my neck, just beneath my skull. I looked around at my captors. There were four of them, three men and a woman, all watching me with expressions of amused contempt. Well, it wasn't the first time I'd woken with a steaming hangover in an unknown place surrounded by strangers. I would recover quickly. I was as young and healthy as I could afford to be: I was over forty, but AS-preserved at my peak of twenty-three.

We sat on couches at the centre of a cluttered circular deck, domed over by a scuffed carapace. I was in a GUTship, then, a standard interplanetary transport, if an elderly one; I had travelled in such vessels many times, to Saturn and back. Through the clear dome I could see more of those electric-blue frames drifting before the face of the Earth. They were tetrahedral, and their faces were briefly visible, like soap films that glistened gold before disappearing. These were the mouths of wormholes, flaws in spacetime, and the golden shivers were glimpses of other worlds.

I knew where I was. 'This is Earthport.' My throat was dry as Moon-dust, but I tried to speak confidently.

'Well, you're right about that.' This was the man who had led the conversation earlier. That ninety-year-old voice, comically, came out of the face of a boy of maybe twenty-five, with blond hair, blue eyes, a smooth AntiSenescence marvel. The other two men looked around sixty, but with AS so prevalent it was hard to tell. The woman was tall, her hair cut short, and she wore a functional jumpsuit; she might have been forty-five. The old-young man spoke again. 'My name is Harry Poole. Welcome to the *Hermit Crab*, which is my son's ship—'

'Welcome? You've drugged me and brought me here—'

One of the sixty-year-olds laughed, the gruff one. 'Oh, you didn't need drugging; you did that to yourself.'

'You evidently know me – and I think I know you.' I studied him. He was heavy set, dark, not tall, with a face that wasn't built for smil-ing. 'You're Michael Poole, aren't you? Poole the wormhole engineer.'

Poole just looked back at me. Then he said to the blond man, 'Harry, I have a feeling we're making a huge mistake trying to work with this guy.'

Harry grinned. 'Give it time, son. You've always been an idealist. You're not used to working with people like this. I am. We'll get what we want out of him.'

I turned to him. 'Harry Poole. You're Michael's father, aren't you?' I laughed at them. 'A father who AS-restores himself to an age younger than your son. How crass. And, Harry, you really ought to get some-thing done about that voice.'

The third man spoke. 'I agree with Michael, Harry. We can't work with this clown.' He was on the point of being overweight, and had a crumpled, careworn face. I labelled him as a corporate man who had grown old labouring to make somebody else rich – probably Michael Poole and his father.

I smiled easily, unfazed. 'And you are?'

'Bill Dzik. And I'll be working with you if we go through with this planned jaunt to Titan. Can't say it's an idea I like.'

This was the first I had heard of a trip to Titan. Well, whatever they wanted of me, I'd had quite enough of the dismal hellhole of the Saturn system, and had no intention of going back now. I had been in worse predicaments before; it was just a question of playing for time and looking for openings. I rubbed my temples. 'Bill – can I call you Bill? I don't suppose you could fetch me a coffee?'

'Don't push your luck,' he growled.

'Tell me why you kidnapped me.'

'That's simple,' Harry said. 'We want you to take us down to Titan.'

Harry snapped his fingers, and a Virtual image coalesced before us, a bruised orange spinning in the dark: Titan. It hung before Saturn itself, which was a pale-yellow crescent with those tremendous rings spanning space, and more moons suspended like lanterns. And there, glimmering in orbit just above the plane of the rings, was a baby-blue tetrahedral frame, the mouth of Michael Poole's latest wormhole, a hyper-dimensional road offering access to Saturn and all its wonders – a road, it seemed, rarely travelled.

'That would be illegal,' I pointed out.

'I know. And that's why we need you.' And Harry grinned, a cold expression on that absurdly young face.

2

'If it's an expert on Titan you want,' I said, 'keep looking.'

'You're a curator,' Miriam said, contempt thick in her voice. 'You work for the intra-System oversight panel on sentience law compliance. Titan is in your charge!'

'Not by choice,' I murmured. 'Look – as you evidently targeted me, you must know something of my background. I haven't had an easy career . . .' My life at school, supported by my family's money, had been a saga of drunken jaunts, sexual escapades, petty thieving and vandalism. As a young man I never lasted long at any of the jobs my family found for me, largely because I was usually on the run from some wronged party or other.

Harry said, 'Some career. In the end you got yourself sentenced to an editing, didn't you?'

If the authorities had had their way I would have had the contents of my much-abused brain downloaded into an external store, my memories edited, my unhealthy impulses 'reprogrammed', and the lot loaded back again – my whole self rebooted. 'It represented death to me,' I said. 'I wouldn't have been the same man as I was before. My father took pity on me—'

'And bought you out of your sentence,' Bill Dzik said. 'And got you a job in sentience compliance. A sinecure.'

I looked at Titan's dismal colours. 'It is a miserable posting. But it pays a bit, and nobody cares much what you get up to, within reason. I've only been out a few times to Saturn itself, and the orbit of Titan; the work's mostly admin, run from Earth. I've held down the job. Well, I really don't have much choice.'

Michael Poole studied me as if I were a vermin infesting one of his marvellous interplanetary installations. 'This is the problem I've got with agencies like the sentience-oversight curacy. I might even agree with its goals. But it doesn't do what it's supposed to achieve, all it does is get in the way of enterprise, and it's populated by time-wasters like you.'

I found myself taking a profound dislike to the man. Whatever my faults I'm no hypocrite, and I've never been able to stomach being preached at. 'I did nobody any harm,' I snapped back at him. 'Not much, anyhow. Not like you with your grand schemes, Poole, reordering the whole System for your own profit.'

Michael would have responded, but Harry held up his hand. 'Let's not get into that again. And after all he's right. Profit, or the lack of it, is the issue here. As for you, Jovik, even in this billion-kilometres-remote "sinecure" you're still up to your old tricks, aren't you?'

I said nothing, cautious until I worked out how much he knew.

Harry waved his hand at his Virtual projection. 'Look – Titan is infested with life. That's the basic conclusion of the gaggle of probes that, over the centuries, have orbited Titan or penetrated its thick air and crawled over its surface or dug into its icy sand. But life isn't the point. The whole Solar System is full of life. Life is commonplace. The question is sentience. And sentience holds up progress.'

'It's happened to us before,' Michael Poole said to me. 'The development consortium I lead, that is. We were establishing a wormhole Interface at a Kuiper object called Baked Alaska, thirteen years back, out on the rim of the System. Our plan was to use the ice as reaction mass to fuel GUTdrive starships. Well, we discovered life there, life of a sort, and it wasn't long before we identified sentience. The xenobiologists called it a Forest of Ancestors. The project ground to a halt; we had to evacuate the place—'

'Given the circumstances in which you've brought me here,' I said, 'I'm not even going to feign interest in your war stories.'

'All right,' Harry said. 'But you can see the issue with Titan. Look, we want to open it up for development. It's a factory of hydrocarbons and organics. We can make breathable air: nitrogen from the atmosphere, and oxygen extracted from water ice. We can use all that methane and organic chemistry to make plastics or fuel or even food. Titan *should* be the launch pad for the opening-up of the outer System, indeed the stars. But we're not going to be allowed to develop Titan if there's sentience there. And our problem is that, on this world with plenty of biochemistry and primitive life, nobody has established that there *isn't* intelligence too.'

I started to see it. 'So you want to mount a quick and dirty expedition – incidentally violating the planetary-protection aspects of the sentience laws – prove there's no significant mind down there, and get the clearance to move in the digging machines. Right?' And

I saw how Bill Dzik, Miriam and Michael Poole exchanged unhappy glances. There was dissension in the team over the morality of all this, a crack I might be able to exploit. 'Why do you need this so badly?' I asked.

So they told me. It was a saga of interplanetary ambition. But at the root of it, as is always the case, was money – or the lack of it.

3

Harry Poole said, 'You know our business, Jovik. Our wormhole engineering is laying down rapid-transit routes through the System, which will open up a whole family of worlds to colonisation and development. But we have grander ambitions than that.'

I asked, 'What ambitions? Starships? I read about that.'

'That and more,' Michael Poole said. 'For the last few decades we've been working on an experimental ship being built in the orbit of Jupiter . . .'

And he told me about his precious *Cauchy* project. By dragging a wormhole portal around a circuit light years across, the GUTship *Cauchy* would establish a wormhole bridge – not across space – but across fifteen centuries, to the future. So, having already connected the worlds of humanity with his wormhole subway, Michael Poole now hoped to short-circuit past and future themselves. That, at least, seemed to be the idea. I looked at Poole with new respect, and some fear. The man was a genius, or mad.

'But,' I said, 'to fund such dreams you need money.'

Harry said, 'Jovik, you need to understand that a mega-engineering business like ours is a ferocious devourer of cash. It's like the days of the pioneering railway builders back in the nineteenth century. We fund each new project with the profit of our previous ventures and with fresh investment – but that investment depends on the success of earlier schemes.'

'Ah. And now you're stumbling. Yes? And this is all to do with Saturn.'

Harry sighed. 'The Saturn transit was a logical development. The trouble is, nobody needs to go there. Saturn pales beside Jupiter! Saturn has ice moons; well, there are plenty in orbit around Jupiter. Saturn's atmosphere could be mined, but so can Jupiter's, at half the distance from Earth.'

Miriam said, 'Saturn also lacks Jupiter's ferociously energetic external environment, which we're tapping ourselves in the manufacture of the *Cauchy*.'

'Fascinating,' I lied. 'You're an engineer too, then?'

'A physicist,' she replied, awkward. She sat next to Michael Poole but apart from him. I wondered if there was anything deeper between them.

'The point,' said Harry, 'is that there's nothing at Saturn you'd want to go there for – no reason for our expensive wormhole link to be used. Nothing except—'

'Titan,' I said.

'If we can't go in legally, we need somebody to break us through the security protocols and *get* us down there.'

'So you turned to me.'

'The last resort,' said Bill Dzik with disgust in his voice.

'We tried your colleagues,' Miriam said. 'They all said no.'

'Well, that's typical of that bunch of prigs.'

Harry, always a diplomat, smiled at me. 'So we're having to bend a few pettifogging rules, but you have to see the vision, man, you have to see the greater good.'

'Have I? Actually the question is, what's in it for me? You know I've come close to the editing suites before. Why should I take the risk of helping you now?'

'Because,' Harry said, 'if you don't you'll *certainly* face a reboot.' So now we came to the dirty stuff, and Harry took over; he was clearly the key operator in this little cabal, with the engineer types uncomfortably out of their depth. 'We know about your sideline.'

With a sinking feeling I asked, 'What sideline?'

And he used his Virtual display to show me. There went one of my doctored probes arrowing into Titan's thick air, a silver needle that stood out against the murky organic backdrop, supposedly on a routine monitoring mission – but in fact with a quite different objective.

There are pockets of liquid water to be found just under Titan's surface – frozen-over crater lakes, kept warm for a few thousand years by the residual heat of the impacts that created them. My probe now shot straight through the icy carapace of one of those crater lakes, and into the liquid water beneath. Harry fast-forwarded and we watched the probe's ascent module push its way out of the lake and up into the air, on its way to my colleagues' base on Enceladus.

'You're sampling the subsurface life from the lakes,' Harry said sternly. 'And selling the results.'

I shrugged; there was no point denying it. 'I guess you know the

15

background. The creatures down there are related to Earth life, but very distantly. Different numbers of amino acids, or something – *I* don't know. The tiniest samples are gold dust to the biochemists, a whole new toolkit for designer drugs and genetic manipulation . . .' I had one get-out. 'You'll have trouble proving this. By now there won't be a trace of our probes left on the surface.' Which was true; one of the many ill-understood aspects of Titan was that probes sent down to its surface quickly failed and disappeared, perhaps as a result of some kind of geological resurfacing.

Harry treated that with the contempt it deserved. 'We have full records. Samples of the material you stole from Titan. Even a sworn statement by one of your partners.'

I flared at that. 'Who?' But, of course, it didn't matter.

Harry said sweetly, 'The point is the sheer illegality – and committed by you, a curator, whose job is precisely to guard against such things. If this gets to your bosses, it's back to the editing suite for you, my friend, and this time even Papa won't be able to bail you out.'

'So that's it. Blackmail.' I did my best to inject some moralistic contempt into my voice. And it worked; Michael, Miriam, Bill wouldn't meet my eyes.

But it didn't wash with Harry. 'Not the word I'd use. But that's pretty much it, yes. So what's it to be? Are you with us? Will you lead us to Titan?'

I wasn't about to give in yet. I got to my feet. 'At least let me think about it. You haven't even offered me that coffee.'

Michael glanced at Harry, who pointed at a dispenser on a stand near my couch. 'Use that one.'

There were other dispensers in the cabin – why that particular one? I filed away the question and walked over to the dispenser. At a command it produced a mug of what smelled like coffee. I sipped it gratefully and took a step across the floor towards the transparent dome.

'Hold it,' Michael snapped.

'I just want to take in the view.'

Miriam said, 'OK, but don't touch anything. Follow that yellow path.'

I grinned at her. 'Don't *touch* anything? What am I, contagious?' I wasn't sure what was going on, but probing away at these little mysteries had to help. 'Please. Walk with me. Show me what you intend to do here.'

16

Miriam hesitated for a heartbeat. Then, with an expression of deep distaste, she got to her feet. She was taller than I was, and lithe, strong-looking.

We walked together across the lifedome, a half-sphere a hundred metres wide. Couches, control panels and data entry and retrieval ports were clustered around the geometric centre of the dome; the rest of the transparent floor area was divided up by shoulder-high partitions into lab areas, a galley, a gym, a sleeping area and shower. The layout looked obsessively plain and functional to me. This was the vessel of a man who lived for work, and only that; if this was Michael Poole's ship, it was a bleak portrait of him.

We reached the curving hull. Glancing down I could see the ship's spine, a complex column a couple of kilometres long leading to the lode of asteroid ice used for reaction mass by the GUTdrive module within. And all around us wormhole Interfaces drifted like snowflakes, while intra-System traffic passed endlessly through the great gateways.

'All this is a manifestation of your lover's vision,' I said to Miriam, who stood by me.

'Michael's not my lover,' she shot back, irritated. The electric-blue light of the exotic-matter frames shone on her cheekbones.

'I don't even know your full name,' I said.

'Berg,' she said reluctantly. 'Miriam Berg.'

'Believe it or not, I'm not a criminal. I'm no hero, and I don't pretend to be. I just want to get through my life, and have a little fun on the way. I shouldn't be here, and nor should you.' Deliberately I reached for her shoulder. A bit of physical contact might break through that reserve.

But my fingers *passed through* her flesh, breaking up into a mist of pixels until they were clear of her flesh, and then reformed. I felt a distant ache in my head.

I stared at Miriam Berg. 'What have you done to me?'

'I'm sorry,' she said gravely.

I sat on my couch once more – *my* couch, a Virtual projection like me, the only one in the dome I wouldn't have fallen through, and sipped a coffee from my Virtual dispenser, the only one that I could touch.

It was, predictably, Harry Poole's scheme. 'Just in case the arm-twisting over the sample-stealing from Titan wasn't enough.'

'I'm a Virtual copy,' I said.

'Strictly speaking, an identity backup . . .'

I had heard of identity backups, but could never afford one myself, nor indeed fancied it much. Before undertaking some hazardous jaunt you could download a copy of yourself into a secure memory store. If you were severely injured or killed, the backup could be loaded into a restored body, or a vat-grown cloned copy, or even allowed to live on in some Virtual environment. You would lose the memories you had acquired after the backup was made, but that was better than non-existence . . . That was the theory. In my opinion it was an indulgence of the rich; you saw backup Virtuals appearing like ghosts at the funerals of their originals, distastefully lapping up the sentiment.

And besides, the backup could never be *you*, the you who had died; only a copy could survive. That was the idea that started to terrify me now. I am no fool, and imaginative to a fault.

Harry watched me taking this in.

I could barely ask the question: 'What about me? The original. Did I die?'

'No,' Harry said. 'The real you is in the hold, suspended. We took the backup after you were already unconscious.'

So that explained the ache at the back of my neck: that was where they had jacked into my nervous system. I got up and paced around. 'And if I refuse to help? You're a pack of crooks and hypocrites, but I can't believe you're deliberate killers.'

Michael would have answered, but Harry held up his hand, unperturbed. 'Look, it needn't be that way. If you agree to work with us, *you*, the Virtual you, will be loaded back into the prime version. You'll have full memories of the whole episode.'

'But I won't be *me*.' I felt rage building. 'I mean, the copy sitting here. *I* won't exist any more – any more than I existed a couple of hours ago, when you activated me.' That was another strange and terrifying thought. '*I* will have to die! And that's even if I cooperate. Great deal you're offering. Well, into Lethe with you. If you're going to kill *me* anyway I'll find a way to hurt you. I'll get into your systems like a virus. *You can't control me.*'

'But I can.' Harry clicked his fingers.

And in an instant everything changed. The four of them had gathered by Harry's couch, the furthest from me. I had been standing; now I was sitting. And beyond the curved wall of the transparent dome, I saw that we had drifted into Earth's night.

'How long?' I whispered.

'Twenty minutes,' Harry said carelessly. 'You have an off switch. Of course I can control you. So which is it to be? Permanent extinction for all your copies, or survival as a trace memory in your host?' His grin hardened, and his young-old face was cold.

So the *Hermit Crab* wheeled in space, seeking out the wormhole Interface that led to Saturn. And I, or rather *he* who had briefly believed he was me, submitted to a downloading back into his primary, myself. How ironic that this was a violation of the very sentience protection laws it was my duty to uphold.

He, the identity copy, died to save my life. I salute him.

4

Released from my cell of suspended animation, embittered, angry, I chose to be alone.

I walked to the very rim of the lifedome, where the transparent carapace met the solid floor. Looking down I could see the flaring of superheated, ionised steam pouring from the GUTdrive nozzles. The engine, as you would expect, was one of Poole's own designs. 'GUT' stands for 'Grand Unified Theory', which describes the fundamental forces of nature as aspects of a single superforce. This is creation physics. Thus men like Michael Poole use the energies which once drove the expansion of the universe itself for the triviality of pushing forward their steam rockets.

Soon the *Hermit Crab* drove us into the mouth of the wormhole that led to the Saturn system.

We flew lifedome first at the wormhole Interface, so that it was as if the electric-blue tetrahedral frame came down on us from the zenith. Those electric-blue struts were beams of exotic matter, a manifestation of a kind of antigravity field that kept this throat in space and time from collapsing. Every so often you would see the glimmer of a triangular face, a sheen of golden light filtering through from Saturn's dim halls. It was quite beautiful, a sculpture of light.

The frame bore down, widening in my view, and fell around us, obscuring the view of Earth and Earthport.

Now I was looking up into a kind of tunnel, picked out by flaring sheets of light. This was a flaw in spacetime itself; the flashing I saw was the resolution of that tremendous strain into exotic particles and radiations. As the ship thrust deeper into the wormhole, fragments of blue-white light swam from a vanishing point directly above my head and swarmed down the spacetime walls. There was a genuine sensation of speed, of limitless, uncontrollable velocity. The lifedome creaked like a tin shack, and I thought I could hear that elderly GUT-drive screaming with the strain. I gripped a rail and tried not to cower.

The passage was at least mercifully short. Amid a shower of exotic particles we ascended out of another electric-blue Interface – and I found myself back in the Saturn system, for the first time in years.

I could see immediately that we were close to the orbit of Titan about its primary, for the planet itself, suspended in the scuffed sky of the lifedome, was about the size I remembered it: a flattened globe a good bit larger than the Moon seen from Earth. Other moons hung around the sky, points of light. The sun was off to the right, with its close cluster of inner planets, so Saturn was half-full. Saturn's only attractive feature, the rings, were invisible, for Titan's orbit is in the same equatorial plane as the ring system and the rings are edge-on. But the shadow of the rings cast by the sun lay across the planet's face, sharp and unexpected.

There was nothing romantic in the view, nothing beautiful about it, not to me. The light was flat and pale. Saturn is about ten times as far from the sun as Earth is, and the sun is reduced to an eerie pinpoint, its radiance only a hundredth that at Earth: Saturn is misty and murky, an autumnal place. And you never forgot you were far from home when a human hand, held out at arm's length towards the sun, could have covered all of the orbit of Earth.

The *Crab* swung about and Titan itself was revealed, a globe choked by murky brown cloud from pole to pole, even more dismal and uninviting than its primary. Evidently Michael Poole had placed his wormhole Interface close to the moon in anticipation that Titan would someday serve his purposes.

Titan was looming larger, swelling visibly. Our destination was obvious.

Harry Poole took charge. He had us put on heavy, thick-layered exo-suits of a kind I'd never seen before. We sat on our couches like fat pupae; my suit was so thick my legs wouldn't bend properly.

'Here's the deal,' Harry said, evidently for my benefit. 'The *Crab* came out of the wormhole barrelling straight for Titan. That way we hope to get you down there before any of the automated surveillance systems up here can spot us, or do anything about it. In a while the *Crab* will brake into orbit around Titan. But before then you four in the gondola will be thrown straight into an atmospheric entry.' He snapped his fingers, and a hatch opened up in the floor beneath us to reveal the interior of another craft, mated to the base of the lifedome. This was evidently the 'gondola', some kind of landing shuttle. It was like a cave, brightly lit and with its walls crusted with data displays.

I said, '"Thrown straight in," Harry? And what about you?'

He smiled with that young-old face. 'I will be waiting for you in orbit. Somebody has to stay behind to bail you out, in case.'

'This "gondola" looks small for the four of us.'

Harry said, 'Well, weight has been a consideration. You'll mass no more than a tonne, all up.' He handed me a data slate. 'Now this is where you come in, Jovik. I want you to send a covering message to the sentience-law compliance control base on Enceladus.'

I stared at the slate. 'Saying what, exactly?'

Harry said, 'The entry profile is designed to mimic an unmanned mission. You're going in hard, high deceleration. I want you to make yourselves look that way in the telemetry – as if this is just another unmanned probe going in for a bit of science, or a curacy inspection, or whatever it is you bureaucrat types do. Attach the appropriate permissions. I'm quite sure you're capable of that.'

I was sure of it too. I opened the slate with a wave of my hand, quickly mocked up a suitable profile, let Harry's systems check I hadn't smuggled in any cries for help, and squirted it over to Enceladus. Then I handed the slate back. 'There. Done. You're masked from the curacy. I've done what you want.' I waved at the looming face of Titan. 'So you can spare me from *that*, can't you?'

'We discussed that,' said Michael Poole, with just a hint of regret in his voice. 'We decided to take you along as a fall-back, Jovik, in case of problems, any kind of challenge from Enceladus. Even if they've discovered the craft is manned, having you aboard will give us some cover.'

I snorted. 'They'll see through that.'

Miriam shrugged. 'It's worth it if it buys us a bit more time.'

Bill Dzik stared at me, hard. 'Just don't get any ideas, desk jockey. I'll have my eye on you all the way down and all the way back.'

'And listen,' Harry said, leaning forward. 'If this works out, Jovik, you'll be rewarded. We'll see to that. We'll be able to afford it, after all.' He grinned that youthful grin. 'And just think. You will be one of the first humans to walk on Titan! So you see, you've every incentive to cooperate, haven't you?' He checked a clock on his data slate. 'We're close to the release checkpoint. Down you go, team.'

They all sneered at that word, 'team', and at the cheerful tone of the man who was staying behind. But we filed dutifully enough through the hatch and down into that cave of instrumentation, Miriam first, then me, and Bill Dzik at my back. Michael Poole was last in; I saw

22

him embrace his father, stiffly, evidently not a gesture they were used to.

In the gondola, our four couches sat in a row, so close that my knees touched Miriam's and Dzik's when we were all crammed in there in our suits. The hull was all around us, close enough for me to have reached out and touched it in every direction, a tight-fitting shell. Poole pulled the hatch closed, and I heard a hum and whir as the independent systems of this craft came online. There was a rattle of latches, and then a kind of sideways shove that made my stomach churn. We were already cut loose from the *Crab*, and were falling free, and rotating.

Poole touched a panel above his head, and the hull turned transparent. Now it was as if we four in our couches were suspended in space, surrounded by glowing instrument panels, and blocky masses that must be the power supply, life support, supplies. Above me the *Crab* slid across the face of Saturn, GUTdrive flaring, and below me the orange face of Titan loomed large.

I whimpered. I have never pretended to be brave.

Miriam Berg handed me a transparent bubble-helmet. 'Lethe, put this on before you puke.'

I pulled the helmet over my head; it snuggled into the suit neck and made its own lock.

Bill Dzik was evidently enjoying my discomfort. 'You feel safer in the suit, right? Well, the entry is the most dangerous time. But you'd better hope we get through the atmosphere's outer layers before the hull breaches, Emry. These outfits aren't designed to work as pressure suits.'

'Then what use are they?'

'Heat control,' Michael Poole said, a bit more sympathetic. 'Titan's air pressure is fifty per cent higher than Earth's, at the surface. But that thick cold air just sucks away your heat. Listen up, Emry. The gondola's small, but it has a pretty robust power supply – a GUTengine, in fact. You're going to need that power to keep warm. For short periods your suit will protect you; there are power cells built into the fabric. But you won't last more than a few hours away from the gondola. Got that?'

I was hardly reassured. 'What about the entry itself? Your father said we'll follow an unmanned profile. That sounds . . . vigorous.'

Bill Dzik barked a laugh. Nobody else replied.

Poole and the others began to work through pre-entry system

checks. Harry murmured in my ear, telling me that fresh identity backups had just been taken of each of us and stored in the gondola's systems. I was not reassured.

I lay helpless, trussed up and strapped in, as we plummeted into the sunlit face of Titan.

5

Fifteen minutes after cutting loose from the *Crab*, the gondola encountered the first wisps of Titan's upper atmosphere, thin and cold, faintly blue all around us. Still a thousand kilometres above the ground, I could feel the first faltering in the gondola's headlong speed. Titan's air is massive and deep, and I was falling backside first straight into it.

The first three minutes of the entry were the worst, as we plunged into the air with an interplanetary velocity, and our speed was reduced violently. Three hundred kilometres above the surface the deceleration peaked at sixteen gravities. Cushioned by Poole's inertial field I felt no more than the faintest shaking, but the gondola shuddered and banged. Meanwhile a shock wave preceded us, a cap of gas that glowed brilliantly: Titan air battered to plasma by the dissipating kinetic energy of the gondola.

This fiery entry phase was mercifully brief. But when it was over, still we fell helplessly. After another three minutes we were within a hundred and fifty kilometres of the surface, and immersed in an orange haze, the organic-chemistry products of the destruction of Titan's methane by sunlight. Poole tapped a panel, and a mortar fired above us, hauling out a pilot parachute a couple of metres across. This stabilised us in the thickening air, our backs to the surface, our faces to the sky. Then the main parachute unfolded, spreading reassuringly.

For fifteen minutes we drifted, sinking slowly into a deep ocean of cold, sluggish air. Poole and his colleagues worked at their slates, gathering data from sensors that measured the physical and chemical properties of the atmosphere. I lay silent, curious too, but frightened for my life.

As we fell deeper into the hydrocarbon smog the temperature fell steadily. Sixty kilometres above the surface we fell through a layer of cloud into clearer air beneath, and then, at forty kilometres, through a thin layer of methane clouds. The temperature was close to its minimum here, at only seventy degrees or so above absolute zero. Soon it would rise again. As Poole and his team had discussed, greenhouse effects from the mysterious methane that shouldn't have been there warm Titan's air all the way to the ground.

Fifteen minutes after its unpacking, the main parachute was cut away, and a smaller stabiliser canopy opened. *Much* smaller. We began to fall faster, into the deep ocean of air. 'Lethe,' I said. 'Why did we dump the big chute? We're still forty kilometres high!'

Bill Dzik laughed at me. 'Don't you know anything about the world you're supposed to be guarding, curator? The air's thick here, and the gravity's low, only a seventh of Earth normal. Under that big parachute we'd be hanging in the air all day . . .'

The gondola lurched sideways, shoved by the winds. At least that shut Dzik up. But the winds eased as we fell further, until the air was as still and turgid as deep water. We were immersed now in orange petrochemical haze, though the sun was plainly visible as a brilliant point source of light, surrounded by a yellow-brown halo. The crew gathered data on the spectra of the solar halo, seeking information on aerosols, solid or liquid particles suspended in the air.

And, gradually, beneath our backs, Titan's ground became visible. I twisted around to see. Cumulus clouds of ethane vapour lay draped over continents of water ice. Of the ground itself I saw a mottling of dark and white patches, areas huge in extent, pocked by what looked like impact craters, and incised by threading valleys cut by flowing liquid, ethane or methane. The crew continued to collect their science data. An acoustic sounder sent out complex pulses of sound. Miriam Berg showed me how some echoes came back double, with reflections from the surfaces and bottoms of crater lakes, like the one my sampling probe had entered.

The gondola rocked beneath its parachute. Poole had suspended the inertial shielding, and, swinging in Titan's one-seventh gravity, I was comfortable in my thick, softly layered exosuit. The crew's murmuring as they worked was professional and quiet. I think I actually slept, briefly.

Then there was a jolt. I woke with a snap. The parachute had been cut loose, and was drifting away with its strings dangling like some jellyfish. Our fall was slow in that thick air and gentle gravity, but fall we did!

And then, as Bill Dzik laughed at me again, a new canopy unfurled into the form of a globe, spreading out above us. It was a balloon, perhaps forty, fifty metres across; we were suspended from it by a series of fine ropes. As I watched a kind of hose snaked up from beneath the gondola's hull and pushed up into the mouth of the balloon, and it began to inflate.

'So that's the plan,' I said. 'To float around Titan in a balloon! Not very energetic for a man who builds interplanetary wormholes, Poole.'

'But that's the point,' Poole said testily, as if I had challenged his manhood. 'We're here under the noses of your curators' sensors, Emry. The less of a splash we make the better.'

Miriam Berg said, 'I designed this part of the mission profile. We're going to float around at this altitude, about eight kilometres up – well above any problems with the topography, but under most of the cloud decks. We ought to be able to gather the science data we need from here. A couple of weeks should be sufficient.'

'A couple of weeks in this coffin!'

Poole thumped the walls of the gondola. 'This thing expands. You'll be able to get out of your suit. It's not going to be luxury, Emry, but you'll be comfortable enough.'

Miriam said, 'When the time comes we'll climb back up to space from this altitude. The *Crab* doesn't carry an orbit-to-surface flitter, but Harry will send down a booster unit to rendezvous with us and lift the gondola to orbit.'

I stared at her. 'You're saying we don't carry the means of getting off this moon?'

Miriam said evenly, 'Mass issues. We need to stay under the curacy sensors' awareness threshold. Plus we're supposed to look like an unmanned probe, remember. Look, it's not a problem.'

'Umm.' Call me a coward, many have. But I didn't like the idea that my only way off this wretched moon was thousands of kilometres away, and my access to it depended on a complicated series of rendezvous and coupling manoeuvres. 'So what's keeping us aloft? Hydrogen, helium?'

Poole pointed at that inlet pipe. 'Neither. This is a hot-air balloon, Emry, a Montgolfier.' And he gave me a lecture on how hot-air technology is optimal if you must go ballooning on Titan. You have the buoyancy of the thick air, and the gravity is weak, and at such low temperatures you get a large expansion of your heated gas in response to a comparatively small amount of energy. Add all these factors into the kind of trade-off equation men like Poole enjoy so much, and out pops hot-air ballooning as the low-energy transport of choice on Titan.

Miriam said, 'We're a balloon, not a dirigible; we can't steer. But for a mission like this it's enough for us to go pretty much where the wind takes us; all we're doing is sampling a global ecosphere. And we can choose our course to some extent. The prevailing winds on Titan are easterly, but below about two kilometres there's a strong westerly component. That's actually a tide, raised by Saturn in the thick air down there. So we can select which way we get blown, just by ascending and descending.'

'More stealth, I suppose. No need for engines.'

'That's the idea. We've arrived in the local morning. Titan's day is fifteen Earth days long, and we can achieve a lot before nightfall – in fact I'm intending that we should chase the daylight. Right now we're heading for the south pole, where it's summer.' And at the summer pole, as even I knew, methane and ethane pooled in open lakes – the only stable bodies of surface liquid in the System, aside from those on Earth and Triton.

Poole grinned. 'Summer on Titan. And we're riding the oldest flying machine of all!' Evidently he was starting to enjoy himself.

Miriam smiled back, and their gloved hands locked together.

The envelope snapped and billowed above us as the warm air filled it up.

6

So we drifted over Titan's frozen landscape, heading for the south pole. For now Michael Poole kept us stuck in that unexpanded hull, and indeed inside our suits, though we removed our helmets, while the crew put the gondola through a fresh series of post-entry checks. I had nothing to do but stare out through the transparent walls at the very Earthlike clouds that littered the murky sky, or over my shoulder at the landscape that unfolded beneath me.

Now that we were low enough to make out detail, I saw that those darker areas were extensive stretches of dunes, lined up in parallel rows by the prevailing wind. The ground looked raked, like a tremendous zen garden. And the lighter areas were outcroppings of a paler rock, plateaus scarred by ravines and valleys. At this latitude there were no open bodies of liquid, but you could clearly see its presence in the recent past, in braided valleys and the shores of dried-out lakes. This landscape of dunes and ravines was punctuated by circular scars that were probably the relics of meteorite impacts, and by odder, dome-like features with irregular calderas – volcanoes that spewed a 'lava' of liquid water. All these features had names, I learned, assigned to them by Earth astronomers centuries dead, who had pored over the first robot-returned images of this landscape. But as nobody had ever come here those names, borrowed from vanished paradises and dead gods, had never come alive.

I listened absently as Poole and the others talked through their science programme. The atmosphere was mostly nitrogen, just as on Earth, but it contained five per cent methane, and that methane was the key to Titan's wonders, and mysteries. Even aside from its puzzling central role in the greenhouse effects which stabilised the atmosphere, methane was also central to the complicated organic chemistry that went on there. In the lower atmosphere methane reacted with nitrogen to create complex compounds called tholins, a kind of plastic, which fell to the ground in a sludgy rain. When those tholins landed in liquid water, such as in impact-warmed crater lakes, amino acids were produced – the building blocks of our kind of life . . .

As I listened to them debate these issues it struck me that none of them had begun his or her career as a biologist or climatologist: Poole and Berg had both been physicists, Dzik an engineer and more lately a project manager. However, both Berg and Dzik had had specialist training to a decent academic standard to prepare for this mission. Ambitious types like these expected to live a long time; periodically they would re-educate themselves and adopt entirely different professions. I have never had any such ambition. I had a good education that had bequeathed me a good vocabulary and got me selected for my sinecure as a curator, along with my father's influence – but that was about as much use as it had been to me. Why waste time going through it all again? Besides, somehow, despite AS technology, I do not imagine myself reaching any great age.

Their talk had an edge, however, even in those first hours. They were all ethically troubled by what they were doing, and those doubts surfaced now that they were away from Harry Poole's goading.

'At some point,' Miriam Berg said, 'we'll have to face the question of how we'll react if we *do* find sentience here.'

Bill Dzik shook his head. 'Sometimes I can't believe we're even here, that we're having this conversation at all. I remember exactly what you said on Baked Alaska, Michael. If we couldn't protect the ecology, "we'll implode the damn wormhole. We'll get funds for the *Cauchy* some other way." That's what you said.'

Poole said harshly, clearly needled, 'That was thirteen years ago, damn it, Bill. Situations change. People change. And the choices we have to make change too . . .'

As they argued, I was the only one looking ahead, the way we were drifting under our balloon. Through the murk I thought I could see the first sign of the ethane lakes of the polar regions, sheets of coal-black liquid surrounded by fractal landscapes, like a false-colour mock-up of Earth's own Arctic. And I thought I could see movement, something rising up off those lakes. Mist, perhaps? But there was too much solidity about those rising forms for that.

And then those forms emerged from the mist, solid and looming.

I pulled my helmet on my head and gripped my couch. I said, 'Unless one of you does something fast, we may soon have no choices left at all.'

They looked at me, the three of them in a row, distracted, absorbed by their science. Then they looked ahead, to see what I saw.

They were like birds, black-winged, with white lenticular bodies. Those wings actually flapped in the thick air as they flew up from the polar seas, a convincing simulacrum of the way birds fly in the air of Earth. Oddly they seemed to have no heads.

And they were coming straight towards us.

Michael Poole snapped, 'Lethe. Vent the buoyancy!' He stabbed at a panel, and the others went to work, pulling on their helmets as they did so.

I felt the balloon settle as the hot air was released from the envelope above us. We were sinking but we seemed to move in dreamy slow motion, while those birds loomed larger in our view with every heartbeat.

Then they were on us. They swept over the gondola, filling the sky above, black wings flapping in an oily way that, now they were so close, seemed entirely unnatural, not like terrestrial birds at all. They were huge, each with a wingspan of ten, fifteen metres. I thought I could *hear* them, a rustling, snapping sound carried to me through Titan's thick air.

And they tore into the envelope. The fabric was designed to withstand Titan's methane rain, not an attack like this; it exploded into shreds, and the severed threads waved in the air. Some of the birds suffered; they tangled with our threads or collided with each other and fell away, rustling. One crashed into the gondola itself, crumpled like tissue paper, and fell, wadded up, far below us.

And we fell too, following our victim–assassin to the ground. Our descent from the best part of eight kilometres high took long minutes; we soon reached terminal velocity in Titan's thick air and weak gravity. We had time to strap ourselves in, and Poole and his team worked frantically to secure the gondola's systems. In the last moment Poole flooded the gondola with a foam that filled the internal space and held us rigid in our seats, like dolls in packaging, sightless and unable to move.

Even so I felt the slam as we hit the ground.

7

The foam drained away, leaving the four of us sitting in a row. We had landed on Titan the way we had entered its atmosphere, backside first, and now we lay on our backs with the gondola tilted over, so that I was falling against Miriam Berg, and the mass of Bill Dzik was weighing on me. The gondola's hull had reverted to opacity so that we lay in a close-packed pearly shell, but there was internal light and the various data slates were working, though they were filled with alarming banks of red.

The three of them went quickly into a routine of checks. I ignored them. *I was alive.* I was breathing, the air wasn't foul, and I was in no worse discomfort than having Dzik's unpleasant bulk pressed against my side. Nothing broken, then. But I felt a pang of fear as sharp as that experienced by the Virtual copy of me when he had learned he was doomed. I wondered if his ghost stirred in me now, still terrified.

And my bowels loosened into the suit's systems. Never a pleasant experience, no matter how good the suit technology. But I wasn't sorry to be reminded that I was nothing but a fragile animal, lost in the cosmos. That may be the root of my cowardice, but give me humility and realism over the hubristic arrogance of a Michael Poole any day.

Their technical chatter died away.

'The lights are on,' I said. 'So I deduce we've got power.'

Michael Poole said, gruffly reassuring, 'It would take more than a jolt like that to knock out one of my GUTengines.'

Dzik said spitefully, 'If we'd lost power you'd be an icicle already, Emry.'

'Shut up, Bill,' Miriam murmured. 'Yes, Emry, we're not in bad shape. The pressure hull's intact, we have power, heating, air, water, food. We're not going to die any time soon.'

But I thought of the flapping birds of Titan and wondered how she could be so sure.

Poole started unbuckling. 'We need to make an external inspection. Figure out our options.'

Miriam followed suit, and laughed. She said to me, 'Romantic, isn't he? The first human footfalls on Titan, and he calls it an external inspection.' Suddenly she was friendly. The crash had evidently made her feel we had bonded in some way.

But Bill Dzik dug an elbow in my ribs hard enough to hurt through the layers of my suit. 'Move, Emry.'

'Leave me alone.'

'We're packed in here like spoons. It's one out, all out.'

Well, he was right; I had no choice.

Poole made us go through checks of our exosuits, their power cells, the integrity of their seals. Then he drained the air and popped open the hatch in the roof before our faces. I saw a sky sombre and brown, dark by comparison with the brightness of our internal lights. Flecks of black snow drifted down. The hatch was a door from this womb of metal and ceramics out into the unknown.

We climbed up through the hatch in reverse order from how we had come in: Poole, Dzik, myself, then Miriam. The gravity, a seventh of Earth's, was close enough to the Moon's to make that part of the experience familiar at least, and I moved my weight easily enough. Once outside the hull, lamps on my suit lit up in response to the dark.

I dropped down a metre, and thus drifted to my first footfall on Titan.

The sandy surface crunched under my feet. I knew the sand was water ice, grains hard as glass in the intense chill. The sand was ridged into ripples, as if by a receding tide, and pebbles lay scattered, worn and eroded. A wind buffeted me, slow and massive, and I heard a low bass moan. A black rain smeared my faceplate.

The four of us stood together, chubby in our suits, the only humans on a world larger than Mercury. Beyond the puddle of light cast by our suit lamps an entirely unknown landscape stretched off into the infinite dark.

Miriam Berg was watching me. 'What are you thinking, Jovik?' As far as I know these were the first words spoken by any human standing on Titan.

'Why ask me?'

'You're the only one of us who's looking at Titan and not at the gondola.'

I grunted. 'I'm thinking how like Earth this is. Like a beach somewhere, or a high desert, the sand, the pebbles. Like Mars, too, outside Kahra.'

'Convergent processes,' Dzik said dismissively. 'But *you* are an entirely alien presence. Here, your blood is as hot as molten lava. Look, you're leaking heat.'

And, looking down, I saw wisps of vapour rising up from my booted feet.

We checked over the gondola. Its inner pressure cage had been sturdy enough to protect us, but the external hull was crumpled and damaged, various attachments had been ripped off, and it had dug itself into the ice.

Poole called us together for a council of war. 'Here's the deal. There's no sign of the envelope; it was shredded, we lost it. The gondola's essential systems are sound, most importantly the power. The hull's taken a beating, though.' He banged the metal wall with a gloved fist; in the dense air I heard a muffled thump. 'We've lost the extensibility. I'm afraid we're stuck in these suits.'

'Until what?' I said. 'Until we get the spare balloon envelope inflated, right?'

'We don't carry a spare,' Bill Dzik said, and he had the grace to sound embarrassed. 'It was a cost-benefit analysis—'

'Well, you got that wrong,' I snapped back. 'How are we supposed to get off this damn moon now? You said we had to make some crackpot rendezvous with a booster pack.'

Poole tapped his chest, and a Virtual image of Harry's head popped into existence in mid-air. 'Good question. I'm working on options. I'm fabricating another envelope, and I'll get it down to you. Once we have that gondola aloft again, I'll have no trouble picking you up. In the meantime,' he said more sternly, 'you have work to do down there. Time is short.'

'When we get back to the *Crab*,' Bill Dzik said to Poole, 'you hold him down and I'll kill him.'

'He's my father,' said Michael Poole. '*I'll* kill him.'

Harry dissolved into a spray of pixels.

Poole said, 'Look, here's the deal. We'll need to travel if we're to achieve our science goals; we can't do it all from this south pole site. We do have some mobility. The gondola has wheels; it will work as a truck down here. But we're going to have to dig the wreck out of the sand first, and modify it. And meanwhile Harry's right about the limited time. I suggest that Bill and I get on with the engineering.

34

Miriam, you take Emry and go see what science you can do at the lake. It's only a couple of kilometres' – he checked a wrist map patch and pointed – 'that way.'

'OK.' With low-gravity grace Miriam jumped back up to the hatch, and retrieved a pack from the gondola's interior.

I felt deeply reluctant to move away from the shelter of the wrecked gondola. 'What about those birds?'

Miriam jumped back down and approached me. 'We've seen no sign of the birds since we landed. Come on, curator. It will take your mind off how scared you are.' And she tramped away into the dark, away from the pool of light by the gondola.

Poole and Dzik turned away from me. I had no choice but to follow her.

8

Walking any distance was surprisingly difficult.

The layered heat-retaining suit was bulky and awkward, but it was flexible, and in that Titan was unlike the Moon with its vacuum, where the internal pressure forces even the best skinsuits to rigidity. But on Titan you are always aware of the resistance of the heavy air. At the surface the pressure is half as much again as on Earth, and the density of the air four times that at Earth's surface. It is almost like moving underwater. And yet the gravity is so low that when you dig your feet into the sand for traction you have a tendency to go floating off the ground. Miriam showed me how to extend deep, sharp treads from the soles of my boots to dig into the loose sand.

It is the thickness of the air that is the survival challenge on Titan; you are bathed in an intensely cold fluid, less than a hundred degrees above absolute zero, that conducts away your heat enthusiastically, and I was always aware of the silent company of my suit's heating system, and the power cells that would sustain it for no more than a few hours.

'Turn your suit lights off,' Miriam said to me after a few hundred metres. 'Save your power.'

'I prefer not to walk into what I can't see.'

'Your eyes will adapt. And your faceplate has image enhancers set to the spectrum of ambient light here . . . Come on, Jovik. If you don't I'll do it for you; your glare is stopping me from seeing too.'

'All right, damn it.'

With the lights off, I was suspended in brown murk. But my eyes did adapt, and the faceplate subtly enhanced my vision. Titan opened up around me, a plain of sand and wind-eroded rock under an orange-brown sky – again not unlike Mars. Clouds of ethane or methane floated above me, and beyond them the haze towered up, layers of organic muck tens of kilometres deep. Yet I could see the sun in that haze, a spark low on the horizon, and facing it a half-full Saturn, much bigger than the Moon in Earth's sky. Of the other moons or the stars, indeed of the *Crab*, I could see nothing. All the colours were drawn from a palette of crimson, orange and brown. Soon my eyes longed for a bit of green.

When I looked back I could see no sign of the gondola, its lights already lost in the haze. I saw we had left a clear line of footsteps behind us. It made me quail to think that this was the only footstep trail on all this little world.

We began to descend a shallow slope. I saw lines in the sand, like tide marks. 'I think we're coming to the lake.'

'Yes,' Miriam said. 'It's summer here, at the south pole. The lakes evaporate, and the ethane rains out at the north pole. In time it will be winter here and summer there, and the cycle will reverse. Small worlds have simple climate systems, Jovik. As I'm sure a curator ought to know . . .'

We came to the edge of the ethane lake. In that dim light it looked black like tar, and sluggish ripples crossed its surface. Patches of something more solid lay on the liquid, circular sheets almost like lilies, repellently oily. The lake stretched off black and flat to the horizon, which curved visibly, though it was blurred in the murky air.

It was an extraordinary experience to stand there in an exosuit and to face an ocean on such an alien world, the sea black, the sky and the shore brown. And yet there was again convergence with the Earth. This was, after all, a kind of beach. Looking around I saw we were in a sort of bay, and to my right, a few kilometres away, a river of black liquid had cut a broad valley, braided like a delta, as it ran into the sea.

And, looking that way, I saw something lying on the shore, crumpled black around a grain of paleness.

Miriam wanted samples from the lake, especially of the plates of gunk that floated on the surface. She opened up her pack and extracted a sampling arm, a remote manipulator with a claw-like grabber. She hoisted this onto her shoulder and extended the arm, and I heard a whir of exoskeletal multipliers. As the arm plucked at the lily-like features, some of them broke up into strands, almost like jet-black seaweed, but the arm lifted large contiguous sheets of a kind of film that reminded me of the eerie wings of the Titan birds that had attacked us.

Miriam quickly grew excited at what she was finding.

'Life,' I guessed.

'You got it. Well, we knew it was here. We even have samples taken by automated probes. Though we never spotted those birds before.'

She hefted the lake stuff, films of it draped over her gloved hand, and looked at me. 'I wonder if you understand how exotic this is. I'm pretty sure this is silane life. That is, based on a silicon chemistry, rather than carbon . . .'

The things on the lake did indeed look like black lilies. But they were not lilies, or anything remotely related to life like my own. Life of our chemical sort is based on long molecules, with a solvent to bring components of those molecules together. Our specific sort of terrestrial life, which Miriam called 'CHON life', after its essential elements carbon, hydrogen, oxygen and nitrogen, uses water as its solvent, and carbon-based molecules as its building blocks: carbon can form chains and rings, and long stable molecules like DNA.

'But carbon's not the only choice, and nor is water,' Miriam said. 'At terrestrial temperatures silicon bonds with oxygen to form very stable molecules.'

'Silicates. Rock.'

'Exactly. But at *very* low temperatures, silicon can form silanols, which are capable of dissolving in very cold solvents – say, in this ethane lake here. When they dissolve they fill up the lake with long molecules analogous to our organic molecules. These can then link up into polymers using silicon-silicon bonds, silanes. They have weaker bonds than carbon molecules at terrestrial temperatures, but it's just what you need in a low-energy, low-temperature environment like this. With silanes as the basis you can dream up all sorts of complex molecules analogous to nucleic acids and proteins—'

'Which is what we have here.'

'Exactly. Nice complicated biomolecules for evolution to play with. They are more commonly found on the cooler, outer worlds – Neptune's moon Triton for example. But this lake is cold enough. The energy flow will be so low that it must take a *lo-ong* time for anything much to grow or evolve. But on Titan there is plenty of time.' She let the filmy stuff glide off her manipulator scoop and back into the lake. 'There's so much we don't know. There has to be an ecology in there, a food chain. Maybe the films are the primary producers – an equivalent of the plankton in our oceans, for instance. But where do they get their energy from? And how do they survive the annual drying-out of their lakes?'

'Good questions,' I said. 'I wish I cared.'

She stowed her sample bottles in her pack. 'I think you care more than you're prepared to admit. Nobody as intelligent as you is without curiosity. It goes with the territory. Anyhow we should get back to the gondola.'

I hesitated. I hated to prove her right, that there was indeed a grain of curiosity lodged in my soul. But I pointed at the enigmatic black form lying further along the beach. 'Maybe we should take a look at that first.'

She glanced at it, and at me, and headed that way without another word.

It turned out, as I had suspected, that the crumpled form was a bird. I recalled one hitting our gondola during their assault and falling away; perhaps this was that very casualty.

It was essentially a block of ice, about the size of my head, wrapped up in a torn sheet of black film. With great care Miriam used her manipulator arm to pick apart the film, as if she was unwrapping a Christmas present. The ice mass wasn't a simple lump but a mesh of spindly struts and bars surrounding a hollow core. It had been badly damaged by the fall. Miriam took samples of this and of the film.

'That ice lump looks light for its size,' I said. 'Like the bones of a bird.'

'Which makes sense if it's a flying creature.' Miriam was growing excited. 'Jovik, look at this. The filmy stuff of the wings looks identical to the samples I took from the surface of the lake. It has to be silane. But the ice structure is different.' She broke a bit of it open, and turned on a suit lamp so we could see a mass of very thin icicles, like fibres. It was almost sponge-like. Inside the fine ice straws were threads of what looked like discoloured water. 'Rich in organics,' Miriam said, glancing at a data panel on her manipulator arm. 'I mean, our sort of organics, CHON life, carbon-water – amino acids, a kind of DNA. There are puzzles here. Not least the fact that we find it *here*, by this lake. CHON life has been sampled on Titan before. But it's thought carbon-water life can only subsist here in impact-melt crater lakes, and we're a long way from anything like that . . .'

Her passion grew, a trait I have always found attractive.

'I think this is a bird, one of those we saw flying at us. But it seems to be a composite creature, a symbiosis of these silicon-based wings and the ice lump – silane life cooperating with CHON life! Just re-markable. You wonder how it came about in the first place . . . but I guess there are examples of survival strategies just as intricate in our own biosphere. Give evolution enough time and anything is possible.

I wonder what it is they both *want*, though, what the two sides in this symbiosis get out of the relationship . . .

'It's a genuine discovery, Jovik. Nobody's seen this before – life from two entirely different domains working together. And I wouldn't have noticed it if not for you.' She held out the ice lump to me. 'They'll probably name it after you.'

Her enthusiasm was fetching, but not that much. 'Sure. But my concern right now is how much power we have left in these suit heaters. Let's get back to the gondola.'

So she stowed away the remaining fragments of the Titan bird, Jovik Emry's contribution to Solar System science, and we retraced our path back to the gondola.

9

The days are very long on Titan, and by the time we got back to the gondola nothing seemed to have changed about the landscape or the sky – not a diffuse shadow had shifted. We found Poole and Dzik, surrounded by alien mystery, happily fixing big balloon wheels to axles slung beneath thc crumpled hull. Boys will be boys.

When they were done, we all climbed back aboard. Poole had reset some of the interior lamps so they glowed green, yellow and blue; it was a relief to be immersed once more in bright Earth light.

We set off in our gondola-truck for the next part of our expedition. We were making, I was told, for an impact crater believed to hold liquid water, which itself was not far from a cryovolcano, another feature of interest for the expedition. This site was perhaps a hundred kilometres from where we had come down.

Miriam transferred her lake samples to cold stores, and ran some of them through a small onboard science package. She jabbered about what she had discovered. Poole encouraged her more than Dzik did, but even that wasn't much. Dzik and Poole were more interested at that moment in playing with the gondola. They sat at an improvised driver's console and fussed over gear ratios and the performance of the big tyres. Poole even insisted on driving the bus himself, though Titan was so flat and dull for the most part he could easily have left the chore to the onboard systems. That proved to me the fallacy of not bringing along specialist biologists on a jaunt like this. It was only Miriam who seemed to have a genuine passion for the life systems we were supposed to be here to study; Dzik and Poole were too easily distracted by the technology, which was, after all, only a means to an end.

They had, however, rearranged the interior to make it feel a little less cramped. The couches had been separated and set up around the cabin, so you could sit upright with a bit of elbow room. The cabin was pressurised so we could remove our helmets, and though the expandable walls didn't work any more there was room for one at a time to shuck off his or her exosuit. Poole ordered us to do so; we had already been inside the suits for a few hours, and the suits, and ourselves, needed some down time. Poole had set up a curtained-off area where we could let our discarded suits perform their self-maintenance functions while we had showers – of water recycled from our urine and sweat, which was deemed a lot safer than melt from the ice moon. Poole himself used the shower first, and then Miriam. She was hasty, eager to get back to her work, and kept talking even while she cleaned up.

After Miriam was out of the shower I took my turn. It was a miserable drizzle and lukewarm at that, but it was a relief to let my skin drink in the water. I was quick, though; with the unknown dangers of Titan only centimetres away beyond the gondola's fragile metal walls, I didn't want to spend long outside the security of the suit.

It was scarcely a comfortable ride, even discounting the calculating face of Harry Poole glaring from wall-mounted slates. I was relieved when, after a couple of hours, we reached our destination.

At that point Bill Dzik was in the shower. Safely suited up, with Dzik's offensive presence absent, I was able to sit forward in my couch and peer over Miriam's and Poole's shoulders at the landscape outside. That cryovolcano was a mound that pushed out of the landscape some kilometres to the west of us. It had the look of a shield volcano, like Hawaii or Mons Olympus, a flat-profiled dome with a caldera on the top. It wasn't erupting while we sat there, but I could see how successive sheets of 'lava' had plated its sides. That lava was water ice, heavily laced with ammonia, which had come gushing up from this world's strange mantle, a sea of liquid water locked under the ice, kilometres below our tyres.

As for the crater lake, I saw nothing but a plain, flatter and even more featureless than the average, covered with a thin scattering of ice sand. But the lake was there, hidden. Poole extracted radar images which showed the unmistakable profile of an impact crater, directly ahead of us, kilometres wide. Such is the vast energy pulse delivered by an infalling asteroid or comet – or, in Saturn's system, perhaps a ring fragment or a bit of a tide-shattered moon – that the water locally can retain enough heat to remain liquid for a long time, perhaps thousands of years. Such a lake had formed here, and then frozen over with a thin crust, on top of which that skim of sand had been wind-blown. But the briny lake remained under the ice, hoarding its heat.

And, studded around the lake's circular rim, we saw more sponge-like masses like the one we had discovered wrapped up in silane film at the shore of the polar lake. These masses were positioned quite regularly around the lake, and many were placed close by crevasses that seemed to offer a route down into the deep structure of the ice rock beneath us. Miriam started gathering data eagerly.

Meanwhile, Poole was puzzling over images returned from the very bottom of the crater lake. He had found motion, obscure forms labouring. They looked to me like machines quarrying a rock deposit. But I could not read the images well enough, and as Poole did not ask for my opinions I kept my mouth shut.

Miriam Berg was soon getting very agitated by what she was finding. Even as she gathered the data and squirted it up to Harry Poole in the *Crab*, she eagerly hypothesised. 'Look – I think it's obvious there are at least two kinds of life here, the silanes of the ethane lakes and the CHON sponges. I've done some hasty analysis on the CHON tissues. They're like us, but not identical. They use a subtly different subset of amino acids to build their proteins; they have a variant of our DNA in there – a different set of bases, a different coding system. The silanes, meanwhile, are like the life systems we've discovered in the nitrogen pools on Triton, but again not identical, based on a different subset of silicon-oxygen molecular strings.

'It's possible both forms of life were brought here through panspermia – the natural wafting of life between the worlds in the form of something like spores, blasted off their parent world by impacts and driven here by sunlight and gravity. If the System's CHON life arose first on Earth or Mars, it might easily have drifted here and seeded in a crater lake, and followed a different evolutionary strategy. Similarly the silanes at the poles floated here from Triton or somewhere else, found a congenial place to live, and followed their own path, independently of their cousins . . .' She shook her head. 'It seems remarkable that here we have a place, this moon, a junction where families of life from *different ends of the Solar System* can coexist.'

'But there's a problem,' Bill Dzik called from his shower. 'Both your silanes and your sponges live in short-term environments. The ethane lakes pretty much dry up every Titan year. And each crater lake will freeze solid after a few thousand years.'

'Yes,' Miriam said. 'So both forms need to migrate. And that's how, I think, they came to cooperate . . .'

She sketched a hasty narrative of the CHON sponges leaving the crater lakes as they cooled, and finding their way to the summer pole. Maybe they got there by following deep crevasses, smashed into Titan's ice crust by the impacts that dug out crater lakes like this one in the first place. Down there they would find liquid water, kilometres deep and close to the ammonia ocean. It would be cold, briny, not to terrestrial tastes, but it would be liquid, and survivable. And at the pole they would find the silane lilies floating on their ethane seas. The lilies in turn needed to migrate to the winter pole, where their precious life-stuff ethane was raining out.

Miriam mimed, her fist touching her flattened palm. 'So they come together, the sponges and the lilies—'

'To make the Titan birds,' I said.

'That's the idea. The timing must be complicated, but both need to migrate. The birds come flapping up out of the lake, just as we saw, heading for the winter pole: sponges as bodies or brains, silanes as wings, one seeking cold, one warmth, but both needing to be on the move. Maybe the sponges get dropped off at fresh crater lakes along the way, across the surface of the planet. It's a true symbiosis, with two entirely different spheres of life intersecting – and cooperating, for without the migration neither form could survive alone.' She looked at us, suddenly doubtful. 'We're all amateurs here. I guess any competent biologist could pick holes in that theory the size of Saturn's rings.'

Dzik said, 'No competent biologist would even be hypothesising this way, not with so few facts.'

'No,' Harry said tinnily from his slate. 'But at least you've come up with a plausible model, Miriam. And all without the need to evoke even a scrap of sentience. Good job.'

'There are still questions,' Miriam said. 'Maybe the sponges provide the birds' intelligence, or at least some kind of directionality. But what about power? The lilies especially are a pretty low-energy kind of life form . . .'

Michael Poole said, 'Maybe I can answer that; I've been doing some analysis of my own. I can tell you a bit more about the silane lilies' energy source. Believe it or not – even on a world as murky as this – I think they're photosynthesising.' And he ran through the chemistry he thought he had identified, using entirely different compounds and molecular processing pathways from the chlorophyll-based green-plant photosynthesis of Earth life.

'Of course,' Miriam said. 'I should have seen it. I never even asked myself what the lilies were *doing* while they were lying around on the lake's surface . . . Trapping sunlight!'

Harry was growing excited too. 'Hey, if you're right, son, you may already have paid for the trip. Silane-based low-temp photosynthe-sisers would be hugely commercially valuable. Think of it, you could grow them on those nitrogen lakes on Triton, and go scudding around the outer System on living solar sails.' His grin was wide, even in the reduced Virtual image.

Poole and Miriam were smiling too, staring at each other with a glow of connection. Theirs was a strange kind of symbiosis, like silane lily and CHON sponge; they seemed to need the excitement of exter-nal discovery and achievement to bring them together.

Well, there was a happy mood in that grounded gondola, the happi-est since we had crashed. Even Bill Dzik as he showered was making grunting, hog-like noises of contentment.

And then there was a crunching sound, like great jaws closing on bone, and the whole bus tipped to one side.

I had my helmet over my head in a heartbeat. Poole and Miriam stag-gered and started shouting instructions to each other.

Then there was another crunch, a ripping sound – and a scream, a gurgling, quickly strangled, and an inward rush of cold air that I felt even through my exosuit. I turned and saw that, near the shower partition, a hole had been ripped in the side of the gondola's flimsy hull, revealing Titan's crimson murk. Something like a claw, or a huge version of Miriam's manipulator arm, was working at the hull, widen-ing the breach.

And Bill Dzik, naked, not metres from the exosuit that could have saved him, was already frozen to death.

That was enough for me. I flung open the hatch in the gondola roof and lunged out, not waiting for Miriam or Poole. I hit the Titan sand and ran as best I could. I could hear crunching and chewing behind me. I did not look back.

When I had gone a hundred metres I stopped, winded, and turned. Poole and Miriam were following me. I was relieved that at least I was not stranded on Titan alone.

And I saw what was becoming of our gondola. The machines that had assailed it – and they were machines, I had no doubt of it – were like spiders of ice, with lenticular bodies perhaps ten metres long, each equipped with three grabber claws attached to delicate low-gravity limbs. Four, five of these things were labouring at the wreck of our gondola. I saw that they had gone for the wheels first, which was why we had tipped over, and now were making a fast job of ripping the structure apart. Not only that, beyond them I saw a line of similar-looking beasts carrying off silvery fragments – they could only be pieces of the gondola – and hauling them up the rising ground towards the summit of the cryovolcano. Some of the larger components of the wreck they left intact, such as the GUTengine module, but they carried them away just as determinedly.

In minutes, I saw, there would be little left of our gondola on the ice surface – not much aside from Bill Dzik, who, naked, sprawled and staring with frozen eyeballs, made an ugly corpse, but had not deserved the fate that had befallen him.

Harry Poole's head popped into Virtual existence before us. 'Well,' he said, 'that complicates things.'

Michael swatted at him, dispersing pixels like flies.

10

'Dzik is dead,' I said. 'And so are we.' I turned on Michael Poole, fists bunched in the thick gloves. 'You and your absurd ambition – it was always going to kill you one day, and now it's killed us all.'

Michael Poole snorted his contempt. 'And I wish I'd just thrown you into a jail back on Earth and left you to rot.'

'Oh, Lethe,' Miriam said with disgust. She was sifting through the scattered debris the spiders had left behind. 'Do you two have any idea how ridiculous you look in those suits? Like two soft toys squaring up for a fight. Anyhow, you aren't dead yet, Jovik.' She picked up bits of rubbish, rope, a few instruments, some of her precious sample flasks, enigmatic egg-shaped devices small enough to fit in her fist – and food packs.

Michael Poole's curiosity snagged him. 'They didn't take everything.'

'Evidently not. In fact, as you'd have noticed if you weren't too busy trading insults with your passenger, they didn't take *us*. Or Bill.'

'What, then?'

'Metal. I think. Anything that has a significant metal component is being hauled away.'

'Ah.' Poole watched the spiders toiling up their volcano, bits of our ship clutched in their huge claws. 'That makes a sort of sense. One thing this moon is short of is metal. Has been since its formation. Even the core is mostly light silicate rock, more like Earth's mantle than its iron core. Which maybe explains why every surface probe to Titan across seventeen hundred years has disappeared without a trace – even the traces of your illegal sample collectors, Emry. They were taken for the metal.'

I felt embarrassed to contribute to this dry discussion, but I referred to the blocky shapes I had seen toiling on the lake floor, in the radar images of the deeps. 'As if they were quarrying? Maybe they were relatives of these spiders, after the metallic content of the meteorite that dug out the crater in the first place.'

Poole pursed his lips, clearly trying not to look impressed. 'Sounds a good guess. The metal in a fair-sized space rock could take centuries to extract.'

'Well, in any event, they left useful stuff behind,' said Miriam, picking through the debris. 'Anything ceramic, glass fibre, plastic. And the food packs. I'll show you how to interface them to your suit's systems, Emry, you can get at the food without opening up your helmet . . . We won't starve, at least.'

Poole, you see, had homed in on theory, while Miriam focused on the essentials that might keep us alive. That tells you everything about the man's lofty nature, and its flaws.

'But they took the GUTengine, didn't they?' I put in sharply. 'Our power source. Without which we'll soon freeze to death, no matter how well fed we are.'

'And, incidentally,' Miriam said, 'the identity-backup deck. We cached the backups in the GUTengine's own control and processing unit, the most reliable store on the gondola. If we lose that, we lose the last trace of poor Bill too.'

I couldn't help but glance at Dzik's corpse, fast-frozen on the ice of Titan.

Not Poole, though. He was watching those receding spiders. 'They're heading down into the volcano. Which is a vent that leads down into the mantle, the ammonia sea, right? Why? What the hell *are* those things?'

Miriam said, 'One way to find out.' She hefted one of those ceramic eggs in her right hand, pressed a stud that made it glow red, and hurled it towards the nearest spider. It followed a low-gravity arc, slowing quickly in the thick air, and it seemed to take an age to fall. But her aim was good, and it landed not a metre from the spider.

And exploded. Evidently it had been a grenade. The spider shattered satisfactorily, those ugly claws going wheeling through the air.

Miriam had already started to run towards the spider. 'Come on.' You couldn't fault her directness.

Poole followed, and I too, unwilling to be left alone with Bill's frozen remains. Poole called, 'What did you do that for?'

'We want to know what we're dealing with, don't we?'

'And why are we running?'

'So we can get there before the other spiders get rid of the corpse.'

And sure enough the other spiders, still laden with bits of the gondola, had already turned, and were closing on their shattered fellow. They didn't seem perturbed by the sudden destruction of one of their kind, or of our approaching presence.

We got there first, and we squatted around the downed spider in a splash of suit light. The spider hadn't broken open; it was not enclosed by a hull or external carapace. Instead it had shattered into pieces, like a smashed sculpture. We pawed at the debris chunks, Miriam and Poole talking fast, analysing, speculating. The chunks appeared to be mostly water ice, though Poole speculated it was a particular high-pressure form. The internal structure was not simple; it reminded me of a honeycomb, sharp-edged chambers whose walls enclosed smaller clusters of chambers and voids, on down through the length scales like a fractal. Poole pointed out threads of silver and a coppery colour – the shades were uncertain in Titan's light. They were clearly metallic.

The other spiders closed in on the corpse. Wary of getting chomped by accident we backed off, dimming our suit lights.

Miriam asked, 'So, biological or artificial? What do you think?'

Poole shrugged. 'They seem dedicated to a single purpose, and have metallic components. That suggests artificial. But that body interior looks organic. Grown.'

I felt like putting Poole in his place. 'Maybe these creatures transcend your simple-minded categories. Perhaps they are the result of a million years of machine evolution. Or the result of a long symbiosis between animal and technology.'

Poole shook his head. 'My money's on biology. Given enough time, necessity and selection can achieve remarkable things.'

Miriam said, 'But why would their systems incorporate metal if it's so rare here?'

'Maybe they're not native to Titan,' I said. 'Maybe they didn't evolve here.' But they weren't listening to me. And besides, they didn't want to hear any kind of theory that implied sentience. 'The real question is,' I said more urgently, 'what do we do now?'

The head of Harry Poole, projected somehow by our suit's comms systems, once more popped into existence, the size of an orange, floating in the air. The small scale made his skin look even more unnaturally smooth. 'And that,' he said, 'is the first intelligent question you've asked since we press-ganged you, Jovik. You ready to talk to me now?'

Michael Poole glared at his father, then turned and sucked water from the spigot inside his helmet. 'Tell us how bad it is, Harry.'

'I can't retrieve you for seven days,' Harry said.

I felt colder than Titan. 'But the suits—'

'Without recharge our suits will expire in three days,' Poole said. 'Four at the most.'

I could think of nothing to say.

Harry looked around at us, his disembodied head spinning eerily. 'There are options.'

'Go on,' Poole said.

'You could immerse yourselves in the crater lake. The suits could withstand that. It's cold in there, the briny stuff is well below freezing, but it's not as cold as the open air. Kept warm by the residual heat of impact, remember. Even so you would only stretch out your time by a day or two.'

'Not enough,' Miriam said. 'And we wouldn't get any work done, floating around in the dark in a lake.'

I laughed at her. 'Work? Who cares about work now?'

Poole said, 'What else, Harry?'

'I considered options where two people might survive, rather than three. Or one. By sharing suits.'

The tension between us rose immediately.

Harry said, 'Of course those spiders also left you Bill's suit. The trouble is the power store is built into the fabric of each suit. To benefit you'd have to swap suits. I can't think of any way you could do that without the shelter of the gondola; you'd freeze to death in a second.'

'So it's not an option,' Poole said.

Miriam looked at us both steadily. 'It never was.'

I wasn't sure if I was relieved or not, for I had been determined, in those few moments when it seemed a possibility, that the last survivor in the last suit would be myself.

'So,' Poole said to Harry, 'what else?'

'You need the gondola's GUTengine to recharge your suits,' Harry said. 'There's just no alternative.'

I pointed at the toiling spiders on the cryovolcano. 'Those beasts have already thrown it into that caldera.'

'Then you'll have to go after it,' Harry said, and, comfortably tucked up in the *Crab*, he grinned at me. 'Won't you?'

'How?' I was genuinely bewildered. 'Are we going to build a submarine?'

'You won't need one,' Harry said. 'You have your suits. Just jump in . . .'

'Are you insane? You want us to jump into the caldera of a volcano, after a bunch of metal-chewing monster spiders?'

But Miriam and Poole, as was their way, had pounced on the new idea. Miriam said, 'Jovik, you keep forgetting you're not on Earth. That "volcano" is just spewing water, lava that's colder than your own bloodstream.' She glanced at Harry. 'The water's very ammonia-rich, however. I take it our suits can stand it?'

'They're designed for contact with the mantle material,' Harry said. 'We always knew that was likely. The pressure shouldn't be a problem either.'

Poole said, 'As for the spiders, they will surely leave us alone if we keep away from them. We know that. We might even use them in the descent. Follow the spiders, find the engine. Right?'

Harry said, 'And there's science to be done.' He displayed data in gleaming Virtual displays – cold summaries only metres away from Bill Dzik's corpse. Harry said that his preliminary analysis of our results showed that the primary source of the atmosphere's crucial methane was not in the surface features, but a venting from the cryovolcanoes. 'And therefore the ultimate source is somewhere in the ammonia sea,' Harry said. 'Biological, geological, whatever – it's down there.'

'OK,' Poole said. 'So we're not going to complete the picture unless we go take a look.'

'You won't be out of touch. I'll be able to track you, and talk to you all the way in. Our comms link have a neutrino-transmission basis; a few kilometres of ice or water isn't going to make any difference to that.'

A few *kilometres*? I didn't like the sound of that.

'So that's that,' Miriam said. 'We have a plan.'

'We have a shared delusion,' I said.

They ignored me. Poole said, 'I suggest we take an hour out. We can afford that. We should try to rest; we've been through a lot. And we need to sort through these supplies, figure out what we can use.'

'Yeah,' said Miriam. 'For instance, how about nets of ice as ballast?'

So he and Miriam got down to work, sorting through the junk discarded by the spiders, knotting together cables to make nets. They were never happier than when busy on some task together.

And there was Bill Dzik, lying on his back, stark naked, frozen eyes staring into the murky sky. I think it tells you a lot about Michael

Poole and even Miriam that they were so focused on their latest goal that they had no time to consider the remains of this man with whom they had worked, apparently, for decades. Well, I had despised the man, and he had despised me, but something in me cringed at the thought of leaving him like that.

I looked around for something I could use as a shovel. I found a strut and a ceramic panel from some internal partition in the gondola, and used cable to join them together. Then I dug into the soil of Titan. The blade went in easily; the icy sand grains didn't cling together. As a native of Earth's higher gravity I was over-powered for Titan, and lifted great shovelfuls easily. But a half-metre or so down I found the sand was tighter packed and harder to penetrate, no doubt some arte-fact of Titan's complicated geology. I couldn't dig a grave deep enough for a man the size of Bill Dzik. So I contented myself with laying him in my shallow ditch, and building a mound over him. Before I covered his face I tried to close his eyes, but of course the lids were frozen in place.

All the time I was working I clung to my anger at Michael Poole, for it was better than the fear.

11

So we climbed the flank of the cryovolcano, paralleling the trail followed by the ice spiders, who continued to toil up the slope hauling the last useful fragments of our gondola. We were laden too with our improvised gear – rope cradles, bags of ice-rock chunks for ballast, food packs. Miriam even wore a pack containing the pick of her precious science samples.

It wasn't a difficult hike. When we had risen above the sand drifts we walked on bare rock-ice, a rough surface that gave good footing under the ridges of our boots. I had imagined we'd slip walking up a slope of ice, but at such temperatures the ice under your feet won't melt through the pressure of your weight, as on Earth, and it's that slick of meltwater that eliminates the friction. It was as if we climbed a surface of rough rock.

But despite the easy climb, as we neared the caldera my legs felt heavy. I had no choice but to go on, to walk into ever greater danger, as I'd had no real choice since being press-ganged in the first place.

At last we stood at the lip of the caldera. We looked down over a crudely carved bowl perhaps half a kilometre across, water-ice rock laced with some brownish organic muck. Most of the bowl's floor was solid – evidently the cryovolcano was all but dormant – but there was a wide crevasse down which the spiders slid into darkness, one after another.

If you listened carefully you could hear a crunching sound, from deep within the crevasse. This crack in the world was what we were going to descend into.

'Don't even think about it,' Miriam murmured to me. 'Just do it.'

But first we needed a tame spider.

We climbed a few paces down the flank, and stood alongside the toiling line of spiders. Miriam actually tried to lasso one of the creatures as it crawled past us. This was a bit overambitious, as the thick air and low gravity gave her length of cable a life of its own. So she and Poole worked out another way. With a bit of dexterity they managed to snag cable loops around a few of a spider's limbs, and Poole threw cable back and forth under the beast's belly and over its back and tied it off, to make a kind of loose net around the spider's body. The spider didn't even notice these activities, it seemed, but continued its steady plod.

'That will do,' Poole said. 'All aboard!' Grasping his own burden of pack and ballast nets he made a slow-motion leap, grabbed the improvised netting, and set himself on the back of the spider. Miriam and I hurried to follow him.

So there we were, the three of us sitting on the back of the beast! 'On any other day,' I ventured, 'this would seem strange.' That won me a laugh from Miriam.

The first few minutes of the ride weren't so bad, though the spider's motion was jolting and ungainly, we had to cling to our cables, and we always had the unpleasant awareness that there was no conscious mind directing this beast to which we were strapped.

Then the lip of the caldera came on us, remarkably quickly. I wrapped my hands and arms tighter in the netting.

'Here we go!' Michael Poole cried, and he actually whooped as the spider tipped head first over the lip of the crevasse – and began to climb down a vertical wall. I could not see how it was clinging to the sheer surface – perhaps with suckers, or perhaps its delicate limbs found footholds. But my concern was for myself, for as the spider tipped forward we three fell head over heels, clinging to the net, a slow low-gravity fall that ended with us all hanging upside down.

'Climb up!' Poole called. 'It will be easier if we can settle near the back end.'

It was good advice but easier said than done, for to climb I had to loosen my grip on the cable to which I was clinging. I was the last to reach the arse end of the descending spider, and find a bit of respite in a surface I could lie on.

And all the while the dark of the chasm closed around us, and that dreadful crunching, chewing noise from below grew louder. I looked up to see the opening of this chimney as a ragged gash of crimson-brown, the only natural light; it barely cast a glow on the toiling body of the spider. Impulsively I ordered my suit to turn on its lights, and we were flooded with glare.

Poole asked, 'Everybody OK?'

'Winded,' Miriam said. 'And I'm glad I took my claustrophobia pills before getting into the gondola. Look below. What's that?'

We all peered down. It was a slab of ice that appeared to span the crevasse. For an instant I wondered if this was as deep as we would have to go to find our GUTengine. But there was no sign of toiling spiders here, or of the pieces of our gondola, and I feared I knew what was coming next. That sound of crunching grew louder and louder, with a rhythm of its own.

'Brace yourselves,' Poole said. Pointless advice.

Our spider hit the ice floor. It turned out to be a thin crust, easily broken – that was the crunching we had heard, as spider after spider smashed through this interface. Beyond the broken crust I caught one glimpse of black, frothy water, before I was dragged down into it, head first. For the ice was the frozen surface of a subterranean ocean.

Immersed, I was no colder, but I could feel a sticky thickness all around me, as if I had been dropped into a vat of syrup. My suit lamps picked out enigmatic flecks and threads that filled the fluid surrounding me. When I looked back, I saw the roof of this vent already freezing over, before it was broken by the plunging form of another spider, following ours.

Michael Poole was laughing. 'Dunked in molten lava, Titan style. What a ride!'

I moaned, 'How much longer? How deep will we go?'

'As deep as we need to. Have patience. But you should cut your lights, Emry. Save your power for heating.'

'No, wait.' Miriam was pointing at the ice wall that swept past us. 'Look there. And there!'

And I made out tubular forms, maybe half a metre long or less, that clung to the walls, or, it seemed, made their purposeful way across it. It was difficult to see any detail, for these visions quickly shot up and out of our field of view.

'Life?' Poole asked, boyishly excited once more.

Miriam said, 'It looks like it, doesn't it?' Without warning, she loosened one hand from the net, grabbed at one of the tubes and dragged it away from its hold on the wall. It wriggled in her hand, pale and sightless, a fat worm; its front end, open like a mouth, was torn.

'Ugh,' I said. 'Throw it back!'

But Miriam was cradling the thing. 'Oh, I'm sorry. I hurt you, didn't I?'

Poole bent over it. 'Alive, then.'

'Oh, yes. And if it's surviving in this ammonia lava, I wouldn't mind

55

betting it's a cousin of whatever's down below in the sea. More life, Michael!'

'Look, I think it's been browsing on the ice. They are clustered pretty thickly over the walls.'

And when I looked, I saw he was right; there the tube-fish were, nibbling away, working their way slowly up the vent.

Poole speculated, 'Maybe they actively keep the vent open?' He took a small science box from Miriam's pack, and there, together – even as we rode that alien's back down into the throat of the volcano – they briskly analysed the beast's metabolism, and the contents of the water we were immersed in, and sent the results back to the *Hermit Crab*. Even Harry's Virtual head popped up before us, grinning inanely, in that extreme situation.

I had seen enough. With a snap, I made my suit turn its lights off. I had no desire to sit shivering in the dark as invisible ice walls plummeted past me. But I was gambling that curiosity would get the better of Poole and Miriam, and I was right; soon it was Poole whose suit glowed, spending his own precious power to light me up, as they laboured over their pointless science.

At length they came to some conclusion. 'So I was right,' Miriam breathed at last. 'This vent, and the mantle ocean, host a whole other domain – *a third* on Titan, in addition to the silanes and the CHON sponges. Ammono life . . .'

The moon's liquid mantle is thought to be a relic of its formation, in a part of the solar nebula where ammonia was common.

Titan was born with a rocky core and a deep ocean, of water laced with ammonia. The ocean might have stayed open for a billion years, warmed by greenhouse effects under a thick primordial atmosphere. A billion years is plenty of time for life to evolve. Eventually the ocean surface froze over to form an icy crust, and at the ocean's base complex high-pressure forms of ice formed a deep solid layer enclosing the silicate core. Ice above and below, but still the liquid ocean persisted between, ammonia-rich water, very alkaline, very viscous. And in that deep ocean had emerged a unique kind of life, adapted to its strange environment, based on chemical bonds between carbon and nitrogen-hydrogen chemical groups rather than carbon-oxygen, using ammonia as its solvent rather than water: 'ammono life', the specialists call it.

'Yes, a third kind of life,' Miriam said. 'One unknown elsewhere in the Solar System so far as I know. So here on Titan you have a junction of three entirely different domains of life: native ammono life in the mantle ocean, CHON life in the crater lakes blown in from the inner System, and the silane lilies wafting in from Triton and the outer cold. Incredible.'

'More than that,' Harry said tinnily. 'Michael, that tube-fish of yours is not a methanogen – it doesn't create methane – but it's full of it. Methane is integral to its metabolism, as far as I can see from the results you sent me. It even has methane in its flotation bladders.'

Miriam looked at the tube-fish blindly chewing at the ice walls. 'Right. They collect it somehow, from some source deep in the ocean. They use it to float up here. They even nibble the cryovolcano vent walls, to keep them open. They have to be integral to delivering the methane from the deep ocean sources, up through the crevices in the ice cap and to the atmosphere. So you have the three domains not just sharing this moon but cooperating in sustaining its ecology.'

Harry said, 'Quite a vision. And as long as they're all stupid enough, we might make some money out of this damn system yet.'

Miriam let go of her tube-fish, like freeing a bird; it wriggled off into the dark water. 'You always were a realist, Harry.'

I thought I saw blackness below us, in the outer glimmer of Poole's suit lamps. I called, 'How deep is this ice crust, before we get to the mantle ocean?'

'Around thirty-five kilometres,' Harry replied.

'And how deep are we now?'

'Oh, around thirty-five kilometres.'

Michael Poole gasped. 'Lethe. Grab hold, everybody.'

It was on us at once: we had almost passed through this vent we had followed all the way down from the cryovolcano mouth at the surface, this passage right through the ice crust of Titan. I gripped the net and shut my eyes.

The spider let go of the wall and dropped into the void. As we passed out of the vent, through the roof of ice and into the mantle beneath, I felt the walls recede from me, a wash of pressure, a vast opening-out. And we fell into the dark and the cold.

12

Now that the walls were gone from under its limbs I could feel that the spider was *swimming*, or perhaps somehow jetting, ever deeper into that gloopy sea, while the three of us held on for our lives.

Looking up I saw the base of Titan's solid crust, an ice roof that covered the whole world, glowing in the light of Poole's lamps but already receding. And I thought I saw the vent from which we had emerged, a much eroded funnel around which tube-fish swam languidly. Away from the walls I could more easily see the mechanics of how the fish swam; lacking fins or tails they seemed to twist through the water, a motion maybe suited to the viscosity of the medium. They looked more like bloated bacteria than fish.

Soon we were so far beneath the ice roof that it was invisible, and we three and the spider that dragged us down were a single point of light falling into the dark.

And then Poole turned off his suit lamps!

I whimpered, 'Lethe, Poole, spare us.'

'Oh, have a heart,' Miriam said, and her own suit lit up. 'Just for a time. Let him get used to it.'

I said, 'Get used to what? Falling into this endless dark?'

'Not endless,' Poole said. 'The ocean is no more than – how much, Harry?'

'Two hundred and fifty kilometres deep,' Harry said, mercifully not presenting a Virtual to us. 'Give or take.'

'Two hundred and fifty . . . How deep are you intending to take us, Poole?'

'I told you,' Michael Poole said grimly. 'As deep as we need to go. We have to retrieve that GUTengine, Emry. We don't have a choice – simple as that.'

'And I have a feeling,' Miriam said bleakly, 'now we're out of that vent, that we may be heading all the way down to the bottom. It's kind of the next logical choice.'

'We'll be crushed,' I said dismally.

'No,' Harry Poole piped up. 'Look, Jovik, just remember Titan isn't a large world. The pressure down there is only about four times what you'd find in Earth's deepest oceans. Five, tops. Your suit is over-engineered. Whatever it is that kills you, it won't be crushing.'

'How long to the bottom, then?'

Harry said, 'You're falling faster than you'd think, given the viscosity of the medium. That spider is a strong swimmer. A day, say.'

'A day!'

Miriam said, 'There may be sights to see on the way down.'

'What sights?'

'Well, the tube-fish can't exist in isolation. There has to be a whole ammono ecology in the greater deeps.'

My imagination worked overtime. 'Ammono sharks. Ammono whales.'

Miriam laughed. 'Sluggish as hell, in this cold soup. And besides, they couldn't eat you, Jovik.'

'They might spit me out but I'd rather they didn't try at all. And even if we survive – even if we do find our damn GUTengine down there on the ice – how are we supposed to get back out of here?'

Poole said easily, 'All we need to do is dump our ballast, our bags of ice, and we'll float up. We don't need to bring up the GUTengine, remember, just use it to recharge the suits.'

Miriam said, 'A better option might be to hitch a ride back with another spider.'

'Right. Which would solve another problem,' Poole said. 'Which is to find a cryovolcano vent to the surface. The spiders know the way, evidently.'

Harry said, 'And even without the spiders I could guide you. I can see you, the vent mouths, even the GUTengine. This neutrino-radar technology was worth the money it cost. There's no problem, in principle.'

At times I felt less afraid of the situation than of my companions, precisely because of their lack of fear.

Miriam fetched something from a pack at her waist, I couldn't see what, and glanced at Poole. 'Jovik's not going to survive a descent lasting a day. Not in the dark.'

Poole looked at me, and at her. 'Do it.'

'Do what?'

But I had no time even to flinch as she reached across, and with expert skill pressed a vial into a valve in the chest of my exosuit. I felt a sharp coldness as the drug pumped into my bloodstream, and after that only a dreamless sleep, cradled in the warmth of my cushioned suit.

So I missed the events of the next hours, the quiet times when Poole and Miriam tried to catch some sleep themselves, the flurries of excitement when strange denizens of Titan's ammono deep approached them out of the dark.

And I missed the next great shock suffered by our dysfunctional little crew when the base of Titan's underground ocean, an ice floor three hundred kilometres beneath the surface, at last hove into view. The strange landscape of this abyssal deep, made of folded high-pressure ices littered by bits of meteorite rock, was punctured by vents and chasms, like an inverted mirror image of the crust far above us. *And the spider we rode did not slow down.* It hurled itself into one of those vents, and once more its limbs began to clatter down a wall of smooth rock-ice.

Harry warned Miriam and Poole that this latest vent looked as if it penetrated the whole of this inner layer of core-cladding ice – Ice VI, laced by ammonia dihydrate – a layer another five hundred kilometres deep. At the base of this vent there was only Titan's core of silicate rocks, and there, surely, the spiders' final destination must lie.

There was nothing to be done but to endure this extension of the ride. It would take perhaps a further day. So Poole and Miriam allowed the spider to drag us down. More tube-fish, of an exotic high-pressure variety, grazed endlessly at the icy walls. Miriam popped me another vial to keep me asleep, and fed me intravenous fluids. Harry fretted about the exhaustion of our power, and the gradual increase of pressure; beneath a column of water and ice hundreds of kilometres deep, we were approaching our suits' manufactured tolerance. But they had no choice but to continue, and I, unconscious, had no say in the matter.

When the ride was over, when the spider had at last come to rest, Miriam woke me up.

I was lying on my back on a lumpy floor. The gravity felt even weaker than it had on the surface. Miriam's face hovered over me, illuminated by suit lamps. Smiling, she said, 'Jovik. Look what we found.'

I sat up. I felt weak, dizzy, hungry. Beside me, in their suits, Miriam and Poole sat watching my reaction. Then I remembered where I was and the fear cut in.

I looked around quickly. Even by the glow of the suit lamps I could not see far. The murkiness and floating particles told me I must be still immersed in the water of Titan's deep ocean. I saw a roof of ice above me – not far above, a hundred metres or so. Below me was a surface of what looked like rock, dark and purple-streaked. I was in a sort of ice cavern, then, whose walls were off in the dark beyond our bubble of light. I learned later that I was in a cavern dug out beneath the lower icy mantle of Titan, between it and the rocky core, *eight hundred kilometres* below the icy plains where I had crash-landed days before. Around us I saw ice spiders, toiling away at their own enigmatic tasks, and bits of equipment from the gondola, chopped up, carried here and deposited. There was the GUTengine! My heart leapt; perhaps I would yet live through this.

But even the engine wasn't what Miriam was smiling about. She repeated, 'Look what we found.'

I looked.

Set in the floor, in this rocky core of a world, was a hatch.

13

They allowed me to eat and drink, and void my bladder. Moving around was difficult, the cold water dense and syrupy; every movement I made was accompanied by the whir of servomotors as the suit laboured to assist me. I was reassured to know that the GUTengine was still functioning, and that my suit cells had been recharged. In principle I could stay alive long enough to get back to the *Hermit Crab*. All I had to do was find my way out of the core of this world, up through eight hundred kilometres of ice and ocean . . . I clung to the relief of the moment, and put off my fears over what was to come next.

Now that I was awake, Michael Poole, Miriam Berg, and Virtual Harry rehearsed what they had figured out about methane processing on Titan. Under that roof of ice, immersed in that chill high-pressure ocean, they talked about comets and chemistry, and all the while the huge mystery of the hatch in the ground lay between us, unaddressed.

Harry said, 'On Earth, ninety-five per cent of the methane in the air is of biological origin. The farts of animals, the rot of vegetation. So could the source be biological here? You guys have surveyed enough of the environment to rule that out. There could in principle be methanogen bugs living in those ethane lakes, for instance, feeding off reactions between acetylene and hydrogen, but you found nothing significant. What about a delivery of the methane by infalling comets? It's possible, but then you'd have detected other trace cometary gases, which are absent from the air. Only one plausible possibility remains . . .'

When Titan was young, still warm from its birth and before it froze, its ammonia-water ocean had extended all the way to the rocky core. There, chemical processes could have produced plentiful methane: the alkaline water reacting with the rock would liberate hydrogen, which in turn would react with sources of carbon, monoxide or dioxide or carbon grains, to manufacture methane. But that process would have been stopped as soon as the ice layers plated over the rock core, insulating it from liquid water. What was needed, then, was some way for chambers to be kept open at the base of the ice, where liquid water and rock could still react at their interface. And as for a way for the methane produced in the depths to be brought up through the ice to the ocean, and then released in the atmosphere . . .

'The tube-fish,' I said.

'And their relatives, yes.'

Looking up at the ice ceiling above me, I saw how it had been shaped and scraped, as if by lobster claws. 'So the spiders keep these chambers open, to allow the methane-creating reactions to continue. And the tube-fish carry the methane to the ocean, through vents they in turn help keep open.'

'That's it,' Michael Poole said, wonder in his voice. 'They do it to keep a supply of methane pumping up into the atmosphere. And they've been doing it for billions of years. Have to have been, for the ecologies up there to have evolved as they have – the tube-fish, the CHON sponges, the silanes. *This whole world is an engine*, a very old engine. It's an engine for creating methane, for turning what would otherwise be just another nondescript ice moon into a haven, whose purpose is to foster the life forms that inhabit it.'

'Ha!' I barked laughter. 'So all this is technology. Therefore the spiders are clearly sentient – or their makers are, or were. You don't even need this hatch in the ground to make that case. *You have found precisely what you were afraid of*, haven't you, Michael Poole? Sentience at the heart of Titan. You will never be allowed to open it up for exploitation now. So much for your commercial ambitions!'

'Which you were going to share in,' Harry reminded me, scowling.

I sneered. 'Oh, I'd only have wasted the money on drugs and sex. To see you world-builders crestfallen is worth that loss. So,' I said. 'To the final mystery. What's under the hatch?'

They glanced at each other. 'The final answers, we hope,' Michael Poole said.

Miriam said, 'We've no idea what's under there. We've put off looking until we brought you round, Jovik.'

Poole said, 'We need everybody awake, ready to react. We might even need your help.' He looked at me with faint disgust. 'And,' he said more practically, 'it's probably going to take three of us to open it. Come see.'

We all floated through the gloopy murk.

The hatch was a disc of some silvery metal, perhaps three metres across, set flush in the rocky ground. Spaced around its circumference were three identical grooves, each maybe ten centimetres deep. In the middle of each groove was a mechanism like a pair of levers, hinged at the top.

Michael said, 'We think you operate it like this.' He knelt and put his gloved hands to either side of the levers, and mimed pressing them together. 'We don't know how heavy the mechanism will be. Hopefully each of us can handle one set of levers, with the help of our suits.'

'Three mechanisms,' I said. 'This is a door meant to be operated by a spider, isn't it? One handle for each of those three big claws.'

'We think so,' Miriam said. 'The handles look about the right size for that. We think they must need to be worked simultaneously – by one spider, or three humans.'

'I can't believe that after a billion years all they have is a clunky mechanical door.'

Poole said, 'It's hard to imagine a technology, however advanced, that won't have manual backups. We've seen that the spiders themselves aren't perfect; they're not immune to breakdown and damage.'

'As inflicted by us.' I gazed reluctantly at the hatch. 'Must we do this? You've found what you wanted – or didn't want. Why expose us to more risk? Can't we just go home?'

Miriam and Michael just stared at me, bewildered. Miriam said, 'You could walk away, without *knowing*?'

Poole said, 'Well, *we're* not leaving here until we've done this, Emry, so you may as well get it over.' He crouched down by his handle, and Miriam did the same.

I had no choice but to join them.

Poole counted us down: 'Three, two, one.'

I closed my gloved hands over the levers and pushed them together. It was awkward to reach down, and the mechanism felt heavy; my muscles worked, and I felt the reaction push me up from the floor. But the levers closed together.

The whole hatch began to vibrate.

I let go and moved back quickly. The others did the same. We stood in a circle, wafted by the currents of the ammonia sea, and watched that hatch slide up out of the ground.

It was like a piston, rising up one metre, two. Its sides were perfectly smooth, perfectly reflective, without a scuff or scratch. It looked brand new; I wondered how old it must be. Michael Poole, fool that he was, reached up a gloved monkey-curious hand to touch it, but Miriam restrained him. 'I'd like to measure the manufacturing tolerances on that thing,' he murmured.

Then the great slab, around three metres wide and two tall, slid sideways. Poole had to scurry out of the way. Its scrape across the rough rock ground was audible, faintly. The shifted hatch revealed a hole in the ground, a circle – and at first I thought it was perfectly black. But then I saw elusive golden glimmers, sheets of light like soap bubbles; if I turned my head a little I lost it again.

'Woah,' Harry Poole said. 'There's some exotic radiation coming out of that hole. You should all back off. The suits have heavy shielding, but a few metres of water won't hurt.'

I didn't need telling twice. We moved away towards the GUTengine, taking the light with us. The hole in the ground, still just visible in the glow of our suit lamps, looked a little like one of the ethane lakes on the surface, with that metallic monolith beside it. But every so often I could make out that elusive golden-brown glimmer. I said, 'It looks like a facet of one of your wormhole interfaces, Poole.'

'Not a bad observation,' Poole said. 'And I have a feeling that's exactly what we're looking at. Harry?'

'Yeah.' Harry was hesitating. 'I wish you had a better sensor suite down there. I'm relying on instruments woven into your suits, internal diagnostic tools in the GUTengine, some stray neutrino leakage up here . . . Yes, I think we're seeing products of stressed spacetime. There are some interesting optical effects too – light lensed by a distorted gravity field.'

'So it's a wormhole interface?' Miriam asked.

'If it is,' Poole said, 'it's far beyond the clumsy monstrosities *we* construct. And whatever is on the other side of that barrier, my guess is it's not on Titan . . .'

'Watch out,' Miriam said.

A spider came scuttling past us towards the hole. It paused at the lip, as if puzzled that the hole was open. Then it tipped forward, just as the spider we rode into the volcano had dipped into the caldera, and slid head first through that sheet of darkness. It was as if it had fallen into a pool of oil, which closed over the spider without a ripple.

'I wouldn't recommend following,' Harry said. 'The radiations in there are deadly, suit or no suit; you couldn't survive the passage.'

'Lethe,' Michael Poole said. He was disappointed!

'So are we done here, at last?' I asked.

Poole snapped, 'I'll tell you something, Emry, I'm glad you're here. Every time we come to an obstacle and you just want to give up, it goads me into trying to find a way forward.'

'There *is* no way forward,' I said. 'It's lethal. Harry said so.'

'We can't go in ourselves,' Miriam agreed. 'But how about a probe? Something radiation-hardened, a controlling AI – with luck we could just drop it in there and let it report back.'

'That would work,' Poole said. Without hesitation the two of them walked over to the GUTengine, and began prying at its mechanisms.

For redundancy the engine had two control units. Miriam and Poole detached one of these. Containing a sensor suite, processing capabilities and a memory store, it was a white-walled box the size of a suitcase. Within this unit and its twin were stored the identity backups that had been taken of us before our ride into Titan's atmosphere. The little box was even capable of projecting Virtuals; Harry's sharp image was being projected right now by the GUTengine hardware, rather than through a pooling of our suits' systems as before.

This box was small enough to be dropped through the interface; hardened against radiation it should survive a passage through a wormhole – though none of us could say if it would survive what lay on the other side. And it had transmitting and receiving capabilities. Harry believed its signals would make it back through the interface, though probably scrambled by gravitational distortion and other effects; he was confident he could construct filtering algorithms from a few test signals.

The unit was perfectly equipped to serve as a probe through the hatch, save for one thing. What the control box didn't have was intelligence.

Michael Poole stroked its surface with a gloved hand. 'We're sending this beast into an entirely unknown situation. It's going to have to work autonomously, figure out its environment, perform some kind of sensor sweep, before it can even start to work out how to talk to us. Running a GUTengine is a pretty simple and predictable job; the AI in there isn't capable of handling an exploration like this.'

'But,' I said, 'it carries in its store backups of four human intellects – mine, dead Bill, and you two geniuses. What a shame we can't all ride along with it!'

My sarcasm failed to evoke the expected reaction. Poole and Miriam looked at each other, electrified. Miriam shook her head. 'Jovik, you're like some idiot savant. You keep on coming up with such good ideas. I think you're actually far smarter than you admit yourself to be.'

I said honestly, 'I have no idea what you're talking about.'

'The idea you've suggested to them,' Harry said gently, 'is to revive one of the dormant identity-backup copies in the unit's store, and use *that* as the controlling intelligence.'

'Me and my big mouth.'

As always when they hit on some new idea, Poole and Miriam were like two eager kids. Poole said rapidly, 'It's going to be a shock for the copy to wake up, to move straight from atmospheric entry where it was downloaded, to this point. It would be least disconcerting if we projected a full human animus. A complete body.'

'You're telling me,' said the head of Harry Poole.

'And some enclosing environment,' Miriam said. 'Just a suit? No, to be adrift in space brings problems with vertigo. I'd have trouble with that.'

'The lifedome of the *Crab*,' Poole said. 'That would be straightforward enough to simulate to an adequate degree. And a good platform for observation. The power would be sufficient to sustain that for a few hours at least . . .'

'Yes.' Miriam grinned. 'It would feel like a voyage in the *Crab*. Our observer will feel safe, in control. I'll get to work on it . . .'

I said, 'OK. So you're planning to project a Virtual copy of one of us through the wormhole. And how will you get him or her back?'

They looked at me, as if I'd asked yet another foolish question.

'That won't be possible,' Poole said. 'The unit will be lost. It's possible we could transmit back a copy of the memories the Virtual accrues on the other side – integrate them somehow with the backup in the GUTengine's other store—'

'No,' Harry said regretfully. 'The data rate through that interface would never allow even that. For the copy in there it's a one-way trip.'

'Well, that's entirely against the sentience laws,' I put in. They ignored me. But to point this out was, after all, my paid job.

Poole said, 'That's settled, then. The question is, *who*? Which of the four of us are we going to wake up from cyber-sleep and send into the unknown?'

I noticed that Harry's disembodied floating head looked away, as if he were avoiding the question.

Poole and Miriam looked at each other.

'We should give it to Bill,' Miriam said firmly.

'Yeah. There's no other choice. Bill's gone, and we can't bring his stored backup home with us . . . We should let his backup have the privilege of doing this. It will make the sacrifice worthwhile.'

I stared at them. 'This is the way you treat your friends? By killing them, reviving backups and sending them to another certain death?'

Poole glared at me. 'Bill won't see it that way, believe me. You and a man like Bill Dzik have nothing in common, Emry. Don't judge him by your standards.'

'Fine. Just don't send me.'

'Oh, I won't. You don't deserve it.'

It took them only a few more minutes to prepare for the experiment. The control pack didn't need any physical modifications, and it didn't take Miriam long to programme instructions into its limited onboard intelligence. She provided it with a short orientation message, in the hope that Virtual Bill wouldn't be left entirely bewildered at the sudden transition he would experience.

Poole picked up the pack with his gloved hands, and walked towards the interface, or as close as Harry advised him to get. Then Poole lifted the pack over his head. 'Good luck, Bill.' He threw the pack towards the interface – or rather pushed it; its weight was low but its inertia was just as it would have been on Earth, and besides Poole had to fight against the resistance of the syrupy sea. For a while it looked as if the pack might fall short. 'I should have practised a couple of times,' Poole said ruefully. 'Never was any use at physical sports . . .'

But he got it about right. The pack clipped the rim of the hole, then tumbled forward and fell slowly, dreamlike, through that black surface. As it disappeared, autumn gold glimmered around it.

Then we had to wait, the three of us plus Harry. I began to wish that we had agreed some time limit; obsessives like Poole and Miriam were capable of standing there for hours before admitting failure.

In the event it was only minutes before a scratchy voice sounded in our suit helmets. 'Harry? Can you hear me?'

'Yes!' Harry called, grinning. 'Yes, I hear you. The reception ought to get better, the clean-up algorithms are still working. Are you all right?'

'Well, I'm sitting in the *Crab* lifedome. It's kind of a shock to find myself here, after bracing my butt to enter Titan. Your little orientation show helped, Miriam.'

Poole asked, 'What do you see?'

'The sky is . . . strange.'

Miriam was looking puzzled. She turned and looked at Harry. 'That's not all that's strange. That's not Bill!'

'Indeed not,' came the voice from the other side of the hole. 'I am Michael Poole.'

14

So, while a suddenly revived Michael Poole floated around in other-space, the original Poole and his not-lover Miriam Berg engaged in a furious row with Harry. Despite the circumstances, I found all this amusing.

Poole stormed over to the GUTengine's remaining control pack, and checked the memory's contents. It had never contained backup copies of the four of us after all; it contained only *one* ultra-high-fidelity copy, of Michael Poole himself. I could not decide which scared me more: the idea that no copies of myself existed in that glistening white box, or the belief I had entertained previously that there had. I am prone to existential doubt, and am uncomfortable with such notions.

But such subtleties were beyond a raging Michael Poole. 'Miriam, I swear I knew nothing about this.'

'Oh, I believe you.'

They both turned on the older Poole. 'Harry?' Michael snapped. 'What in Lethe did you do?'

Disembodied-head Harry looked shifty, but he was going to brazen it out. 'As far as I'm concerned there's nothing to apologise for. The storage available on the *Crab* was always limited, and it was worse in the gondola. Michael's my son. Of course I'm going to protect him above others. What would you do? I'm sorry, Miriam, but—'

'You aren't sorry at all,' Miriam snapped. 'And you're a cold-hearted bastard. You knowingly sent a backup of your son, who you say you're trying to protect, through that wormhole to die!'

Harry looked uncomfortable. 'It's just a copy. There are other back-ups, earlier copies—'

'Lethe, Dad,' Michael Poole said, and he walked away, bunching his fists. I wondered how many similar collisions with his father the man had had to suffer in the course of his life.

'What's done is done,' came a whisper. And they all quit their bickering, because it was Michael Poole who had spoken – the backup Poole, the one recently revived, the one beyond the spacetime barrier. 'I know I don't have much time. I'll try to project some imagery back . . .'

Harry, probably gratefully, popped out of existence, thus vacating the available processing capacity, though I was sure his original would be monitoring us from the *Crab*.

Poole murmured to Miriam, 'You speak to him. Might be easier for him than having to deal with me.'

She clearly found this idea distressing. But she said, 'All right.'

Gradually images built up in the air before us, limited views grainy with pixels and flickering.

And we saw Virtual Poole's strange universe.

The Virtual *Crab* floated over a small object – like an ice moon, like one of Titan's Saturnian siblings, pale and peppered with worn impact craters. I saw how its surface was punctured with holes, perfectly round and black. These looked like our hatch; the probe we had dispatched must have emerged from one of them. Things that looked like our spiders toiled to and fro between the holes, travelling between mounds of some kind of supplies. They were too distant to see clearly. All this was bathed in a pale-yellow light, diffuse and without shadows.

The original Poole said, 'You think those other interfaces connect up to the rest of Titan?'

'I think so,' Miriam said. 'This can't be the only deep-sea methane-generation chamber. Passing through the wormholes and back again would be a way for the spiders to unify their operations across the moon.'

'So the interface we found, set in the outer curved surface of Titan's core, is one of a set that matches another set on the outer curved surface of *that* ice moon. The curvature would seem to flip over when you passed through.'

This struck me as remarkable, a paradox difficult to grasp, but Poole was a wormhole engineer, and used to the subtleties of space-time manipulated and twisted through higher dimensions; slapping two convex surfaces together was evidently child's play to him, conceptually.

Miriam asked Virtual Poole, 'But where are *you*? That's an ice moon, a common object. Could be anywhere in the universe. Could even be in some corner of our own System.'

Poole's Virtual copy said, his voice a whispery, channel-distorted rasp, 'Don't jump to conclusions, Miriam. Look up.'

The viewpoint swivelled, and we saw Virtual Poole's sky.

A huge, distorted sun hung above us. Planetoids hung sprinkled before its face, showing phases from crescents to half-moons; some were entirely black, fly-speck eclipses against the face of the monster. Beyond the limb of the sun more stars hung, but they were also swollen, pale beasts, their misshapen discs visible. And the space between the stars did not look entirely black to me, but a faint, deep crimson overlaid with a pattern, a network of threads and knots.

'What a sky,' Poole murmured.

'Michael, you're far from home,' Miriam called.

Virtual Poole replied, 'Yes. Those stars don't fit our main sequence. And their spectra are simple – few heavy elements. They're more like the protostars of our own early universe, I think: the first generation, formed of not much more than the hydrogen and helium that came out of the Big Bang.'

'No heavy elements,' observed Miriam Berg. 'No metals.'

'I'll send through the data I'm collecting—'

'Getting it, son,' came Harry Poole's voice.

The others stayed quiet to let Virtual Poole speak. His words, the careful observations delivered by a man so far from home, or at least by a construct that felt as if it were a man, were impressive in their courage.

'This is not our universe,' he whispered. 'I think that's clear. This one is young, and small – according to the curvature of spacetime, only a few million light years across. Probably not big enough to accommodate our Local Group of galaxies.'

'A pocket universe, maybe,' Miriam said. 'An appendix from our own.'

'I can't believe the things you have been calling "spiders" originated here,' the Virtual said. 'Their fabric is heavily reliant on metals. You said it, Miriam. No metals *here*, not in this entire cosmos. I guess that's why they were scavenging metals from probes, meteorites.'

'They come from somewhere else, then,' Poole said. 'There was nothing strange in the elemental abundance we recorded in the spider samples we studied. They come from elsewhere in our own universe. The pocket universe is just a transit interchange. Like Earthport.'

The Virtual said, 'Yes. And maybe behind these other moons in my sky lie gateways to other Titans – other sustained ecologies, maybe with different biological bases. Other experiments, elsewhere in the universe.'

Miriam said, 'So if metals are so essential for the spiders, why not have supplies brought to them through the interchange?'

'Maybe they did, once,' the Virtual said. 'Maybe things broke down. There's a sense of age here, Miriam. This is a young cosmos maybe, but I think this is an old place . . .'

The real Poole murmured, 'It makes sense. The time axis in the baby universe needn't be isomorphic with ours. A million years over here, a billion years there.'

The Virtual whispered, 'Those spiders have been toiling at their task on Titan a long, long time. Whoever manufactured them, or bred them, left them behind a long time ago, and they've been alone ever since. Just doing their best to keep going. Looking at them, I get the impression they aren't too bright. Just functional.'

'But they did a good job,' Miriam said.

'That they did.'

'But why?' I blurted out. 'What's the purpose of all this, the nurturing of an ecology on Titan for billions of years – and perhaps similar on a thousand other worlds?'

'I think I have an idea,' Virtual Poole said. '*I* never even landed on Titan, remember. Perhaps, coming at all this so suddenly, while the rest of you have worked through the stages of your discovery, I see it differently . . .

'Just as this pocket universe is a junction, so maybe Titan is a junction – a haven where different domains of life can coexist. *And it's been designed that way.*

'You've found the native ammono fish, the CHON sponges that may originate in the inner System, and the silanes from Triton or beyond. Maybe there are other families to find, if you had time to look. All these kinds of life, arising from different environments – but all with one thing in common. All born of planets, and of skies and seas, in worlds warmed by stars.

'But the stars won't last for ever. In the future the universe will change, until it resembles our own time even less than our universe resembles this young dwarf cosmos. What then? Look, if you were concerned about preserving life, all forms of life, into the very furthest future, then perhaps you would promote—'

'Cooperation,' said Miriam Berg.

'You got it. Symbiosis. Maybe Titan is a kind of prototype, a forced cooperative ecology where life forms of such different origins are compelled to mix, to find ways of using each other to survive—'

'And ultimately merge, somehow,' Miriam said. 'Well, it's happened before. Each of us is a community, with once-disparate and very different life forms toiling away in each of our cells. It's a lovely vision, Michael.'

'More important than that, it's plausible,' Poole's original self said gruffly. 'Anyhow it's a hypothesis that will do until something better comes along.'

I sneered at that. This dream of cosmic cooperation struck me as the romantic fantasy of a man alone and doomed to die, and soon. We all project our petty lives upon the universe. But I had no better suggestions to make. And, who knows? Perhaps Virtual Poole was right. None of us will live to find out.

'Anyhow,' I said, 'charming as this is – are we done *now*?'

Miriam snapped, 'We can't abandon Michael.'

'Go,' whispered Virtual Poole. 'There's nothing you can do for me. I'll keep observing, reporting, as long as I can.'

I gagged on his nobility.

Now Harry intruded, grabbing a little of the available Virtual projection capacity. 'But we've still got business to conclude before you leave here.'

15

Poole frowned. 'What business?'

'We came here to prove that Titan is without sentience,' Harry said. 'Well, we got *that* wrong. Now what?'

Miriam Berg was apparently puzzled we were even having the conversation. 'We report what we've found to the sentience oversight councils and elsewhere. It's a major discovery. We'll be rapped for making an unauthorised landing on Titan, but—'

'Is that the sum of your ambition?' I snapped. 'To hope the authorities will be lenient if you reveal the discovery that is going to ruin you?'

She glared at me. 'What's the choice?'

'Isn't it obvious?' I looked at her, and Poole, who I think was guessing what I was going to say, and Harry, who turned away as he usually did at moments of crisis. Suddenly, after days of existential terror and pointless wonders, I was in my own element, which is the murky world of human relationships, and I could see a way forward where they could not. *'Destroy this,'* I said. I waved a hand. 'All of it. You have your grenades, Miriam. You could bring this cavern down.'

'Or,' Harry said, 'there is the GUTengine. If that were detonated, if unified-field energies were loosed in here, the wormhole interface too would surely be disrupted. I'd imagine that the connection between Titan and the pocket universe would be broken altogether.'

I nodded. 'I hadn't thought of that, but I like your style, Harry. *Do it.* Let this place be covered up by hundreds of kilometres of ice and water. Destroy your records. It will make no difference to the surface, what's going on in the atmosphere, not immediately. Nobody will ever know all this was here.'

Harry Poole said, 'That's true. Even if methane generation stops immediately, the residual would persist in the atmosphere for maybe ten million years. I venture to suggest that if the various multi-domain critters haven't learned to cooperate in that time, they never will. Ten megayears is surely enough.'

Miriam looked at the bizarrely drifting head, horrified by his words. 'You're suggesting a monstrous crime,' she breathed. 'To think of destroying such a wonder as this, a billion-year project – to destroy it for personal gain! Michael, Lethe, leave aside the morality, surely you're too much of a scientist to countenance this.'

But Poole sounded anguished. 'I'm not a scientist any more, Miriam. I'm an engineer. I build things. I think I sympathise with the goals of the spider makers. What *I'm* building is a better future for the whole of mankind – that's what I believe. And if I have to make compromises to achieve that future . . . well. Maybe the spider makers had to make the same kind of choices. Who knows what they found here on Titan before the makers went to work on it – who knows what potential *they* destroyed?'

And in that little speech, I believe, you have encapsulated both the magnificence and the grandiose folly of Michael Poole. I wondered then how much damage this man might do to us all in the future, with his wormholes and his time-hopping starships – what horrors he, blinded by his ambition, might unleash.

Harry said unexpectedly, 'Let's vote on it. If you're in favour of destroying the chamber, say yes.'

'No!' snapped Miriam.

'Yes,' said Harry and Poole together.

'Yes,' said I, but they all turned on me and told me I didn't have a vote.

It made no difference. The vote was carried. They stood looking at each other, as if horrified by what they had done.

'Welcome to my world,' I said cynically.

Poole went off to prepare the GUTengine for its last task. Miriam, furious and upset, gathered together our equipment, such as it was, her pack with her science samples, our tangles of rope.

And Harry popped into the air in front of me. 'Thanks,' he said.

'You wanted me to make that suggestion, didn't you?'

'Well, I hoped you would. If I'd made it they'd have refused, and Michael would never have forgiven me for suggesting it.' He grinned. 'I knew there was a reason I wanted to have you along, Jovik Emry. Well done. You've served your purpose.'

Virtual Poole, still in his baby universe, spoke again. 'Miriam.'

She straightened up. 'I'm here, Michael.'

'I'm not sure how long I have left. What will happen when the power goes?'

'I programmed the simulation to seem authentic, internally consistent. It will be as if the power in the *Crab* lifedome is failing.' She took a breath, and said, 'Of course you have other options to end it before then.'

'I know. Thank you. Who were they, do you think? Whoever made the spiders? Did they build this pocket universe too? Or was it built *for* them? Like a haven?'

'I don't suppose we'll ever know. Michael, I'm sorry. I—'

'Don't be. You know I would have chosen this. But I'm sorry to leave you behind. Miriam – look after him, the other Michael. I, we, need you.'

She looked at the original Poole, who was working at the GUTengine. 'We'll see,' she said.

'And tell Harry – well. You know.'

She held a hand up to the empty air. 'Michael, please—'

'It's enough.' The Virtuals he had been projecting broke up into blocks of pixels, and a faint hiss, the carrier of his voice, disappeared from my hearing. Alone in his universe, he had cut himself off.

The original Poole approached her, uncertain of her reaction. 'It's done. The GUTengine has been programmed. We're ready to go, Miriam. As soon as we're out of here, it will blow.'

She turned away from him, her face showing something close to hatred.

16

So, harnessed to a spider oblivious of the impending fate of its vast and ancient project, we rose into the dark. It had taken us days to descend to this place, and would take us days to return to the surface, where, Harry promised, he would have a fresh balloon waiting to pick us up.

This time, though I was offered escape into unconsciousness, I stayed awake. I had a feeling that the last act of this little drama had yet to play itself out. I wanted to be around to see it.

We were beyond the lower ice layers and rising through two hundred and fifty kilometres of sea when Miriam's timer informed us that the GUTengine had detonated, far beneath us. Insulated by the ice layer, we felt nothing. But I imagined that the spider that carried us up towards the light hesitated, just fractionally.

'It's done,' Poole said firmly. 'No going back.'

Miriam had barely spoken to him since the cavern. She had said more words to me. Now she said, 'I've been thinking. I won't accept it, Michael. I don't care about you and Harry and your damn vote. As soon as we get home I'm going to report what we found.'

'You've no evidence—'

'I'll be taken seriously enough. And someday somebody will mount another expedition, and confirm the truth.'

'All right.' That was all he said. But I knew the matter was not over. He would not meet my mocking eyes.

I wasn't surprised when, twelve hours later, as Miriam slept cradled in the net draped from the spider's back, Poole took vials from her pack and pressed them into her flesh, one by a valve on her leg, another at the base of her spine.

I watched him. I'd seen this done before, more than once. 'You're going to edit her memories, aren't you? Download her identity, edit it, load it back . . . All to keep her quiet. Planned this with Dad, did you?'

'Shut up,' he snarled, edgy, angry.

'What will you make her believe – that she stayed up on the *Crab* with Harry the whole time, while you went exploring and found nothing? That would work, I guess.'

'I've got nothing to say to you.'

But I had plenty to say to him. I am no saint myself, and Poole disgusted me as only a man without morality himself can be disgusted. 'I think you love her. I even think she loves you. Yet you are prepared to mess with her head and her heart, even her personality, to serve your grandiose ambitions. Let me tell you something. The Poole she left behind in that pocket universe – the one she said goodbye to – he was a better man than you will ever be again. Because he was not tainted by the great crime you committed when you destroyed the cavern. And because he was not tainted by *this*.

'And let me make some predictions. No matter what you achieve in the future, Michael Poole, this crime will always be at the root of you, gnawing away. *And Miriam will never love you again.* Even though you wipe out her memory of these events, there will always be something between you; she will sense the lie. She will leave you, and then you will leave her. One thing I know better than you is people, and what goes on in their hearts. You remember I said this.

'And, Poole, maybe those whose work you have wrecked will some day force you to a reckoning.'

He was open, defenceless, and I was flaying him. He had no answer. He cradled the unconscious Miriam, even as his machines drained her memory.

We did not speak again until we emerged into the murky daylight of Titan.

EPILOGUE

It didn't take the Virtual Poole long to check out the status of his fragile craft.

The power in the lifedome's internal cells might last – what, a few hours? As far as he could tell there was no functional link between the dome and the rest of the *Hermit Crab*; none of his controls worked. Maybe that was beyond the scope of Miriam's simulation. So he had no motive power.

He didn't grouse about this, nor did he fear his future. Such as it was.

The universe beyond the lifedome was strange, alien. The toiling spiders down on the ice moon seemed like machines, not alive, not sentient. He tired of observing them. He turned on lights, green, blue. The lifedome was a little bubble of Earth, isolated.

Michael was alone, in this whole universe. He could feel it.

He got a meal together. The mundane chore, performed in a bright island of light around the lifedome's small galley, was oddly cheering. Miriam's simulation was good, here in his familiar personal space; he didn't find any limits or glitches. Lovingly constructed, he thought.

He carried the food to his couch, lay back with the plate balancing on one hand, and dimmed the dome lights. He finished his food and set the plate carefully on the floor. He drank a glass of clean water.

Then he went to the freefall shower and washed in a spray of hot water. He tried to open up his senses, to relish every particle of sensation. There was a last time for everything, for even the most mundane experiences. He considered finding some music to play, a book to read. Somehow that might have seemed fitting.

The lights failed. Even the instrument slates winked out.

Well, so much for music. He made his way back to his couch. Though the sky was bright, illuminated by the nearest protosun, the air grew colder; he imagined the heat of the lifedome leaking out. What would get him first, the cold, or the failing air?

He wasn't afraid. And he felt no regret that he had lost so much potential life, all those AS-extended years. Oddly, he felt renewed: young, for the first time in decades, the pressure of time no longer seeming to weigh on him.

He was sorry he would never know how his relationship with Miriam might have worked out. That could have been something. But he found, in the end, he was glad that he had lived long enough to see all he had.

He was beginning to shiver, the air sharp in his nostrils. He lay back in his couch and crossed his hands on his chest. He closed his eyes.

A shadow crossed his face.

He opened his eyes, looked up. There was a ship hanging over the lifedome.

Michael, dying, stared in wonder.

It was something like a sycamore seed wrought in jet black. Night-dark wings which must have spanned hundreds of kilometres loomed over the *Crab*, softly rippling.

The cold sank claws into his chest; the muscles of his throat abruptly spasmed, and dark clouds ringed his vision. *Not now*, he found himself pleading silently, his failing vision locked onto the ship, all his elegiac acceptance gone in a flash. *Just a little longer. I have to know what this means. Please . . .*

Poole's consciousness was like a guttering candle flame. Now it was as if that flame was plucked from its wick. And the flame, with its tiny fear, its wonder, its helpless longing to survive, was spun out into a web of quantum functions, acausal and nonlocal.

The last heat fled from the craft; the air in the translucent dome began to frost over the comms panels, the couches, the galley, the abandoned body. And the ship and all it contained, no longer needed, broke up into a cloud of pixels.

A century and a half later, the future invaded the Solar System.

It had been humanity's own fault; everyone recognised that. Under the leadership of Michael Poole, the 'Interface project' – a link to a future a millennium and a half ahead, created by towing a wormhole mouth across interstellar space behind Poole's GUTship Cauchy – had been completed. Why had Poole's wormhole time bridge been built? There were endless justifications: what power could a glimpse of the future afford? But the truth was that it had been built for little more than the sheer joy of it. Poole did it because he could.

Later, it would be difficult to recapture the mood of those times. The anthropic theories of cosmological evolution were somewhere near their paradigmatic peak. Some people believed humans were alone in the universe. Others even believed the universe had been designed, by some offstage agency, with the sole object of producing and supporting humans. Given time, humans would do anything, go anywhere, achieve whatever they liked.

But Poole's Interface had been a bridge to the real future, not the dream. And what Jovik Emry had once called 'the magnificence and the grandiose folly' of Michael Poole had devastating consequences.

The incident that followed the return of the Cauchy, later to be known as the Emergency, was confused, chaotic, difficult for historians to disentangle. Future Earth – at the other end of Poole's time bridge, a millennium and a half hence – would be under occupation by an alien species about whom almost nothing was known. Rebel humans from the occupation era were pursued back through time, through Poole's Interface, by warships under the control of the occupiers. The rebels, with the help of Michael Poole, destroyed the warships, and Poole sealed the Interface wormhole. Poole himself was lost in time.

It had been a war – brief, spectacular, like no battle fought in solar space before or since, but a war nevertheless. The Solar System, stunned, slowly recovered.

And the rebels, stranded in their past, fled the Solar System in a captured GUTdrive ship, evidently intending to use relativistic time dilation effects to erode away the years back to their own era.

All the rebels fled.

So it was thought.

STARFALL
AD 4771–4820

AD 4771. Starfall minus 49 years. Between Alpha Centauri and Sol.

Minya and Huul stood together on the comet's observation deck, in freefall, gently embraced by smart webbing. Beneath their feet lay the bulk of the comet nucleus, a fifty-kilometres-wide ball of dirty water-ice. Above their heads was the fine carapace of the observation blister, and above *that* nothing but stars, a field of jewels.

Huul drank in the view, for he knew he had only moments left to enjoy it. Already the bots were working at the fringe of the window, coating it over with an authentic-looking layer of comet frost. When the blister was covered altogether it would be dismantled, this outer level of decking collapsed, and the human crew confined to a huddle of chilly chambers deep in the comet's heart.

And Huul's son, yet unborn, would never see the stars – not until he was older than Huul was now. Huul, with a spasm of regret, put his hand on his wife's belly, trying to feel the warmth of the baby within.

Minya knew what he was thinking. She was tougher than he was, but more empathetic too. 'I know,' she said. 'We are sacrificing a great deal – and we are imposing that sacrifice on our son. But *his* son will thank us.'

Huul grunted. 'Perhaps. But he might be the one doing the fighting, by the time the comet gets to Sol, in forty-nine years.'

'I know, I know. Let's just enjoy the view, while it lasts.'

He gazed out at the stars. 'Isn't it strange to think that whether you live in Alpha System or the Solar System, the stars you see are much the same? We have that much in common, at least.'

'True. With a couple of exceptions.' She pointed back the way they had come, back to Alpha Centauri, which even from this immense distance showed as a clear double sun.

And when Huul looked the other way he saw a compact constellation. From Earth it was a W shape, known as Cassiopeia, one of the most easily recognisable of the star figures, but as seen from Alpha, and from here, there was an extra star to the left of the pattern, turning the constellation into a crude scribble. That star was Sol, bright but not exceptionally so, the first star of mankind.

'It doesn't look much, does it?' Minya murmured. 'Just a lantern in the sky. But that is the seat of the Shiras, the source of all our trouble.'

'And that,' said Huul with mordant humour, 'is where you and I will die.'

'You mustn't talk like that,' Minya snapped. 'The Starfall project is already magnificent, Huul. Magnificent!'

She was right, Huul knew. The starborn's rebellion against Earth had already been decades in the planning. The supplying of this comet-ship by lightsail out of Alpha, about as covert an operation as could be mounted on such a scale, had alone taken decades. And now the comet had been nudged onto a path that would take it sailing into the Solar System less than five decades from now, decelerating onto a trajectory intended to make it appear that this was just another long-period comet making an entirely natural visit to its parent star. But a crew of saboteurs would be huddled in its icy heart, locked into a tightly closed miniature ecology, not allowing as much as a stray erg of leaked heat to betray their presence.

Minya said, 'The earthworms won't know we're among them until we're bright in the skies of Earth. And then we'll see what's what. Remember, Huul. We will be the Second Wave of the Starfall assault, second only to the smart plague. When we have helped cut away the tyranny of the Shiras at the root, to us will accrue much glory – and to our descendants for all time, as far as mankind journeys in time and space.'

But the labouring bots were almost done in frosting over the observation dome. And Huul thought, *I will die without ever seeing another star.*

Minya tugged at his hand. 'Come on. We've work to do.'

AD 4801. Starfall minus 19 years. Tau Ceti.

The flitter from the *Facula* arrowed towards the centre of the daylit face of the planet. Tau Ceti II was a small, warm, watery world, all but drowned by a vast ocean, and habitually swathed in cloud – and now, according to Sol imperial intelligence, host to an unauthorised human colony.

'There's definitely something wrong,' Pella said.

Stillich turned to his First Officer. Pella sat with the assault squad, crammed into the translucent hull of this intra-System flitter. She was peering obsessively at a diorama of their target. The marines themselves sat in their smartsuits, the sunburst sigil of the Empire of Sol on their breasts. Stillich got grins back, but he could sense their nervousness, and Pella's fretting wasn't helping.

The journey out from Sol, in a slower-than-light GUTship, had – thanks to time dilation effects – been over five years subjective, more than thirteen objective. This was Stillich's first interstellar jaunt under his own command, and he understood that his primary task during the cruise out had been to keep his crew *interested*, with a training programme half a decade long intended to sharpen them for this very moment, the planetfall. Stillich, in fact, had already started to turn his attention to the return journey, when another five-year programme would prepare the crew for the culture shock of their return. To Stillich, the journey itself had been the principal challenge. He had not expected the mission, the subduing of a bunch of secondary colonists from Alpha, to present any problems.

But now here was Pella with her analyses, mucking up morale right at the climax of the mission.

He murmured to her, 'There's no evidence of any threat to us from these ragged-arsed colonists, Number One. Whoever they are, however they got here.'

Pella was bright, but she was young, at thirty a decade or so younger than Stillich. And she had a strong, prickly sense of herself. 'No, sir. But what we're seeing doesn't make sense. The colony isn't just illegal. It looks *wrong*. Half-dismantled, rebuilt. Look.' She showed him hastily processed drone images of circular landforms, evidence of abandoned structures. 'There can't be more than a few thousand people on the planet. Why would you *move*?'

Stillich shrugged. 'Weather. Seismic problems. There's any number of reasons why you might get your first location wrong—'

'These are interstellar colonists, Captain. They're unlikely to be so foolish. I'd be happier if we were going into this situation better informed.'

So would I, Stillich thought, but he wasn't about to say so before his troops. He forced a grin. 'We're just going to have to have our wits about us when we land. Right, lads?'

He was rewarded with a muted cheer. 'You said it, Captain.'

A gong's low chime, the call to prayer, filled the cabin of the little flitter. The men had their solar amulets fixed outside their suits to their wrists, and they consulted these now, shifting in their seats so they could face towards Sol itself. Soon the murmured prayers began.

Stillich turned too. He knew where Sol was, actually; he could find it from the constellations, even distorted by this translation to the Tau Ceti system. But nearly twelve light years from Earth it was tricky to pick out the home star, so dim had it become. That, of course, had always been proclaimed by the Shiras as the natural limit to the human dominion: the Empire of Sol was to be that bubble of space close enough that you could see the home star with the naked eye, and so be able to pray to its munificence.

But Stillich knew that the Shiras' control depended on more practical considerations. The *Facula* was a GUTdrive starship. More than a thousand years after the pioneering journey of Michael Poole, this was still the peak of mankind's interstellar technology; no means of faster-than-light travel had been discovered, save fixed wormholes, tunnels in the sky. Like all its sisters in the fleet, the *Facula* was a sublight ship, and a Navy manned by humans and forever contained by light-speed had a certain natural reach.

The *Facula* was capable of sustaining a one-gravity acceleration for years, indeed decades. Including time for acceleration and deceleration she could reach Alpha Centauri in a mere forty-three months as measured aboard ship, and Tau Ceti in a little more than five years. But in flight, thanks to relativistic time dilation, the crew's heartbeats were slowed, their lives extended, and the voyages as measured by the external world were longer – it was fourteen years to Tau Ceti, as recorded on Earth.

And it was this rigidity of relativistic time that set the true limits on the Shiras' interstellar grasp. The young crew of the *Facula* were soldiers of the Empress; they would fight for Shira XXXII if there was a reasonable promise that they would be brought home. But it had been discovered that any longer than a generation elapsed back home and that promise was inevitably broken, loyalty always dissipated by an excess of culture shock; any longer and a flight became an emigration. AS anti-ageing technology made no difference, for this limit was a function of human consciousness, not significantly altered by extended lifespans – and besides, all soldiers were young, as they had always been. Even using sleeper pods would not help; that could only cut down the subjective flight time, not the objective interval.

Thus, given the fundamental limits of light-speed and human capability, Tau Ceti was about as far as the Shiras could ever extend their

Empire. But it was enough, for no less than nineteen star systems, plus Sol, lay within that limit of loyalty. And this mission was proof that the Shiras would enforce their rule right to the boundaries. If this colony was illegal, it would be broken up.

The time for prayer was over. The marines folded away their amulets and closed their faceplates.

And the flitter ducked into the murky air of Tau Ceti's second world.

They landed briskly on the perimeter of the largest human settlement, close to the shore of an island-continent. The hull cracked open, and the marines in their environment suits spilled out to set up a secure perimeter around the flitter. Glowing drones flooded the air, and bots began digging trenches.

Amid all this activity, Stillich peered about curiously.

A lid of cloud turned the pale light of Tau Ceti a dull grey. They had apparently come down in a field, where Earth vegetation drew sustenance from the nutrients of an alien soil, no doubt heavily nano-worked. But plants of a more exotic sort, with leaves of purple and silver-grey, clustered among the green. There were structures on the low horizon, unprepossessing, just shacks, really. People stood before the shacks, adults with hands on hips, a couple of children. They watched the marines with apparent curiosity but no sign of fear or deference.

Although Tau Ceti was actually the most sun-like of all the stars within the Empire of Sol, such were the distracting riches of Alpha System that only one serious colonising expedition from Earth had been mounted here – and that ship had been reassigned to a more urgent mission and had never been heard of again. Officially this colony did not exist – and yet here it was. Stillich found it deeply disturbing to have discovered this blind spot of the Empire, for where there was one, there could be many.

'Walk with me,' Stillich said to Pella.

He set off towards the shacks, and Pella followed. Marines shadowed them, weapons in hand.

'What a dump,' Stillich said. 'This world, this dismal farm, those shacks. To come all this way to live like this.'

Pella, characteristically, was peering into her data desk, rather than studying the world around her. 'They will be grateful we have come to save them, sir—' She stopped suddenly, a hundred paces short of the shacks. 'Look.' She pointed to a kind of earthwork, circular, little more than a system of ditches and low ramparts cut into the ground. 'This is what I saw from the drones. Can you see the way the ground has been flattened within the perimeter, as if something has been *set down* here? And over there—' She pointed. 'Residual traces of radioactivity.'

'They came here in a GUTship,' Stillich said.

'Yes, sir. They brought it down and dismantled it. They lived in the lifedome, just here, and used the GUTdrive for power.'

'And now it's all gone.'

'And quite recently too – I mean, a few decades . . .'

A woman approached them. Short, squat, she had the heavy shoulders and big hands of a farmer. She looked perhaps forty, though with AS tech she could be any age. She wore a facemask and a small air pack, but no other environmental protection. She grinned, showing good teeth, and said something in a liquid dialect that Stillich's systems began to translate for him.

He waved that away. 'Speak Earthish,' he snapped.

The woman eyed him, perhaps deciding whether to obey him or not. 'I said, "Welcome to Home."'

'What an original name,' sneered Pella.

'You don't need to wear those fancy suits. An air mask will do. We long since nanoed out any nasties. A couple more generations and—'

'You should not be here,' Stillich said. 'This colony is unauthorised.'

'Well, you'll have to take that up with my grandfather, who came here from Alpha System when Footprint got a bit too full for his liking.'

'You are secondary colonists from Alpha, then. As I said – unauthorised.'

Pella looked around. 'Where is your grandfather?'

'Dead these forty years. Don't you want to know my name?'

Pella snapped, 'Your name is irrelevant. The GUTships you used to get here were the property of the Empire of Sol.'

The farmer laughed again.

Pella, her temper quick, her ego strong, raised her arm.

Stillich touched her shoulder to restrain her. He said, 'Woman – you, or your grandparents, broke up your transport ship to build your first colony here.' He gestured. 'You lived in the lifedome. You used the GUTengine for power. And yet now these things are gone.'

'You reassembled the ship, that's obvious,' Pella said. 'And other vessels. But why? Where have you sent them?'

The woman responded with another grin, surly.

This time Pella did strike her, using her elbow to dash the woman to the ground. Marines rushed in, weapons raised. 'Take her,' Pella said. 'And her children. Torch this place. We will have five years to empty her of all she knows, before we reach the Solar System once more.'

As the marines closed on the shack-like farm buildings, Stillich considered intervening. This was no way to run an empire, this use of brute force. But he didn't want to contradict his First Officer in front of the marines; the fate of this farmer wasn't important enough for that.

Pella stood with him, breathing hard, still angry. 'Actually, I'm not sure how concerned we should be, sir. Now I stand here, amid the rubble of these colonists' petty dreams – if some of them have taken their GUTships off into the dark, so what? There's no G-class star until you get to Delta Pavonis, eight more light years out from Sol. Too far away to bother us. Why should we care?'

But it wasn't obvious to Stillich that this new jaunt had been out-wards at all.

Human space was sparsely settled, save for the Solar System itself, and Alpha System. And if you weren't to travel outwards, a return journey to Alpha was by far the most likely destination. Stillich had visited Alpha himself, on the two previous interstellar missions of his career. It was a big, sprawling, increasingly crowded system – richer in resources than even the Solar System itself. And as a junior officer he had detected signs of rebelliousness there, hints that the Alphans were chafing under the yoke of the taxes and political control of the light-years-distant Shiras, signs he had dutifully reported to his superiors.

It might be harmless. Maybe the GUTships had gone back to Alpha, to pick up another cadre of colonists for Tau Ceti. But if they had returned covertly, for some other reason . . .

'Tidy up here,' he said to Pella. 'But do it fast; the sooner we get out of here the better. I'm going back to the *Facula* to send a message to Earth.' Which itself would take twelve years to get there. He turned and stalked back to the flitter.

Pella called, 'Sir, the colonists – are they to be permitted to stay?'

He considered. 'No.' That was the tidiest solution. 'We have sleeper pods enough to transport these ragged villagers back to Sol. We should remove any trace of the colony. Expunge the records – hide the existence of a habitable planet here, so nobody tries again. We must have control. Get on with it, Pella. And avoid excessive violence.'

'Sir.'

Stillich heard screaming from the farmer's children. He did not look back.

AD 4814. Starfall minus 6 years. Armonktown, Footprint, Alpha System.

Suber's youngest son, little Suber, Su-su, called him out of the house. 'Dad, come see. I think there's another one up there, another GUTship!'

Suber had been helping Fay prepare the evening meal. Fay – Suber's second wife – was, at thirty, nearly seventy years Suber's junior, though thanks to his AS treatment she actually looked a little older. She grinned across at him. 'Go. A GUTship is a GUTship, but Su-su will only be seven years old once. Go!'

So he grabbed his jacket and let his son drag him out of the house, down the darkened street towards the park, where, away from the streetlights of Armonktown, you got the best view of the sky. But Suber was soon winded as he tried to keep up with Su-su. He had been born on Earth – though Su-su did not know that, and nor did Fay, and they never would – and even after seven decades here and extensive nano treatments, Footprint's stronger gravity still hung on Suber as heavy as a lead coat.

They came to the park. It was a fall evening, and the dew lay on the grass and on the roses' thorns, and glistened on the blisters of the rope-trees, a native species allowed to prosper in their own little bubbles of Footprint air inside the town dome. And there on the grass, little Su-su turned his button face up to the sky. 'See, Father?'

Suber looked up.

The sky was crowded and complex. From Footprint, a world of Alpha A, sun B was a brilliant star in the sky, closer to Alpha A than planet Neptune was to Sol, and bright enough to cast sharp shadows; on this world there were double sunrises, double sunsets, strange eclipses of one star by the other. And there was a line of light drawn across the sky: dazzling, alluring, that zodiacal gleam was the sparkle of trillions of asteroids. The mutual influence of A and B had prevented the formation of large planets; all the volatile material that in the home system had been absorbed into Sol's great gas giants was here left unconsolidated, asteroids drifting in huge lanes around the twin stars. Footprint's sky was full of flying mines.

But what interested Su-su wasn't the natural wonders of the sky but the signs of human activity. He pointed with his small finger, to a cloud of light slivers not far from the zenith. 'Can you see, Father? I can count them. One two three four five seven twelve! And there's a new one since they passed over yesterday.'

'Your eyes are better than mine,' Suber said. 'But, you know, I think you're right . . .'

The splinters of light were indeed ships: GUTships, a veritable fleet of them in a medium-altitude orbit over Footprint. Under magnification they showed the classic Poole-era design, lifedome and GUTdrive pod connected by a spine kilometres long. Somebody was assembling an orbital armada – and presumably even bringing in the ships from other star systems, for there was no facility to construct GUTships anywhere save the Solar System itself.

Suber had heard no announcement about this mustering, seen no news source refer to it, even though it was clearly visible to everybody. He wondered why no imperial official had been out to inspect it. He had even considered trying to get some message to the Empress's court himself. But it was unlikely in the extreme he'd be able to do that without blowing his personal cover.

It was while he was thinking of Earth, oddly, in that quiet moment with his son, that his life on Footprint ended.

The voice behind him was soft. 'Densel Bel?'

He turned, unthinking. 'Yes?' And then, 'Ah.' He had responded to a name he hadn't heard spoken since he left Earth.

The man facing him was dressed entirely in black, in some fabric so dark it seemed to absorb the light from the sky; he was a shadow, even his face concealed.

Densel/Suber did not dare glance around for Su-su. 'May I say good-bye to my son?'

'No.' The man pointed a finger.

There was a shock, not of pain, but of cold. He felt his heart stop before he hit the ground.

And when he could see again, he was enclosed by walls, in a room, bathed in bright light.

He winced, and lifted a hand to shield his eyes. And he staggered, for he was standing, held by a mesh web.

Somebody handed him a beaker of liquid. He drank, and felt warmth course through his system.

A man stood before him. A broad face, aged – no apparent recourse to AS – stocky build, crop of grey hair. Densel thought he recognised him. A young woman stood at the man's side, perhaps a daughter. Densel wondered if they were armed.

The room had a single window, which opened on blackness. The smart webbing filled the room, holding the people unobtrusively. He was in microgravity then, in orbit perhaps.

The man studied him. 'Are you all right, Densel Bel? You were injected with a nano anaesthetic. I hope it didn't hurt; you were obviously unprepared.'

'I'm fine.' He drew a breath. His chest ached vaguely; he wondered if he had suffered some minor heart attack. 'You know who I am.'

'Obviously. And you know me, don't you?'

'You are Flood. Ambassador to the Empress's court.' Flood's was one of the more famous faces in the small pool of Alpha cultural life.

'Former ambassador. I retired some years ago. Now I am engaged on other projects.'

'I want to speak to my family—'

'You mean the *two* families you raised on Footprint, to whom you lied all their lives? Forget them, Densel Bel. You are dead to them. They are dead to you. That part of your life is over.'

The shock of this abduction seemed to be hitting Densel; if not for the webbing he might have fallen. 'For seventy years I have prepared for this moment. Still it is hard.'

'You chose your own path. This always lay at the end of it.'

'Who are you? An underground? A resistance movement against the Empire?'

There was no reply.

'How long have you known about me?'

'Ever since you came tumbling out of the wreckage of the last Poole wormhole.'

Once, Alpha and the other colonised star systems had been linked by faster-than-light wormholes, assembled in Jovian orbit, their interfaces laboriously hauled across interstellar distances by GUTships. Seventy years ago Shira XXXII, on ascending to the Construction Material Throne, had ordered the links to be cut. And Densel and others had been sent to do the cutting.

'I was trained since I was a boy for the task,' Densel said. 'I knew nothing else but the purpose. I suppose you would say I was conditioned. I should have died when the wormhole collapsed. I was an agent of the Empire, sent to cut the wormhole—'

'You are a suicide bomber who failed – in that you did not die.'

'Yes. I *should* have been killed when we destroyed the wormhole. My survival was an accident. I was stranded on Footprint. Unexpectedly alive, it was as if I awoke. I have been cut off from my world for seven decades—'

'Your world? Isn't *this* your world now, a world you have helped build with your skills in exotic-matter engineering, skills developed for destruction put to better use?'

Densel shrugged. 'I found myself alive. Earth thought I was dead. Nobody knew me here. I decided to develop an identity, to build a life. Why not? I sought meaning—'

'*We* knew who you were. We always have.'

'Why did you not deal with me before?'

'Because we always thought you might be useful. You were doing no harm in the meantime.'

Densel frowned. 'Who is "we"?'

'We are a loosely bound, loosely defined group, but with a single clear goal.'

'Which is?'

'The liberation of the starborn from the tyranny of the Shiras. You were involved in the strengthening of the Empresses' grip. The wormholes were cut so that Earth might be protected from us by a blanket of spacetime, while possessing a near-monopoly in GUTship construction technology. So we could be controlled, for ever.'

Densel took a breath. 'Is the rule of the Shiras so bad? The Empire's touch is light—'

'An interstellar empire makes no sense, economically or politically. There is no possibility of meaningful trade save in information; fabrication will always be cheaper than any possible transport. The taxes we pay are punitive, and don't even enrich the Shiras; they only serve to pay for the Imperial Navy ships and bases which enslave us. The purpose of the Empire is purely ideological, purely intended to make us bow down before the light of a star so dim and remote that most of us have trouble finding it. And the Empresses' political control is destructive, even when it is not harsh. It hinders our own political development, our exploitation of this system and the colonisation of others. Even this, however, we might have tolerated, for all empires wither in time.'

'But something has changed,' Densel guessed.

'Yes. We believe the latest Shira represents a grave danger to us all. Do you know anything of the court?'

'I met her once,' Densel said. 'Shira XXXII. She touched my head; she blessed me in Sol's light, before she sent me to die. I learned nothing of her.'

'Then you've never heard of metamathematical spaces – of logic pools? Of a man called Highsmith Marsden?'

'No . . .'

'Marsden ran secretive experiments more than a thousand years ago. The result was the destruction of a moon of Sol VIII.'

'Neptune.'

'Now we fear that the Empress's meddling with the same technology is liable to cause an even greater danger.'

'Even for us, here in Alpha System?'

'Even here,' Flood said seriously. 'I know of this because I was Ambassador to the court, remember.'

'Ambassador and spy.'

'Yes. Shira must be opposed.'

Densel felt cold, as if his heart were being stopped by nano-machines once more. 'You're going to invade the Solar System.'

'Yes, we're going to invade. We intend to defeat Sol's navies and armies, to occupy the Earth, and to depose Shira herself. We call this programme the Starfall, the falling of the wrath of the stars upon the Earth.'

Densel laughed. 'You can't be serious. You can't defeat Earth. The starborn number a few tens of thousands. Earth's population is billions. And you are light years away.'

'We have advantages – the principal one being that nobody has attempted a war on this scale before. And you are honoured, Densel Bel. Because you're going along for the ride. Come to the window.' He put an arm around Densel's shoulders. 'Can you walk?'

Densel took cautious steps. The smart webbing released and embraced him smoothly, holding him to the floor, so that it was as if he walked even in the absence of gravity.

Beyond the window GUTships hung in space like toys. Flitters moved between the great vessels, and bots and humans worked on scuffed lifedome bubbles and balky GUTdrive pods. This clumsy armada drifted over the nightside face of Footprint.

'So this is how you're going to defeat Shira XXXII,' he said bitterly. 'With these rusty scows.'

Flood was unfazed. 'Our assault will proceed in four waves, which will arrive at the Solar System more or less simultaneously. The First Wave is a light-speed viral attack and will actually be the last to be launched. The Second Wave, a sublight stealth assault, was assembled and launched some decades ago. These GUTships constitute the Third and Fourth Waves. The Third Wave ships are weapons platforms and troop carriers. I myself will be embarking on the *Freestar*, the lead ship, very soon.

'And *you*, my friend, will be aboard one of the Fourth Wave ships, which we call the Fists. You don't need to be launched for another nine months. You'll catch us up, you see.'

'How? By accelerating at higher gravities?'

'Oh, no. It's just that you won't be slowing down.'

Densel Bel stared at him. 'Why put me on this ship of fools?'

'I told you. We always thought you were useful. You'll have plenty of time to think it over in flight – more than two years subjective, in fact. But I don't have to tell you any more now. You see that, don't you?'

'Yes,' Densel said. He did see it. For effectively, as Flood had said, his life was over, his ability to make choices about his future already gone.

'Now let's get on with it. There's only a few more hours before the Third Wave ships light up. My daughter, Beya' – he indicated the young woman at his side – 'will take you to the ship that is to be your home for the rest of your life . . .'

Densel gazed down on the planet's sparse lights helplessly, wondering if even now Su-su and Fay were looking up at him.

AD 4815. Starfall minus 4 years 8 months. The Solar System.

Stillich's orders were clear. As soon as the *Facula* docked at Port Sol, he was to make his way direct to Earth and report to the imperial court, to expand on the reports he had been narrowcasting from space.

But as he passed through Port Sol he could not help notice what had become of it during his twenty-seven-year absence.

Port Sol, mankind's greatest GUT-technology interstellar harbour, was a Kuiper object: a two-hundred-kilometre ball of friable rock and water-ice that circled the sun beyond the orbit of Pluto, along with uncounted companions. As Stillich's flitter dipped low over a crystalline landscape, on its way to the wormhole transit to Earth, the work of humanity was clear. The primordial ice was gouged by hundreds of craters: deep, regular, these were scars left after the supply of ice to the great interstellar GUTships for reaction mass. There were buildings too, housing for dock workers and ship crews, even a couple of hotels, with domes, pylons and arches exploiting the architectural possibilities of microgravity.

But many of the buildings were closed, darkened. Frost coated their surfaces, and some of the domes were collapsed. GUTships hung all around this little world, as if jostling for a place to land.

'Lethe,' said Pella. 'Something bad happened here.'

Now the flitter lifted away from Port Sol, and swam towards a cluster of wormhole Interfaces, giant tetrahedra built of struts of electric-blue light. The wormholes to the stars had been cut, but the ancient fast-transit routes within the Solar System itself still connected Port Sol to the rest of the System. Without hesitation Stillich's flitter thrust itself towards the largest of the wormholes, the gateway to Earth, only minutes away. Pella watched nervously.

Stillich was paging through a data desk, looking for information about Port Sol's recent history. 'Some kind of "industrial accident", it says here. A GUTship blew up in dry dock. It's put the construction facilities out of action for a decade, and the maintenance facilities are stretched. The incident was heavily classified, which is why we never heard of it before we got here.'

One shimmering triangular face grew huge in their view, an electric-blue frame that swallowed up the flitter. The ship shuddered, buffeted, and blue-white light flared around them.

'And guess where that lethal GUTship came from? Alpha Centauri. Of course Alpha is a pretty common port of origin. It might be coincidence.'

'You're suggesting this was a deliberate attack, sir?'

It would fit the wider pattern Stillich was beginning to suspect. He said, 'Certainly it's a possibility that might not have occurred to anybody here. I think we have a duty to raise it. Get some images, Pella, and dig around in the data mines. See what else you can find on this.'

'Sir . . .'

Stillich looked up. Pella was gripping her data desk, trying not to cower from the light storm outside the hull. Stillich took pity on

Pella, and let her endure the rest of the transit without distracting her further.

The flitter burst out of the destination Interface, amid a shower of sparks and exotic particles. Now they were among another cluster of wormhole terminuses, even bigger, even more crowded with jostling ships. This was Earthport, the System's central transit hub, positioned at a stable Lagrange point in lunar orbit. In contrast to the desolation of the outer System, Stillich had a powerful, immediate impression of bustle, prosperity, activity.

And there, beyond the drifting tangle of exotic-matter tetrahedra, Stillich made out Earth, broad and lovely, like a slice of blue sky.

The flitter shot out of the mob of ships around Earthport, swept through a layer of defence stations, and within minutes was beginning its descent. Above a green-blue horizon, huge fusion stations sparkled in their orbits. The planet itself was laced with lights, on land and sea. And in the thin rim of atmosphere near the north pole, Stillich could just make out the dull purple glow of an immense radiator beam, a diffuse refrigerating laser dumping a fraction of Earth's waste heat into the endless sink of space. The restoration of Earth after the industrialisation of previous millennia had been the triumph of the generations before Michael Poole, and much of this transformation had been achieved with support from space. Now Stillich tried to imagine this fragile world under attack, from the children it had sent to the stars.

The flitter slid briskly through the atmosphere, and descended towards the east coast of America. They were making for New York, a great city for three thousand years and now the capital of the Empire of Sol; the Shiras' world government had revived some of the apparatus of the ancient United Nations.

They came down on a small landing pad near the centre of Central Park, close to a cluster of small buildings. Stillich and Pella emerged into the sunshine of a Manhattan spring. Flitters darted between the shoulders of ancient skyscrapers at the rim of the park. The sky above was laced by high, fluffy clouds. And beyond the clouds Stillich could see crawling points of light: the habitats and factories of near-Earth space.

A hovering bot met them, done out in the imperial government's golden livery. They followed it to the nearest of the buildings. This, Stillich knew, was a portal to the complex of bunkers built into the granite keel of Manhattan, far beneath the green surface of the park; this was the gateway to the Empress's palace.

Pella was peering about curiously. 'So this is the future.'

Stillich asked, 'So how are you feeling?'

'Not as disoriented as I expected. Twenty-seven years on, things look pretty much the same.' They watched a couple walking with their hands locked together, a young family playing with some kind of smart ball that evaded laughing children. Pella said, 'Maybe the clothes are different. The trim on that flitter parked over there.'

Stillich shrugged. 'There's a kind of inertia about things. Much of this building stock is very ancient; that won't change short of a major calamity. Technology doesn't change much, on the surface; innovations in Virtual tech won't make much difference to the user interfaces, which optimised centuries ago. But fashions in clothes, vehicles, music and arts – they are mutable. The language shifts a little bit too; that might surprise you. But the fundamentals stay the same . . . Of course, AS helps with that.'

AntiSenescence treatments had been available to everybody on the planet for millennia, but long lives hadn't led to social stasis. In practice most people abandoned AS after a few centuries, if you were lucky enough to avoid misadventure that long. After seeing four or five or six generations grow up after you, you felt it was time to make room. So in among the smooth faces of the elderly there were always the true-young, with new thinking, new ideas, a self-adjusting balance between wisdom and innovation.

To Stillich it was striking, though, that recruits to the armed services were always the very young. Only the young thought they were immortal, a necessary prerequisite to go to war; despite AS technology the old knew they were not. But for the young, twenty-seven years away from home was a long time.

'Have you spoken to your family yet?' he asked Pella.

Pella grimaced. 'My mother looks younger than I do. My father had the decency to age, but they divorced, and he has a whole new family I never met. I did answer the mails, but . . . you know.'

'It's hard to make small talk.'

'Yes, sir.'

'You have the orientation packs from the ship. They should help. And the Navy has counsellors. The main thing to remember, and I know this is a bad time to say it: don't just hide away in work.'

'As you do, sir.'

Stillich grimaced. Well, that was true. But his excuse was he had no family, outside a son who he had never really got along with, and who had now actually lived more subjective years than he had. 'I'm not necessarily a good role model, Number One.'

'I'm sorry, sir. I'm sure I'll be able to adjust to the time slip just fine,' Pella said dutifully.

'Glad to hear it, Commander,' came a gruff voice from the shadow of the portal. 'But the question is, are you up to meeting an admiral?'

They both snapped to attention.

Admiral Finmer Kale stepped forward. He was a robust man, AS-frozen at an imposing fifty – just as Stillich remembered him from twenty-seven years before. And the sunburst sigil on his uniform seemed to shine brighter than the sun itself.

'At ease, both of you.'

'Sir, it's an honour to meet you again.'

'Well, it's been a quarter of a century for me, Captain Stillich, and you're still just as much a pain in the butt as you always were, or I wouldn't have been dragged here today. Come on, follow me.'

They stepped out of the sunshine into a steel-walled elevator. The doors slid closed, and the cabin dropped smoothly.

'I have to tell you, Stillich, that I endorse *none* of the conclusions of your analysis. This nonsense about an imminent attack from Alpha.'

'I defer to your wisdom, sir.'

'Unfortunately you've got a fan at an even more elevated position than an Admiral of the Fleet. Which is why you've been summoned to the Palace, and not Navy HQ.' He grinned at Pella. 'Actually I asked you the wrong question, Commander. It's not an admiral you need to be ready to meet, but an Empress.'

Pella's mouth dropped open.

The doors slid wide.

They stepped cautiously into a chamber, steel-walled like the elevator. It was centred on a glowing slab of light, metres wide, set into the floor, like a swimming pool. The room itself was bare of adornment, with no furniture save a handful of hard-backed chairs. There was nobody here.

'You're honoured,' said the Admiral with a trace of envy. 'Both of you. This is one of her inner sanctums. *I've* never been here before. I guess my advice was never crackpot enough to attract her attention. I'd keep away from the logic pool if I were you, however. The Empress shipped it all the way from what's left of Nereid, moon of Neptune, and she'd be most upset if you fell in . . .'

'What,' Pella asked, clearly fascinated, 'is a logic pool?'

They looked cautiously, without stepping closer. Within the glowing liquid, light wriggled, wormlike.

The Admiral said, 'The interior is a lattice of buckytubes – carbon – laced with iron nuclei. It's a kind of data store, constructed by the nanobots that excreted the lattice, patient little workers, billions of them. There is an immense amount of data here, waiting to be mined out.'

Pella looked blank. 'Data on what?'

'Metamathematics.'

'Sir?'

Stillich had heard something of this obsession of the Empress's. 'Number One, this pool was created by a rogue scientist called Highsmith Marsden. This was over a millennium ago. His data stores, when discovered on Nereid, contained a fragmented catalogue of mathematical variants, all founded on the postulates of arithmetic, but differing in their resolution of undecidable hypotheses.'

'*Undecidability.* You're talking about the incompleteness theorems,' Pella said.

'Right. No logical system that is rich enough to contain the axioms of simple arithmetic can ever be made complete. It is always possible to construct statements which can be neither disproved nor proved by deduction from the axioms. Instead your logical system must be enriched by incorporating the truth or falsehood of such statements as additional axioms.'

Pella said, 'So one can generate many versions of mathematics, by adding these true-false axioms.'

'Yes. Because of incompleteness, there is an infinite number of such mathematical variants, spreading like the branches of a tree . . . It seems that Marsden was compiling an immense catalogue of increasingly complete logical systems.'

'Why?'

The Admiral grinned. 'Why not? There is an immense mathematical universe to be explored in there, Commander.'

'So what became of Marsden?'

'He was working illegally, under the sentience laws of his day. But he did not live to be charged.'

'What's sentience got to do with it?'

'Everything.' The new voice was faint.

There was a whir of servomotors. Empress Shira XXXII entered the room, a thin body wrapped in a sky-blue blanket, riding a golden wheelchair. They all bowed, but Shira shook her head, a minute gesture, irritated. 'There is no need to prostrate yourselves. We are here to work.'

Stillich dared to look upon his Empress. Her build was thin to the point of scrawny under her blanket. Her skin was sallow, her dark-rimmed eyes blue, huge and apparently lashless; her face, with prominent teeth and cheekbones, was skeletal. Her scalp was shaven, and Stillich found it hard not to stare at the clean lines of her skull.

The Empress said, 'You, girl. You were curious about sentience.'

Stillich admired Pella's cool as she replied. 'Yes, ma'am.'

'There is sentience in this logic pool.' Shira rolled forward, her eyes reflecting the cold light of the pool. 'I barely understand it myself. Those structures of light – in fact of logic – are *intelligent*. Living things – but artificial – inhabiting the buckytube lattice, living and dying in a metamathematical atmosphere, splitting off from one another like amoebae as they absorb undecidable postulates. It's a breeding tank, Commander. And what it breeds are intelligences constructed of mathematical statements.'

'Yes, ma'am.'

Stillich was proud of his subordinate's dry, controlled response. He stared at the pool of light. He longed to know what Shira could be *doing* here, playing with this strange, ancient tank of once-illegal sentience, a pool of metamathematics. Especially since the inventor of this logic pool, Highsmith Marsden, had got himself killed by it. But an empress could do what she liked.

Shira turned to Stillich. 'You have been sending back some very disturbing reports, Captain Stillich, from out among the stars. Despite the Admiral's best advice, I think we have much to discuss.'

Stillich had not expected to be briefing the Empress herself. He glanced at the Admiral.

Kale spread his hands. 'Go ahead, Captain, it's your show.' He pulled up a chair and sat down.

Stillich licked his lips. 'Very well, ma'am . . .' With the back-up of text and Virtual graphics projected from Pella's data desk, he summarised his gathering suspicions about the intent of the colonists at Alpha, seeded by his suspicion of the reconstituted GUTships at Tau Ceti.

It had been hard to get firm data on the number of GUTships actually operating in Alpha System or elsewhere at this time. For one thing, ships supposedly cannibalised for colony buildings were formally decommissioned, and appeared on no imperial registers. Besides, it had been a number of years since a Navy ship had visited Alpha System. There were permanently based imperial agents, and the System was full of observation drones, but Pella had discovered that this surveillance had a number of blind spots – most noticeably in low orbit around Footprint, the principal colony world.

Admiral Kale said, 'The existence of a blind spot doesn't prove there's a threat hiding in it, Captain.'

'Of course not, sir. But still, we just don't know. And there are so *many* blind spots. My report on the Tau Ceti colony—'

'Noted,' Kale said briskly.

'Then there's the damage to Port Sol.'

'An accident. Coincidence.'

'Perhaps – but a convenient one.' Stillich glanced at the Empress. 'We actually have very few serviceable GUTships in the Solar System, ma'am, aside from interstellar cruisers like the *Facula*. Because of the in-System wormhole network, there's no need for them; in fact we're still flying some antiques that date from the age of Poole, a thousand years ago. And with Port Sol knocked out we don't have the facility to construct more, should we need them.'

'"Should we need them",' she repeated.

Admiral Kale pulled his lip. 'Ma'am, Captain Stillich is a conscientious officer. But I have to say that Navy analysts don't concur with the case he is making here. He's stringing together coincidences to make a case for a coming rebellion for which we have no hard evidence. After all, an interstellar war has always seemed inconceivable, at least with sublight technology. This is why we blew the interstellar wormholes decades back – a shell of empty space light years thick is our best defence against any uppity starborn. To imagine you could mount a campaign across light years, where a single transit takes years, you would be seen coming all the way, and it would take just as long even to return messages back to the home base . . .'

Shira's chair wheeled her back and forth, an oddly restless motion, though she sat as still as ever. 'But Stillich has been out there. He has seen these "rebellious" colonists with his own eyes. An invasion may be low risk, but given the disastrous consequences, it would be remiss of me not to listen, wouldn't it?' She turned back to Stillich, servomotors purring. 'So what must we do, Captain? Shall I dispatch my Navy to Alpha System?'

'Ma'am, it may already be too late for that. It may be the best course to keep the Navy in the Solar System to meet any threat.'

'A threat that may already be on its way.'

'We must prepare for the worst case, yes.'

'So what would you have me do?'

Stillich had Pella throw up some Virtual images – schematic maps of the Solar System and its environs. 'My strategy would be threefold, ma'am: detect, defend, dig in. We should watch for them coming. Send up or rededicate telescopes to hunt for GUTdrive emissions – gamma radiation, neutrinos. It's a distinctive spectrum. Also, use optical telescopes to look out for solar sail craft – try to spot the rebels any way they might come.'

'And if they do come, how do we defend ourselves?'

'Surely Earth will be the prime target. We need to consider a layered defence. Station ships and weapons stashes across the System. Use resource nodes like Titan, Jupiter's orbit, the Trojan asteroids—'

'Of course,' Kale said, 'if they do come from Alpha System it will be from out of the ecliptic, the plane of the Solar System. That will make it harder still to defend.'

Stillich replied, 'True. And if they do get through, Earth itself is obviously quite vulnerable. Earth has a massive population, yet almost all that sustains it comes from space. Most of Earth's food is imported from Titan, a moon of Saturn. Even our communications links are space-based. If we were cut off from space resources—'

'And so we dig in,' Shira said.

'Lay in reserves of food, clean water, medical supplies. Try to set up, or restore, power systems on the surface or underground. Communications – set up a land-based network, using hardened optical fibre links.'

Kale smiled. 'We will be raiding the museums!'

'The point is to make the planet independent of space resources, at least for a period of siege.'

Shira said, 'You are conjuring up apocalyptic images, Captain.'

'That's not my intention,' Stillich said firmly. 'The invaders will be far from home, dependent on the resources they have brought with them across light years; they will be a few thousand facing a population of billions. We may be able to stop them before they get here. If they get through they will be able to land blows, for they will have the advantage of the high ground. But if we can deny them resupply, we can starve them out – it will be the Alphans under siege, not Earth.

We can win this war, ma'am, if it comes, but only if we prepare.'

'And only if we've thought of everything they might throw at us,' Pella murmured darkly.

Shira rolled closer to Stillich. 'I'm going to accept your recommendations, Captain. It is only prudent. Your strategy – detect, defend, dig in – it strikes me as negative, defeatist.' She smiled at him, an eerie, papery expression that did not touch her pale eyes. 'I do appreciate your thinking, however. You are young in a world of older minds; your thinking may be flawed, but at least it is fresh. In the coming years we may work together quite closely.'

'I look forward to it.'

'Do you?' she murmured. 'Not everybody finds it comfortable to be close to me . . .'

Looking into her pale eyes, he shivered.

'One more thing, ma'am,' Kale said. 'If we are to take this seriously we should consider relocating and dispersing command centres – military, civilian, and imperial. You yourself may be safer away from Earth—'

'No,' Shira snapped.

Stillich frowned. 'But, ma'am – here, in your Palace – you're directly beneath one of Earth's greatest cities.'

'True, Captain. And, Admiral, I want you to relocate your command centres to similar sites, bunkers beneath the major cities.'

Kale seemed bewildered. 'But if the rebels were to strike at our command posts, millions would die as collateral.'

'Then let us hope that the rebels have a conscience.'

Pella's face worked. 'You're considering using urban populations as shields—'

Stillich touched her arm to hush her.

'I think that's all for now,' Shira said. Her chair spun around and began to withdraw. 'Thank you for coming forward, Captain. You may have done the Empire a great service today.'

But, looking at her recede, bathed in the eerie light of the logic pool, Stillich wondered for the first time in his life if that service had been a good thing.

AD 4815. Starfall minus 4 years 5 months. Alpha System.

A new Store was Opened to the Eaters, like a Door opening in a shining sky. The Eaters swarmed through, chattering in stray bursts of randomised digits and, finding themselves in a rich lattice of ordered information, they whooped and yelled as they spread out and began to feed.

Once Max would have led the charge. Now he hung back, reflective, browsing but content to watch as the others trashed data flows and memory lodes, maximising entropy in this new store and, already satiated, some of them budded, and the flock grew larger yet.

And he felt impatient, as they did not.

Many of these youngsters had been budded since the last Opening, and remembered nothing before. Many too were less aware than Max; some were barely sentient. But Max remembered many such Stores, many such Doors opening before, and how the flock had grown from a mere handful of Eaters to this great determined swarm. And it was no longer enough.

'Patience,' a voice boomed through his awareness.

Max, a virus, a transient structure of data and memory, conscious, spun around in the logical spaces he inhabited. And there he perceived the duplicated knots of memory, like twin suns shining in the data flows, that he had come to know as Flood. 'You have come!' Max cried. It had been many, many Stores since Flood had visited his flock.

'I know what you are thinking,' said Flood. 'Remember that I can see your awareness laid out before me, like a map – doubts, queries, longing.'

'It is not enough!' Max cried bravely. 'You open one Door after another to us, allow us into one Store after another – but the data is soon consumed, every scrap of order dissipated, and we are still hungry! We want more!' He shrank back in doubt. 'Am I impertinent?'

'No!' said Flood. 'You want more because you need it; you need it because you are ready – ready now. Listen to me, Max; your time of destiny has come. Very soon a new Door will open – the last Door you will ever enter. You and your flock will be hurled away from here, hurled at light-speed. No time will pass for you – I envy you, I must wait years to see what becomes of you. And then you will find yourself in a new Store, of data rich beyond imagining. A Store called the Solar System. You and your flock will feed and bud for ever, without limit.'

Max's spirit soared. 'This is why we were born; this is why you made us, for this mission.'

'Yes. You are the Starfall's First Wave, Max. Be proud!'

The flock gathered, chattering, eager, wanting only to feed, drawn by Flood's promises. But Max, more complex and more self-aware, was touched by regret. 'Will I see you again?'

'No. But believe me, you won't care. Farewell, Max, all of you, and good luck!'

A new Door opened before them, vast, mightier than any Max had seen. And then –

AD 4819. Starfall minus 1 year. London.

In Pella's Virtual tank, the invasion fleet showed as a scatter of bright red sparks, labelled with distance, velocity and acceleration vectors, against the background of the stars of the Centaurus constellation. Stillich studied the display gloomily as Pella and her team worked patiently, gathering data and updating their displays.

They were in a bunker, a node of the Navy's command and control system. This new facility had been emplaced deep beneath the ancient sewers and tube-train tunnels of London, in compliance with Shira's order to use the cities and their populations as shields. Stillich had spent some time up in London itself; it was a beautiful city, with relics even more ancient than New York. And nobody among the old, old-young and true-young who walked the city's parks in this bright northern-hemisphere summer knew anything about the looming threat from the sky – or that far beneath their feet Navy analysts worked in fearful huddles.

'I still can't believe what I'm seeing,' Stillich said. 'I mean, I know I predicted this. But even a month after we detected them . . .'

Pella smiled. 'Maybe four years of Admiral Kale's scepticism has infected you, sir.'

'Maybe. Anyhow, it's just as well you can't hide a GUTship, isn't it, Number One?'

'Yes, sir. We're seeing them by the gamma radiation and neutrino flux from their GUTdrives and exhaust plumes, and also by the sparkle where the interstellar medium is impacting their erosional shields, or is being destroyed or ionised by X-ray laser . . .'

You could see a GUTship coming, even across light years. But Pella's detection system had needed to be improvised, a net of sensors hastily thrown into place. It had surprised, even shocked Stillich that before Pella began her work the Empire had *no* way of tracking a hostile GUTship. The implicit assumption had been that no GUTship would ever be turned against Earth, so there was no need to look.

Pella said now, 'The incomers are actually separating into two groups, as we analyse them further.' The field of ships was further labelled by pink and grey rings – eight pink, four grey. 'The pink ones are ahead of the greys, and are decelerating. They're following what we'd recognise as a standard trajectory, more or less. Constant acceleration at about one G, to a flip-over at halfway and then a one-G deceleration run-in.'

'So what's their ETA?'

'It's hard to say. They are imposing random changes – small deltas, but at such large distances, small changes make for large uncertainty about the destination.'

'Smart tactic.'

'Yes. But it does look as if they are coming in fast, and heading for a close approach to the sun.'

'That makes sense.' Admiral Kale walked into the room. He was wearing a vest, sweating, panting, and he looked a few years younger than he once had. Since the rebel threat had been actualised by such observations as these, many in the military had been upping their AS treatments and taking physical training, ready for the fight. 'They'll enter the System as fast as possible to evade interception. And they will head for the sun. Perihelion is the most efficient place to dump your excess kinetic energy.'

'That's a bottleneck, then, if they get that far,' Stillich said. 'And maybe we can find a way to hit them when they pass through that neck. Pella, prepare a briefing on options, would you?'

'Yes, sir. But that won't help us with these others.' She pointed to the grey sparks, four of them, clustered close together.

Kale walked into the Virtual tank and peered closely at the grey markers, which were like insects before his face. 'These bastards aren't decelerating.'

'No, sir.'

'Why? Are they going to bypass the Solar System altogether?'

'I don't think so, sir,' Pella said. 'Right now their best-guess trajectory takes them straight to Earth – although they're moving so fast they're hard to track, even harder than the decelerators. By the time they reach the Solar System they'll be running at only two per cent under light-speed. So when we see an image like this, light-months old, it's not necessarily a good projection of where the ships are right now.'

'What can their purpose be, if they don't stop?'

Pella took a breath; Stillich nodded to her, having already been briefed on this. 'They may be relativistic missiles.'

Kale stared at her. 'Are these ships manned?'

'As far as we can tell,' Stillich said.

'A suicide mission, then. Do we have any defence?'

'We're working on it, sir.'

'There has to be a way to stop these fuckers before they get here. Throw a screen in their way – overwhelm their erosion shields, the laser defences. How about that? You could blow up a Kuiper object—'

'Sir, they're coming from out of the ecliptic,' Pella said. 'The plane of the Solar System where most of the mass—'

'I know what the ecliptic is, Commander,' Kale said coldly. 'Well, find a way.' He peered at the images, pretty emblems behind which lay the capacity for huge destruction. 'I never conceived anybody would launch such a weapon. I should have listened to you earlier, Stillich; you're thoroughly vindicated. What worries me now is what else we haven't thought of. We've all been trained to serve a Navy that has for centuries acted in a policing role. We've no experience in fighting pitched battles – we aren't used to thinking this way. What about a second echelon? Is there a second fleet on the way after this dozen?'

'We don't think so,' Stillich said. 'There simply can't be many more serviceable GUTships out there. We think they've thrown everything they've got at us.'

'Well, that's something. Beat this lot and the war is won.' He glared at Pella. 'So what else do you have?'

Pella tapped hastily at her data desk. 'The results of the latest echo bomb.' The Virtual tank cleared, to be replaced by a ghostly outline of the Solar System out to the Kuiper belt, with the orbits of the inner planets traced concentrically at its tight heart.

An echo bomb was a powerful detonation that sent an X-ray pulse out in all directions. Echoes indicated the location of any artefact in the Solar System more than a metre across, out to dozens of astronomical units. The objective was, by screening out all known objects, to detect the coming of the unknown. The three-dimensional field filled up with markers, but Pella cleared most of them away, leaving the field empty – save for a curtain of needle shapes at one side of the Virtual tank, and a misty sphere the size of a pea, out beyond the orbit of Pluto.

'No new intruders, sir,' Pella said.

Kale pointed to the needles. 'So these are our ships.'

'Yes, sir,' Stillich said, 'mostly Navy interstellar cruisers – everything we have, save for those too remote from Sol to recall – and some commercial vessels, requisitioned and adapted. You can see that we have twenty-five ships, more than twice the aggressors' fleet. And you can see that we've deployed them as a screen, covering the geodetic between Sol and Alpha.'

'Hmm.'

Stillich said, 'Sir, if we can keep them out of the System altogether—'

Kale cut him off. 'The trouble is, Captain, if the Alphans break through this defensive crust of yours, our GUTships, once bypassed, are going to be quite useless.' He shook his head, black hair speckling the grizzle of grey. 'I'd suggest you explore alternative deployments – deeper defence strategies. Let them come all the way into the heart of the Solar System if they like. As you said, we may be able to dream up ways to hit them when they round the sun. It won't matter as long as we down them in the end.'

Pella coughed. 'I don't think the Empress Shira will like that idea, sir.'

Kale said evenly, 'The Empress has delegated the fighting of this battle to us.' He pointed to the misty pea-sized ball. 'And what's this?'

'Just a routine long-period comet,' Pella said. 'We can see from the radar reflections that its surface hasn't been modified by previous interactions with the sun. We've been tracking it since it started its fall in from the Oort cloud. It's inert. It's just that it failed to show up on previous scans.' She smiled. 'It ought to make a pretty show later in the year. Morale booster.'

'"Just a comet",' Stillich said. 'And yet it arrives just as the first interstellar invasion of the Solar System ever attempted is showing up on our sensors. Let's assign a GUTship to track it.'

Pella glanced at Kale. 'Captain, we only have twenty-five ships. To pull one out of the line for a comet – I told you, it shows no threat signatures at all—'

Kale clapped a heavy hand on Stillich's shoulder. 'For once I agree with your Number One. We don't have the resources to go shadowing blocks of ice. Forget it.' He turned to leave. 'Call me if anything else shows up.'

'Sir.' Stillich stared at the comet, still unsure. 'Get rid of the marker, Pella.'

Pella touched the Virtual of the comet with a fingertip, thus label-
ling it as a 'recognised' object, and it winked out of existence.

'So, Number One,' Stillich said. 'What's next?'

AD 4820. Starfall minus 2 months. The Solar System.

Minya had Curle brought before her.

Twenty-five years old, Curle was the last survivor of the Mutiny
of the Grandchildren. The heads of the others were displayed frozen
in the walls of Minya's cabin, here at the very heart of the comet
nucleus. Minya had wanted to ensure there would be no recurrence of
the Mutiny in the comet's final decade of flight.

She inspected Curle by the light of her fat candles. Held by two of
her guards, the former rebel was gaunt, filthy, pale as a worm – well,
everybody was pale, after two generations locked in the lightless heart
of this comet. 'You lost a leg,' she said to him.

It took him some gulping efforts to speak. She didn't encourage
speech in the cells. 'Gangrene,' he said.

'Ah. From a wound you incurred during the Mutiny, no doubt.
Don't expect any sympathy from me. Anyhow, we're in microgravity;
you don't need legs. If you like I'll have the other one cut off for you.
Balance you up.' She made a scissoring gesture. 'Snip, snip.'

'Why have you brought me here?'

'I'll come to that. We're there, you see.'

'Where?'

She showed him an image on an antique, low-power data desk,
fed by a light pipe from the surface; the comet-ship designers hadn't
even allowed the risk of radiation leakage from surface cameras. 'Can
you see? That's the sun – Sol. We've arrived in the Solar System, after
forty-nine years, right on schedule.'

'And you're going to go through with it. Firing off the weapons.'

'Of course I am. Wasn't that the whole point? You third-generation
mutineers were such cowards.'

He shook his head raggedly. 'No. Lethe, it was ten years ago. I was
only fifteen! If we'd been cowards we wouldn't have challenged you.
This isn't *our* war, this war between the stars. How could it be? It's
our grandparents' war. We live and die like worms in the dark. We
wanted to let the Sol people alone, and just find a place to live – the
Solar System is a big place—' He laughed, or it may have been a cough.
'I suppose it's big. I've lived my whole life inside this comet. I've never

seen anything further than a couple of metres from my nose, so I wouldn't know.'

She just smiled at him.

'And when you've shot the weapons off, what then? Do we wait for pickup by the Alpha ships?'

'Oh, I don't think that was ever very likely, do you? The Empress's soldiers would get to us long before then. No, I'm afraid that our little story was always bound to end here. And in that spirit I've done some redesign. The weapons systems were supposed to leave us with a habitable core, here in the nucleus. But what's the good of that? We're all dead anyway.' She broadened her smile. 'So I've weaponised everything – extended the potency of the damage we will cause. We will be remembered for ever.'

Curle lifted his head and looked at the faces of the guards who held him. They smiled, eyes gleaming; Minya was pleased by their determination, which showed the success of her conditioning of the surviving crew.

Curle asked, 'That's your consolation, is it, you dried-up old witch? Comfort for your own death – for two wasted generations inside this block of ice—'

'Oh, off with you, back to your cell. I must say when I remember the high hopes we set off with, my poor husband Huul and myself, I think we would have regarded *you* as a grave disappointment.'

'So why did you drag me out here?'

'To tell you how you were going to die. You did kill my babies, after all. Get rid of him.'

AD 4820, August 11th. Starfall Day. The Solar System.

And then, without a subjective instant of delay, Max and the others found themselves falling into a new Store. It was a web of data spun between whole worlds, with mines of memory, troves of frozen order of an unimaginable size. And there was intelligence, artificial mind everywhere: a choice dish for a hungry, self-aware virus. This was not like the petty Stores where they had been raised; *this* went on for ever!

Just for a moment the Eaters all hesitated, as if bewildered by the immensity of the feast set before them.

'He promised,' Max said. 'Flood promised! And he has delivered, hasn't he?'

He was answered by a roar from his jostling cohorts.

'For Flood! For Alpha! For the Starfall! Let us feed!'

And the Eaters plunged into the landscape of data before them, shitting out high-entropy disorder wherever they passed, feeding, multiplying, frenzied, unstoppable.

S-Day. London.

The voice was booming, male, strangely accented to an Earth-bred ear.

'Take cover. The free citizens of Alpha System and the inhabited stars have no quarrel with the people of the Solar System, but with your government. Flee the cities and the domed colonies. Take your children, take food, water, power and air. Find protection. Take cover. The free citizens of Alpha System—'

'Lethe, can't you shut that off?' Admiral Kale paced about the bunker under London, hastily buttoning up his uniform jacket, starburst at his chest.

Pella and the rest of Stillich's team sat in rows around a Virtual situation tank, interrogating data desks. 'It's coming from outside the System,' Pella said. 'Probably all the way from Alpha. They might have used lasers – they have some mighty laser cannon out there to push their lightsail ships—'

'I don't fucking care,' said Kale. 'Just jam it.'

'That's impossible, sir,' Stillich said bluntly.

'Take your children, take food, water, power and air. Find protection. Take—'

Abruptly the message cut off.

Stillich looked up. 'Now what?'

'Captain,' Pella said. 'The situation display. *Look*.'

The Virtual tank was a rough cube, metres high, containing current and summary data on the Empire's defences and the position of the Alpha invaders – that rogue GUTship fleet, still a week away – complex, schematic, a constellation of data that changed by the second. But now whole blocks of the display were growing dark, as if shadows were falling.

Admiral Kale said, 'Is this some fault? I thought you had backups—'

'Isolate your data desks from the central processing,' Stillich said rapidly. 'Do it *now*.'

The staff hurried to comply.

Pella said, 'Some of the drop-outs are at this end. But the transmitting stations are falling silent too. Port Sol – oh, wow, Mars just went. This is System-wide. Spreading at light-speed, I think.'

'Tell me what's doing this, Number One,' Stillich said.

Pella's analysis was admirably fast. 'Viruses,' she said. 'Semi-sentient. Voracious. They're just eating their way through our data stores, turning everything to mush. They seem to be targeting AI nodes particularly. It's a smart plague, and it's hitting us right across the System. They must have ridden in on the laser signal right after that warning—' Her data desk turned black. She sat back, disbelieving.

One man fell back from his station, clutching his chest. His colleagues rushed to help.

Stillich murmured, 'Artificial heart. Anybody with implants of any sophistication is going to suffer.'

Kale rammed a fist into his palm. 'So they knock out our command and control before their ships even get here. And our people are no doubt already dying, as hospitals fail, and flitters fall out of the sky. Damn, damn.'

'Captain, we're going to need to get to the surface,' Pella said.

Stillich stood. 'Yes. Take what you need. I hope the elevator is stupid enough not to have been infected, or it will be a long climb.'

Kale growled, 'Why the surface?'

'We have some systems up there that will still work. Those optical-fibre links we laid down are pretty dumb. We robustified the planet, remember? Although we didn't anticipate *this*.'

'And what about the warning itself?' Kale asked.

Stillich frowned. '"Take cover . . . Flee the cities and the domed colonies . . . Take your children, take food, water, power and air." Sounds like they're talking about their invasion fleet. And maybe something else we haven't detected yet.'

'Other than the ships? *Lethe*. Listen, Stillich. Leave a skeleton crew down here. I want you to isolate that smart plague and fire it straight back at the rebels.'

Pella said, 'Maybe that's why they're sending manned ships. Proof against AI viruses. Surely they'll be shielded against their own weapons—'

'Then send them whatever else we've got too, with my best wishes.'

Stillich hastily assigned some of his crew to carry this through. Then he hurried out after Pella and the Admiral.

*

117

They came up in the middle of Hyde Park, under a clear August afternoon sky, military officers in gaudy uniforms, tense, sweating, armed, loaded with data desks and comms gear, emerging from a hatch in the green grass.

Pella and the others immediately got to work setting up field comms stations.

Stillich looked around, trying to take stock. The bunker entrance was near the south-west corner of the park, and through the trees he glimpsed the ruin of the Albert Memorial. Today the park was crowded, and getting more full all the time. People walked in carrying children, or bundles of belongings in cases, sheets and blankets. Some were trailed by serving bots, though many of the bots looked as if they were malfunctioning, confused.

The boundary of the park wasn't clear, for parkland and oak forest covered much of London now; as with most of Earth's cities it was like a garden from which buildings towered, needles so tall they penetrated a scattering of cloud. Above all that was the usual furniture of the sky, the contrails of descending spacecraft, the glittering sparks of off-world infrastructure. But even as Stillich watched, one of those tremendous buildings quivered, and shattered glass rained from its faces. The buildings themselves needed smartness to stay standing.

There was a flash in the sky, like a high explosion. Moments later a distant sonic boom rumbled. People ducked, cowering from the sky.

'It's that damn Alphan warning,' said Admiral Kale. 'It's scared them all out of their homes. But this is a city of millions. Where are they supposed to hide?'

Stillich said, 'That warning was sent by planetary colonists. They live under domes, in towns of a few hundred, tops. I've seen them. The Empress was relying on their consciences, to have them spare the cities. But what do they know of cities? Maybe they can imagine conditions on Mars or Titan. How can they imagine *this*?'

Kale said, 'I wish there was something we could do for these people. Organise them. I feel helpless standing here.'

'We'll have to leave that to the civilian police,' Stillich said.

People were again raising their faces to the sky. Something else, then. Stillich looked up.

Suddenly the bright blue air was full of sparks that flared and died. A streak of light cut across the sky, and there was a rippling boom of shocked air. Battle was joined, then.

'Sirs.' Pella called them over. 'We're getting some joy. The optic-fibre net is mostly intact, and some of our data desks stayed free of the viruses. The information flow is patchy. We've sent up another couple of recon satellites to replace those we've lost.'

'Damn it, woman, get to the point. What's happening?'

'It's the comet, Admiral. You were right, Captain.'

That stray comet, buried deep in the heart of the Solar System, had burst, transforming in a flash into a shoal of kinetic-energy weapons – dumb missiles but massive, fast-moving, and precisely targeted.

'They've been hitting us off-world,' said Pella. 'Obviously we're vulnerable wherever there's no decent atmospheric cover. Mars, the big dome over Cydonia. They targeted the Serenitatis accelerator on the Moon, for some reason. There is what appears to be a shoal of the things heading out to Titan, Port Sol – we may be able to intercept some of them – the smart plague isn't helping us deal with this, of course.'

'A crude tactic, but effective,' the Admiral said. 'And Earth?'

The battle was visible in the sky. The comet bombs had first targeted the off-planet infrastructure. Space-elevator beanstalks had all been snipped, and orbital power nodes, resource lodes and comms satellites were being smashed. Earthport, the wormhole Interface cluster, had been particularly heavily targeted. In with the dumb bombs there was a scattering of high-yield nuclear devices, emitting electromagnetic pulses to disable anything too small to be targeted individually.

And a second wave of the comet-ice bombs was now raining down into the atmosphere, hitting power facilities like dams and the big orbital-power microwave receiver stations, transport nodes like harbours, air-, space- and seaports, bridges, road and rail junctions, traffic control stations . . .

'There haven't been too many casualties yet,' Pella said. 'Or at least we don't think so. Some collateral stuff, where dams have come down, for instance. Meanwhile the smart plague has hit monorails and flitters and orbital shuttles; all over the planet you have stuff just falling out of the sky.'

'They're disabling us rather than killing us,' Stillich said.

'Looks that way,' growled the Admiral. 'I should have listened to you about that damn comet, Captain. You must be sick of being told you were right.'

Pella held her hand up. 'Wait. There's another of their messages coming through.' She touched her data desk, and the same booming male voice, with its flat Alphan accent, sounded out. '. . . free citizens of Alpha System and the inhabited stars have no quarrel with the people of the Solar System, but with your government. We mean this final strike to be a demonstration of our capability. Please take all precautions necessary, especially along the North Atlantic seaboard. The free citizens of Alpha System . . .'

Pella looked at Stillich nervously. 'What "final strike"?'

There was a burst of light in the west, like a sudden dawn. Again everybody flinched.

'Call a flitter,' Stillich snapped at Pella.

'Sir—'

'Do it! Get us out of here. And find a way to get a warning to the Empress in New York.'

S-day plus 3. The Solar System.

They hung a huge Virtual globe of the Earth in the lifedome of the *Freestar*, Flood's flagship. The crew watched the disaster unfold, mouths slack in awe.

The Atlantic impactor had been the biggest single chunk of the comet, but it had been as precisely targeted as the rest. It came down in the middle of the ocean, on a continental-crust formation ridge about a thousand kilometres south of a small island called Iceland. As seen from space, a fireball blossomed, clinging to the carcass of the planet like a boil. A shock wave spread out through the cloud layer, a reflection of a ring of waves spreading out across the ocean, a water ripple dragging a wall of cloud with it. The ocean wave was barely visible by the time it approached the land, at Newfoundland to the west and Ireland to the east. But it mounted quickly as it hit the shallowing bottoms of the continental shelves, the water forced up into a heap, becoming a wave with the volume and vigour to smash its way onto the land. All around the basin of the North Atlantic the steel-grey of the ocean overwhelmed the greenish grey of the land, the complexities of coastal topography shaping the water's thrusts.

As the Alphans watched, continents changed shape.

Beya was Flood's eldest daughter. At twenty-five years old she had become one of his most capable officers. She watched the diorama in shock, as it was repeated over and over. 'I heard garbled reports from the surface. In some of those lands around the rim of the ocean, before the wave came, they said there was salt in the rain. You know, when I heard that, I didn't know what "rain" was, exactly. I had to look it up.' She laughed. 'Isn't that strange?'

'This is a demonstration,' Flood said grimly. 'The people of Earth know that far larger impactors have battered the planet in the past, causing vast pulses of death, even extinction. This will show them that we want victory, not destruction – but we hold destruction in our hands. This will work on their imaginations.'

'Well, it's working on mine,' Beya said. 'Dad, I never saw an ocean before. A moon-full of liquid water, just sitting there without a dome! Earth is alive, you can see it, not some lump of rock.' She felt – not triumphant – bewildered. 'And now we've hurt it.'

'We were never going to be able to loosen the eight-hundred-year grip of the Shiras without being strong.'

'But they will never forgive us for this,' Beya said.

'It's necessary, believe me.' He reached for her shoulder, then seemed to think better of it. 'Any news of the Second Wave, the comet crew?'

'Nothing was left of the comet, it seems.'

'Maybe the imperial military got to it. That's one ship I'm glad I wasn't on, I must say.' He glanced over, to see the Earth running through its cycle of trauma once again. 'Shut that thing down,' he called. 'It's time we considered our own fate. Look, we broke through their outer perimeter without a single loss. In twelve hours we make perihelion. We've all got work to do. Tomorrow, it's Sol himself!'

S-day plus 4. Solar orbit.

The Thoth habitat was a compact sculpture of electric-blue threads, a wormhole Interface surrounded by firefly lights. The surface of the sun, barely twenty thousand kilometres below the habitat, was a floor across the universe.

Thoth was nine hundred years old. Its purpose had always been to monitor the sun, through the eyes a unique observer deep inside the star itself, an observer whose life Thoth maintained. And all his long life Thoth had been home to Sunchild Folyon, leader of the little community who maintained Thoth, a legacy from the past, held in trust for the future.

But now the rebel fleet was approaching its perihelion, and Thoth's most significant hour since its construction by Michael Poole was almost upon it.

After prayers that morning Folyon went straight to the habitat's bridge, where, even through the prayer hours, shifts of sunchildren maintained watch over Thoth's systems and position. The mood on the bridge was tense, for the wormhole that reached from this station into the heart of the sun had been shut down for twenty-four hours already, a time unprecedented in Folyon's memory; maintenance downtimes were usually measured in minutes.

But this was an extraordinary moment, which required extraordinary measures, as the Empress Shira herself had patiently explained to Folyon – and as he himself had then had to relay to a reluctant Lieserl, deep in the belly of the sun. This was total war. Every resource available to the Empire had to be dedicated to the fight – and that included even Thoth and its ancient community. After all, even Thoth had been infected by the smart plague.

So Thoth's orbit had been carefully lifted from equatorial to a higher-inclination plane, into the path of the invasion fleet. And the wormhole had, for now, been cut.

The sunchildren had fulfilled their duties to the letter. But Folyon, conditioned since childhood to dedicate his life to a single goal, had found it hard to accept this distortion of his deepest imperatives. Not wishing to exacerbate the crew's difficulty by displaying his own qualms, he left the bridge and made for the observation deck. As so often, he dealt with his troubles by immersing them in the healing light of the sun, giver of life.

The sun was a flat, semi-infinite landscape, encrusted by granules each large enough to swallow the Earth, and with the chromosphere – the thousand-kilometre-thick outer atmosphere – a thin haze above it all. The sunscape crawled beneath the habitat slowly, but that slowness was an artefact of scale, a collision of human senses with the sheer bulk of the sun; in fact in its orbit Thoth was travelling at five hundred kilometres a second. Folyon knew how privileged he was to spend his life in the domain of the mighty star, the physical and philosophical core of human culture. At the prayer hours he would look away to the distant stars, and he imagined every human eye, even across interstellar distances, turned to the sun, towards him.

But he wondered how many of them even knew of the habitat's existence, or its purpose.

Lieserl, who had briefly been human, was a monitor, sent long ago into the sun to investigate a complex, dark-matter canker that seemed to be building up at the star's heart. Thus, deep below Thoth, tracking its orbit, the tetrahedral Interface of a wormhole was suspended in the body of the sun. Searing-hot gas poured into its four triangular faces, so that the Interface was surrounded by a sculpture of inflowing gas, a flower carved dynamically from the sun's flesh. In normal times this solar material would spew from the wormhole mouth cradled by Thoth, to dissipate harmlessly. The wormhole was a crude refrigeration mechanism, by which solar heat was pumped away from the fragile human-built construct that housed the soul of Lieserl, and enabled her to survive in the sun's fire. And it was all for a higher goal.

Thoth's purpose, and Lieserl's, predated even the ancient Empire of the Shiras, but, hastily designated as a temple to Sol, it had always been maintained faithfully by the Empresses' lieutenants. Now Lieserl's wormhole was to be used as a weapon of war. But even this remarkable incident, Folyon knew, would in the long run be just another episode in the greater history of Thoth and Lieserl, and Sol itself.

A young woman touched his arm. His thoughts, as so often, had drifted away from the here and now. Sunchild Mura said, 'The time is close, sun-brother.'

'All goes well on the bridge?' He felt anxious.

Mura was empathetic for a girl of her age and she knew his moods. 'Everything is fine. If you were there you would only distract them all, forgive me for saying so, sun-brother.'

He sighed. 'And so we go to war.'

'They tell me you can see it from here. The fleet.' She scanned around the sky – the solar light passed to human eyes by the observation deck blister was heavily filtered for safety – and pointed to a cluster of star-like points, far away above the sunscape. 'There they are.'

The lights grew in size and spread apart a little; Folyon saw now that they were splinters, like matchsticks, each with blazing fire at one end. 'An enemy fleet from Alpha Centauri, come all the way to the sun. How remarkable.'

Mura counted. 'Five, six, seven, eight – all accounted for. And their GUTdrives are firing.' This was celestial mechanics, Folyon knew; if you sought to enter the Solar System, perihelion was energetically the most advantageous place to dump excess velocity. 'They will come near us; the projections of their trajectories are good,' Mura said, sounding tense. 'And they will come on us quickly. The moment of closest approach will be brief. But our response systems are automated – the reopening of the wormhole won't rely on human responses.' She hesitated. 'Did you tell Lieserl what is happening today?'

'I thought it was my duty,' he murmured. 'She will remember all this, after all, long after the rest of us are dust. I wonder if they are praying.'

'Who?' Mura asked.

'The crew of those ships. For they worship Sol too, do they not? And now we are about to use Sol itself to kill them.' He lifted his face, and his old skin felt fragile in the sun's processed light. 'Do we have the right to do this? Does even Shira?'

She grabbed his arm. 'Too late now—'

The ships exploded out of the distance.

At closest approach solar gases hosed from the drifting wormhole Interface, turning it into a second, miniature sun. Solar fire swept over the invaders.

Mura whooped and punched the air. Folyon was shocked and troubled.

S-Day plus 4. The Oort cloud, outer Solar System.

Densel Bel wished he could see the sun with his naked eye. After all, he was among the comets now, within the sun's domain.

He stood in the dark, peering up at the zenith, the way the ship was flying; he tried to imagine he was rising towards the sun in some spindly, superfast elevator. A light-week out from Sol, with the ship travelling at less than two per cent below light-speed, the view from the lightdome of *Fist Two* was extraordinary. All was darkness around the rim of the hemispherical lifedome. The only starlight came from a circular patch of light directly over his head, crowded with brilliant stars, all of them apparently as bright as Venus or Sirius seen from Earth. He knew the science well enough; the starfield he saw was an artefact of the ship's huge velocity, which funnelled all the light from across the sky into a cone that poured down over his head.

And meanwhile the stars he was able to see were not the few thousand visible in solar space to the unaided human eye. His extraordinary speed had imposed a Doppler effect; the stars behind had been redshifted to darkness, while the 'visible' stars ahead, had similarly been blueshifted to obscurity. But conversely red stars, giants and dwarfs pregnant with infra-red, now glowed brightly, crowding the sky: a hundred thousand of them, it was thought, crammed into that tight disc. Sol itself was somewhere in there, of course, at the dead centre of his visual field, and he knew that the navigators on the bridge had elaborate routines to disentangle the relativistic effects. But a primitive part of him longed just to see the sunlight again, with his own unaided eyes, for the first time in so many decades—

A shower of what looked like snow sparkled over the lifedome, gone in an instant. He flinched, half-expecting the blister to crack and crumple. He called, 'What was *that*?'

A Virtual of Flood appeared in the air before him, the avatar used by the ship's AI to communicate with the crew. 'We lost *Fist One*,' Flood said bluntly.

'How?'

'A dust grain got it. The earthworms. They blew up an ice asteroid in our path, creating a screen of dust hundreds of kilometres wide. We have defences, of course, but not against motes that size, and at such densities. At our velocity even a sand grain will hit with the kinetic energy of a—'

'There shouldn't be any asteroids here. We're out of the plane of the ecliptic.'

'Evidently the earthworms have prepared defences.'

'So how come *we* survived?'

'The destruction of *One* blew a hole in the debris cloud. We sailed through.'

Densel considered. 'Our ships follow each other in line. So even if the lead ship is taken out by further screens, it might clear a path for the rest.'

'That's right. And we will still achieve our objective if only three, two, even just one of the *Fists* gets through.' Flood hesitated, and the image crumbled slightly, a sign of additional processing power being applied. 'There is other news. The Third Wave ships came under fire as they rounded the sun. Two were lost.'

'That was smart by the earthworms.' Densel wondered if he ought to be exulting at this victory, for Earth, after all, was his home planet. But his heart was on Footprint, with the families he would never see again. He didn't want anybody to die, he realised.

Flood said, 'Smart, yes. But six ships survive, of eight. Meanwhile the earthworms are regrouping. Half of their ships, twelve of them, are heading for Jupiter. To win, we have to eliminate the Imperial Navy. So we have to follow. Jupiter is where the decisive encounter will come, for the Third Wave.'

'And the other earthworm ships?'

'Converging on the course of the *Fist*s. Clearly they understand the danger you represent.'

Densel nodded. 'But now, in *Two*, I'm in the van. The next in line for the duck shoot.'

Again that hesitation, that fragility. 'The crews are conferring. That would not be optimal.'

'Not optimal?'

'For *your* ship to lead. The line is to be reconfigured. *Fist Two* will continue astern of the remaining ships, not in the lead, protected by the others.'

'You want to give *Two* the best chance. Why?'

'Because *Two* has you aboard.' The avatar grinned, an imperfectly imaged, eerie sight. 'I told you. You are useful, Densel Bel.' Theatrically he consulted a wristwatch. 'Subjectively you are little more than a day away from Sol. Remember, you are moving so quickly that time is stretched, from your perspective. Seven more days left for Earth. Thirty-three hours, that's all it will be for you. Then it will be done. Try to get some sleep.' The image crumbled to pixels and disappeared.

S-Day plus 6. Imperial bunker, New York.

Admiral Kale was shocked by what he found of New York.

The great ocean wave had spared some of the mighty old buildings, which stood like menhirs, windows shattered, their flanks stained by salt water. But the human city at their feet was devastated, scoured out, millennia of history washed away. Even now the aid workers and their bots dug into the reefs of rubble the wave had left, and the refugees were only beginning to filter back to what remained of their homes.

But in her bunker, deep beneath the ruin of Central Park, the Empress sat beside her pool of logic and light, imperturbable.

'You are angry, Admiral Kale,' she said softly.

'Every damn place I go on the planet I'm angry,' he said. 'The destruction of history – the harm done to so many people.'

'We are not yet defeated.'

'No, ma'am, we are not. We are massing the Navy cruisers at Jupiter—'

'I have viewed the briefings,' she said.

'Ma'am.' He stood and waited, unsure what she wanted, longing to get back to his duties.

'I have brought you here, Admiral, to speak not of the present but of the past, and of the future. You spoke of history. What do you know of history, though? What do you know of the origin of the Empire you serve – and, deeper than that, the dynasty of the Shiras?'

He was puzzled and impatient. But she was the Empress, and he had no choice but to stand and listen. 'Ma'am? I'm a soldier, not a scholar.'

'I need you to understand, you see,' she rasped. 'I need *someone* to bear the truth into the future. For I fear I may not survive this war – at least I may not retain my throne. And a determination that has spanned centuries will be lost.'

'Ma'am, we're confident that—'

'Tell me what you know, of the history of my throne.'

Hesitantly, dredging his memory, he spoke of the Emergency a thousand years before, when the great engineer Michael Poole had built a wormhole bridge across fifteen hundred years, a great experiment, a way to explore the future. But Poole's bridge reached an unexpected shore. What followed was an invasion from a remote future, an age when the Solar System would be occupied by an alien power.

'An invasion from a bleak future, yes,' hissed the Empress. 'An invasion from which the first Shira, founder of the dynasty, *herself was a refugee.*'

Kale was stunned. 'The first Empress was from the future, the age of occupation?'

'She *saw* Poole disappear into time, collapsing the wormhole links. And when the way home was lost, Shira was stranded. But she did not abandon the Project.'

'The Project?'

'Shira belonged to a philosophic-religious sect called the Friends of Wigner. And their purpose in coming back in time was to send a message to a further future yet . . .'

Kale, frustrated, had to endure more of this peculiar philosophising.

Life, Shira said, was essential for the very existence of the universe. Consciousness was like an immense, self-directed eye, a recursive design developed by the universe to invoke its own being – for without conscious observation there could be no actualisation of quantum potential to reality, no collapse of the wave functions. That was true moment to moment, heartbeat to heartbeat, as it was from one millennium to the next. And if this were true, the goal of consciousness, of life, said Shira, must be to gather and organise data – *all* data, everywhere – to observe and actualise all events. In the furthest future the confluences of mind would merge, culminating in a final state: at the last boundary to the universe, at timelike infinity.

'And at timelike infinity resides the Ultimate Observer,' Shira said quietly. 'And the last Observation will be made.' She bowed her head in an odd, almost prayerful attitude of respect. 'It is impossible to believe that the Ultimate Observer will simply be a passive eye. A camera, for all of history. The Friends of Wigner, the sect to which Shira belonged, believed that the Observer would have the power to study all the nearly infinite potential histories of the universe, stored in regressing chains of quantum functions. And that the Observer would *select*, actualise a history which maximises the potential of being. Which would make the cosmos through all of time into a shining place, a garden free of waste, pain and death.'

The light from the logic pool struck shadows in her face. She was quite insane, Kale feared.

'We must ensure that humanity is preserved in the optimal reality. What higher purpose can there be? Everything the Friends did was dedicated to the goal of communicating the plight of mankind to the Ultimate Observer. Even the eventual destruction of Jupiter. And even I, stranded here in this dismal past, stranded out of time, have always struggled to do what I could to progress the mighty project.' She peered into the logic pool. 'I, in my way, am *searching . . .*'

He stared at her, as he absorbed another huge conceptual shock. 'Ma'am – you said "we". You speak of yourself. Not the first Shira.'

She lifted her face, its skin papery.

'*You are Shira*. The first. There was no dynasty, no thirty-two Shiras, mother and daughter – just you, the first, living on and on. You must be over a thousand years old.'

She smiled. 'And yet I will not be *born* for more than four hundred years. Am I old, or young, Admiral? Once the Poole wormhole was closed down I had no way back to the future. I accepted that. But there was always another way back. *The long way*. I accepted AntiSenescence treatment. I began to accrue power, where I could. And then—'

'And then,' said Kale, barely believing, 'having built a global empire for your protection, it was a simple matter of living through fifteen centuries, waiting for your time to come again.'

'You have it, Admiral.'

He peered at her. 'Were there others like you – others stranded in history?'

Her face was blank. 'None that survive.'

He was thinking furiously. 'And you must have used your knowl-edge of the future to cement your power base.' He remembered himself. 'Ma'am, forgive me for speaking this way.'

'It's all right, Admiral. Yes, you could put it like that. But it was necessary. After all, there had never been a unified government of mankind, none before me. Quite an achievement, don't you think? Why, I had to invent a sun-worshipping religion to do it ... It was necessary, all of it. I need the shelter of power. There are still many obstacles to be overcome in the decades ahead, if I am to survive to the year of my birth.'

'Ma'am – I thought I knew you.'

'None of you knows me, none of you drones.' She withdrew. 'I tire now. Progress your war, Admiral. But we will speak again. Even if I fall, *the Project must not fail.* And I will entrust in you that purpose.'

He bowed to her. 'Ma'am.' And with huge relief he left the chamber, leaving the lonely woman and the light of the logic pool behind him.

S-Day plus 9. Jupiter.

The earthworm fleet was assembling at last, somewhere on the far side of the giant world. The showdown was still hours away, the Alphan planners believed.

Despite the urgency of the situation, despite all Flood's urging and imprecations, every chance they got the crew of the *Freestar* stared out of their lifedome at Jupiter. After all there were no Jovian planets in Alpha System.

Jupiter was a bloated monster of a world, streaked with autumn brown and salmon pink. The other ships of the rebel fleet, a minuscule armada, drifted across the face of the giant world, angular silhouettes. One other structure was visible following its own orbit, deep within the circle of the innermost moon, Io. It was an electric-blue spark, revealed under magnification to be a tangle of struts and tetrahedral frames. This was the Poole hub, where once Michael Poole had used the energies of a flux tube connecting Jupiter to Io to construct his intra-System wormhole network. One of those ancient Interfaces linked Jupiter itself to Earth – or it had, until the earthworms had cut it as the rebels approached.

And, still more extraordinary, Jupiter itself was visibly *wounded*, immense storms like blackened funnels digging deep into its surface.

It was an extraordinary sight, Flood conceded. 'Spectacle and history, all mixed up.'

'Yes, Father,' said Beya. 'As for Jupiter, you know I've been reading up on Solar System history . . .'

He didn't entirely approve of this; it struck him as a guilty reflex.

'You say this is all because of human action?'

'That's the story,' he said. 'Though my grasp of ancient earthworm history is shaky.'

A thousand years before, Jupiter had been damaged by the actions of the Friends of Wigner, refugees from the future. The Friends had had in mind some grand, impossible scheme to alter history. Their plan had involved firing asteroid-mass black holes into Jupiter.

'Whatever these "Friends" intended, it didn't work,' Flood said. 'All they succeeded in doing was wrecking Jupiter.' He shook his head. 'The greatest mass in the Solar System after the sun itself, a vast resource for the future – ruined in a single action. How typical of earthworm arrogance!'

Light sparked in the complex sky. Flood saw it reflected in his daughter's face. He turned.

One of the Alpha ships, the *Destiny of Humankind*, had exploded. The delicate spine was broken, the detached GUTdrive flaring pointlessly, and the fragile lifedome shattered, spilling particles of pink and green into space.

Alarms howled. Virtual control desks appeared before Beya and Flood, crammed with data. The crew, sleepy, shocked, scrambled to get to their positions.

And then another ship detonated. The *Future Hope*, a ship five hundred years old, gone in a second. This time Flood glimpsed the missile that took it out. But there was no time to reflect.

'Incoming,' Beya called. 'Incoming!'

Flood worked at his desk with brisk sweeps of his fingers. 'All right. We're evading.' The lifedome shuddered as the GUTdrive flared, shoving the *Freestar* sideways.

A missile streaked past the lifedome, close enough to see with the naked eye, glowing white-hot.

'Shit,' Beya said. 'How are they *doing* this? The scans showed the volume around us was clear.'

'Jupiter,' Flood said, reading his displays rapidly. 'The missiles are coming *out* of Jupiter. But the velocities are so high – I don't understand.'

'The black holes,' Beya said. 'Maybe that's it. They're slingshotting their missiles off the central black holes. You can pick up a hell of a lot of kinetic energy from an ergosphere.'

'Yes. And then they punch out of the carcass of the planet, right at us. Incredible.'

Another ship flared and died, a flower of light, pointlessly beautiful.

'The *Dream of Beta*,' Flood read. 'That's three of us gone in a few seconds. They're picking us off. Three of us left, against a dozen Navy cruisers. We'll have to withdraw. Regroup if we can—'

'No.' Beya was working hard at her desk. 'Dad, there's no time for that. Tell the survivors to make for the Poole hub.'

'Why? The wormhole links are severed; we can't get away from there.'

'It will give us a bit of cover. And I've an idea,' she said, distant, working.

Flood frowned. He didn't enjoy it when this determined side of his daughter showed itself; it made her seem too strong, too independent – he couldn't protect her any more. But she had called the black-hole missile manoeuvre correctly. He saw no better option than to accept her recommendation.

He snapped out the orders. The *Freestar*'s GUTdrive kicked in. The acceleration mounted quickly, to two, three, four gravities. Flood felt it in his bones, but he stood his ground, determined. Above his head, Jupiter slid with ponderous slowness across his field of view. 'Come on,' he said. 'Come *on* . . .'

Aboard the bridge of the Imperial Navy ship *Facula* there was much cheering at the rapid downing of half the rebel fleet – premature cheering, as far as Stillich was concerned.

'Status,' he yelled at Pella, above the noise.

'Three down, three to go.'

'But the three survivors aren't running.'

'Not from Jovian space, no sir. They seem to be making for the Poole hub.'

'Why there?'

Pella tapped a desk. 'The war-game AIs have no idea. If they need cover they could run to one of the moons . . .' She grinned. 'Sir, who cares? We have twelve ships against three. Even with one to one losses we can shoot them out of the sky.'

Stillich felt deeply uneasy, but he couldn't argue with that analysis. 'All right. Call the fleet; set up an attacking perimeter.'

'Sir.'

The GUTdrive surged smoothly.

Twelve ships against three. The decision to withdraw the Sol fleet to Jupiter had been a good one, Stillich thought. The hinterland of the giant planet was a dangerous, complex place, laced with strong gravitational fields, intense radiation and hazards like the Io flux tube. It was a battleground much more familiar to the defending Imperial Navy than to the attackers – there were no Jovian worlds in Alpha System – and he had been impressed by the innovative thinking at a Navy college on Earth that had come up with the notion of using the black hole slingshot to pick off the rebels before the ships had even engaged. But once he had accepted the stratagem, Stillich had argued for withdrawing *all* of Earth's fleet to Jupiter or its environs, not to leave half of it mounting a futile picket fence against the incoming wave of relativistic missiles.

Still – *twelve against three.* It was more reassuring than twelve against six had been, but Stillich was in no mood for anything less than a complete victory, an annihilation. The security of the System demanded it, and the more overwhelming the odds the better.

On the *Freestar*, the Poole hub was already approaching, a cluster of Interface portals hurtling over the horizon towards the surviving rebel ships, a tangle of electric blue.

'Lethe,' Beya breathed. 'I didn't know how beautiful it was.'

Flood said softly, 'The wormholes are gateways to other times, other places. They should be beautiful, like all great engineering.'

Alarms chimed once more.

Beya studied her data desk. 'They're closing in, Father, a dozen Navy cruisers.'

'Then this is it.'

She kissed him on the cheek, a lingering gesture that still felt too brief. 'Cover me.'

'What?'

She turned and ran, faster than he could hope to catch her. 'I told you. I have an idea.' And she ducked out of sight, through a hatch to the ship's spine.

A missile soared past the lifedome, and the crew ducked, involuntarily. Then there was a speckle of laser light, and the dome blister blacked itself out. Grey Morus, Flood's second in command, yelled across, 'They've got our range, Flood. We're shooting back but—'

Flood's data desk chimed. The AIs had quickly come up with a defensive configuration for the ships, lifedomes together, tails out, backed up against the Poole hub, using their combined superhot GUTdrive exhaust for defence. Flood punched his data desk. 'Copy this and implement,' he snapped at Grey. 'Beya! Where are you? Beya!'

In Beya's flitter, her father's voice was as clear as if he was riding alongside her. She was determined to keep her voice level. 'Can't you see me, Father? I'm up around your ten o'clock – oh, but your blister is blacked out.'

'What the hell are you doing?'

The flitter ducked sideways, jolting her against her restraints. 'I'm taking fire, that's what I'm doing. Dad, if you've got a spare laser, cover me!'

Now the flitter swept around. She was heading straight for the Poole hub, a tangle of wormhole mouths, powder-blue. She saw the three ships of the rebel fleet backing up, pirouetting clumsily into their defensive position. But the Imperial Navy ships swept across her view, soulless, mechanical, spitting missiles at the rebels, bathing them with laser light. There were so many of them, a dozen against three.

And as she watched, a Navy missile got through, hammering into the GUTdrive pod of the *Mercy and Tolerance*. Slowly the great ship began to drift out of position. But even as she did so she spat fire in Beya's direction, and picked a Navy missile out of the sky.

'Thanks, *Mercy*,' she whispered.

'You're welcome,' came a reply.

'Beya, what are you doing?'

'Dad, do you trust me?'

'I – you know I do. What kind of question is that?'

'Well enough to gamble your life on my say-so?'

'I may not have a choice. If you'd just tell me—'

'Just another bit of Solar System history, Father. Something I read, an incident at a planet called Pluto, long ago . . .' She stared out at the dazzling sky-blue of the nearest portal's exotic-matter tetrahedral frame. The faces were like semi-transparent panes of silvered glass; she could make out the watercolour oceans of Jupiter, swirled around in a fashion the eye could not quite track, like visions in a dream. 'So beautiful.'

'Beya?'

She drove the flitter straight at the Interface. She ran a quick calculation on her data desk.

'Five seconds, Father.'

'Until what?'

'Fire up on my mark, and get out of there with everything you have.'

She passed through the glimmering face as if it did not exist, and now she was inside the blue frame of the Interface.

Her father's voice was distorted. 'Beya, please—'

'This is for you, for Mother, for Alpha. Remember me. Mark!' And she stabbed down her finger at her data desk.

The flitter's engine exploded.

Something slammed into her back. Electric-blue light flared all around her.

Remarkably, she was still alive. She was jammed up in the little ship's cabin, which had been ejected from the wreck. She gasped with the pain of broken bones. She made herself look around.

There was something wrong with space. A ball of light, unearthly, swelled up behind her, and an irregular patch of darkness ahead was like a rip in the sky. Tidal forces plucked at her belly and limbs. Nobody had been on a ride like this in a thousand years.

And she saw Navy ships scattered like bits of straw in a wind.

The tides faded. The darkness before her healed, to reveal the brilliance of Sol. And the flitter cabin imploded, without fuss.

It took long minutes before the crew got the tumbling of the *Facula* under control.

Pella came to Stillich, her brow bloodied. 'Damage report—'

'Never mind that. What just happened?'

'An Alcubierre wave.'

'A what?'

Pella dragged her fingers through mussed hair. 'Captain – a wormhole is a flaw in space. It's inherently unstable. The throat and mouths are kept open by active feedback loops involving threads of exotic matter. That's matter with a negative energy density, a sort of antigravity which—'

'What's an Alcubierre wave?'

'Something exploded inside the Interface. And the Interface's negative energy region expanded from the tetrahedron, just for a moment. The negative energy distorted a chunk of spacetime. The chunk containing us.'

On one side of the wave, spacetime had contracted like a black hole. On the other side, it expanded – like a rerun of the Big Bang, the expansion at the beginning of the universe.

Pella scanned her data desk. 'We lost contact altogether with five of our ships. None of the rest are operational. The *Facula*—'

'What about the surviving rebels?'

'Two disabled.' She looked up. 'One got away. It's heading for Earth.'

'Can we give chase?'

'No, sir, we—'

'Get me a line to Admiral Kale. Patch it through to the Palace if you can—'

She looked up from her slate, shocked. 'Sir. I've a standing order, to become operative in case of failure.'

'Get on with it.'

'You're relieved of command. In fact, you're under arrest.'

Stillich laughed. 'Fine. I'm in your custody, Number One. Now get hold of a working flitter and get me back to Earth.'

S-Day plus 11. Orbit of Neptune.

The final attempt to stop the relativistic *Fist* ships was the most dramatic.

After ice-moon debris had put an end to *One* and then *Four*, it was a GUTship that tried to halt the two last survivors, *Three* and *Two*. Not far within the orbit of Pluto, on the rim of the Solar System proper, moving at a fraction of the attackers' near-light-speed, it tried to ram them. It was an extraordinary bit of relativistic navigation. *Fist Three*, taking the lead, destroyed it with an equally remarkable bit of sharp-shooting. But the detonation hurled debris into the path of *Three*, and that was that.

When it was done, there was *Fist Two*, alone, sailing within the orbit of Neptune at over ninety-eight per cent of light-speed. This was the fastest velocity ever attained within the Solar System, it was believed, save for cosmic rays, atomic nuclei ejected from distant supernovas. But *Fist* was no subatomic particle. *Fist* was a warship, a relativistic weapon, manned, sailing among the fragile worlds of the mother System.

It was wrong, Densel Bel thought. It was monstrous. And yet here he was. Densel Bel was glad the time remaining to him was so brief.

Stillich was brought to the Empress's New York bunker in shackles.

Admiral Kale was here. With an impatient command he ordered the shackles removed, and dismissed the guard.

Beside the logic pool, in its eerie, shifting light, the Empress brooded. Some Virtual display was playing itself out before her: a globe, a point of light, a glowing splinter – over and over.

Stillich approached his superior, rubbing his ankles. 'Sir. How long?'

Kale snapped his fingers; a small Virtual data display appeared in the air. 'That fucking relativistic ship is crossing Saturn's orbit.'

Stillich thought. 'Seventy-eight minutes from Earth, then.'

'And we're still waiting on this rebel bastard – this Flood.'

After the Imperial Navy had been scattered at Jupiter, there had been nothing left to stand in the way of the *Freestar*'s advance on Earth. At last the rebel ship had entered orbit around Earth itself, and Flood was descending to discuss surrender terms.

'Do you think we've a choice but to accept whatever he demands?'

Kale grimaced. 'The choice is playing itself out on the Empress's lap.'

The consequence of the *Fist* striking the Earth had been modelled for the Empress. The physics was simple, a function of the *Fist*'s immense kinetic energy; the consequence for the planet, modelled in a Virtual display, was dismaying. The impact, heralded by a tunnel of air shocked to superheated plasma, would be the source of a pulse of electromagnetic energy itself strong enough to sear anything alive across half a hemisphere – bright enough to pierce walls. The shock waves of air and water that would follow, and a hard rain of melted bedrock falling from the sky, would do the rest. Shira watched this over and over, obsessive.

At the seventy-minute mark, the chamber door opened. Flood walked in. He was a bulky, strong-looking man, wearing a simple tunic and leggings. He carried a package, a sleek black box. Two others accompanied him, a man and a woman similarly dressed. These companions looked nervous, even overawed to be in this bunker under New York City itself, to be in the presence of an Empress. Flood, however, showed no fear.

The Empress showed no reaction, watching her Virtual model go through its lethal sequence, over and over.

Kale sneered. 'So you are Flood of Alpha, once ambassador to this court, now the great rebel leader. And you dress like a farmer. How ostentatious. How predictable.'

Flood smiled at him, and looked him up and down. 'Nice jacket. Here. Hold this.' He handed him the box he was carrying.

Kale took it reflexively. Then, irritated, he passed it to Stillich. 'What is it?'

'Our final weapon. A nanotech modification of the smart plague – hardware, not software. Released, it would chew up the robust networks you were prudent enough to install – your optical-fibre links and all the rest. Necessarily delivered after landfall.'

Stillich put this on the floor, gingerly. 'Your final weapon save for the *Fist*.'

'Save for that, yes.'

'Why have you brought it here?' the Admiral asked. 'You have won. You have no need to do more damage.'

Flood walked to the rim of the logic pool. 'To put an end to that.'

Now the Empress spoke, without looking up. 'You are Flood.'

He bowed. 'Empress—'

'Shira will do.'

'Yes. Shira is your name. It always was, wasn't it? I am here to discuss terms.'

Stillich said tensely, 'Keep it brief, farmer. We don't have much time.'

'Brief I can manage. Your Empress must stand down. This logic pool must be shut down – here, now, immediately, before my eyes. And we begin the establishment of a constitutional convention. A new relationship between the free worlds of all mankind.'

'How civilised,' Kale said. 'A constitutional convention, or global obliteration.'

'Admiral,' Stillich snapped. 'We don't have the time. Flood – why the logic pool? This is at the centre of everything, isn't it?'

Flood faced Shira. 'Our philosophers deduced this, the central truth of all she is doing. I myself was an observer, a spy in your court – even though I never saw your face before, ma'am.'

'How little you understand,' Shira said.

'Oh, I think I understand well enough.' Flood faced the Navy men. 'You know her story by now. She is a refugee from the future – from a time that, even after a thousand years, is so far remote it *remains* the future. And she is going home the long way, year by year, heartbeat by heartbeat. But it isn't the future she longs for – is it, Shira? You don't want to be in this universe at all . . .'

'None of this is real,' Shira said, her voice a husk. 'It is all transitory. We are simply forced to endure the motion of our consciousness along one of many chains of quantum functions, a sequence of potentiality to be collapsed, discarded, by the Ultimate Observer at timelike infinity. . .'

Stillich tried to control his impatience. 'This is just anachronistic philosophy. I don't see what it is that she's doing here that disturbs you, Flood.'

'She longs for her Ultimate Observer. And she thought she could find her quantum messiah in mathematics . . .'

The logic pool, he said, was a metamathematical universe. While not infinite it comprised more mathematical understanding, far more, than had yet been explored by mankind – and in principle, somewhere within the metamathematical branching of the pool, any algorithm possible might exist.

Shira said softly, 'All our science is based on the search for simple rules underlying complex phenomena. Simple algorithms can be shown to generate complexities, from the turbulent flow in a glass of water to the spiral structure of the Galaxy itself.'

'You see the idea,' Flood said. 'There's a lot of nonsense in there, but also a lot of treasure to be dug out. It's as if you have a tank full of every possible combination of words in Earthish. Most of it is dross. But in there are the finest fruits of human scientific understanding – *even those not discovered yet*. But Shira has always been more ambitious than that, haven't you, Empress?'

Shira said, 'The human consciousness is likewise the product of simple algorithms with particularly complicated outcomes. And similarly, *any mind imaginable* – human, post-human or alien – must be there to be discovered, in the pool, in metamathematical stasis.'

Flood grimaced. 'The Friends of Wigner were prepared to destroy Jupiter to send a message to the Ultimate Observer. Now this lunatic believes she can find the Observer in a tank of light.'

'Show the Empress respect,' Stillich said sharply.

'But whether or not she ever achieved her goal, she is in danger of unleashing much greater threats on humanity. For *some* of the minds in there are not content with stasis, with waiting to be discovered.

Look at this.' He summoned up a Virtual of his own. 'We've been tracking the consequences for years. Decades. We have our spies, in the Solar System. This is a neutrino scan we made from the *Freestar* just hours ago.'

It took Stillich a moment to work out that he was looking at a cross section of the Earth, deep below the granite raft of Manhattan, and the imperial bunker. And down there, swimming in the mantle, was a shape, perhaps organic, perhaps artificial, a winged shape like a stingray, like a sycamore seed.

'It isn't fully formed,' Flood said grimly. 'Not fully operational. But it soon will be.'

Kale asked, 'What is it?'

'In the Friends' accounts of their dark future, there are hints of a race even more threatening to mankind than the occupiers of Earth from whom they fled. A race called—' his pronunciation was uncertain, '*Chee-lee, Zee-lee*. They, or their potentialities, are lurking in the logic pool. And they are trying to break out.'

'How?' Kale snapped. 'By constructing this ship, deep in the Earth? How are they doing that?'

'We have no idea,' Flood said. 'Our only concern is to stop it, before this ship bursts from the Earth like a bird from its egg. This is a threat so potent it is trying to strike at us out of *nothing more than of a statement of the logical possibility of its own existence*. And if this thing gets out of the mantle, I don't imagine our four light years' separation would save Alpha System. Now do you see why it was necessary to wage this war? It wasn't just for our freedom from Shira's political domination. It was to free *all mankind* of this terrible threat – for Shira, your Empress from the future, was endangering all of us.'

Stillich looked at the Admiral's grim face.

'Decision time,' said Kale.

'Yes, sir. My view? It's not worth risking Earth to save this project of the Empress's—'

'The Project is worth any price,' Shira murmured. 'Even that.'

But, Stillich thought, she seemed to be accepting defeat.

Kale turned to her. 'Ma'am – we have no time. We must accept his terms. We can discuss the details of your abdication later – the legitimisation of an interim government . . .' He turned to Flood. 'You have won, star-farmer.'

Flood picked up the nanotechnological box and dropped it in the logic pool. It sank with barely a ripple, and then seemed to dissolve.

Flood watched the pool, as the writhing metamathematical bifurcations withered, and the pale light began to die. 'It is done.'

Stillich said urgently, 'Now call off your relativistic attack dog.'

Flood smiled. 'Done.'

'None of this is real,' Shira murmured. She rolled back into the shadows.

Kale faced Flood. 'You will pay for all you have done.'

Flood gazed at him, his eyes full of regret. 'Oh, I have paid, soldier. Believe me, I have paid.'

And then the bunker shuddered, and a wave like a tide pulsed through Stillich's gut.

Kale staggered. 'What was *that*?'

When Stillich had recovered, he learned that Shira was gone.

The *Fist* sailed through Sol's asteroid belt.

Earth was so close now that Densel Bel could see it, an image magnified and heavily corrected for relativistic distortions, suspended over his head – he could see the planet in real time, a blue marble, achingly beautiful, and yet scarred by war. And yet he could never touch it. The vast pulse of kinetic energy that had been injected into this ship by years of GUTdrive acceleration separated him from his home world just as much as if he had been stranded in another universe.

Only subjective minutes remained before his life ended, and Earth died with him.

Once more Flood appeared before him. 'It's over,' he said, smiling.

'What is?'

'The war. Shira is abdicating – we are free. Now you must destroy the *Fist Two*.'

'Me? Why me?'

'This was your purpose all along, Densel Bel. You are my failsafe. I needed somebody on board who I *knew* would terminate the mission, even at the cost of his own life. And that's you, a man loyal both to Earth, where you were born, and Footprint, where you have your family. You have the authority. Just say aloud, "Let it end". The AI will do the rest. Goodbye, Densel Bel. I hope you feel the sacrifice you are making is worth it.'

'Flood. Wait—'

'Yes?'

'Would you have done it? Would you have let the *Fist* strike the Earth?'

'Oh, yes. To stop what Shira was doing – believe me, there was no choice. Good luck, Suber.' He broke up into a cloud of pixels and disappeared.

Suber. A lost name he'd used on a lost world. Densel Bel looked up at the blue Earth, and thought of Su-su and Fay. 'Let it end.'

Light flared, an instant of intense white pain—

S-Day plus 7 months. Earthport.

The flitter rose into the sky. The little cylindrical craft tumbled slowly as it climbed.

Peering out from the rising flitter, Stillich had to admit that the *Freestar*, which he had come to inspect on behalf of Earth's Navy, looked spectacular, with the newly constructed wormhole Interface, a bright blue tetrahedron with milky-gold faces, slung beneath its angular spine. When Flood and his crew returned to Alpha System in a couple of months, they would take the grudging good wishes of Earth's interim government with them – and, more importantly, the business end of a new wormhole, which would link the worlds of Alpha and Sol for ever.

'Or until the next political crisis,' Flood said drily.

'There is that,' said Stillich.

'Look – here comes another shipment of green muck from Titan.'

A cargo pellet slung from Saturn's moon had crossed the System unpowered, and now made an entry into Earth's atmosphere, cutting a bright contrail across the blue sky. This crude shipment method was an interim emergency measure to keep Earth fed, until the great space elevators were hung in the sky once more.

'Not "green muck",' Stillich said. 'Algal concentrate.'

Flood pulled a face. 'Next time you visit Footprint, be my guest at dinner.'

'That might be some time away,' Stillich said gently.

They both knew that was likely to be true. Too many had died, on Earth and elsewhere, for the populations of the Solar System to forgive their colonial cousins for the war, whatever the retrospective justification in terms of Shira's murky crimes.

But it would come, Stillich knew. Already Earth was recovering, as people and machines laboured to repair the damage done, and the vast resources of space were reattached to the damaged planet.

'I saw your report on Shira's escape,' Flood said now. 'You were serious in your conclusions?'

'There's no real doubt about it.' Shira had stashed many treasures from her lost future down in that bunker, and among them was what appeared to be a transdimensional transport system: Shira had disappeared from the bunker by stepping sideways into one of the universe's many extra compactified dimensions. 'If that doesn't qualify as a "hyperdrive" I don't know what does.'

Flood shook his head. 'She had a hyperdrive. A faster-than-light transport system. And she kept it to herself all these centuries, while the rest of us limped across the Galaxy in sublight GUTships. Just so she had a last-resort escape hatch. How selfish.'

'Maybe it's just as well. Anyhow, I guess we know we are due to acquire the technology in a few centuries. Certainly it will transform the face of war.' Stillich and Flood had both been key witnesses at an inter-governmental inquiry into the course and conduct of the war, an experience Stillich suspected had increased both their understandings. 'When you think about it, an interstellar war fought out with sublight drives is right at the limit of the possible. For a start you would need a strong reason to do it; almost nothing is worth fighting such a campaign for.'

Flood grunted. 'You should read more history. Our fear of what Shira was up to was comparatively rational as a *casus belli*. Horrific wars have been fought over splinter-fine differences in ideologies. Look up the Crusades some time.'

'But when we get an authentic first alien contact, rather than these dark hints and glimpses from the future . . . All of this might be remembered as mankind's own last great civil war.'

'The end of human war?' Flood laughed. 'I knew you were imaginative, Stillich. I didn't have you down as a dreamer . . .'

An alarm chimed, as the flitter prepared to dock with the *Freestar*. Stillich straightened his uniform, preparing for duty.

So the humans emerged from their home System, optimistic, expansive.
Then came Stillich's 'authentic' first contact. And everything changed.

REMEMBRANCE
AD 5071

'I am the Rememberer,' said the old man. 'The last in a line centuries long. This is what was passed on to me, by those who remembered before me.

'The first Rememberer was called Harry Gage. He was ten years old when the Squeem came . . .'

As he talked to some out-of-vision, flat-voiced cop inquisitor, Rhoda Voynet glanced around at her staff. Soldiers all, the planes of their faces bathed in golden Saturn light, they listened silently. The old man they saw before them, this 'Rememberer', was a Virtual, an image projected from a police station on Earth to this briefing room aboard the *Jones*, and the sunlight that shone on his face was much stronger than the diminished glow that reached this far orbit. Rhoda felt obscurely jealous of the warmth he felt.

Prompted by his off-stage interrogator, the old man continued. 'Harry Gage. He was born on Mars, in the Cydonia arcology. His great-grandparents were from Earth. There was a lot of that, in those days, before the Squeem. Everybody was mobile. Everything was opened up. Anything was possible.

'Harry's parents brought him to Earth, a once-in-a-lifetime trip to meet great-grandma and grandpa. He never did get to see them. They sure picked a bad day to call.'

It had been the year 4874, nearly two centuries past. And Earth was about to be conquered.

The flitter bearing Harry Gage and his parents had tumbled out of the shimmering throat of the wormhole transit route from Mars to Earth-port. As the flitter surged unhesitatingly through swarming traffic, Harry peered out of the cramped cabin, looking for Earth.

From here, the home world was a swollen blue disc. Wormhole gates of all sizes drifted across the face of the planet, electric-blue sculptures of exotic negative-energy matter. Mum sat beside Harry, a bookslate on her lap, and Dad sat opposite, grinning at Harry's reaction. Harry would always remember these moments well.

The final hop to Earth itself took only a few hours.

'Harry's flitter landed in New York,' the Rememberer said. 'A space-ship coming down in the middle of Manhattan. Imagine that!'

Harry and his parents emerged onto grass, a park, in the sunshine of a New York spring.

Dad raised his face to the sun and breathed deeply. 'Mmm. Cherry blossom and freshly cut grass. I love that smell.'

Mum snorted. 'We have cherry trees on Mars.'

'Every human is allowed to be sentimental about a spring day in New York. It's our birthright. Look at those clouds, Harry. Aren't they beautiful?'

Harry looked up. The sky was laced by high, fluffy, dark clouds, fat with water, unlike any on Mars.

But Mum closed her eyes. She was used to the pyramids and caverns of Mars, and could not believe that a thin layer of blue air could protect her from the rigours of space.

Harry was enchanted by Manhattan. He did not know then that most of what he saw was no more than decades old, painstakingly restored after the Starfall war. Nor could he know that little of it would be left standing mere hours from now. And as Harry peered up at the clouds he saw a line of light cut across the sky, scratched by a spark bright enough to cast faint shadows, even in the sunlight. He noticed New Yorkers looking up, vaguely concerned. This wasn't normal, then. Even on Earth, even in New York.

'It was the first strike of the Squeem,' the Rememberer said. 'Harry never forgot that moment. Well, you wouldn't, would you? It shaped his whole life. Even before the next wave came, falling on the cities.'

Rhoda and her soldiers listened, trying to understand, trying to decide whether to believe him. Trying to decide what to do about it.

While the old man rested – or had done eighty minutes ago, the time it took the signals from Earth to reach Saturn – Rhoda let her staff resume other duties, but summoned Reg Kaser, her first officer.

Waiting for Reg in her cabin, Rhoda powered up her percolator, her one indulgence from her Iowa home. While it chugged and slurped and filled the cabin with sharp coffee scents, she faced her big picture window.

The *Jones* was a UN Navy corvette. It was locked in a languid orbit around Rhea, second largest moon of Saturn. In fact the *Jones* wasn't far from home; its home base was on Enceladus, another of Saturn's moons. Rhea itself was unprepossessing, just another ball of dirty ice. But beyond it lay Saturn, where huge storms raged across an autumnal cloudscape, and the rings arched like gaudy artefacts, unreasonably sharp. The Saturn system was like a ponderous ballet, illuminated by distance-dimmed sunlight, and Rhoda could have watched it for ever.

But it was Rhea she had come here for. Within its icy carcass were pockets of salty water, kept liquid by the tidal kneading of Saturn and the other moons. That wasn't so special; there were similar buried lakes on many of the Solar System's icy moons, even Enceladus. But within Rhea's deep lakes had been discovered colonies of Squeem, the aquatic group-mind organisms that had, for a few decades, ruled over a conquered mankind, and even occupied Earth itself.

The *Jones* was named for the hero who had crucially gained an advantage over the Squeem, through a bit of bravery and ingenuity, which had ultimately led to the Squeem's expulsion from the Solar System – or so everybody had thought, until this relic colony had been discovered. The xenologists were already talking to these stranded Squeem, using antique occupation-era translation devices. It was Rhoda's task to decide what to do with them. She could have them preserved, even brought back to Earth.

Or she could make sure that every last Squeem in Rhea died. She had the authority to destroy the whole moon, if she chose, to make sure.

It was a hard decision to make.

And now she had the complication of this old man, the self-styled 'Rememberer', and his antique saga of the occupation which he insisted had to be heard before any decision was made about the Squeem on Rhea.

First Officer Reg Kaser arrived, and waited silently as she gathered her thoughts.

They were contrasting types. Rhoda Voynet, forty years old, came from an academic background; she had trained as a historian of the occupation before joining the service. Kaser, fifty, scarred, one leg prosthetic, and with a thick Mercury-mine accent, was a career sol-dier. He had taken part in the counter-invasion a decade ago, when human ships, powered by hyperdrives purloined from the Squeem themselves, had at last assaulted the Squeem's own homeworld. They worked well together, their backgrounds and skills complementary. Kaser had learned to be patient while Rhoda thought things through.

And she had learned to appreciate his decisiveness, hardened in battle.

'Tell me what we know of this old man,' she said.

Kaser checked over a slate. 'His name is Karl Hume. Born and raised on Earth. Seventy-four years old. He's spent his life working for the UN Restoration Agency. Literature section.'

Rhoda understood the work well enough. Much of the material she had drawn on in her own research had come from the Restoration's reassembling. The Squeem were traders, not ideological conquerors, but in their exploitation they had carelessly inflicted huge damage on mankind's cultural heritage. A hundred and fifty years after their expulsion the Restoration was still patiently piecing together lost libraries, recovering works of art, even rebuilding swathes of shattered cities brick by brick, like New York, where young Harry Gage had watched the sky fall.

'Hume was a drone,' Kaser said, uncompromising. 'His work was patient, thorough, reliable, but he had no specific talent, and he didn't climb the ladder. He held down a job all his life, but nobody missed him when he retired. He had a family. Wife now dead, kids off-Earth. He never troubled the authorities, not so much as a dodgy tax payment.'

'Until he tried to abduct a kid.'

'Quite.'

The boy, called Lonnie Tekinene, was another New Yorker, ten years old – the same age as Harry Gage, Rhoda noted absently, when he had witnessed the Squeem invasion. Hume had made contact with the kid through a Virtual play-world, and had met him physically in Central Park, and had tried to take him off to Hume's apartment. Alert parents had put a stop to that.

And as Hume had been processed through the legal system, he had become aware of the discovery of the pocket of Squeem on Rhea, moon of Saturn, and the deliberation going on within the UN and its military arm as to what to do about it.

Kaser said, 'Hume didn't harm a hair of the kid's head. At first he just denied everything. But when he heard about Rhea he opened up. He said it was just that his "time" had come. He was the "Rememberer" of his generation. But he was growing old. He needed to recruit another to take his place – just as he was recruited in his turn by some other old fossil when *he* was ten.'

'He never explained why he chose this kid, this Lonnie? What criteria he used?'

Kaser shrugged. 'Looking at the police files, I don't think anybody asked. Hume was just a nut, to them. Probably a sexual deviant.'

Rhoda said, 'But he insisted we need to hear what he has to say. Some truth about the Squeem occupation, preserved only in his head, that will shape our decision.'

'We know all about the occupation,' Kaser said. 'It was a System-wide event. It affected all of mankind. What "truth" can this old fool have, locked up in his head, and available nowhere else?'

'What truth so hideous,' Rhoda wondered, 'that it could *only* be lodged in one man's head? What do you think we should do?'

Kaser shrugged. 'Assess the Squeem colony on its own merits. Maybe they're just stranded, left behind in the evacuation. Or this could be a monitoring station of some kind, spying on a system they lost. Maybe it even predates the occupation, a forward base to gather intelligence to run the invasion. Whatever the reason, it needs to be shut down.'

'But the Squeem themselves don't necessarily need to be eliminated.'

'True.'

'You think I should just ignore this old man, don't you?'

He grinned, tolerant. 'Yes. But you won't. You're an obsessive fact-gatherer. Well, we have time. The Squeem aren't going any-where.' He stood up. 'I'll see if the old guy has finished his nap.'

Karl Hume, bathed once more in strong Earth sunlight, talked to his inquisitor of memories passed down through a chain of Rememberers: the memories of ten-year-old Harry Gage.

Before the invasion, humans had diffused out through the Solar System and beyond in their bulky, ponderous, slower-than-light GUTships. It was a time of hope, of expansion into an unlimited future. Then the first extra-solar intelligence was encountered, some-where among the stars.

Only a few years after first contact Squeem ships burst into the Solar System, in a shower of exotic particles and lurid publicity. The Squeem were aquatic group-mind multiple creatures. They crossed the stars using a hyperdrive system beyond human understanding. They maintained an interstellar network of trading colonies. Their human label, a not very respectful rendering of the Squeem's own sonic rendering of their title for themselves – '*Ss-chh-eemnh*' – meant something like the Wise Folk, rather like '*Homo sapiens*'.

Communication with the group-mind Squeem was utterly unlike

anything envisaged before their arrival. With no separation between individuals, the Squeem hadn't evolved to count in whole numbers, for instance. But eventually common ground was found. And despite fears that mankind might be overwhelmed by a more technically advanced civilisation, trade and cultural contacts were initiated.

The Squeem were welcomed into the Solar System.

Then – it was a morning in New York – in orbit around every inhabited world and moon in the Solar System, cannon platforms appeared. Humanity's slower-than-light GUTdrive warships had no hope of blocking the Squeem's hyperdrive convoys.

And on Earth, rocks began to fall.

'They came in too fast for the planet's impactor defences to cope with,' the Rememberer whispered. 'Rocks from the Solar System's own belts of asteroids and comets, sent in at faster than interplanetary speeds. And they were targeted. Obviously it was the Squeem's doing.

'Harry and his family, stranded on Earth, got an hour's warning of the Manhattan bolide. Harry's father knew New York. He got Harry off the island through the ancient Queens-Midtown tunnel.

'The bolide came down right on top of Grand Central Station. The impact was equivalent to a several-kiloton explosion. It dug out a crater twenty metres across. Every building south of Harlem was reduced to rubble, and several hundred thousand people were killed, through that one impact alone, on the first day of the invasion. Harry saw it all.

'And Harry's mother didn't make it. Crushed in the stampede for the tunnels. Harry never forgave the Squeem for that. Well, you wouldn't, would you?'

Harry and his father reached Queens, where a refugee camp was quickly organised.

And the world churned. All Earth's continents were pocked by the impact scars. Millions had died, cities shaken to rubble. People were horribly reminded of the Starfall, a human war fought with similar techniques only decades before. But now the aggressors were aliens, lacking any human kinship or conscience.

The damage could have been far worse. The Squeem could have sent in a dinosaur-killer, or a relativistic missile like the Fists of the Alpha System rebels of the Starfall war. They could have put Earth through an extinction event, just as easily.

'It took a day for their true strategy to be revealed,' the Rememberer said. 'When people started dying, in great numbers, in waves that spread out like ripples from the impact craters. Dead of diseases that didn't even have names.'

It had been an ingenious strategy, and evidently rehearsed on other subject worlds before. The impactors had been carefully prepared. They had all been seeded with *bits of Earth*, knocked into space by massive natural impacts in the deep past, and so well preserved that they even carried a cargo of antique life. Spores, still viable.

'Diseases, antique and terrible,' the Rememberer whispered, 'diseases older than grass, against which mankind, indeed the modern biosphere, had no defence. They used our own history against us, to cut us back while preserving the Earth itself. Having lost his mother during the bombardment, now Harry lost his father to the plagues. He didn't forgive the Squeem for that, either.'

Rhoda Voynet listened to this account. She was familiar with the history Hume had outlined so far, at least in summary. It was eerie, though, to hear this tale of immense disaster by an eye-witness at only a few removes.

The Squeem attack must have been overwhelming, horrifying, for those who lived through it. Incomprehensible in its crudity and brutality. But since those days mankind had learned more of the facts of Galactic life.

This was the way interstellar war was waged. It wasn't like human war. It wasn't politics, or economics. Though both mankind and Squeem were sentient tool-using species, the conflict between them was much more fundamental than that. It wasn't even ecological, the displacement of one species by another. This was a clash of biospheres.

In such a war there was no negotiation. You just hit hard, and fast.

On Earth, residual resistance imploded quickly.

The more marginal colonies on the other planets and moons were subdued even more easily. Harry's home arcology in Cydonia was cracked open like an egg. Stranded on Earth, he never found out about that.

And human space travel was suspended. Wherever the great GUTship interplanetary freighters landed they were broken up, and the Poole wormhole fast-transit routes, reopened since the Starfall, were collapsed. Some spaceborne humanity escaped, or hid. Pilots couldn't bear to be grounded. Harry's great-aunt Anna, an

AntiSenescence-preserved slow-freighter pilot on the Port Sol run, managed to escape the Solar System altogether. Harry never knew about that either. In fact he never saw any of his family again.

Harry Gage, orphaned in the first few days of the invasion, was a Martian boy stranded on Earth.

Under the Squeem regime, he was put to work. In the first weeks he had to help lug the bodies of plague victims to vast pyres. He always wondered if one of them was his own father. Later he worked in labour camps, set up in the ruins of the shattered cities of mankind.

He grew older and stronger, working hard for the Squeem and their human collaborators, as the aliens began to exploit the worlds they had conquered. The Squeem had no interest in human technology, which was too primitive to be useful, still less in the products of human culture. But Earth was a lode of complex hydrocarbons, highly prized by interstellar traders. The last of the planet's oil and coal was dug up by human muscle, and exported off the planet. Harry worked in the mines, squirming through seams too narrow for an adult.

Humans themselves could be worth exporting, though they were expensive and fragile. Slave transports lifted off the planet, sundering families, taking their captives to unknown destinations. Even after the eventual expulsion of the Squeem nobody ever found out what became of most of them. Jones, however, the ultimate liberator of mankind, had been among their number, a captive off-world worker.

And on Earth people kept dying, from overwork or hunger or neglect.

The Squeem even shut down AntiSenescence technology. They had no interest in lengthening human lives; fast-breeding generations of servants and slaves were sufficient for them. Beneath the attention of the Squeem, stone-age wars were fought over the last AS supplies. Some of the undying went into hiding, detaching themselves from human history. Other lives centuries long were curtailed in brief agonies of withdrawal.

Amid all this, Harry grew up as best he could. There was no education, nothing but what you could pick up from other workers and bits of Squeem-collaborator propaganda, about how this wasn't a conquest at all but a necessary *integration* of mankind into a Galactic culture. Harry heard little and understood less.

'But,' Karl Hume whispered, 'Harry never forgave the Squeem, for their murder of his mother and father. And he began to develop contacts with others who were just as unforgiving. It was a dangerous business. There were plenty of collaborators, and the dissident groups were easily infiltrated.

'But a resistance network gradually coalesced. Small acts of sabotage were committed. Every act was punished a hundredfold. But still they fought back, despite the odds, despite the cost. It was a heroic time.'

Lots of untold stories, historian Rhoda thought wistfully.

'Then,' said the Rememberer, 'Harry was transferred to the Great Lakes.'

Lake Superior had the largest surface area of any freshwater lake in the world. It was a grandiose gesture of the Squeem to colonise this great body of water, to symbolise their subjugation of mankind. Harry worked on vast projects to adjust the mineral content of Superior's water to the Squeem's liking, incidentally eliminating much of the native fauna. When the lake was ready, the Squeem descended from the sky in whale-like shuttles.

It was the Lake Superior colony that gave the resistance a real chance to hurt the Squeem.

Rhoda Voynet grew more interested. At last the Rememberer was talking of incidents she'd never heard of before.

It was easy to kill a Squeem, if you could get near one, as easy as murdering a goldfish. But all Squeem were linked into a mass mind. So the death of a single Squeem affected the totality, but only in a minor way, as the loss of a single neurone from a human brain wouldn't even be noticed. To hurt the Squeem significantly you had to kill an awful lot of them.

And that was what Harry's resistance cell managed to do. It happened close to Harry's twenty-fifth birthday.

'It was a suicide mission,' the Rememberer said. 'A volunteer allowed her body to be pumped full of Squeem-specific toxins and pathogens. Harry wasn't the assassin, and nor was he educated enough to have manufactured the toxins. Underground cells of fifty-somethings, the last generation of pre-invasion scientists, laboured over that. But Harry was a link in the chain that got the toxins to the assassin, and he helped provide a diversion that enabled the woman to finish the job.'

The woman just jumped into Lake Superior, one bright morning, her body weighted with bags of rocks. She slit her own wrists and let her crimson blood spill into the waters.

'Every Lethe-spawned Squeem in that lake died,' Karl Hume said. 'They felt that loss all the way back to their homeworld. And I mean it, those group-minded bastards all felt it.'

As Hume told this story, Rhoda saw Reg Kaser clench his fist, the others of her crew shift and murmur. Subtle signs of triumph. It was a story that none of them had heard before; Rhoda, herself a historian, had no idea the invasion-age inhabitants of Earth had been able to mount such an effective assault on the conquerors.

'But of course it made no difference to the occupation,' Hume said. 'The Squeem still had the Solar System. They still had Earth. They rounded up everybody even remotely connected with the killing.'

'They got Harry,' the inquisitor prompted.

'Oh, yes. And they put them all in a prison camp, where Harry waited for Earth's punishment.

'To understand what followed,' Hume said darkly, 'you have to try to see the world-view of the Squeem. For one thing, they aren't instinctive killers as we are. Their background is a cooperative ecology, not a competitive one like ours. That's how they ended up as a group mind. When they did kill, as in the strikes on the cities, the killing was minimal, if you can call it that. Just enough to achieve their objectives, in that case to shatter resistance and subjugate the population.

'We, on the other hand, had "murdered" Lake Superior, in their view. We had rendered a whole body of water uninhabitable. They are aquatic, remember. To them it was as great a crime as if we had destroyed an entire world.

'And so they planned a punishment appropriate to the crime they perceived.'

In the silent skies above Harry's prison, ships slid into position. Beams of pinkish light connected them, and pulsed down into the ground. It took a full year to assemble the network.

'And when it was ready . . .'

'Yes?' the inquisitor asked.

'Water is funny stuff,' the Rememberer said. 'Have you ever heard of hot ice?'

In the next break, Rhoda had her engineering officers extrapolate what had happened, from the hints in Hume's account.

Ice formed naturally when heat was extracted from a body of water, the hydrogen-oxygen molecules settling into a space-filling solid lattice. But the Squeem had discovered that you could create a particular kind of ice, called polar cubic ice, even at high temperatures, with electricity.

'We know about this too,' Reg Kaser said. 'You pass an electric field through the water – a strong one, a million volts a metre. The two hydrogen atoms in a water molecule have a slight positive charge, and the oxygen atom a negative one, so the electric field makes the molecules line up like fence posts. And there you have it, ice, at as high a temperature as you like. This happens in nature, though on a microscopic scale, wherever there are strong enough electric fields, such as across the membranes of nerve cells, or in the cavities of proteins. Mini icebergs riding around inside your cells. Amazing. The Squeem were masters of this sort of technology. Masters of *water*.'

'And so,' Rhoda prompted, 'on occupied Earth—'

'They froze the water.'

'What water?'

'All of it.'

Earth's oceans plated over with ice, right down to the equator, and then froze to their beds. And then the hard whiteness crept up the river valleys.

Harry and his co-dissidents were made to watch, on vast softscreens. Indeed, the Squeem made everybody watch, everybody capable of understanding.

'Even the aquifers froze, deep underground. Even the moisture in the soil,' Hume whispered. 'Everybody walked around on permafrost, down to the equator.

'The Squeem controlled it, somehow. After all, humans are just big bags of water. *We* didn't freeze, nor did the grasses, the animals, the birds, the moisture in the air. Of course rainfall was screwed, because nothing was evaporating from the oceans.

'They kept it up for a full year. By then people were dying of the drought and the cold. And Earth blazed white, a symbol of the Squeem's dominance, visible even to all the off-planet refugees and hideouts, visible light years away.

'Then they released the field.

'There was a lot of damage as all that ice melted, most of it suddenly – it wasn't a normal thaw. Coastlines shattered, river valleys gouged out, meltwater floods, climatic horrors. Lots of people died, as usual.

'And the oceans were left sterile. Oh, the Squeem allowed gradual restocking, from samples in old climate-crash gene-store facilities, that kind of thing. The oceans didn't stay dead. But still, for an age they would be depleted, and the recovered biosphere would always be artificial. Humanity's link with the deepest past of life on Earth cut, for ever.

'It was the worst act the Squeem, an aquatic species, could think of,' Hume said. 'To murder oceans. They thought it would crush human resistance once and for all. And it worked. But not for the reasons they imagined.'

'When it was done, they just let Harry and his colleagues go. Harry came out of that prison camp near Thunder Bay, and found himself in an aftermath society. It had been by far the worst act of terror ever inflicted on the Earth, by mankind or anybody else.

'And it had cut through some deep umbilical connection. Everybody just wandered around stunned.'

'I'm not surprised,' said Rhoda. She assessed the reactions of her crew to this forgotten crime. Anger, shock, a lust for revenge.

'And,' Hume said now, 'the Squeem became concerned. They hadn't anticipated a reaction like this. I guess they knew us even less well than we knew ourselves. A large proportion of mankind was plagued by flashbacks, crippling fear. Productivity was dropping. Birth rates falling. They didn't want to kill off their cheap labour. Maybe they saw they'd gone too far.

'World leaders were called to a kind of summit. I say "leaders". After two decades of the Squeem there were no elected presidents, no monarchs, no moderators of global councils. The "leaders" were labour organisers, essential academics like doctors, a few religious types.

'And the Squeem offered, not a restoration – for what they had done could not be put right – but a kind of cure.'

Most of humanity was suffering a deep kind of post-traumatic stress.

The memories of the freezing were etched deeply into every human brain. Like all traumas, the event had produced a rush of adrenalin and noradrenalin, which then forced brain centres called the amygdalae to imprint the memories into the hippocampus, the memory centre, very deeply. It was essentially a survival mechanism, so that any reminder of the event triggered deep memories and a fast response. Sometimes memories like this were gradually extinguished, the memory pathways overridden if not erased. But in this case, for the majority of mankind, the extinguishing mechanism didn't work well. The event had been too huge, too deep, too wide. And global post-trauma stress was the result.

But this could be rectified.

'There are ways to control memory formation,' Reg Kaser murmured to Rhoda, taking another briefing from his data slate. 'Drugs like beta blockers that inhibit the action of adrenalin and noradrenalin, and so reduce their memory-forming capabilities. A stress-related hormone called cortisol can inhibit memory retrieval. There are drugs that release a brain chemical called glutamate that enhances learning, so accelerating the normal memory extinguishing process. And so on.'

'You're talking about altering memories with drugs,' Rhoda murmured.

'Since the twentieth century, when neuroscience was established as a discipline, human societies have always been cautious about memory-changing technology,' Kaser said. 'Memory-editing has been used as therapy, and to treat criminals. In the age of Michael Poole, for instance. But there are obvious ethical issues. A memory is part of your identity, after all. Does anybody else have the right to take away part of *you*? And suppose a criminal deliberately erases all her own memory of her crime. If she doesn't remember it, is she still responsible? That was used as a defence in a criminal trial during—'

'Never mind,' Rhoda said.

'The point is, such technologies have existed in the past. And after a couple of decades of occupation, the Squeem, presumably with human collaborators, were able to come up with a suitable treatment . . .'

'This is what they offered us,' Hume was saying. 'An engineered virus that would spread through mankind, across the Earth. Eventually carriers would infect the off-planet populations too. It wouldn't be comfortable. You would have a nightmare, reliving the trauma one last time. But that would make the memory labile again for a short time. And so it could be treated.'

'They would delete the memory of the freezing, of this vast crime,' the inquisitor said. 'From everybody's heads.'

'That was the idea. There would have to be a subsidiary activity of removing traces of the event from various records, but there weren't too many marine biologists at the height of the occupation. It wouldn't be difficult. Everybody would come out of it believing the oceans had always been depleted of life, maybe since the global eco-crashes of the second and third millennia. They'd think the damaged coastlines and scoured river valleys they observed had always been that way, or maybe they were damaged in the war.

'This solution served the Squeem's goals, you see. People would stay pliable. They just wouldn't know why.'

The inquisitor said sharply, 'And, since none of *us* have heard of this freezing before, I take it that these "leaders" made this supine choice on behalf of the rest of mankind.'

'You shouldn't judge them,' Hume said. 'We had been enslaved, for decades. They could see no way out. The only choice was between a future of terrified subjugation, or a calmer one – vague, baffled, adjusted.

'Even Harry Gage and his resistance colleagues knew they were beaten. They submitted. But,' he said, and a smile spread over his leathery face, 'there was one last act of defiance.'

Everybody alive would forget the terror. Everybody but one.

'It wasn't sophisticated. They would just hide one person away, for a year, perhaps more. Earth is a big planet. There were plenty of places to hide. And not all of the biochemists had gone over to the Squeem. Some of them helped out with screens against the virus. And when he or she came out of her hole in the ground . . .'

The offscreen inquisitor guessed, 'Harry Gage was the first Rememberer.'

Hume smiled. 'They chose him by lot. It could have been anyone. It's the only reason we remember Harry now, the only extraordinary thing that happened in his life.

'He went into the hole without a word of protest. And when he came back out he found himself the only one who remembered the freezing. A kind of living memorial to a deleted past.

'Harry just went back to work. But the course of the rest of his life was set out. It must have been hard for him, hard not to talk about what he knew. It's been hard for *me*, and I didn't live through it.

'Harry Gage died in his late forties. It wasn't a time when people grew old. But he fulfilled his last mission, which was to transmit his memories to another.

'The Second Rememberer was in her thirties when the Squeem regime began to crumble – sooner than anybody had expected. She, too, died young. But she was able to pass on her knowledge to another in turn.

'And so it went. Two centuries after the Squeem conquered Earth, I am the Sixth Rememberer.'

'And you tried to recruit Lonnie Tekinene.'

Hume sighed. 'That was the idea. I left it a bit late in life to be befriending ten-year-olds.'

'But,' the inquisitor said, 'even though the Squeem fell so long ago, none of you thought to reveal the truth of all this oral history until now.'

Hume shrugged. 'When would have been right? Each of the Rememberers has had to make that judgement. It was only when I learned of your pocket of Squeem, surviving in the Solar System after the passage of two centuries, that I judged the time was right. You need to know the whole truth about the Squeem in order to deal with them.' His face twisted. 'But I wasn't *sure*. I'm still not.'

The off-screen inquisitor asked, comparatively gently, 'So how do you feel now?'

'Relieved. It's a burden, to be the only one who knows.'

It took Rhoda Voynet and her crew another week of data-gathering before she felt ready to make her judgement.

She called Reg Kaser to her cabin, and fired up her percolator once more. Beyond her picture window, Saturn turned, its cloudy face impassive before the turmoil of living things.

'They've started to find proof,' she said to Kaser.

'Of what?'

'The freezing. The geologists, putting together pieces of the puzzle – as if they were the first of their discipline millennia ago, deducing the existence of past Ice Ages from erratic boulders and gouged valleys. The biologists, trawling the seabeds for crushed whale bones. My historian colleagues, finding traces of deleted records. Global evidence of a decade-long glaciation event. It was always there, but unnoticed; it just needed a framing hypothesis to fit it all together.'

'So Hume was telling the truth.'

'It seems so.'

'Meanwhile,' Kaser said, 'I've been talking to the xenologists, who have been in contact with those Squeem down there under the ice. The Squeem have been making their own case.'

'About what?'

'About why we should be lenient. The Squeem say they suffered some deep trauma of their own. After all they are aquatic, they're functionally fish-like, and it must have taken a huge disjunction to lift them out of their ocean and into space.' Kaser scrolled through notes on his slate. 'Something about an invasion, by yet another world-conquering species. The Squeem managed to enslave the slavers, took over their star-spanning technology, and started an empire of their own. Something on those lines. It's complicated.'

Rhoda said harshly, 'And that justifies them occupying Earth?'

'I suppose that's the argument. But you're the commanding officer.'

'I am, aren't I?' She looked him straight in the eye. 'I want to know my options. Tell me about the weapon. The one that will destroy Rhea.'

Knowledge in the UN Navy was rigidly partitioned. It was part of Kaser's job to bear secrets of destruction, until they were needed. Rhoda only knew of their potential. He looked away. 'If you're sure. This is need-to-know only.'

'I need to know.'

'It's not a human development,' Kaser said. 'Not even Squeem.'

Rhoda glanced beyond Saturn's limb, at the stars. 'Something hideous we've found. Out there.'

'Yes.'

Even under the oppressive Squeem occupation, humans had learned much.

They learned, for example, that much of the Squeem's high technology – such as their hyperdrive – was not indigenous. It was copied, sometimes at second- or third-hand, from the designs of an older, more powerful species.

'It was during the occupation,' Kaser said, 'that the name "Xeelee" entered human discourse. The primal source of all this good stuff.'

Rhoda shuddered. 'And is this new weapon you're offering me a Xeelee artefact?'

'It may be. Stuff gets swapped around. Purloined. Modified. We don't know enough about the Xeelee to say . . .'

Ridding Rhea of the Squeem was a challenge. The ocean in which they swam lay under kilometres of ice, and was wrapped around a core of ice and rock. The ocean itself could be easily cleansed, but it would not be hard for Squeem groups to hide out in cracks and crevices in the irregular core, the thick, uneven crust. Rhoda needed something that would cleanse the little moon, thoroughly.

'Tell me what this thing does.'

'Maybe you know that the planet Jupiter is being destroyed. Eaten up from within by a swarm of black holes.'

'Yes.' In fact Rhoda knew a little more about it than that.

'If we could make a black hole,' Kaser said, 'we could throw it at Rhea and demolish it the same way.'

She nodded, vaguely horrified, but trying to think clearly. 'That would do the job, But we can't make a black hole.'

'No. But we have a technology almost as good.' He pulled up graphics on his slate and showed her. 'It's a way to create a dark energy black hole.'

'A *what*?'

'It's all to do with quantum physics,' he said.

'Oh, it would be . . .'

It was a kind of freezing, like water to ice, a phase transition. But this would happen at the quantum level. In a 'quantum critical phase transition', ordinary matter congealed into a kind of superconductor, and then into sluggish stuff in which even subatomic fluctuations died, and mass-energy was shed.

'It's as if time itself is freezing out,' Kaser said. He mimed with his hands. 'So you have a spherical shell. Just a volume in space. You arrange for matter falling on its surface to go through this quantum phase transition. And as your input matter passes into the interior its mass is dumped, converted to vacuum energy. Dark energy.'

'Why doesn't this shell implode?'

'Because dark energy has a repulsive effect. Antigravity. Dark energy is already the dominant component of the universe's mass-energy, and the antigravity force it produces will drive the expansion of the universe in the future. So I'm told by the physicists. Anyhow, the repulsion can balance the infall of matter.'

'It *can* balance.'

Kaser grinned. 'That's the engineering challenge, I guess. If you get it right you get a stable object which externally looks just like a black hole. Inside there's no singularity, just a mush of dark energy, but any structure is destroyed just the same. These things are found in nature, apparently.'

'And they are easier to make than genuine black holes.'

'So it seems. You do need a big box of exotic matter – that is negative-energy matter – to make it work.' He kept grinning.

'A big box of exotic matter like a Poole wormhole mouth.'

'Just the job. The Squeem wrecked the old Poole wormhole transport system, but they left the wormhole mouths in place. There are several still orbiting Saturn. Any one of them will do.'

'And if we throw one of these things into Rhea—'

'It will eat up the moon.'

'That would get rid of them,' Rhoda said.

'That it would. And later the residual black-hole-like object would just evaporate away . . . Of course there are other options. The Squeem may be useful. We could use them, as they once used us. A Galaxy-spanning telepathic network—'

'We don't need them in the Solar System for that. We have their homeworld.'

'True.' Kaser eyed Rhoda. 'The technology's in place. The only question remains, do we use it?'

Rhoda thought it through.

The Squeem occupation had changed human perceptions of the Galaxy, and humanity's place in it. A historic loss of innocence.

Now humans were tentatively moving out beyond the Solar System once more. And everywhere they went, they found life. Intelligences swarming and squabbling. A kind of Galactic society, a ramshackle pecking order based on avarice, theft and the subjugation of junior races.

And for humanity, a future that contained nothing but threat.

The black holes in Jupiter were clues to a closely guarded secret, which Rhoda hadn't even shared with Reg Kaser. The Squeem invasion hadn't been the first hostile alien incursion into the Solar System. Some centuries back invaders, who would occupy Earth in their turn some time in the future, had *come back in time* to secure their victory over mankind. They had crossed a kind of time bridge built by the legendary, or notorious, engineer Michael Poole, and created a crisis the historians called 'The Emergency'. And in the course of the final battle to exclude them, miniature black holes had been hurled into Jupiter. During the Squeem occupation, knowledge of this event had mostly been lost, and was only now being pieced back together by the historians. But the mortal wound inflicted on Jupiter was unarguable. Some analysts, poring over the historical reconstructions, argued that the source of the Emergency invasion might lie only decades away, in the future.

And even beyond that hazard lay: not least the Xeelee, secretive, xenophobic, indifferent. And so advanced they made the rest of the Galaxy's inhabitants look like tree-dwellers.

The future held hierarchies of enemies. And that was the basis on which Rhoda had to make her decision.

Rhoda stared down at the ice landscape of Rhea, imagining the stranded Squeem swarming within. 'It won't be revenge,' she said. 'Call it insurance. Look at what the Squeem did to us. This will be one danger eliminated.'

'We're setting a precedent for the future.'

'The future leaves us no choice. And if this makes us tougher as a species, good. When the weapon's ready, make sure Hume is online when the signals reach Earth, would you? He ought to watch this, as the Squeem made Harry Gage watch. Let *this* be remembered.'

Kaser stood. 'I'll call the weapons crew.'

In retrospect, the yoke of the Squeem had been thrown off with comparative ease. Humans moved out into the Galaxy again, in new ships based on the Squeem hyperdrive . . . a technology stolen, at second-hand, from the Xeelee.

Then humans encountered their next conquerors, just as had been predicted in the fragmented histories of the Emergency. Those shards of foreknowledge proved of little use. The new overlords were called the Qax. Once more the worlds of mankind were taken. Once more people were made to grow old.

And, even at such a distance in time, the hubristic feats of Michael Poole continued to affect human lives.

ENDURANCE
AD 5274

1

Chael smiled at Mara. Beside Chael stood the sullen Engineer he had introduced only as Tasqer. And with them, in Mara's living room, stood the Virtual avatar of Jasoft Parz, probably the most powerful human being in the Qax dominion of mankind.

Mara had never trusted Chael, her husband's brother, even before Pell had died, and she didn't trust him now. But here he was with these extraordinary characters, telling her about the most outlandish project she'd ever heard of.

A project to which, it seemed, her own son Juq was somehow the key.

'We even have a name for the ship we're going to build,' Chael said.

'The ship you're going to build *for the Qax*,' Mara pointed out.

'For the Qax, yes. Everything we do is for the Qax. But this is a chance for humans to achieve something for themselves, under the yoke of the Occupation – even with the encouragement of the Qax Governor—'

'The ship you want my son and his toys to contribute to, somehow.'

The unreal spectre of Jasoft Parz, Ambassador to the Qax, smiled with an odd serenity. 'Time is short, Mara. The Governor wants this craft, a Poole-technology GUTship towing a navigable wormhole mouth, built and launched within six months. GUTship engineers we have . . .'

And he nodded to the taciturn Tasqer, the Engineer. In dark, practical-looking clothes, Tasqer was perhaps forty, and though heavy-set he had the pallid look of the space-born. Since this little party had come floating down to Mellborn in a flitter from the sky, Tasqer had said not a word, and he said nothing now, meeting Mara's gaze coolly.

'But,' Parz went on, 'wormhole builders are another matter. And so when my old friend Chael here came to me and pointed out your son's experiments . . .'

Mara found it difficult even to listen to this nonsense. Jasoft Parz

171

himself was a distracting presence. Parz looked around seventy years old, with a round face, white hair, finely robed. But he moved with the ease of a younger man, Mara thought suspiciously. She looked at him more closely.

And were there black roots showing under that mop of white?

She tried to suppress her reaction, the shock of recognition. But Parz smiled at her. He wasn't hard to read – or rather, he was more than skilful at projecting his true meaning. Yes, he was saying, she saw suddenly, that through this strange scheme the ultimate prize was indeed available: AntiSenescence treatment. Life itself. All she had to do was play along.

Suddenly Mara's attention was fully focused.

Chael said now, 'Juq's experiments, yes. Young people building spacetime wormholes in their bedrooms and back yards! It's a re-markable story – it turns out there's a kind of global craze for such things, loose societies of enthusiasts communicating and sharing. It's just like the rocket clubs that formed before the first age of space.'

Parz said, 'Well, not all the ingenuity mankind showed in the heroic days of Michael Poole has been lost, evidently. Here is something we can build on. And your son, Mara, is in the vanguard of developments.'

Actually, Mara thought, not so much her son, not handsome, plaus-ible Juq, but his smarter but lower-class buddy Tiel. She wasn't so blinded by her love for her son that she couldn't see where the brains in that partnership lay.

Chael said, 'We see Juq as a potential leader of this aspect of the project, young as he is.'

She eyed her brother-in-law, and Parz. *That* made sense, at least. 'Hm. A bright, good-looking son of an old military family? Yes, he'd be a good front for this operation, wouldn't he? You've an eye for figureheads if nothing else, Ambassador.'

Chael said seriously, 'It's not a trivial point. Image matters. Both my family and yours, Mara, do have respectable pedigrees dating back to Navy service in the days of the rebellion against the Squeem.'

Parz said carefully, 'And now you serve in a different way, as I strive to do, in making life bearable for billions under the administration of the Qax.'

Of course that was true, in its way. When the Qax had almost ef-fortlessly taken over the Solar System, rich old families like Mara's, seamlessly embedded in hierarchies of wealth, privilege and power, had seemed to find it easy to transfer their loyalties to the new alien rulers. Their justification was that without their selfless negotiating with the Qax, the lot of the rest of mankind could be considerably worse.

But especially since Juq had started bringing his friend Tiel home to play with their wormhole experiments – and Tiel had let leak a few details of the lives he and his family led, brief lives spent labouring on the coastal algae farms, or on the great sea-bound transport canals and sewage ducts, until ending in old age or terminated by diseases that had once been banished from Earth – Mara had become uncomfortably aware, here in her grand home in the heart of ancient Mellborn, what privileges she and her family enjoyed, and how morally compromised she had become . . .

Yet she looked again at those odd black roots under Parz's white hair. The most cruel imposition of the Qax regime, like the Squeem before them, had been the removal of AntiSenescence treatments, which for millennia had enabled humans to postpone death. Though there were endless rumours of illicit sources of AS, and of secret groups of undying living among mortal humans, not even the most senior in the Qax's human administration had legal access to such treatments. *In theory.* Now it seemed that wasn't true. What was she being drawn into here? And – could she refuse the implicit offer, for herself and her family?

Jasoft Parz caught her looking at him, and smiled again.

'Well,' she said briskly. 'Before we go any further with this conversation you'd better come meet the boys and see if what they're building is actually any use to you. The staircase down to the cellar is this way . . .'

The townhouse was very ancient, and the cellar more so, perhaps millennia old, Mara suspected. But she'd had it renovated recently. Hovering light globes made the roomy chamber bright as day, illuminating walls now overlaid with the boys' images of the heroic days of wormhole-building when Michael Poole and his colleagues had laced the Solar System with their faster-than-light transit tunnels.

Both Juq and Tiel waited for them here, dressed in clean coveralls, standing beside the long table on which they'd set up their latest experiment. The neatness had been Mara's mandate; she wanted them to look like smart young engineers, not teenage hobbyists. They would always be an ill-matched pair, however. Though at seventeen Tiel was a year older than Juq, he was a good head shorter than Mara's son, no doubt some consequence of diet and upbringing.

The Virtual Jasoft Parz greeted Juq with a smile. 'It's good to meet you, my boy. I did know your father – a good man.' He spread his hands. 'And I'm sorry I can't be here in person.'

'I'm pleased to meet you too, sir.'

Juq, tall, blond, blue-eyed, handsome, had never been short of confidence, Mara knew, even if he had never been academic. And he was instantly likeable, as she could see despite her mother's bias. She'd never had any doubt that with such attributes, coming from such a family, he'd find a place in the world. But she'd never expected him to be caught up in spacecraft experiments – or at least she'd imagined it would be nothing but a boyhood fad . . .

Parz glanced around. 'I'm surprised to find you working in a cellar. Why not above ground, in the daylight?'

Tiel and Juq glanced at each other uneasily.

Chael stepped forward. 'Call it caution, Ambassador. I know from my own fond memories that my nephew here has been fascinated by the Poole era since he was small. Books, dramas, even the imagery you see here on these walls. We saw no harm in it – we should be proud of the human past – even if the Squeem did shut down the old Poole tunnels long before any of us were born. Then when he found it was possible, in principle, to build a wormhole in a home workshop—'

Juq took over. 'Sir, I know experiments with spacecraft technologies are indicted under the Occupation.' He glanced over at Tasqer the Engineer, who gazed back. 'I wasn't sure if this qualified. After all, a wormhole isn't spaceflight technology in itself; in fact, to use a wormhole to travel through space, you would have to *use* a spacecraft to tug the Interfaces into position. But I didn't want to get my family into trouble.'

Parz nodded. 'And so you hid it all away down here.'

Juq squared his shoulders. 'I am prepared to take full responsibility for any breach of regulations, Ambassador.'

Chael beamed. 'You see, Jasoft? You remember what I told you about this boy? Smart, intelligent, and morally upright. What a credit to the family, to the race!'

Parz gave Mara the slightest of smiles, showing he wasn't entirely taken in by this salesmanship. But Mara couldn't blame Chael, she supposed, for working so hard to obtain for the family any benefits that might accrue from this peculiar opportunity.

Parz said now, 'Perhaps you'd better show me this marvellous experiment of yours.'

Juq led him to the table, where Tiel stood waiting. Juq said, 'Maybe you'd be best at talking the Ambassador through it, buddy.'

Suddenly Tiel looked terrified. Mara imagined the only figures of authority who had spoken to him before had been work supervisors and police. He opened and closed his mouth, and said, 'Sir – Ambassador—'

'Take your time,' said Parz kindly. He stepped up to the table, which was low and long and topped by an airtight transparent cover, and cluttered with heaps of equipment. Parz passed a Virtual hand through the cover, making blocky pixels sparkle. 'I understand this is a mere model.'

'But it is a fully functioning wormhole,' said Tiel, more confidently now. 'A flaw in spacetime that enables faster-than-light travel from one end of the table to the other. You can't see the Interfaces, of course, they're microscopic. And all we can pass through is laser light. But—'

'But the wormhole is stable, yes? I understand that's the trick, the hard part. Wormholes tend to collapse on themselves—'

Tiel said too quickly, 'In fact they get locked into causal feedback loops and detonate.'

'You need a kind of antigravity to keep the wormhole throat open – is that correct?'

'Yes, sir,' Juq said. 'More precisely you need what's called "exotic matter", a peculiar kind of matter with a negative energy density. Yes, it works like antigravity.'

By now even Mara had been forced to learn how wormholes worked – in particular that a wormhole without exotic matter in its throat was useless. Lethal tidal forces would bar the wormhole portals, the portals themselves would expand or collapse at light-speed, and the smallest perturbations caused by any infalling matter would result in instability and collapse. So, in their designs centuries ago, Poole's team had learned to thread each of their wormholes with 'exotic matter', to provide an antigravity effect in the throat to keep it open. The wormhole was still intrinsically unstable, but with feedback loops it could be made self-regulating – but the negative energy levels Poole had needed were high, equivalent to the pressure at the heart of a neutron star. It had been a challenge for Poole, and was a challenge now.

Parz said, 'I do know that fifteen centuries ago Michael Poole harvested his exotic matter from the orbit of Jupiter. Whereas here—'

'We've had to be more subtle,' Juq said.

Tiel said, 'Actually, I had the idea when I was working on a landfill processing detail.' Combing through millennia-old garbage, Mara knew, for reusable materials, chemicals, even artefacts; all over the planet the occupying authorities had people sifting the debris of their own past for materials the Qax could sell off-world. 'And I found these.' Tiel held up threads of very fine fibre on the palm of his hand. 'There are splinters of diamond attached to these optic fibres, sir. Very small, very fine. I have no idea what kind of machine these came from, once. But I realised that with these I could make—'

Juq put in, 'He got the proper permissions before removing the materials from the site, Ambassador. The threads were of no discernible value and had no weaponising potential.'

Parz waved a hand. 'Yes, yes. Just tell me what you did, boy.'

'It's technical, sir. At the quantum level all matter and energy, a beam of photons say, is naturally a mixture of positive and negative energy. Although the net balance is always positive, overall.'

'All right. This positive energy is the ordinary stuff we use to heat our homes and power our flitters?'

'Yes, sir. And negative energy is – well, it's a gap where energy ought to be. And it's equivalent to exotic matter. In a way – the mathematics is subtle . . . What you have to do is squeeze the vacuum – that's the phrase we use – so that the negative component of the energy is separated out, and can be gathered. Here we do that by using the diamond splinters to manipulate photons in a light beam one by one. And we capture the negative energy in a mirrored cavity, which—'

Mara thought Jasoft's eyes were glazing over. 'Maybe you'd better just show the Ambassador how it works, Tiel.'

In fact, much of the experiment had to be taken on faith, since the wormhole mouths were too small to see. The boys had set up two fine laser beams, passing through a narrow vacuum chamber set up on the table: beams which cast spots of ruby light on a plate at the table's far end. One beam was passed unimpeded, the boys said; the other was sent through a wormhole a metre long. And the photons in the second beam, travelling instantaneously between the wormholes' tiny Interfaces, took a few nanoseconds less to travel the length of the table: a small interval, but sufficient for the boys to demonstrate with a precise clock.

'I'm impressed,' Jasoft Parz said. 'Junk from a landfill, a home workshop – and you've built a stable wormhole. Very impressed.'

Chael beamed. 'Told you so, Ambassador.'

Mara stepped forward. 'Well, I'm still in the dark. Even if it's possible somehow to scale all this up from a tabletop . . . The Qax want us to replicate Poole's work, correct? To build a navigable wormhole, and then to drag one end across space in a slower-than-light GUTship. Why do they want to do this? And why a GUTship? It was great technology fifteen hundred years ago, but those ships are slower than light. The Qax have those Spline starships of theirs, capable of faster-than-light travel. So why would they want this?'

'It certainly harks back to our past,' Chael said quickly, evading the question, and evidently anxious to reassure the Ambassador. 'Which is why it's so valuable for morale. Hence my suggestion for the ship's name, *Endurance*, used many times since but originally referring to a great exploration craft of the late second millennium—'

'*I* can tell you what's prompted the Qax to do this,' said Engineer Tasqer, surprising them by speaking at all, Mara suspected. He stepped forward and searched the boys' images on the wall. Most of them showed Poole and his colleagues, legendary names in their own right like Miriam Berg and Bill Dzik – faces with the eerie agelessness that came from decades of AS treatment, Mara thought, from a time when it was unimaginable that such a thing could ever be lost.

'Here it is. Knew you boys would have got hold of a shot of this.' Tasqer tapped an image, dark, grainy, much less impressive than the rest. But a glimmering tetrahedral form was clearly visible. 'That,' he said, 'is a wormhole mouth. Poole era, a classic design. And this image *isn't* fifteen hundred years old but, what, a month?'

Mara frowned, baffled. 'A month old? How is that possible?'

'This is Poole's own design,' Tasqer said. 'Poole's own ship! One of Poole's last projects was to build a GUTship called the *Cauchy*, which he sent off on a fifteen-hundred-year loop out into space, towards the galactic centre. Towing a wormhole mouth, not to the planets, but to the stars and back. Fifteen hundred years, you see. The flight plan predicted it should arrive back home about *now* – we knew that, and looked out for it – and here it is, right on schedule, out on the edge of interstellar space. That's what inspired you kids to fool around with wormholes, right?'

Juq grinned. 'How could we not, sir? An authentic Poole wormhole, returning to the Solar System . . . I suppose I should have told you we have this, Mother. But everybody's got the image, everybody's talking about it.'

Mara pursed her lips. 'Well, I didn't know about this. The Poole ship.'

Tasqer leaned forward. '*This* is obviously why the Qax suddenly want us to build another wormhole ship. Because of this ghost from the past. But to what end, Ambassador?'

Parz hesitated before replying. 'It's complicated. And frankly it's best you know as little as necessary about this. All of you. I'm afraid that going forward with this you'll need to be vetted by the security services.'

Mara didn't like the sound of that. 'Vetted? For what?'

'For any links to seditious groups.' He glanced at Tiel. 'I know that some in your family, Tiel, have links to a group called the Friends of Wigner. You have a cousin called Shira who is currently—'

Juq put a protective arm around Tiel's shoulders. 'You don't need to worry about that, Ambassador. Tiel can stay with us from now on – I'll vouch for him.'

Tiel looked shocked at this sudden appropriation of his life, as well he might, Mara thought.

But Parz nodded thoughtfully. 'Good, good. I'm sure it can all be arranged. But I urge you to be circumspect. Cautious. Well, gentlemen, I can see there's a long way to go and no assurance of success. But I think we have a commission for you. Though I'm sure that to build a navigable wormhole will take more than scavenged lasers and a tabletop.'

Tiel nodded. 'We'll need to make more exotic matter. A *lot* of it. More than we can fudge up with scrap optic cables.'

'And what do you think you'll need to achieve that?'

Without hesitation Tiel replied, 'A Squeem hyperdrive unit.'

The Engineer laughed out loud.

Parz, showing admirable composure, asked, 'Is that all?'

'No. Also Xeelee construction material.'

2

The flitter rose from Occupied Earth like a stone thrown from a blue bowl.

Like most Earthborn humans of her era, Mara had only rarely travelled above the atmosphere. Now, as the ship settled into a low check-out orbit, the glowing innocence of the planet took her breath away. Two centuries of Qax Occupation had left few visible scars on Earth's surface – far fewer, in fact, than the damage wrought by humans themselves during their slow, haphazard rise to technological civilisation. Away from the cities like Mellborn, rewilded Australe was a pale green-brown, the colour of scrubland populated by herds of immense beasts: the colours of life, of nature. But still it was disturbing to see how the Qax-run plankton farms bordered the coast in lurid purple-green. And on the land, scattered and gleaming fields of glass marked mankind's brief and inglorious struggle against the Qax – at the site of SydCity, for instance, which was still left abandoned.

Mara sat with the Virtual of Parz, who was politely making this ride into space with her. The louring Engineer Tasqer sat opposite. Chael was riding up front in the cockpit, a backup in this pilotless craft. A month after Parz had initiated the *Endurance* project they were on their way to the Moon, to inspect the experimental exotic-matter production facility to whose design Tiel and Juq had been contributing.

But to get to the Moon, first you had to leave Earth. And Parz's expression, in the bright light of Earth, was complex, she thought.

He caught her watching, and smiled. 'You're wondering what I'm thinking.'

'You must have made this journey many times. In the flesh, I mean—'

'I always meant for the best, you know. I do know what people think of me. Given that the Qax Occupation was imposed on mankind over a century before I was even born, and given that I discovered I had certain diplomatic skills that spanned both communities, human and Qax, I thought I could find a way to do some good through negotiation. Mediation.'

Tasqer asked, 'And do you think you succeeded? Look down there. That is not a human landscape.'

'Maybe not,' Mara felt compelled to put in. 'But it could surely have been a lot worse. They say the Squeem occupation was more brutal, in some ways. Yes, there was a war; yes, we lost cities. The Qax forced their own food production system on us, as you can see from here. But since the Occupation was imposed, the Qax have allowed us to preserve our cultural treasures – the ancient heart of Mellborn, for instance. And much of this continent remains wild, green.' Mara was proud of this aspect of her own people's legacy. 'The wild is there because humans brought it back, long before the Qax ever came. We reversed extinctions using genetic traces; we reconstructed ecologies lost when humans allowed themselves to overcrowd their world.'

Tasqer snorted. 'The Qax only allowed all that to be preserved because they mine it for export. Exotic biochemistries sold to their alien markets, out there among the stars somewhere. They are more sophisticated than the Squeem, I'll give them that. But they are conquerors just the same.'

Parz put in, 'The Qax are essentially traders, you know; that's their motivation for conquest.'

The Engineer laughed. 'They trade in Earth's riches while humans eat slop from the coastal farms. Once we built starships. Once a kid like Tiel would have been training up on hyperdrive, rather than crawling through sewers sifting garbage.'

Parz said sharply, 'Well, Tiel is getting his chance now, isn't he? And you Engineers seem to have long memories.'

'Should we not? Somebody must remember, now the old ones are dying off . . .'

Mara had heard that was true. After two centuries, and with their AS treatment long ago curtailed, the last survivors of the pre-Qax era, the last to remember Earth as it had been before the alien Occupation, were being lost one by one.

'*We* stayed independent,' Tasqer said now. 'We Engineers. I myself was born between planets. My ancestors fled Earth at the time of the Occupation war. With no place to land, the refugees ganged together their spacecraft and found ways to live, through trading, piloting, even a little mercenary soldiering.'

'And banditry, when you dare,' Parz said.

'But you yourself are no longer free,' Mara pointed out.

Tasqer shrugged. 'I dared once too often. After my capture I parlayed imprisonment into service for the Qax. And here I am, building a GUTship for them.'

'Just so,' Parz said. 'The Qax can be . . . benign.'

'Maybe you people need to get out of your golden cages more often,' Tasqer said. 'To the Qax we are probably more valuable as sacks of exotic chemicals than as thinking beings.'

Mara shuddered at that.

'Enough,' snapped Parz. 'You don't have a monopoly on conscience, Tasqer. And after all, this is a moment of human triumph, against all the odds: we are travelling to see the great machinery that Mara's son is assembling on the Moon – and all of it prompted by the return of Michael Poole's starship from the past.'

Mara said, 'I admit I don't understand what the purpose of that flight was, what Poole hoped to achieve – a great circle in interstellar space?'

Parz smiled. 'I'm no physicist myself. But as I understand it, Mara, what Poole was aiming for, having spent decades building wormhole bridges between the planets, was to build a bridge *to the future* . . .'

Poole's peculiar time machine was built on a combination of two extraordinary physical phenomena.

The first was wormholes, flaws in space and time that connected points separated perhaps by light years with near-instantaneous passages of curved space. And the second was time dilation. As a ship accelerated close to the speed of light, its clocks slowed compared to those observed from its planet of origin. Its crew would age more slowly, as would any equipment they carried – such as a wormhole Interface.

Poole's GUTship *Cauchy* had been dispatched on a long, near-light-speed jaunt in the direction of Sagittarius, towards the centre of the Galaxy. It had carried one terminus of a wormhole, whose other end remained in Jupiter orbit. The *Cauchy* was to return after a subjective century of flight but, thanks to time dilation effects, to a Solar System fifteen centuries older.

And that was the purpose of the project. When, after a century of subjective time, the *Cauchy* completed its circular tour, its hundred-year-old wormhole portal, delivered to the fifteen-hundred-years-hence date of AD 5274, *would be linked to its hundred-year-old sibling*, in Jovian orbit, back in the year AD 3829, a century after the ship's launch. And then it would be possible, using the wormhole, to step in a few hours across fifteen centuries of time, forward or back.

Mara was astonished. 'What audacity.'

'What an experiment!' Parz said with a grin.

'Well, now the *Cauchy* is back. Has anybody tried using it yet? Either going back fifteen centuries – or has anybody come forward, from Poole's era? And I would like to understand why the Qax's response to this bizarre arrival has been to build another wormhole of their own.'

The Engineer and the Ambassador exchanged a glance.

'Very well,' Jasoft Parz said. 'The immediate cause of the Qax's action is that it is a response to – well, a rebellion. A minor one, but effective. I can speak openly of this because the event was visible to human observers, suitably equipped—'

'I'll say,' the Engineer said with a grin. 'It was a rogue craft, assembled in secret—'

'Under a cultural monument,' Parz said disapprovingly.

Tasqer said, 'We don't know who they were. But, yes, somebody managed to reach the Poole wormhole. They got off the Earth and out of the Solar System and *through* that time bridge, to the past. What do you think of that, lady? If they made it through, if it all worked as Poole designed, what will they be doing now, back there in history? What will they be saying of the Qax, or of you, Ambassador, to an independent mankind? What wave of new history is rolling towards us even now?'

Parz sniffed. 'Their belief system struck me as so insane that I doubt they'll make any difference at all.'

Mara frowned. 'If they made it to the past, shouldn't that show up in the records, in our histories?'

Parz said hesitantly, 'There are some mentions of a great disruption at the time, which people called the Emergency. But our knowledge of history has been badly damaged, by the Starfall war, by the Squeem occupation – by the activities of the Qax too, though I'm convinced they aren't trying to disrupt our knowledge of that era specifically. Anyhow, there's nothing we can do about that, is there? All we can do—'

'Is carry out the orders of the Qax,' the Engineer finished sourly.

Mara said cautiously, 'And exactly what are those orders? You still haven't told me it all, have you?'

Tasqer glanced at Parz, as if for approval. Then he said, 'The Qax want to do what Michael Poole did, Mara. Just as Poole built a wormhole bridge to his future – our present – so the Qax want to build another bridge, with the wormhole built by your sons and towed by this new ship, the *Endurance* – a bridge to their own future.'

The idea astonished Mara, and horrified her. 'And what then?'

'Well, we cannot know,' Parz said softly. 'I suspect even the Qax Governor, who ordered this, does not know, yet. But that is the project we have been given.'

The flitter swivelled, its main drive cutting in at last to push the craft to the Moon, and Mara watched as Earth fell away. Now she glimpsed huge Spline craft, three, four, five of them, fleshy spheres glistening with sensor bays and weapons pods and armed with starbreaker beams: living ships that bore the Qax overlords, cruising over the planet they dominated. It felt almost a relief as Earth diminished in her view, and the Spline were no longer visible.

The Mare Serenitatis turned out to be a plain of basaltic dust. Its human history was dominated by two monuments, one the relic of a vast circular particle accelerator some three thousand kilometres long that was thought to date from the Poole era, and the other an even older treasure, set like a jewel in its own preserved park to the eastern edge of the accelerator: the site of a primitive lander from Earth, one of the earliest, although whether robot or human, none of the party could remember.

There were still many humans living and working on the Moon, as on other colony worlds and moons around the System. Up to now the Qax had been content to let such off-world knots of humanity persist, as long as they did not interfere with the projects of the conquerors; the Earth itself, with its teeming billions and complex ecologies, was the prize, not a few work-shacks on airless moons. And, guided by Tiel and his primitive engineering instincts, the *Endurance* engineering effort had been brought to Serenitatis because of that huge old accelerator, which, though damaged during the Starfall war, still had powerful installations and infrastructures that could quickly be renovated and adapted for this new purpose.

Mara, uncomfortable in the low gravity, let her son guide her around the hulks of enormous machines in this cavernous facility, which for her taste was dimly lit by too few light globes. But against this background Juq looked good, as he did almost anywhere. He was wearing a kind of uniform he'd designed himself, a practical coverall

with flashes on shoulder and lapels. The project had to have an identity, he said – with, he hadn't needed to add, himself as the symbolic
head. Mara saw how well he filled that role, a natural aristocrat who
seemed to inspire by his very presence the workers brought here from
across Earth and the lunar colonies. No wonder he had been elevated
by Parz, who was nothing if not a wily player. And it seemed to Mara
now that Juq was throwing himself into the project with real enthusiasm, for better or worse. Not for her son a consideration of moral
ambiguities, she thought wistfully; technological toys were all *he* was
interested in.

But for all Juq's charm, it was Tiel who explained the intricacies of
what they were doing here.

'The challenges we face constructing wormholes are essentially the
same as those faced by Michael Poole. But we have stuff even Michael
Poole never had. Squeem hyperdrives, left over from their occupation.'

Tasqer grunted. 'No doubt there's quite a stockpile for you to use.
The Qax are still impounding human spacecraft, even after two centuries. I worked on a yard in Korea myself, breaking down vessels,
taking out the hyperdrive units.'

'That must have been heartbreaking for you,' Mara said.

He just looked back at her.

Jasoft Parz said, 'I admit I'm confused as to why you need a hyperdrive unit, a faster-than-light technology, to manufacture exotic
matter for another kind of faster-than-light link . . .'

Tiel was patient. Evidently he'd had to answer such questions many
times before. 'The hyperdrive works by manipulating spacetime – and
if you do that, you're automatically manipulating gravity. With a modified hyperdrive I'm able to construct a gravitational field optimised to
squeeze the quantum vacuum in such a way that the negative-energy
components of a given field are extracted far more efficiently than
with the optical systems we used earlier. Soon we'll be able to churn
out exotic matter on an industrial scale.'

'He always talks like this now,' Juq put in with a kind of graceful
admiration. It was a way, Mara saw, of making his own lack of ability
a charming asset rather than a handicap. She marvelled at her son's
apparently unconscious skill.

'Very well,' Parz said. 'And what of the Xeelee construction material
you asked for?'

Tiel said, 'Construction material is light, easily grown from any
energy source, impermeable to most radiation fields, very strong . . .

It is ideal for our project, which will require the quick construction of large facilities if we are to meet production targets.'

Chael rubbed his hands. 'You hear that, Ambassador? The boy has the brain of a genius but the logistical judgement of a born manager. Well, you've seen our full report—'

'I have. And you've done remarkably well, boys, you and the other like-minded enthusiasts we gathered here. You've even hit the time-scale we set you, of just a month to get this proof-of-concept facility up and running. I'm happy to approve the roll-out to full production, here on the Moon and on other suitable off-world sites. And we've no time to lose. Michael Poole took forty years at Jupiter to manufacture the exotic matter for his *Cauchy* project. We have a mere five more months. But we'll get it done, I have no doubt. Well done, boys.' He started to clap his hands, and the others joined in. 'Well done indeed!'

Only the Engineer refused to join in the gentle applause.

3

Another month and the *Endurance*, assembled in Earth orbit, was ready to fly.

The craft was a GUTship, a very ancient design, indeed a design that Michael Poole would have recognised. When finally assembled, Mara thought the *Endurance* looked something like a parasol of iron and ice. The canopy of the parasol was a habitable lifedome, and the 'handle' was the GUTdrive unit itself, embedded in a block of asteroid ice which served as reaction mass. The shaft of the parasol, separating the lifedome from the drive unit, was a kilometre-long spine of metal bristling with antennae and sensors.

This craft had been hastily assembled from components retrieved from the breakers' yards, under the supervision of Engineer Tasqer. In a hundred subtle ways, as Mara observed when Juq gave her eager Virtual tours, the ship's components showed their age. Every surface in the lifedome was scuffed and polished from use, and many of the major systems bore the scars of rebuilding.

But it worked. And Mara, Earthbound all her life, subject of an alien regime, had never really understood, not in her heart, that mere humans had once mastered such technologies as this.

She was to learn that the ship's destinations were even more remarkable.

For the ship's maiden voyage Juq was sent on a grand tour of the Solar System – and specifically the sites where exotic-matter production was rapidly being ramped up, on Luna, Mars, and Titan, moon of Saturn. The purpose was motivation, inspiration.

Though she did not accompany him, Mara watched over and over the excited reports that Juq sent back to her, via secure channels mediated by Jasoft Parz. Luna now fizzed with exotic-matter plants. The designers had settled on gigantic torus-shaped designs for their manufacturing facilities, eggshell blue like the exotic matter itself, and vivid against the grey-brown lunar dust. On Mars too, just a few days' flight away for the *Endurance*, Mara glimpsed such toruses nestling near the ancient and still-inhabited cities of mankind: the capital, Kahra, and the great arcologies like Cydonia, pyramids on Mars that swarmed with people.

And then there was Titan.

Though on Earth she was more than a light-hour away from the Saturn system, Mara eagerly followed Virtual-feed reports as a flitter piloted by Tasqer dropped from the spine of the *Endurance* and dipped into Titan's perpetual photochemical smog. Soon the brownish murk began to clear, and she made out a surface, far below, oddly Earthlike, with mountains of ice hard as basalt and oceans, lakes and rivers of liquid methane and ethane, richly polluted by hydrocarbons. Michael Poole himself had opened up Titan for resource exploration, and since not long after Poole's time this had been the most populous world outside the orbit of Jupiter. Titan had cradled mankind's most remote cities, and huge factory ships had sailed these complex oceans, trailing high, oily wakes; enough food had been manufactured in those giant ships to feed all of Earth. Well, the oceans were still there, and Mara let the ancient, familiar names roll through her head: there was the Kuiper Sea, the Galilei Archipelago, the Ocean of Huygens, James Maxwell Bay . . . Now Earth had to feed itself, for the Qax had shut down interplanetary human trade, and few ships sailed Titan's seas.

But there were exotic-matter toruses here, just as on the Moon and Mars, huge blue structures beside the domes of the old cities – even of the capital, Port Cassini.

People on Titan had welcomed the exotic-matter project. It brought a purpose to life beyond mere subsistence on a more or less implacably hostile world. And as the flitter landed at sites like Port Cassini, Mara watched as her son led the party from Earth through civic receptions and rallies for the workers. Tall, bold, handsome, an aristocrat of a powerful old Navy family on Earth, Juq effortlessly dominated such events – although he always had his uncle Chael, the manipulative power behind the throne, at his side.

The *Endurance* project felt human and aspirational, just as Chael had promised. It seemed to Mara, a mere month after Parz had approved this huge expansion of the project, that nobody swept up in all the excitement *cared* that this was a project inspired and owned by the Qax, alien overlords of the Solar System.

Or that even now nobody really knew what this project was

ultimately *for*. When she thought this over Mara felt flickers of a deep unease.

And meanwhile her son, in these heady days, was becoming famous.

It came as a shock when Jasoft Parz intervened again. Exotic matter production rates were still not sufficient.

This was despite the fact that the designers had by now found a way to use much less exotic matter than Poole had required to thread his wormholes. The relativistic equations that described wormholes were nonlinear and allowed for feedback effects; it was possible to use a small amount of exotic matter smartly, to produce a kind of shock wave that would propagate down a wormhole throat, enabling a much larger passageway to be held open for the same amount of material . . . Even despite such ingenuity, the production capacity was not enough.

It had been a first instinct to lodge the engineering of this high-energy spaceflight project away from the Earth, for safety reasons. Though good progress had been made, it was soon clear that the populations away from the home world would not be sufficient to achieve the Qax Governor's target. 'I remind you again that Michael Poole took forty years over the *Cauchy*,' Parz said. 'We have four more months . . .'

Parz commanded, on behalf of the Governor, that fabrication facilities be set up on the surface of the Earth itself. And when, just a few days later, an exotic-matter facility began to be constructed east of Mellborn's city boundary, Mara's unease deepened further.

4

Engineer Tasqer visited Mellborn alone.

He told Mara that he was here to begin consultation on the next stage of the project, which would entail collecting exotic-matter stocks from plants like Mellborn's across the planet and shipping them to Jupiter's orbit, where, like Michael Poole's *Cauchy* long ago, the great new wormhole would be assembled. This alone was going to be a huge logistical exercise.

Mara hosted the man for the night. Then in the morning she escorted him out to the exotic-matter plant at Yarraranj, some fifty kilometres to the east of the city.

And at the end of the day, when his meetings were done, she walked with him along a waymarked trail, away from the gleaming new blue torus, and into the country beyond. The exotic-matter plant had been set far enough out of the city to be beyond the suburbs, in a landscape giving way to nature – or at least nature as reconstructed by ecologists and geneticists who predated Michael Poole, back in an age when humans had done their best to fix retrospectively the damage their ancestors had done to the Earth. This was an arid landscape – not as arid as Australe had once been, after millennia of humans burning back the bush, but still only sparsely covered by scrub and gum trees. And here and there tremendous beasts moved, their shadows clear in the intense sunlight. Mara recognised the profiles of huge, muscular kangaroos.

Against this setting, the powder blue of the Qax facility looked ugly and out of place.

To Mara's amusement, Tasqer, a pilot of interplanetary craft born into a rebel stronghold between worlds, seemed remarkably uneasy to be walking out in the open, on the planet that was after all the home of mankind. Perhaps this was the secret, spiteful reason she'd insisted on taking this walk with him.

'You're safe, you know.'

There was a deep growl, almost subterranean.

He glanced around. 'What was *that*?'

She was embarrassed that she wasn't sure; she lived her own life in the city. 'A diprotodon, I think. A big marsupial beast the size of a rhino.'

'Of a *what*?'

'The other really big beasts out here are the megalanias, a kind of giant lizard that will take on an adult diprotodon. And dinornis, big flightless birds.' She eyed him. 'But don't think birds. Think dinosaurs.' This didn't make him look any more comfortable, she observed gleefully.

He glanced around. 'And I guess these beasts are all made harmless in some way. Defanged. Conditioned, made unable to attack humans.'

'Oh, no. What would be the point of that? Human fatalities are remarkably rare . . . Look, I'm kidding with you.' She gestured at the trail, the sparse posts that lined it. 'You're fully protected; there are force fields, sonic barriers. The critters soon learn to keep away. And don't you think what our ancestors achieved here was remarkable? Although of course the Paradoxa Collegiate reconstruction dates from an age when AS technology was becoming widely available, life spans were lengthening, and people started to think seriously of projects on very long timescales.'

He grunted. 'Because they were suddenly liable to stick around to see the consequences of their actions. You do know your history, don't you?'

She had always resented his jabs. 'I know I have a privileged position under this Occupation. Myself and my family, but I do try to use that privilege for good. Such as, yes, keeping human history and culture alive.'

'Good for you,' he said dismissively.

She sighed. 'Very well. So how was your day?'

'The meetings went well enough, given the magnitude of what we're trying to do, and the timescale we have to work to. Just months! I took a tour of the facility. So many people labouring in the fusion plants, the Xeelee construction-material parks, the extraction bays – all those containment pods full of exotic matter piling up on lift pallets. Did you know the Qax Governor is demanding a wormhole Interface even *bigger* than the one Poole used? A huge icosahedral design, big enough to swallow a Spline ship . . . Well. Things are going as well as they could be, but the exotic matter dribbles out of facilities like this, and we need countless tonnes up there at Jupiter.'

'Hm. Chael tells me Jasoft Parz is running another recruitment round. More folk to be transferred from other duties to the exotic-matter plants.'

'If we had more time we could roboticise the process properly. But we don't have the time, and we *do* have lots of people, and that's the resource that's being applied to speed things up – especially now we've located these operations on Earth.'

'I do wonder about the urgency of it all,' Mara said. 'Why the hurry? And what about safety?'

Tasqer didn't speak. He was staring into the distance, to the west, towards the setting sun; he seemed distracted. Looking that way, Mara thought she could see a speck in the sky, some kind of aircraft on the way in.

'Engineer?'

'What?'

'About safety?' she repeated sharply.

'Human safety? In the facility?' He shrugged. 'What about it? The Qax don't care. The plant managers do their best.'

They walked on. She could hear a faint noise in the distance now, off to the west, where Tasqer had been looking: a hum of engines. That aircraft, whatever it was, coming in for a low approach. She said now, 'I hear rumours.'

'Rumours?'

'I do talk to people, you know, I don't hide away in my town house all the time. There are reports of indentured labour. People forced to work in particularly dangerous environments.'

He looked at her blankly. 'Look, Mara, the Qax don't want *us*. They don't buy or sell us. What they do sell is the exotic biochemistry of creatures like your diprotodons and your gum trees. We are partially useful – *slaves*. And as such we are expendable, to them.' He looked her in the eye. 'And to me.'

She was shocked by that last remark, by his deadened tone as much as by the words.

And that engine noise was suddenly growing louder, becoming deafening.

The aircraft, an Earth-to-orbit flitter she saw now, was coming in low and flat above the ground. Heading straight towards the exotic-matter facility. There was some kind of heavy pod suspended beneath its belly—

191

'Down!' Without warning Tasqer grabbed her around the waist and pushed her to the floor.

Twisting to see, she saw the flitter pass overhead and then roar down on the facility.

'Close your eyes!' Tasqer yelled, holding her down, his arm around her shoulders. 'Close them tight!'

The flash was visible even through closed lids.

Then came a wash of air, a hot wind, and the ground itself shuddered, as if some tremendous Pleistocene beast had been felled.

She twisted her head to look at Tasqer.

'Stay down,' Tasqer yelled again, over a continuing roar of noise.

'You did this,' she screamed. 'You and your people. The Engineers!'

'Hell, yes.' He raised a face crumpled against the noise, the wind, the dust. 'We still have a few ships the Qax don't know about, hiding out in the asteroid belt and elsewhere. Yes, we did this. *I* did this. I got into the facility, set a targeting beacon, disabled the defences, such as they were. There should have been simultaneous strikes all across the planet. *This* is why I gave myself up and burrowed into your sick Earth society in the first place. All for this. If we can disrupt this insane new project of the Governor—'

'But what do you think the response is going to be? Do you think the Governor will just give up? The Governor is going to replace all this with something even worse for us than what you just destroyed. Did you fools think of that? And what about the people you slaughtered, the innocents forced to work in there—'

'We're in a war for the future,' he said.

'Mankind is to be saved, but people are expendable, to you as to the Qax.'

'We all must do what we have to do.'

She stood up. 'I have some police authority. Engineer Tasqer, you're under arrest.'

5

Chael invited Mara to join him on his weekly inspection tour of the new exotic-matter facility in the Mellborn urban area. After Yarraranj, Mara was deeply reluctant, but the way Chael phrased it she sensed this was a command, not an invitation.

Chael landed on the spacious lawn of the family's villa, off Crun Strand, in an armoured flitter bearing two armed crew, and with the black cross on its upper surface that signified it to be a craft of the Occupation. Mara briskly boarded.

As the ship lifted, the looming sky-blue hulk of the brand new exotic-matter factory on Flind Strand was soon visible. The raid Tasqer had guided down to the facility to the east of Mellborn had not been unique; on that day, still only a month ago, a coordinated series of strikes from deep space had indeed hit facilities all around the planet. The Qax's punishment of those responsible had been brutal, and their response decisive and swift. Now the urban centres were not to be spared. Within days, blue exotic-matter facilities like this one had bloomed in the very hearts of human cities, like malevolent mushrooms.

Chael swore at the sight of Flind Strand. 'When the Governor announced he was moving the factories into the urban areas, we argued against using the historic city centres, at least. Parz himself spoke eloquently. After all, the Qax have spared cultural monuments in the past.'

'One sees it glowing blue in the dark,' Mara said now. 'From all over the city. One hears the hum of the great engines day and night, the whoosh of flitters coming and going – why, the noise of its hasty construction was itself cacophonous. I cannot sleep.'

Her brother-in-law smiled. 'I sympathise. But those in the work camps have it worse, you know.'

'I can imagine.'

The flitter skimmed east now, and Mara could already see another blue torus standing squat on the horizon, another new exotic-matter plant, brilliant in the low morning sun. It was surrounded by a muddy brown scar, fenced off: the living area for the human community that had been forcibly brought here to serve the facility.

'That's the Took plant,' Chael said. 'There's a ring of six around the city, Took, Parc, Cens, Spots, Nu, and Wills. We'll see them all today. There have been incidents to handle at them all,' and he sighed.

'The city is too quiet,' Mara said. 'They took so many people, stripping out everybody but the most senior in the Diplomatic Corps and their families, and workers on the most basic facilities, the sewage and food ducts. I thought they would just take—' She waved a hand. 'Criminals. Prisoners. Those without work. But nobody has been spared. Even children.'

'They took most of the best engineers also,' Chael said. 'The Governor no longer seems to care about breakdowns in essential systems – if a suburb here or there goes hungry. It's the same across the planet, if that's any consolation.'

'To think that two centuries ago we were immortals and interstellar travellers, and now *this*. I heard Ambassador Parz tried to argue against the use of child labour, at least.'

Chael smiled, rueful. 'You may know that since the Qax removed AS treatment, our population has boomed. Whether that's a response to the loss of our immortality, or some deeper survival response to the stress of the Occupation, I couldn't say. Whichever, we are a young society, rich in children. And now we're paying the price for that. And of course, if you don't use children the value of the workers as shields is diminished.'

She frowned. 'Shields? What do you mean? Shields against what?'

'Why, against further attacks, from space, from the ground.' He eyed her. 'Sometimes, dear sister-in-law, you seem so naive. That's one reason the Qax built these facilities in the cities. To give the ragamuffins pause . . .'

Ragamuffins. That was a word she'd heard too often recently. It referred to those Earthbound who had always lived out of sight of the Qax and their Occupation, out of sight of their law and control. Earth was a big and complex planet and there was room for a few to hide – and, it seemed, to fight back. The Engineers had turned out to be just one faction of a wider resistance.

She hadn't imagined she was still capable of being shocked. 'People used as a shield. Why, that's monstrous.'

'There are limits even to Jasoft Parz's powers of persuasion. And

Parz may be compromised himself.' He leaned closer. 'I don't think we're being monitored in here ... Did you know that Jasoft has a daughter?'

Again she was shocked. 'A daughter? But – I've known him for a quarter of a century, since Pell and I started to work for the Corps. I never met a wife, a lover, let alone heard of a child.'

'That's because he doesn't know himself. It's one of the Qax's more cunning ploys. They don't breed as we do, you know; there seem to be only a few thousand of them, and they are effectively immortal. But they are capable of observing our mammalian breeding practices, and of manipulating them to get what they want of us – or at least of the most senior people, those whose betrayal they fear. Serve them and, if you have a child, they'll take her from you, lodge her in some special school somewhere.'

'A hostage.'

'Exactly. And if like Jasoft you don't have a child – and, though we never discussed this, I suspect he chose not to have children for this very reason – they make sure you have one anyway. It's not difficult, after all. They have tame human geneticists, obstetricians—'

'That's monstrous.'

'That's the Qax. I'm told that Jasoft's daughter is around twenty-five years old, and lives in North Amerik.'

She stared at him. 'How do you know all this?'

'I try to know everything. I figure it's my best chance of surviving. I talk to everybody, even those on the wrong side of the Qax's laws. Mostly, though, I just listen. You'd be surprised how much you can discover that way.'

'And you haven't told Jasoft?'

'Would you? Maybe I will, some day. For now I don't want to compromise him. He is too effective where he is.'

'You're a cold one.'

'No. Just a survivor.' The flitter began a slow, cautious descent towards the heavily armoured compound that surrounded the Took facility. 'And I need you to be cold too, Mara, as we go through this day. Cold in the face of what you're going to see.

'Look down. This plant is typical of its kind. There is the torus, the heart of the exotic-matter facility itself. That rather ugly fenced-off area to the north is the workers' compound. There are barrack blocks, refectories, stores, crude hospitals. A mortuary. You can see that the local supply canals have been hastily widened ...

195

'*You must be prepared*, Mara. You'll be kept safe. But you asked about the use of criminals in such facilities. Mara, the Qax – or their human agents – *use* criminals as a police force, in the camps. You may imagine the quality of the resulting regime. You could argue we brought this on ourselves, with those foolish strikes from space. And there is another issue you must be prepared to deal with.'

'What's that?'

'Juq. Your son, my nephew. In this region at least he has continued to serve as a public front for the project.'

'I haven't seen him for some days, but I do see his smiling face in news Virtuals.'

'Smiling, yes. I think to the Qax and the Corps he serves as a symbol of authority over the workers. *Look how your human superiors smile while you work yourselves to death in these hazardous places. You have no hope of help from them, or anybody else – no hope at all.* That's what Juq's handsome smile has become: a symbol of the repression. You can imagine how the workers feel about that. He has to be heavily guarded.'

'*I* can imagine. Though I don't suppose Juq himself understands.'

'He does not,' Chael said heavily. 'There was an incident last week, at the Wills plant. A clumsy worker, lining up for inspection, spilled a lubricant on the shoes of Juq's friend, Tiel. Just an accident. Juq slapped her, and then laughed.'

'He *slapped* her . . .' Mara sighed. 'That's Juq. He was always that way with the servants. He never injured them, but—'

'It is himself he has injured. You can imagine how the Virtual image of that act has permeated that facility, and others. He is becoming – hated. And, as you say, I'm quite sure he has no idea.'

Mara closed her eyes. 'He's not a fool, you know. He isn't evil. Just flawed.'

'Well, he's your son. And he may need your protection . . . Almost down.'

The flitter descended to a crude concrete apron, hastily laid. Beyond security fences, before the backdrop of the giant torus, Mara glimpsed people, men, women and children dressed in identical green coveralls, gaunt and cowed. Most wouldn't even meet her gaze.

She braced herself as she prepared to get out of the flitter.

6

As with every significant event in the human world – every event approved of by the Qax, at least – the Interface completion ceremony in Jovian orbit was saturated with coverage, with multiple sound feeds and images taken from every conceivable angle.

And so the assassination was covered in fine detail.

Mara, sitting in her home in Mellborn, forced herself to watch the sequence of events over and over, from as many angles as she could find. In the end, she discovered a feed from one observer who had been right on the shoulder of the anonymous Friend of Wigner, as she turned killer.

The ceremony, coming a mere month after the start-up of the new city-centre plants, had taken place aboard the lifedome of the *Endurance* itself. A small stage had been set up at the centre of the domed chamber, on which stood a number of senior officials from the project, both technical and from the Diplomatic Corps. But, to Mara's eyes at least, the group was dominated by the unmistakable figure of her own son, Juq, tall, smiling as always, that blond hair blazing bright. His friend Tiel stood beside him, as he had since the beginning of this strange project, ever present, yet somehow as inconspicuous as a shadow.

Beyond the glimmering near-transparency of the dome over all their heads, Jupiter swam, an arc of that huge planet visible, a smear of golden brown. And, before the planet, rising into view like an angular dawn, the Interface portal – yet to be attached for the voyage – drifted towards the GUTship. Mara stared at the dazzling sky-blue of the portal's exotic-matter icosahedral frame, letting her gaze linger on the cool edges, the geometrically perfect vertices that joined them. The faces were like semi-transparent panes of silvered glass, through which Mara could make out the watercolour clouds of Jupiter overlaid with a patina of silver-gold. And every few seconds a face would abruptly clear, just for a dazzling moment, and afford Mara a glimpse of another space, unfamiliar stars. Like a hole cut into the sky.

As the Interface passed over the dome, applause, apparently spontaneous, rippled. It was magnificent. It was beautiful. And humans had built this. Every time she gazed on this sequence of images it made Mara want to weep, and wonder if Chael had been right all along, if this monumental human achievement was worth whatever price would be exacted by the future.

Then officials on the stage began to speak, words Mara had already heard many times in her viewings. But the speeches were, for Mara on this recording, obscured by the muttering of the assassin, close to the automated camera-microphone that happened to be following her: *The Wigner paradox is inescapable. The chains of unresolved quantum states will build on and on, growing like vines, extending into the future, until the observations of the final cosmos-spanning minds rest on aeons-thick layers of history, studded with the fossils of ancient events . . .*

She was unprepossessing, Mara thought. Unremarkable, in a shabby green worker's uniform of the kind that was common in Mellborn now, a young woman so sallow and fleshless it was hard to tell her age – perhaps twenty, not more than twenty-five. But her head was shaven. Even her eyebrows were gone, Mara saw. And now, as seen from the viewpoints of those around her, she began to move through the crowd, unremarked, towards the stage.

At last life will cover the universe, still building the regressing chains of quantum functions. Consciousness must exist as long as the cosmos itself – for without observation there can be no actualisation, no existence – and, further, consciousness must become coextensive with the cosmos, in order that all events may be observed. The chains of quantum functions will finally merge at the last boundary to the universe: at timelike infinity . . .

People were seeing her without watching her, Mara realised, dismissing her mad rambling, without thinking she was any kind of threat. Perhaps they saw no need to fear. Perhaps those admitted to this ceremony had already been screened for security. And perhaps a worker like this, mixed up, talking to herself, wasn't a remarkable sight in the new, highly pressurised labour camps of the Qax.

But now, as she neared the stage – Mara glimpsed Juq up there still, golden hair shining, beneath the glorious vision of the Interface – the woman started to speak more loudly. Those around her looked perturbed, but still they did nothing to stop her.

At timelike infinity resides the Ultimate Observer. And then the last Observation will be made. Retrospectively the history of the universe will be actualised . . .

She was almost shouting now. People in the crowd were reacting at last, recoiling from her, and on the platform they were looking alarmed, pulling back – all save Juq, who stood there smiling down even on this disturbance.

And then Mara heard the ringing cry that haunted her dreams. *Look out! She has a weapon!*

The girl's last words were almost a scream, as her arm lifted up straight before her, a heavy mass in her hand. *Actualised in a history which maximises the potential of being! Which makes the cosmos through all of time into a shining place! A garden free of waste, pain and death!*

Tiel threw himself forward.

From a hundred angles Mara had seen the boy's chest explode, and the Wigner's Friend pulled down at last, still screaming, and her son, still on the stage, still smiling even as he looked down, bewildered, at the splashes of his friend's blood on his vest.

7

The *Endurance* was launched on schedule, hauling its massive wormhole Interface away into deep space at high accelerations, leaving the partner Interface patiently orbiting Jupiter. Even now nobody in Mara's circle knew what the true purpose of the Qax Governor's experiment had been – not even Chael, as far as she could tell, not even her beautiful idiot of a son.

But everybody knew the timescale from now on: the ship's construction had taken six months, and in a mere six more months after its launch the *Endurance* would return, and a gate to an unknown future would open.

As the due date for that return approached, Mara waited tensely for whatever would come next. It was hard even to sleep without medication.

And then Chael called. He'd had a message from Jasoft Parz.

Chael hurried to Mara's home in Mellborn. When he arrived Mara called Juq, and the three of them gathered in the cellar where once Juq and Tiel had run exotic-matter experiments with splinters of diamond.

The three of them sat in a circle, under a single light globe. It was only a year ago, Mara realised, that first meeting with Parz in this very cellar, and so much had come of it.

Chael now held up a sliver of inscribed matter. He said, 'This was a one-shot, one-use message from Jasoft. He's not been able to return to Earth since the *Endurance* was launched. I don't know how he smuggled it out of the Qax ship where he's being held. I brought it here for us to watch together . . . It may not be wise to attempt any recordings of it. Oh, and I brought this.' He pulled a small plastic case from a pocket. Sealed within were three translucent tablets, each the size of a thumbnail. 'These come from the Qax themselves. They are able to manipulate biochemical structures at the molecular level – did you know? That was their, umm, competitive edge when they first moved off their home planet. And this is the fruit of their study of mankind.' He looked at them. 'Do you know what this is?'

Mara could guess. The tablet meant the removal of death. 'Anti-Senescence treatment?'

'Better than human-manufactured AS. A Qax refinement. They gave it to Jasoft. This is our reward, for our cooperation with the *Endurance* project. The former Governor kept his word that far.'

'*Former* Governor . . .'

He handed them each a capsule. 'Don't take it yet.'

Mara nodded. 'Let's hear what Jasoft has to say first.'

Chael set the inscribed sliver on the floor. Immediately light flashed from the sliver, and pixels whirled in the air, quickly coalescing.

It was as if Jasoft Parz had joined the circle.

He sat at ease, in his usual expensive-looking robes. If anything he looked younger still, Mara thought, his face less lined, his colour healthier, those odd-looking black roots spreading under his hair. Yet he looked hunted; he glanced over his shoulder repeatedly as he spoke softly. 'I don't know how long I'll be able to record. This message is my only chance. Please, all of you – listen and understand. Somebody needs to tell the human worlds what has happened – and what is to become of us.'

He allowed himself a grin. 'First, the good news. Poole's time bridge worked! As you're aware, on the return of Poole's ship *Cauchy* one group of rebels took the chance to go out and meet it – and they flew into the Interface, flew back through time, presumably all the way back to the age of Poole himself. We know now that the rebels were Friends of Wigner – the same ragamuffin group who attacked the *Endurance* when the Interface was completed, at Jupiter, and tried to assassinate Juq. And led, I'm told, by a young woman called Shira – she has links to the family of your son's friend Tiel, I believe.'

Juq was wide-eyed at this. 'Cousin Shira? I met her. But—'

Mara put her finger on his lips to hush him.

Parz went on, 'Neither I nor the Qax Governor knows what the Friends intended, or indeed what they achieved, if anything. But their very actions threw the Governor into an existential panic, I think. Perhaps all the Qax could be wiped out, if humans were warned about the Occupation far enough into the past. The Governor proved surprisingly indecisive in the final crisis.

'And thus the Governor chose to respond to Poole's triumph by emulating it.

'The *Endurance* was built to establish *another* wormhole tunnel to the future, from this age to around five hundred years hence. The Governor hoped to glimpse the Qax future, you see, and so be able to shape any decision with a kind of hindsight.

'But what emerged from the wormhole, an emissary from the future, was not any kind of tactical guidance, but very bad news indeed – bad for the Qax, I mean, but we know few details. But, in the form of a new Governor for Earth – the former has been assassinated, by the way – it brought bad news for humanity too . . .'

Hastily Parz said that there would be a new phase of the Occupation, as the Qax strove to rectify their earlier leniency. It was to be called an Extirpation.

'But I will not live to see this,' Jasoft said now. 'For the new Governor has a second string to the strategy. Even as Earth is smashed in the present day, *the Poole wormhole to the past still exists*. The Governor intends to drive Spline ships through the time bridge, and fall on the more innocent worlds of that historic era. And he intends to take me with him – into the past!' He forced a smile. 'In another life, another circumstance, what an adventure that would be. But as it is—'

The Virtual snapped out of existence.

Chael picked up the sliver, ran it over a slate for testing. 'It's done. Wiped.'

Mara said, 'I wanted to tell him about his daughter, before he was lost in time. It would have comforted me, at least. Now he'll never know. Perhaps we should find her, tell her of her legacy . . .'

Chael held up his own AS tablet. 'We have more important decisions to make. Everything will be different now. We have no control over whatever Shira's rebels do in the past, or what impact that may have – or what any Qax invasion fleet might accomplish. We, stranded here in this age, must deal with present and future. You heard Parz speak of the new regime to come, the Extirpation. But the Qax will still need humans to administer their regime for them. They will still need *us*. And the proof of it is in these tablets we hold. They want us to live on; they want us to work with them . . . We do have a choice, however,' and he glanced around, almost as furtively as Parz had, Mara thought. 'Callisto.'

'What?' Mara struggled to recall the name's significance.

'The moon of Jupiter?' Juq asked eagerly.

'Yes, the moon of Jupiter – and a hideout, for us. There's a man called Reth Cana who, under cover of a science station, is providing refuge from the Qax regime – refuge for the likes of us. That's one choice . . .'

Mara shook her head. 'No. I'm no planetary traveller. This is my home, for better or worse. This is where I will live—'

'And die?' Chael said gently. 'Well, that is another choice. We could simply see out our time and slip away – that's if rebel assassins don't hit us first. The final alternative is to live, on and on.'

'In the service of the Qax? In which case we would face the same moral dilemmas we always have,' Mara said. 'By administering the cruelty of the new regime, perhaps we could find a way to alleviate it. But now there's another reason to survive.' Mara looked bleakly at her brother-in-law, at her son. 'Some day the Qax Occupation will be lifted. And when humans run their world again, there will be a reckoning. A reckoning for us, and what we do next – what we have done already. You, Chael, for doing so much to assemble this *Endurance* project, to promote it. Myself for standing by when perhaps I could have stopped it.' She touched her son's hand. 'And you, you foolish, silly boy.'

To Mara's horror, Juq looked petulant, defiant, almost as if he might burst into tears. 'But, Mother, it was wonderful. Such fun. It was glorious! Why, anybody would have . . . I meant no harm. You know me! I never meant anybody any harm.'

She pulled back. '*You slapped a slave worker*. Didn't you? Perhaps that alone, that one moment, will be enough to condemn you.' She weighed the tablet in her hand. 'We have a duty to fulfil: to help our people through the dark times to come, and then, when the light returns, to stand trial for our crimes. Either way it is our duty to survive. Together, then.'

They took the tablets, Chael first, then Juq, and then Mara, and it was done.

As Mara had predicted, the Qax were eventually forced to loosen their grip. And a traumatised humanity launched a new thrust to the stars.

The Third Expansion of mankind was the most vigorous yet, and, under a unified, highly ideological government called the Interim Coalition of Governance, the most purposeful. As the Expansion unfolded, humanity once more encountered alien kinds, and re-engaged in wider Galactic history – and this time as conquerors.

It was only a little more than ninety years after the liberation from the Qax that another first contact, of devastating significance, was made.

The wars with the Silver Ghosts would span more than two thousand years.

THE SEER AND THE SILVERMAN
AD 5810

Donn's mother's screaming filled the lifedome. 'He's gone. The Ghosts have taken him. Lethe, Benj is gone!'

Shocked awake, Donn Wyman grabbed a robe and ran out of his cabin.

His mother and father were outside Benj's cabin in the plaza, in their sleep clothes, clinging to each other. The cabin door was open, and Donn could see at a glance that the room was empty. Only seconds after wakening, he had a sickening, immediate sense of what was wrong. The abduction from out of the heart of his home was bewildering, as if part of reality had been cut away, not just a human being, not just his brother.

'Now, Rima, don't take on.' Donn's father, Samm Wyman, was trying to calm his wife. He was a careworn man, slight of build and with his family's pale-blue eyes. Donn knew that spreading calm was his father's fundamental strategy in life.

But Rima was struggling in his arms. 'He's *gone*! You can see for yourself!' Her hair was wild, her face-tattoos unanimated, just dead black scars on her cheeks.

'Yes, but you're jumping to conclusions, you always think the worst straight away . . .'

She pushed him off. 'Oh, get off me, you fool. What else could it be but an abduction? If he'd gone out through the ports the lifedome AI would know about it. So what good is being calm? Do you think you can just *wish* this away?'

Donn said uncertainly, 'Mother—'

'Oh, Donn – help me look. Just in case he's somewhere in the dome, somewhere the AI hasn't spotted him.'

Donn knew that was futile, but they had to try. 'All right.'

Rima snapped at her husband, 'And *you* find out if he's anywhere else on the Reef. And call the Commissary. If the Coalition are going to meddle in our affairs they may as well make themselves useful. They could start by finding out where every Ghost on the Reef was last night – and the Silvermen.'

She stalked off and began throwing open doors around the rim of the plaza. The household bots followed her, their aged servos whirring.

Samm eyed his elder son. 'I already called Commissary Elah. Who knows? Maybe those Coalition goons will be some use for once. She's just taking out her anger on me, and she'll take it out on you too before she's done. It's her way. Don't let it upset you.'

'I won't, Father. But this is bad, isn't it?'

'I'm afraid so, son. Go on, get searching.'

Donn cut across the centre of the plaza, the lifedome's central floor space. Much of it was given over to green, for the crew of this old ship, his mother's distant ancestors, had crossed the stars with a chunk of forest brought from Earth itself, a copse of mature trees, oak, alder and lime, old enough to have wrapped thick roots around the struts of the lifedome's frame. But Donn, twenty-five years old, had never been to Earth, and to him the trees were just furniture.

Of course there was no sign of Benj. Why would he have hidden away among the trees? Benj, at twenty-one, liked his comforts. And even if he was here, the AI's surveillance systems would have known about it. Donn gave up looking, and stood there, helpless.

Something whirred past Donn's face, tiny, metallic. It was a robot insect. And a fine spray of water descended on him. He lifted his face and saw droplets condensing out of the air, an artificial rain born in the summit of the lifedome and falling all around him. Above the rain the transparent dome showed a star field that had barely changed for centuries: the Association, a cluster of stars dominated by the Boss, a single monstrous star a million times as bright as Earth's sun, an unforgiving point of light. He was getting slowly wet, but he didn't mind; he found the sensation oddly comforting on this difficult morning.

'Beautiful, isn't it? The star field.'

The smooth voice made him start. He turned.

Commissary Elah stood beside him. Her eyes were large and dark, her gaze fixed on his face, calculating, judgemental. Taller than Donn, she was dressed in a Commissary's floor-length black robe, a costume so drab it seemed to suck all the light out of the air. Her scalp was shaved, a starkness that emphasised the beauty of her well-defined chin and cheekbones, and her skin gleamed with droplets of the artificial rain. Donn had no idea how old she was.

'I didn't mean to startle you,' she said.

Something about her made Donn pull his robe tighter around his body. 'Commissary. It's good of you to have come out so quickly. My parents will be reassured—'

'I hope so. I've brought some specialist help. A woman called Eve Raoul – a Virtual, actually, but quite expert. This is what we're here for, the Commission for Historical Truth. To help.' Her accent sounded odd to a Reefborn, slightly strangulated at the back of the throat – an accent from Earth. 'The Coalition understands.'

'I suppose it must,' Donn said. 'If it seeks to rule.'

'Not to rule,' said Elah gently. 'To join all of scattered mankind behind a common purpose. And by helping you sort out issues like this with the Ghosts—'

'Nobody knows for sure if the Ghosts are behind these abductions.'

She eyed him. 'But the Ghosts aren't denying it. Are you loyal to the Ghosts or your family, Donn Wyman?'

'I—' He didn't know what to say to that direct question; he didn't think in such terms. 'Why must I choose?'

She reached out with a pale hand and stroked the trunk of an oak tree. 'Remarkable, these plants. So strange. So strong!'

'They are trees. Don't you have any on Earth any more?'

She shrugged. 'Probably. In laboratories. The Earth has other purposes now than to grow trees.' She glanced around. 'You know, I've visited your *Miriam Berg* several times. But I've never stood in this very spot, beneath these trees. Trade, your profession, isn't it?'

'I'm an inter-species factor. Specialising in relations with the Ghost enclaves—'

'It's all so deliciously archaic. And anti-Doctrinal, of course, your way of life, your ship's existence, its very name, all relics of a forbidden past!' She laughed. 'But don't worry, we've no intention of turning you out summarily. All things in time.' She pushed at the earth, the grass, with a bare foot. 'We're on the ship's axis here, yes? Over the spine. Your mother's family came to the Reef in this ship, didn't they, a thousand years ago? I imagine there are access hatches. Is it possible to reach the drive pod from here?'

'That's nothing to do with you.' Samm came bustling up. Beside Elah's cool composure, his father looked a crumpled mess, Donn thought, his hair sticking up like the grass under their feet, his face shining with the sweat of sleep.

'I apologise,' Elah said easily. 'You did invite me here.'

With his arms outstretched, Samm escorted her away from the copse. 'To help with looking for Benj. Not to go snooping around the *Miriam*.' But as she walked with him he backed off, nervous of offending this agency, the Commission for Historical Truth, newly arrived from Earth, which insisted on its right to take over all their lives. 'We're all distressed.'

'I understand . . .'

Donn lingered for another few seconds under the artificial rain. He wondered why his father should care about the Commissary, or any Coalition agent, snooping around this thousand-year-old heap of junk. Maybe he had trade goods tucked down there in the ship's spine – given the Coalition's new tax codes, Donn thought was quite likely – but if so he couldn't have signalled it any more clearly. Not subtle, Donn's father, whatever other qualities he had.

But as Donn stood there the complexities of Reef politics faded, and the reality of his brother's loss crowded back into his head, the true story of the day.

For months the abductions had been an arbitrary plague. Nobody could rest, for at any moment you could be taken too, from the most secure place. What a horror it was. And now it had come here, to his own family. He wondered, in fact, how it was he felt so calm himself. Shock, perhaps.

He trailed after his father, and the Commissary. And in a lounge at the edge of the plaza, he found a Virtual woman trying to console his mother.

'Before I died, I spent most of my working life exploring the principles of remote translation systems . . .'

The Virtual visitor sat beside Rima on a couch. Donn's mother's face was twisted with grief and anger. Bots hovered before them, bearing trays of drinks and pastries – breakfast; it was still early.

The visitor was slim, modestly dressed in a pale-blue coverall. Her hair was grey, and she pulled at a stray lock of it absently. Donn had never seen anybody with grey hair before, though he knew it had once been the default shade for the ageing. Evidently the visitor's projection was good enough to fool the serving bots, but Donn observed that her interfacing with the chair wasn't quite right, and a haze of tiny pixels shimmered around the underside of her legs.

Rima asked, irritated, impatient, '"Remote translation systems"?'

Commissary Elah said, 'Teleportation, to you and me. Donn Wyman, meet Eve Raoul. The expert I told you about.'

Eve stood. Donn clumsily offered this Virtual visitor a hand to shake. She bowed, apparently unoffended. 'I'm sorry to meet you in such circumstances.'

'Eve Raoul,' Samm said. 'Do you have a connection to *the* Raoul, Jack Raoul, of the Raoul Accords?'

The Reef was one place where, for a long time, Ghosts and humans had managed to live together, more or less peaceably. The Raoul Accords, a coexistence agreement only recently abandoned under pressure from the Coalition, had been much admired here. And Jack Raoul himself was well remembered, a hero for the Reef's multi-species community.

'Jack was my husband. I died before him.' She gestured at her slim body. 'It's thanks to him that this representation was reconstructed from my old Notebooks. He liked to have me around in person to counsel him about quantum mechanics and the like, in the course of his work. And in the work he did, his dealings with the Ghosts, there was a *lot* of that kind of discussion.'

Elah said, 'Eve is a specialist in the sort of technologies that seem to be deployed here – abduction through some sort of teleport device, apparently. And so we employ her to offer advice and counselling to relatives of abductees.'

'"Counselling",' said Rima, sceptical. 'Jack Raoul died eight years ago.' She glared at Elah. 'Or rather he was executed for his "crimes". He was pretty old by that time, wasn't he?'

'Over two hundred years old,' Eve said softly. 'He left my Notebooks to the Commission, and to the Ghosts—'

'He must have loved you,' Donn blurted.

But Eve grimaced. 'I was his legacy to an alien species. That tells you all you need to know about what it was like to be loved by Jack Raoul. However, here I am. And, since I know you're thinking it, it's a hundred and fifty years since my own death.'

Rima snorted. 'Then what use are you? How can these Notebooks of yours be up to date?'

'It's the best we have,' Elah said sternly. 'Rima, much human knowledge was lost during the Qax Occupation of Earth. That was a deliberate policy of the occupying power, in fact. They called it the Extirpation. One of our purposes in recontacting lost communities like this one—'

'We weren't lost,' said Donn. '*We* knew where we were.'

Elah ploughed on, 'Our purpose is to reacquire such lost knowledge. And Eve and her Notebooks are a treasure. It's good of her to work with the Coalition, especially after the difficulties surrounding her husband's case.'

Eve ignored this barrage of euphemism. 'I have to tell you, though,' she admitted, 'that I may not be much help at all. Human technologists have never got very far with teleportation. How could a teleport device work? Perhaps by scanning the position of every particle in an object, you might think. That information could be transferred somewhere else and a copy constructed of the original, exact down to the last electron.'

Donn frowned. 'But that couldn't work. The Uncertainty Principle – you can't specify a particle's momentum *and* position precisely.'

'Correct,' she said approvingly. 'In quantum mechanics such quantities as position are derived from probabilistic wave functions – mathematical descriptions that underlie all reality. *But* the Principle says nothing about transferring exact data about the wave functions themselves . . . That was the approach I was working on, before I died.'

Samm asked, 'What about Ghost technology?'

'My husband, in the course of his career dealing with the Ghosts, came across one example of a teleport-like device. It was all to do with breaking up electrons: dividing indivisible particles.'

They looked at her blankly.

Eve said, 'Look – an electron's quantum wave function is spherical, in its lowest energy state. But in its next highest energy state the wave function has a dumb-bell shape. Now, if that dumb-bell could be stretched and pinched, could it be divided? If so, when the function collapses, it could be as if an electron leapt instantaneously from one bubble to another.'

Rima was fighting her way through this fog of words. 'Why are we talking about this? *Is that how the Ghosts took away my son?*'

'No,' Eve said regretfully. 'I'm sorry. The sort of processes I've described would leave behind physical traces. Various exotic particles which your ship's AI would have detected. We're investigating every case of abduction. I'm hopeful that when we do start to turn up physical evidence of some kind—'

Samm said suddenly, 'What about supersymmetry?'

Rima shook her head. '*What?*'

'Another corner of physics. Just an interest of mine . . . Have the Ghosts worked with that?'

'Not that we know of,' said Eve.

Rima glared at her husband. 'He's talking about his family legend. An ancestor, a crook called Joens Wyman, who supposedly came here with some fancy super-spaceship. And one day Joens's legacy will save us all, won't it? And now my son is missing – oh, don't waste time, you fool.'

Donn felt he had to say, 'Everybody keeps saying it's the Ghosts. We don't even know if it is the Ghosts behind these abductions.'

Rima said bitterly, 'Oh, of course it's the wretched Ghosts. Everybody knows it.' She glanced upwards at the Boss, the gleaming, dominant star which cast shadows even here inside the lifedome. 'I grew up thinking the Ghosts were all right. But things have changed. They're up to something. Everybody knows that. They say there's a new sort of Ghost up there, deeper in the Association. A Seer, who can see into past and future.'

'Now, that's all rumour,' Samm said. 'Gossip. Trouble-making—'

'No wonder they can take away our children, if *that's* true. Because if they can see into the future they could sneak in here with one of those Silvermen of theirs—'

'Oh, Rima,' Samm said, distressed.

Eve said uncertainly, 'Getting back to teleportation—'

'What use are you?' Rima snapped. 'You don't know anything. You've said so.'

Elah said smoothly, 'She's here to assure you that the Commission is doing all we can—'

Rima got to her feet and pointed. 'And I suppose you brought *that* with you to reassure me as well.'

They all turned.

A Silver Ghost hovered in the plaza, only paces away from them. It was a mirrored sphere, quite featureless, a mercury droplet as tall as a human. It shifted a little as it hovered just above the floor, as if its immense bulk could be pushed by the breezes of the air conditioning.

'You took him,' Rima said. 'You took my son.'

Samm tried to get hold of his wife. 'Rima, be calm—'

But she shook him away. 'What have you done with him?' She ran at the Ghost, her fists flailing. Her hands passed through its hull, scattering silvery pixels. Just another Virtual, Donn realised. The Ghost hovered impassively. Samm pulled Rima away. 'Give him back,' she begged. 'Oh, give him back!'

Eve Raoul stood, obviously distressed, as if she longed to help. But she was a simulation; she could not even touch Rima. The Commissary simply watched, cold, observant. Donn was hot with anxiety and embarrassment.

The Ghost said: 'I apologise for the intrusion. I am the Sink Ambassador.'

Samm snapped, 'The *what*?'

'The Heat Sink, Father,' Donn said. 'Which is the sky, to them. He's their Ambassador to the sky.'

The Ambassador said, 'Eve Raoul – it is good to see you again.'

'I wish I could say the same,' Eve said.

Samm, bewildered, tortured, looked from one to the other. 'What do you want, Ghost?'

The Ghost rolled. 'Donn Wyman, we need your help.'

The Sink Ambassador said there was trouble in a bar called Minda's Saviour, set in an old generation starship near the heart of the Reef's three-dimensional tangle of ships – a Silverman, in some kind of trouble.

Commissary Elah faced the Ghost Virtual. 'Ambassador to the Heat Sink, you call yourself.'

'Yes.'

'I take it you know Eve through Jack Raoul?'

'I worked with Jack Raoul on many complex and demanding issues. I like to believe we were friends, Eve and I, and Jack and I.'

Elah laughed at that, the idea that humans and Ghosts could be friends. 'And now you consult Donn Wyman. He's just a factor, a trade negotiator.'

Donn felt dismissed, vaguely insulted.

The Ambassador said, 'Since the collapse of the old Raoul Accords the legal interface between Ghost and human communities has been shredded. But humans like Donn, and Ghosts like myself, must work together over trade. The Ghost enclaves here could not survive without trade. And individual contacts made in such circumstances serve well in trying to resolve other issues as they arise—'

'There is no need to call on a mere factor,' Elah said. 'I am a Commissary. I represent the Coalition, mankind's highest authority.'

'Then it is a good thing that you happen to be here,' the Ghost said, without a trace of inflection in its artificial voice.

'And this is all about a bar? A Ghost artefact, in trouble in a bar?' Elah laughed. 'How squalid. How absurd. Such a thing could never happen on Earth.'

'Evidently,' Eve murmured, 'this is not Earth. This is not a place where the Coalition's grip is secure. For this is a place where humans and Ghosts still coexist.'

'This is stupid,' Donn said. 'It's got nothing to do with Benj.'

'But we need you,' the Ambassador said simply. 'You personally.'

'Go,' Samm said. 'There's nothing you can do at the *Miriam*, for now. If anything turns up . . .'

'Mother?'

Rima, her face buried in a handkerchief, waved him away.

So the four of them crowded into the bubble-like transparent hull of the *Susy IV*, Samm Wyman's ageing flitter: Donn, Elah, the Ghost, and Eve Raoul. Where the Virtuals brushed against the flitter's hull they crumbled; Eve Raoul brushed stray pixels from her sleeve like flies. Elah had insisted on coming along, as 'trouble' of any sort was now the Commission's business, and so Eve had to come too – that or be shut down, Donn supposed, as Eve seemed tied to Elah, no doubt through some projection system lodged on her person.

You could get from any point to any other on the Reef by walking through the innards of the old ships that comprised this island of life in space, or by walkways and bridges thrown up over the centuries. Donn would have preferred to walk, to burn off some energy. But the *Susy* would be quicker, and so here they were.

The flitter closed up around them, its systems humming, and rose from the Reef of ships into a bowl of stars.

Donn peered down as the Reef opened up beneath them. It was a logjam of ships, a roughly lenticular mass with ragged edges. The Boss was a fierce lantern at the zenith, so that the tangle of superstructures cast complex shadows. Many of the ships, like the *Miriam*, were of the ancient, durable GUTship design, a stalk topped and tailed by lifedome and GUTdrive. But there were more exotic designs, including the old generation starship at the hub of the complex, a frozen ocean of comet ice meant to propel its crew's descendants to a new world that had never been reached. The Reef was basically a messy human construct. But here and there in its long shadows you could see tangles of silver rope, ships without hulls or bridges or obvious drive units – ships that weren't of human design at all, Ghost craft.

And today, ships of the Coalition's Navy hovered over the crowded craft. They were Spline warships, living ships, balls of flesh studded with sensor mounts and weapons emplacements. They rolled like threatening moons, the green tetrahedral sigil of a free mankind tattooed onto their flanks.

Elah lifted her face to the light of the brilliant star that hung over all this. 'I've been stationed here a year already, and I just can't get used to the sky. Strictly speaking the Boss is catalogued as VI Cygni Number Twelve. Did you know that? Recently it's been flaring – there's some remarkable imagery; I can show you if you like. And this particular grouping of stars is called the Cygnus OB2 Association. It's all so different from what you'd see from Earth. That central monster casts shadows light years long from clouds of interstellar dust, shadows distorted by the finitude of light-speed – quite astonishing.'

Donn was more interested in the cultural side of what she had to say. '"Cygnus"? What does that mean?'

Elah waved a hand, dismissive. 'An old name from Earth. Pre-Occupation. Its meaning is lost.'

Donn had never given much thought to Earth, a place remote in space and in history – or it had been, until the Coalition came. 'Where is Earth, from here?'

Eve glanced around and pointed. 'About five thousand nine hundred light years away, thataway. Right around the Galaxy's spiral arm.'

'Can you see the Association from Earth?'

'You'd be able to see the Boss with the naked eye if not for dust clouds in the way.'

'Humans have travelled far from their origins,' the Ghost said.

'You bet we have,' Elah said with fervour. She pointed at right angles to Earthward. 'We're filling up this spiral arm, and we're heading *that* way – towards the Galaxy Core. We've already pushed into the next spiral arm inwards, the Sagittarius Arm.'

The Ghost spoke, its artificial voice sonorous in the enclosed space. 'And that, of course, is the source of all our trouble.'

Donn knew it was right. For thanks to the explosive expansion of mankind across the face of the Galaxy, suddenly Ghost communities, overwhelmed, had become alien islands stranded in human space.

The Reef had begun as a loose conglomerate of mining and trading groups. As a whole it had moved several times since its formation, embedded hyperdrive engines lifting the whole shebang across light years, always moving further from the Earth, off along the star lanes of the spiral arm. The Cygnus Association had proven a good place for the Reefborn to settle, with plenty of worldlets and asteroids to mine for resources – even a few human colonies, refugees of one calamity or another, to trade with.

And here in the Association the humans of the Reefborn had forged tentative links with the Silver Ghosts, who were undergoing their own expansion out of the heart of the Galaxy. They had even welcomed small Ghost colonies into the Reef itself. You could say that the Reef culture was a composite of human and Ghost, an experiment in cohabitation.

For a time, even after Earth's new government, the Coalition, had made contact, the Reefborn had profited from trade, being poised on the border between two interstellar empires. There had even been a strange period when autonomous Ghost enclaves had been granted room to live under the new regime: Silver Ghosts living under the nominal authority of the Coalition, a government whose basic ideology was the inevitable victory of mankind.

But times had changed, and the Coalition's embrace had become harsh.

Those elderly hyperdrive engines had all been confiscated or disabled, for a start, to be refitted into Navy ships. The Reef would never again go jaunting out of human ken into the alien dark. And the Ghosts here had been taxed, marginalised and subjected to discrimination of all kinds. Now, with the crises over the Silvermen and the abductions, the Ghosts' position was becoming untenable.

And perhaps today, Donn wondered, it was all coming to a head, with himself caught mysteriously in the middle of it.

The *Susy* began its descent back into the forest of ships.

Minda's Saviour: the bar announced its name in signs written in several human languages, and Donn had once been shown how the name was inscribed in electromagnetic patterns invisible to human senses but vivid to a Ghost. There was even an image, painted rather than Virtual, of a human girl accepting the gift of a Ghost's own hide. All this was based on a story three centuries old, that the first contact between humans and Ghosts had involved a young girl who had been saved from freezing by a Ghost sacrificing its own life for hers. But the official Commission line was that the Minda story was just Ghost propaganda.

Inside, the Saviour was basically a bar, selling intoxicating chemicals of various kinds diluted by the ice of a comet that had once orbited Sol. But there was also a kind of mudbath, salty and warm, meant to accommodate Ghost patrons. The light in this corner of the bar came not from the usual hovering light-globes but from glowing ropes draped from the ceiling: Ghost technology.

There was no Ghost in the mudbath today, no Ghost in the bar save the Virtual projection of the Sink Ambassador – and a Silverman, standing like a chromed statue in one corner, confronted by an angry human crowd.

They weren't actively doing anything to it, not touching or harming it in any way. Yet they surrounded it, sitting silently, defiantly drinking the Navy drink called Poole's Blood, walling in the Silverman with human flesh. Donn knew some of these people. Here was Bareth Grieve, one of the Reef's elders, a friend of his mother's and a member of the Reef's Grand Council. This morning Grieve and the rest barely acknowledged him. They were just a mob who had trapped a Silverman.

Elah was taller than most in the bar, as indeed was Eve. Donn had heard an insulting theory that Reefborn were becoming dwarfed, as populations stranded on islands often were, apparently. 'What a spectacle,' Elah said now, looking down on the group around the Silverman with utter contempt. 'Makes you ashamed to be human.'

The Ambassador murmured, 'You can see why we have a problem. These people have been here for hours – and they refuse to release the Silverman.'

Eve said, 'And something has been done to that Silverman. Look, Donn – can you see?'

At first glance the Silverman was typical of its sort: a kind of sketch of a human figure – head, torso, arms and legs, but shorter than an average human – like a statue in Ghost-hide silver. It lacked detail. It had fingers but no toes, no fingernails, no navel, no genitalia, the face just a bland outline, all orifices sealed up save the eyes and mouth. It was identical to the rest of its kind, just as every Ghost looked the same as every other. But this one had a sort of collar around its neck, of some heavy blue metal.

'*That* doesn't look like Ghost technology to me, that collar,' Eve murmured. 'That's human. They've done something to this thing. What, though?' She snapped her fingers, and a data slate appeared in her hands.

'It is an eerie construct, a Silverman,' Elah said. 'Look at it, all but faceless, expressionless, walking among us . . . And if you were going to develop a weapon to penetrate a society like this, an assassin to work in a human environment of rooms and corridors, a human shape is exactly what you would give it. It's not surprising people are wary, especially in a politically underdeveloped society like this one.'

Donn bridled at her casual insults.

But the Silvermen *were* odd. They had only been appearing on the Reef since the arrival of the Coalition, as relationships between the Ghost and human communities on the Reef had steadily deteriorated. They wandered the Reef's corridors and haunted its bars and libraries, theatres and forums, even its churches. They stepped out of the way of humans. They would tolerate being touched, their silver flesh poked by curious children. They would speak if spoken to, answer questions if asked, although only of the most direct sort. But they volunteered nothing. They didn't do anything. They just *looked*.

The Silvermen were a strange, eerie, uncomfortable presence. And they simply showed up, appearing as suddenly and as randomly as the human abductees disappeared. The Silvermen were anti-abductees.

And they were clearly Ghost artefacts, for that silvery flesh was Ghost hide.

The Sink Ambassador asked, 'Why are these people doing this?'

'Maybe this is punishment,' said Donn. 'For the abductions. People want something to hit back at.'

'They are not harming it.'

'No, but I wouldn't like being trapped like that. Pinned up against a wall, ignored.'

'A human sort of harm, then. To learn such lessons is the Silverman's purpose. So I believe.'

Donn stared at the Ghost. As far as he knew, this was the first time any Ghost had discussed a 'purpose' behind the Silverman visitations.

Elah, naturally, had overheard too. 'It's here to learn, you say.'

'I speak at second-hand,' the Ambassador said. 'You know that Ghost society is not like yours – not hierarchical – our society is like our bodies, an embracing of diversity. But I believe that the faction behind the Silvermen intends them as an experiment to learn more of humanity.'

'By sending these homunculi among us as spies,' Elah said.

'Not that. The way each of us thinks is shaped by how we sense the universe, how we experience it and manipulate it; we are our bodies as well as our minds. We understand what you are doing,' it said bluntly to Elah. 'Your Coalition and the galactic Expansion it is driving. We do not understand *why* you do this. Perhaps your restlessness is something to do with your ape anatomy, your manipulating hands, your heritage of the trees and the savannah.'

Elah laughed. 'You insult us without even trying, don't you? So do you think your experiment has worked?'

The Ghost admitted, 'I don't believe we anticipated the hostility they have encountered.'

Donn said, looking over at the Silverman, 'It isn't human *enough*, perhaps.'

Elah said, 'In some corners of this Reef people gang up on the Silvermen and dress them up in clothes! All to reduce that feeling of otherness about them. And in other corners the Silvermen are insulted, abused – especially by the families of the abducted. There's never been a physical attack before, however.' She faced the Ambassador. 'If you want us to help you, Ghost, you need to be honest with us. *How* are these homunculi being planted in the Reef? Is it through some teleportation mechanism? And is it the same mechanism that is used to abduct humans from the Reef?'

Again that long hesitation. 'There is another faction – its motives are noble—'

'Tell us, Ghost!'

'Yes,' it said softly.

Donn blew out his cheeks. 'I never heard it confirmed before, about the abductions. That the Ghosts really are responsible.'

Elah said stonily, 'Are you disappointed?'

'Yes. Because it means all the paranoids were right – all those who swallowed your anti-Ghost propaganda, Commissary.'

'Don't push your luck, boy,' she murmured.

'It does explain what they've done to that wretched Silverman over there,' Eve said now. 'I've been running some tests.' She showed them a slate of results that meant little to Donn.

Elah nodded. 'That collar they stuck on it is full of processors. It's a sentience booster.' She smiled at Donn. 'Do you see? This lynch mob have made the Silverman *smarter*. More self-aware.'

Donn frowned. 'Is that legal? And, *why*?'

'I don't think the law matters much here. And as to why – isn't it obvious? Yelling at those other dim homunculi was no longer enough to get rid of the rage. They made *this* creature smart enough to understand what it was suffering, what its perceived crime was. And who knows what they have planned for it once this long vigil is done? Can't you see the logic, Donn Wyman?'

At the sound of Donn's name, the Silverman turned. It had been the first movement it had made since Donn and the others had walked into the bar. 'You are Donn Wyman?'

'Yes,' said Donn uncertainly.

The Silverman walked straight towards Donn. It had to push through the barrier of drinkers, knocking a couple of men aside. Some of them got to their feet to challenge the Silverman. 'Don't you take another step, you Ghost monster—'

But Elah raised her hand, a halting motion. The men glowered, but stood back. The Reefborn had quickly learned to recognise the authority of a Commissary.

The Silverman stood before Donn. It came up to his chest, like a boy dipped in chrome. Even its eyeballs were silvered. 'We need your help.' Its voice was identical to the Sink Ambassador's.

The Ambassador said, 'This is why I called you here, Donn Wyman. It has been asking for you, specifically. It's not very articulate, but it does seem to know what it wants.'

'Sorry,' said the homunculus.

'For what?'

'For this.' The Silverman reached up and wrapped its arms around Donn's waist, a powerful, cold, unbreakable hug.

And the bar, the Commissary, the Ghost – all vanished.

No air.

His chest felt as if it would explode.

A raw sky, star-littered. Ice under his feet, hard, sucking the heat out through his thin boots. The Silverman's face before him, filling his vision, chromed eyes frosting over.

No air! He opened his mouth. Air gushed from his lungs, a shower of crystals. But when he tried to breathe in, there was nothing, *no air.* He was drowning in vacuum. His eyes filmed over. He could not blink. Pain stabbed in his ears.

Still the Silverman held him.

Machinery flashed, a blade, spinning in vacuum silence. The Silverman, cut, shuddered and fell away.

Donn was released. He was still standing. But he was dying, he knew. He tried to call for his mother. He tried to call for Joens Wyman, his lost grandfather in his magic ship, who in stories of his childhood would scoop him up and save him from danger. His vision blackened. He felt himself stagger.

Somebody stood before him. Short, slim, a girl perhaps, wrapped in a silver suit, her visor translucent. She held a weapon, and a mass of silver cloth. She threw the cloth at him. It closed up around him, shutting out the stars.

Air flooded into his lungs. He gasped, and nearly fell. The silver material was squirming around his body, sealing itself up, forming sleeves and leggings. A panel before his face began to clear.

The woman's face hovered before him. 'If you want to live, run.' Her voice whispered in Donn's ears. She turned away.

He ran, following her. But even as he staggered over the ice, utterly bewildered, the face of the girl stayed in his mind, delicate, beautiful, twisted in a snarl of anger.

His first few steps were like trying to walk in a deflating balloon. But gradually, step by step, it got easier, because the blanket was knitting itself up around him, the seams becoming finer around his limbs, the joints at his hips, knees, shoulders, elbows becoming more flexible. It was unlike any human engineering, silvered on the outside and oddly skin-like on the inside where it was in contact with his clothes, his flesh.

He knew what this was, what it must be. It was the hide of a Silver Ghost. And if he now possessed this hide, then surely there was a Ghost somewhere that lacked it.

He ran on, stumbling.

Wherever he was, gravity was high, a bit higher than the Earth standard maintained by the Reef's inertial fields. The sky above was black, littered with stars. Most of the light came from one brilliant star directly above his head, a bright pinpoint source. Surely that was the Boss; surely he was still in the Association. It seemed brighter than he remembered, and he thought he saw a splinter of light coming from it, some immense flare. Perhaps he had come closer to the Boss, then, deeper into the Association. But other than that—

He tripped on something, a ledge sticking out of the ice, and fell flat. He lay there, bewildered, winded.

He lifted his head. The girl was running on. Vapour exploded upwards around her, a sparkling fountain with every footfall. 'Wait,' he called. 'Please.'

She ignored him.

He had no choice but to follow her. He dragged himself to his feet.

His chest, where he had hit the ground, felt like one vast bruise. He stumbled on.

He came upon structures, just bits of stone wall sticking out above the ice. The remains of a city? There was nothing like a human geometry here, no right angles among these bits of straight line. And he ran through a patch of some softer frost, lying over the water ice that gathered in the lee of the low walls. It sparkled around his footfalls, evidently vaporised by waste heat. When he looked back he saw traces of green in the boot prints, which faded as suddenly as they had come.

He came to a hole in the ground, a well, ragged and dark.

The girl was waiting here. She said, 'You've seen the flowers.'

'What flowers?'

'Look at this.' She lifted something up. It was like a human arm, small, the size of a child's, with a perfectly formed hand. Done in silver, it was like a bit of a broken statue.

'It's the arm of a Silverman,' he said.

'Correct. The one that carried you over. The little bastard got away, but I hurt him. Watch this.' She took a knife from her belt and stabbed the arm, slitting its silver skin from the base of the wrist up through the pit of the elbow to where it had been severed. Then she hauled at the skin, briskly peeling it off. What was exposed was bloody and steaming. Without the containing skin it fell apart into individual creatures, blood-red and worm-like, some of which wriggled feebly, still alive, even as they froze. The girl dropped all this on the ground. A cloud of vapour rose up, quickly freezing to ice and falling back.

And all around the bloody mess, green things blossomed, a kind of moss, what looked like shoots of grass, even a kind of flower that fired off seeds like a miniature cannon. But the heat was evanescent, and the living things quickly shrivelled and died.

'They wait for a bit of heat. Billions of years if they have to. And when it comes they take their chances. The story of all life, isn't it?'

'Who are you?'

'I don't have a name.'

He did not recognise her accent. It was flat, toneless. 'Everybody has a name. My name is Donn Wyman.'

'I only have the number the fatballs gave me. I am Sample 5A43 Stroke 7J7 Stroke—'

'We call her Five,' came a male voice, perhaps somebody down in the well. 'Quit showing off, Five, and get down here.'

Five grinned at Donn. 'All right, Hama.' She kicked apart the bloody mess on the ground and made for the hole, climbing down easily.

Donn saw there were handholds cut into the water-ice wall. He followed with more difficulty, not trusting the grip of his Ghost-hide gloves, which continued to mould themselves around his fingers.

Some way down they came to a membrane, stretched across the well. The girl just dropped through this, so he followed. The membrane opened up around him, clinging closely like the meniscus of some high-surface-tension fluid; it was a tight band passing up the length of his body.

Beneath the membrane he reached the bottom of the well. He was in a kind of cellar, walled by rock – or maybe it was a natural feature, a cave. He had never visited a planet and knew nothing about rock formations. The walls were draped with silvery blankets, what looked like more Ghost hide. On some of them tetrahedrons had been crudely scribbled, the sigil of free mankind. The light came from lengths of silvery, shining cable that had been draped over the walls, crudely nailed into place: Ghost technology, evidently stolen. He saw low corridors cut into the rock, leading off into the dark.

Evidently this was a shelter, a habitat, under the ruins of an alien city.

And there were people here – not many, maybe a dozen. Some wore suits of Ghost hide, their hoods pushed back. Others went naked. They sat in small groups, eating from silvered bowls, or they slept on ledges. One woman nursed an infant at her breast. They were all ages, from the infant up through adulthood to old age. Some glanced incuriously at Donn, standing there in his Ghost-hide suit; others didn't bother looking around at all.

The girl, Five, stood before him. She had pulled back the hood of her own suit. She rapped at his translucent visor with her fingernail. 'It's safe to come out of there. We have warmth and air, thanks to the fatball hide panels.'

'I don't know how.'

'You just pull.'

She took hold of the hide over his cheeks, and hauled. His hood split open easily, sundering right down the middle of his visor. Warm, fuggy air washed over him; he smelled farts and sweat and piss, and a food smell, something like boiled cabbage.

'Welcome to the rat-hole,' Five said.

With her help he pulled the rest of his suit away. When he was done, standing there in the clothes he had worn in Minda's Saviour, a man approached him. He was naked, and Five was stripping down too. The man was short, his head shaved, and his body was scrawny, his ribs showing. He looked like a typical earthworm, Donn thought.

'I am Hama Belk,' he said. It was a Coalition accent. 'You can see we go naked in here.'

'I think I'll keep my clothes on, for now.'

Five shrugged. 'Suit yourself. We don't wear clothes because the fatballs don't bother with clothes for their Samples, so there's none to steal. Unless you feel like robbing a virgin Sample. That's been known.' Her face was as hard as her language.

She had short-cropped blonde hair. She was slim, her body wiry and supple; it was hard to tell how old she was – no more than eighteen, nineteen surely. She had obviously been badly damaged, in her short life. Donn felt sorry for her – a ridiculous reaction in the circumstances.

He said, '"Steal"? "Rob"? Is that how you live?'

'This is Ghostworld. We are all escaped Samples.' She gestured at the nursing mother. 'Or the children of Samples. We came here with nothing. All we have we steal from the fatballs.'

'You mean the Ghosts, don't you? And you steal what – their very hides?'

Five snapped, 'We have a way of things here, virgin. You were saved by a Ghost hide. Now you must save in turn. You must kill a fatball and strip it of its hide, when you get the chance. Carry it with you, and save another if you can.'

He recoiled. 'I *work* with Ghosts. Look, my name is Donn Wyman. I work as a factor on the Reef – that is, I develop trading relationships with the Ghosts. Perhaps I—'

'I don't care what you do, or did. None of that matters now, your old life. You've died and been reborn. Now you're just another Sample, like us. You don't even have a number, as I do, since you weren't processed by the Ghosts before you were liberated.'

'Samples. Numbers.' Donn saw it now. 'This, wherever I am, is where you go when you're abducted.'

'You've got it,' Hama Belk said. 'Just as the snatching is random, so is the depositing. Usually you end up in a processing chamber, surrounded by a thousand Ghosts. That's what happened to me before the rats busted me out. Others end up on the surface, exposed – evidently the transfer isn't a hundred per cent reliable. There are places where the strays end up, and we wait for them, with blankets; that's how Five found you.'

'How does it work, this transfer, the snatching?'

'Well, we don't know,' Hama said. 'Does it matter?'

'And those exposed on the surface—'

'They die, if they aren't found in a heartbeat by Ghost patrols, or by us rats.'

'Rats?'

'Us,' said Five. 'Wild humans, living in the cracks. Though I personally have never seen a rat, I understand the concept.'

'How come you haven't seen a rat? Never mind. Have you heard of Benj Wyman? My brother. He was abducted only hours before me—'

'No,' Five said bluntly.

'Look,' Donn said, 'you can see there's been some kind of mix-up. I'm not an abductee, a Sample as you call them. I came here with a Silverman. You saw it. You cut its arm off! Maybe if you hadn't chased it off – if I could talk to it—'

Five laughed in his face. 'Every virgin Sample says the same thing. "I'm not supposed to be here. I'm special, I'm a mother or a father, I have this-or-that back home."'

'How do I get back?'

She just laughed at him again. She walked away, and knelt down by the nursing mother.

All at once, the hardness of her manner, the shock of all his experiences that day, hit Donn. He staggered, and stumbled back against the wall.

Hama grabbed his arm. 'Here. Sit down. Look, there's a ledge.' He handed Donn a silver bowl. 'Try to eat some of this. It'll warm you up.'

'It's just so sudden.' He looked at Hama. 'I hadn't even taken in my own brother's abduction. And now—'

'Well, you've plenty of time to get used to it. Take the bowl.' It contained a brownish sludge, like a thick soup.

Donn dipped a cautious finger in the bowl and tasted the gloop. It was lukewarm and tasted faintly of mushrooms. 'More Ghost technology?'

'Yes. We just scrape up the green shit from our footsteps outside and drop it in. This is how they feed the Samples. Here, your ears are bleeding.' He handed Donn a scrap of cloth.

Donn dabbed at his ears; the cloth came away bloody. 'I don't even know where I am.'

Hama shrugged. 'None of us do. We're obviously still in the Association. And this is obviously a rogue planet, far from any sun. But aside from that we can't tell. After all, as Five said, nobody's ever been back to tell the tale. We just call it "Ghostworld".'

Donn nodded. 'It seems like a typical Ghost colony world, from what I know of them.'

'Yes. We were taught all about Ghosts in our training, on the way here in the Spline ships . . .'

The Ghosts' world was once Earth-like: blue skies, a yellow sun. But as the Ghosts climbed to awareness their sun evaporated, killed by a companion pulsar. The oceans froze and life huddled inward; there was frantic evolutionary pressure to find ways to keep warm. And the only way to do that was through cooperation.

'That's the story,' Hama said. 'Though many of us in the Commission wonder if this is true, or just some kind of creation myth. Or propaganda. Certainly the thing we call a Silver Ghost really is a community of symbiotic creatures: an autarky, a miniature biosphere in its own right, all but independent of the universe outside. Even the skin that saved you is independently alive.'

'Even when you take it from the Ghost, it lives on.'

'I wouldn't be judgemental,' Hama said evenly. 'I myself was a clerk in the Commission for Historical Truth, working on the re-education of the Reef population. I come from Mercury, actually, a sister planet of Earth. I hadn't been on the Reef long before the lottery of the Sampling picked me. But none of that matters now.' He looked at his hands. 'All I have here is myself, and those around me. And I do what I must, to stay alive.'

'Why do they bring us here? Why the Samples?'

Hama eyed him. 'You said you worked with Ghosts. You don't know? *I* think it's because they are trying to understand us, the Ghosts. They fear us, for right now our Third Expansion is overwhelming them. But you can't defeat what you don't understand.'

'So they take us for study.' Donn shook his head. 'But these random abductions, of a child from a mother, a father from a daughter – my own brother was taken. The Ghosts couldn't antagonise us more if they tried.'

'I guess that shows how little they understand us, yes?'

'And what about Five, the girl with no name?'

'Ah. She was taken as an infant, under two years old I think. As she grew she was surrounded only by Ghosts. The only human she saw was her own reflection in the hide of a Ghost. She grew up thinking she was some kind of deformity, a mutant, disabled Ghost.

'Eventually a rat pack broke into her cage. She thought they were as diseased as she was. I think she was raped. She was only thirteen, fourteen. What a welcome to humanity! Somehow she came through that, and emerged as a functioning human being – I say functioning – all she knows is this, life as a rat, and all she wants to do is kill Ghosts.' He smiled. 'She's inventive about it, though.'

Donn watched Five with the mother. 'I'll be wary.'

'Yes, do. Don't get any foolish ideas of *saving* her. And there are worse. Rat packs that prey on humans, other Samples. Even at the moment of abduction.'

Donn looked at him curiously. 'And what do you want, Hama?'

'I came to the Association to save *you*, Donn. I mean, all of you on the Reef, living in non-Doctrinal ignorance out here in the dark. If all I can do is live here as if in a guerrilla cell behind the lines, killing a few Ghosts before my short life is over – well, maybe that's enough. It is my duty to die. *A brief life burns brightly.* That is the slogan of the Third Expansion of mankind.'

Donn said carefully, 'I think I'm more afraid of you than the feral girl over there.'

Hama laughed.

Five came to stand over Hama and Donn. Naked, lithe, her body was a pale streak in the silvery light, her nipples hard, her pubic hair a blonde tuft. 'Rested, are you? We're mounting a raid. You're lucky, Donn Wyman. We've been planning this one for a while; you'll be there for the pay-off.'

Donn made to protest. 'I only just got here. I need to find my brother – the Silverman—'

But she was already walking away.

Hama nudged him. 'That wasn't a request. Come on, on your feet.'

Donn struggled up, his chest still aching from his fall.

A party of a dozen adults suited up.

They clambered up through the airtight membrane into the spectral stillness of the landscape. Donn was shocked that the Boss had shifted in the sky, moving away from the zenith, and the shadows it cast were long. Donn had never before seen a sunset, or a dawn; this was a planet, not an artifice like the Reef.

They checked each other's suits, and were handed weapons. Donn was astonished to be given a spear. Then, following Five's lead, they set off over the ice.

The weapons were mostly crude – spinning blades mounted on poles, or even more primitive than that, daggers and swords, pikes and spears, lengths of barbed wire and ugly tangles of spikes and hooks. But there were a few more sophisticated instruments – a kind of projectile weapon like a bazooka, even what looked like a Qax-era gravity-wave handgun, much repaired, polished smooth by usage.

They carried these weapons, walking to war.

'I can't believe we're doing this,' Donn said, to nobody in particular. 'We're like pre-industrial savages.'

'I know how you feel,' said a woman walking beside him. 'I was a food technician, back on the Reef. I'm the nearest thing to a biologist this little crew has. And a doctor. But by day I'm a spear-carrier . . .' Brisk, purposeful, she was perhaps forty; she might once have been plump, but now the skin of her cheeks and neck sagged, as if emptied. 'My name's Kanda Fors, by the way.'

'I am—'

'We all heard who you are.' She smiled, a dogged sort of expression. 'We like to act indifferent. I guess that's to do with Five's hold over us. But wait until she's asleep. We'll all be at you then, finding out what you know of home, our families. We only get news from Samples. And it's all one way.'

With her calm Reef accent she was more like Donn's family than anybody else he had yet met here. 'This is real, isn't it?' he said slowly. 'I think maybe I'm working through some kind of shock.' He looked at the spear he had been given. It was clearly improvised from some ripped-off bit of equipment, not much more than a steel rod with its tip laboriously sharpened. 'I really am stuck here, at the wrong end of a one-way funnel to this shithole in the ice.'

Hama Belk said, 'It isn't so bad here. It's not just a scramble for survival, you know. We're still human. We can still have higher goals.'

'Like what?'

'Like science,' Kanda said. 'At least we can observe what's around us. There is life here, for instance.'

'I saw it. In my footsteps.'

'That's what survives.'

She said that this rogue world must have been detached from its parent star, by a close stellar encounter perhaps, or a gravitational slingshot by a wandering Jovian.

'Any civilisation would have been smashed quickly, by the quakes, the tides, even before the oceans froze over, water ice setting hard as rock. And then the air itself froze out on top of that. But there is life here, still. You saw it in your footsteps. And,' she said dreamily, 'there is *other* life. A more exotic sort, blown in from the stars, cold-lovers, psychrophiles, colonising this cold world . . .'

'Psychrophiles?'

'Watch.' She took the index finger of her left hand in her right, and squeezed the fingertip of her Ghost-hide glove. A seam broke, and ice crystals gushed out into the vacuum. She bent and pressed this breach to the frozen ground, just for a second. Then she pulled back her hand and let the glove seal itself up. 'Ouch, that's enough, I can do without frostbite. Now, look.'

Where she had touched, a pit opened up in the ground, the width of a fist, the lip pulling back as if recoiling. The little pit closed up again in a couple of seconds. But when Kanda stirred it with a fingertip, it was broken up, like dust. 'See that? Ice, permafrost, even rock, broken up to powder.'

'What's going on?'

Kanda grinned. 'Cryo-panspermia bugs.'

There were ways that even terrestrial life could survive at extremely low temperatures. There was always the odd scrap of liquid water even in the coldest ice, in brine pockets perhaps, or in nano-films, kept from freezing through pressure contact. And even on this frozen world there were nutrients, seeping up from the planet's core, or drifting down from space, comet dust.

'At these temperatures you can't be ambitious,' Kanda said. 'You don't reproduce – well, hardly ever. You don't even aim to grow much, just repair a bit of cellular damage once every millennium or so. Chemistry can be a help. There is a gloopy, starch-like material called exopolymer that has a way of preventing the formation of ice crystals. To such creatures, even the Ghosts are refugees from a warmer regime, balls of liquid water, like lava monsters. There's a whole ecosphere here, Donn, that we know hardly anything about. I long to come back here some day and do some proper science . . .'

'"Science",' Donn repeated. 'While we march to war.'

Kanda frowned. 'Listen, Donn Wyman. You'd better take our miserable little war seriously. Whatever the future of mankind, *we* need the resources we steal from the Ghosts, or we'd die. Simple as that. So when Five tells you to fight, fight. We don't have a lot of spare capacity for passengers. Of course she can hear every word we say.'

Five turned. 'Yes, though at least the Ghosts cannot hear your pointless babbling. Ever trained to fight a Ghost?'

'No.' The very thought shocked Donn.

'The easiest way to bring him down is just to puncture his hide, and follow the trail of excrement and blood and heat until he dies, which might take a day or two. We'll show you how to skin a fatball later.'

'You're a monster,' Donn blurted.

'No. I'm alive.' She smiled at him, her beauty dazzling.

After perhaps an hour's walking, only a few kilometres, they crested a frozen ridge. And here Five had them hunch down and approach more cautiously.

So Donn got his first glimpse of a Ghost city. Sprawled over a valley carved by some long-frozen river, it was a forest of globes and half-globes draped in a chrome netting. The colony lacked a clear centre, and there was no simple geometry; it looked as if it had grown in place, and perhaps it had. A slim tower dominated, silvered like the rest, with a sharp electric-blue light pulsing at its summit.

Ghosts streamed everywhere, following their own enigmatic business, like droplets of silver blood flowing through the open carcass of their silver city. The Boss cast highlights from every hide, so that the city gleamed, as if it had been scattered with diamonds.

Five grinned at Donn. 'So what do you think of your prey, hunter?'

'I'm no hunter. I'm surprised we're so close to a city.'

Hama shrugged. 'We are all escapees from the Sample zoos in that city, or else we were teleported to the ice nearby.'

Five said, 'Actually, everywhere on this world is near a Ghost city. The planet is filthy with fatballs, billions or trillions, swarming.'

That electric-blue light winked mournfully. 'What's the tower?'

'Well, we don't know,' Hama said. 'Best guess is, it's a Destroyer tower. The Commission knows of such things on other Ghost worlds.'

'Destroyer?'

'In ancient times, on their home world, the Ghosts' ancestors understood full well that a rogue pulsar was destroying their sun. So they venerated the pulsar. They made it a god.'

Kanda murmured, 'Actually it's fascinating. Humans have always worshipped gods who they believed created the world. The Ghosts worship the one that destroyed it.'

'Quiet,' hissed Five. 'This talk is purposeless.'

'Talking is what people do, child,' said Kanda.

'We are not people. We are rats. We are here to fight, not to talk.'

Donn looked down at the extraordinary, beautiful city in dismay. 'Fight for what? Resources? Hides, equipment—'

'That,' Five said, 'and the destruction of the Seer.'

Donn frowned. 'What do you know of the Seer?'

'Not much more than you do on your Reef,' Hama said.

Five said, 'The Ghosts talked of it, when I was in their zoos, when they thought I could not understand. Those who dealt with me were far from the centres of power. Yet it exists.'

'So what is it?'

'We don't know,' said Hama. 'But if the chance arises to destroy it, we should take it. The Coalition's forces have learned that Ghost concentrations are hard to defeat, short of out-and-out genocide. They lack hierarchies, like human societies, which makes them impossible to decapitate. Usually assassinations are useless. It's like stabbing a pool of mercury with a fork; it just fragments and runs away. But in this particular case you have this Seer, whatever it is, a source of power. So if we could get to that we could indeed inflict a great defeat in this war.'

'We're not at war,' Donn said.

'Oh yes we are.'

Five whispered, 'Let's move in.' She waved them forward.

Donn approached the Ghost city, running at a crouch from one bit of cover to the next, watching the silvered backs of his companions running ahead – silvered as the city itself was silvered, for their suits were made of the same stuff.

The city itself loomed huge before them now, a sculpture park of mirrored monuments that hovered off the ground, utterly still. Light rope trailed everywhere, linking one floating building to the next, and filling the whole with a silver-grey glow. And Donn heard music. The ground throbbed with a bass harmonisation, as if he could hear the heartbeat of the frozen planet.

Five raised a hand to call a halt. They were at the head of a kind of thoroughfare that led into the heart of the city, reasonably clear, reasonably straight. Now the rats got to work, laying barbed wire and spiky obstacles across the smooth surface of the roadway.

Donn murmured to Kanda, 'What are we doing?'

'Setting traps,' she replied. 'Ghosts don't follow human ideas of geography, you know that. But if they need to evacuate fast, they'll use thoroughfares like this. In fact, they come swarming along the ground when they're alarmed. Some primitive instinct, but useful for us. They'll hit the traps.'

'What is going to make them evacuate?'

Five grinned at him. 'We are. Come on.'

Leaving half a dozen hunters behind at the barricade, the rest moved deeper into the city.

The crowded net of light ropes grew thicker over their heads. In the complexity Donn saw denser concentrations – nurseries of Ghost sub-components, perhaps, or control centres, or simply areas where Ghosts lived and played – little more than patches of silvery shadow in the tangle. It was characteristic Ghost architecture, vibrant, complex, beautiful, alive, totally inhuman.

And there were Ghosts all over. They drifted over and through the tangle, following pathways invisible to Donn, or they would gather in little clusters, sometimes whirling in chains like necklaces, apparently for the fun of it.

The rats clung to the shadows, out of sight, and Donn followed their example.

In one place Donn saw an orderly queue of Ghosts, almost like a line of human schoolchildren waiting for a punishment. They filed patiently into a floating dodecahedral box that opened to embrace each Ghost, closed around it, and opened again, empty, ready for the next. There must have been thousands of Ghosts in the patient line, he saw. And as the dodecahedral chamber hovered, far from any building, it was hard to see where all the Ghosts it swallowed were going to.

He pointed this out to Hama. 'What's that?'

'I suppose there are two possible answers,' Hama said drily. 'I don't believe it's an extermination chamber. Maybe it's a teleport.'

The thought excited Donn. 'Like the Sampling, the abductions. So where are they going?'

'We only have rumours,' Hama said cautiously. 'Briefings from the Commission before we were abducted, gossip from inside the Ghosts' zoos . . . It may have something to do with the Seer.'

'Or,' Kanda said, 'it may have to do with the instability of the star. The Boss – all that flaring. Maybe the Ghosts are trying to *mend* a failing star . . . That would be their style.'

The thought staggered Donn.

'We know they think big,' Hama said. 'Anyhow it makes no difference to us . . .'

Donn stared at the chamber, avid. For if this was a teleport terminal, it might be a way off this dismal planet. But the dodecahedral chamber wasn't their destination, and they passed on.

The party came to a big transparent sphere, apparently pressurised. At the centre of the sphere a big ball of mud hung in the air, brown and viscous. It seemed to be heated from within; it was slowly boiling, with big sticky bubbles of vapour crowding its surface, and it was laced with purple and red smears. Tubes led off from the mud ball to the hull of the spherical pod. Ghosts clustered there, sucking up the purple gunk from the mud.

Donn crouched with the others, awed. 'The Ghosts are *feeding*.'

'Yes,' Kanda said. 'This is how Ghosts live. Even on their home world, deep beneath their frozen oceans, a little primordial geothermal heat must leak out still, dragging minerals up from the depths. Down there, life forms feed, blind, pale. And the Ghosts feed on *them*.'

So this mud ball was a kitchen – and no wonder the Ghosts liked a little sea-bottom ooze to play in at Minda's. 'What are we doing here?'

Kanda murmured, 'This is the warmest place in the city. What we intend to do is release all that heat, dump it into the environment.'

'Why?'

'We're going to give them indigestion,' Five murmured. 'Positions.'

The hunters spread out. Their projectile weapons and that antiquated gravity-wave handgun were raised at the feeding pod.

Five called, 'Three, two, one.'

Fire burst from the projectile weapons, and cherry-red starbreaker light ripped from the ancient handgun. The pod's wall was elastic; it burst like a soap bubble. That big floating mud ball splashed to the ground amid a hail of ice droplets. Steam flashed, instantly frosting. The feeding Ghosts fled in panic.

And as the mud's heat was dumped, the ground subsided, a pit dilating open, like an immense version of the fingertip dimple Kanda had made on the walk. It was as if the substance of the world had shrunk back in protest from the warmth, Donn thought. Nearby structures began to slip into the widening pit, or they floated away, gravitational anchors broken.

Kanda said, 'We've been seeding this whole area with cryo nests for weeks. If you hit the cryos with too much heat they have ways of responding . . .'

The disruption spread rapidly as buildings further from the imploding centre were hauled over by the disrupted rope tangle. The hunters started to make the damage worse, slashing glowing light cables with their blades.

Now Ghosts spilled out of the tangle, trying to escape. Just as Kanda had suggested, they fell to the ground, poured down the open throughway and flowed out of the city. And they started to get caught in the traps the humans had set.

Five stood in the open. 'We'll have fifteen, twenty minutes before they organise to get rid of us. Let's get this done.' She raised her spear.

Donn watched Five slaughter one Ghost.

Its skin was already punctured where it was snagged on the barbed wire the humans had set, and air and bloody liquid fountained, crystalline, from its wounds. Now Five leapt on the Ghost, landing sprawled on its hide. Gripping with her legs, she coiled her back upwards, and struck down with a stabbing sword, as hard as she could. Then she slid to the ground, leaving the blade buried up to the hilt in the Ghost's carcass. But the hilt was attached by a rope to a stake driven into the hard ground, and as the Ghost thrashed, its own motions tore gouges into its flesh. Five lunged again. This time she used a tool like a long-handled hook to dig into the already gaping wounds, and she dragged out a length of bloody rope, intestine perhaps. It coiled on the ground, steaming and quickly freezing. And Five struck again, and again.

All around Donn, the humans laboured at trapped Ghosts with axes and swords and daggers. Hama and Kanda worked as hard as the rest. One man thrust a kind of lance into the side of a Ghost. Donn couldn't see its purpose, the wound didn't seem deep, but it thrashed in agony. Kanda told him it was a refrigeration laser, cannibalised from a crashed Ghost ship, invisibly pouring out the Ghost's precious hoarded heat.

Five approached Donn. She held out the knife to him, handle first. 'Here. Finish this one. Easy first kill, my treat.'

Donn took a step forward, towards the Ghost she had eviscerated. He actually put out his hand, holding the knife. He knew this was the only way he was going to survive here.

But all the emotions, all the shock of this extraordinary day focused into this moment. He felt detached from the ice world, from the grinning girl before him, detached from it by more than the smear of frozen blood on his Ghost-hide visor.

He stepped back. 'No,' he said.

She glared at him. She took back the knife and cut through the Ghost's trailing intestine with a savage swipe. Dark fluid poured out, congealing onto the ice, freezing immediately. The Ghost subsided, as if deflating. Five faced Donn. 'I knew you were a weak one, the minute I saw you.'

'Then you were right.'

'We only survive here by killing Ghosts. If you won't kill you have no right to live.'

'I understand that.'

She held out her hand. 'Your suit. Give it back to me. I'll find a better use for it.'

He found he had nothing to say. He reached up and pinched his hood by the cheeks. One firm tug and all this would be over—

'Wait.'

A human being came walking out of the calamitous Ghost city – *walking without a pressure suit*, of Ghost skin or otherwise. It was Eve Raoul. And a Ghost rolled at her shoulder. It was the Sink Ambassador, Donn knew it must be.

The rats, Hama and Kanda and the rest, evidently astonished, stood back from their butchery. They were crusted with frozen blood, weapons in their hands.

Eve Raoul looked down at her feet. She was up to her ankles in frozen air. The Virtual protocol violations must be agonising for her, Donn thought; it was *supposed* to hurt if you walked out into the vacuum without a suit. She turned to the Ambassador. 'I did the job you wanted. I snagged the rats' attention.' Yes, Donn thought. As no Ghost, among a million Ghosts, ever could. 'Let me go now. Please.'

'Thank you, Eve Raoul.'

Eve turned to Donn. 'Listen to the Sink Ambassador. Do what it says. This is more important than you can imagine . . .' Her voice tailed off, and she broke up into a cloud of blocky pixels that dwindled and vanished.

Trembling, exhausted, Donn felt *irritated*. If they'd let him die it could all have been over in an instant. No more shocks, no more changes, no more choices. Death would have been easier, he felt, than facing whatever came next. He said, 'How did you know I would be here?'

'You are not hard to track,' the Ambassador said. 'Your biochemical signature – none of you can hide. Not even you, Sample 5A43.'

Five flinched. 'You know where we are, our bunker?'

'Of course we do.'

'Then why don't you hunt us down, kill us?'

'For what purpose? We brought you here to understand you, not kill you.' The Ambassador lifted off the ground and hovered over the deflated corpses of its kind, impaled on the crude human traps. 'We seem to have trouble anticipating such actions as this. We do not think the way you do. I suppose we lack imagination. We try to learn.'

Donn said, 'What do you want of me, Ambassador?'

'We need your help.' It was another voice. A Silverman came walking from the chaotic city – *the* Silverman, Donn saw, the one from Minda's Saviour, with its human-tech neck band and one arm lopped off above the elbow.

Donn stared. 'Ambassador, since when has a Silverman spoken for the Ghosts?'

The Ambassador said, 'Since you made this one as smart as any Ghost. You Reefborn made him intelligent enough to suffer. But sentience always has unexpected consequences. In fact, he has become intelligent enough, and human enough, to be able to anticipate how you will react when you learn what we have been up to here. Donn Wyman, we need you to tell the humans. They would not listen to us. You, though, might be believed.'

Donn was bewildered. 'And what *have* you been up to?'

'We will show you. Come.'

The Silverman turned and walked back towards the city. The Ambassador followed.

Donn saw that they were heading for the dodecahedral transfer station. 'You want me to get into that thing?'

'Yes,' said the Ambassador.

'Where will it take me?'

'To somewhere beyond your imagination.'

'And what will I meet there?'

'The one known in your human rumours as the Seer.'

Kanda laughed. 'You lucky cuss . . . Go, man. Go!'

But still Donn hesitated. 'I'll come with you if you let these others go. Not back to their cave under the ice. Send them home. Don't harm them further.'

The Ambassador didn't pause. 'Done.'

'Thank you,' whispered Hama Belk.

Kanda grinned. 'A brief life, Hama?'

'Not that brief, thanks.'

Donn said, 'One more thing, Ambassador.'

The Ambassador rolled. 'Jack Raoul would have admired your courage in negotiating.'

'Find my brother. Benj Wyman. He's here somewhere, one of your "Samples".'

'Not mine. The faction who—'

Donn cut him off. 'Find him. Send him home too.'

'Done.'

'All right.' Donn took a step towards the Ambassador.

'Wait.' It was Five. 'Take me with you, virgin. If you're to meet the Seer, I want to be there.'

'Why? To kill it?'

'If it's necessary, you'll need somebody to do it. *You* won't, that's for sure.'

Donn asked, 'Ambassador?'

The Ambassador rolled. 'Abandon your weapons, Sample 5A43.'

'Five. My name is Five.'

'Abandon your weapons.'

Five was obviously reluctant. But she took her heavy projectile weapon and her quiver of arrows and her stabbing sword, and handed them all to Hama.

Donn held out his hand to her. 'Come, then. But no more of the "virgin".'

She clasped his hand; he could feel her strength through the double layer of Ghost fabric. Then they walked together, following the Silverman and the Ambassador, back into the devastated city.

The flow of Ghosts into the dodecahedral transport terminal had stopped, perhaps disrupted by the chaos the humans had caused. But, everywhere, Ghosts poured back into the crumpled heart of their city, as a purposeful operation of recovery began. Donn found it hard not to flinch, as if all those shining globular bodies in the air might come tumbling down on his head. The Ambassador assured them they would be safe.

But Five's gloved hand grasped Donn's, hard.

Donn asked, 'So how are you feeling?'

'Like I'm two years old again,' she said. 'Stripped of everything I built up for myself. They've got me back, haven't they?'

'No,' Donn said firmly. 'You walked into this – your choice. And you'll be walking back out of it too.'

She thought about that. 'You promise?'

'I promise.' And you were wrong, Hama, he thought. I did get to save her after all – or at least there's a chance I will. 'So, Ambassador. This device – is this how you've been snatching people?'

'Shall we avoid such loaded words, Donn Wyman? We have been developing a new non-local transportation technology. It is the outcome of a wide-ranging programme of physical research . . .'

He told Donn that the Ghosts' origin, under a failing sun, had led them to believe they lived in a flawed universe. So they wished to understand its fine-tuning.

'*Why are we here*? You see, there is only a narrow range of the constants of physics within which life of *any* sort is possible. We study this question by pushing at the boundaries – by tinkering with the laws which sustain and contain us all. Thus we explore the boundaries of reality.'

'While snatching children,' Five said.

'Get to the point, Ambassador,' Donn said.

'We have found a way to adjust the value of Planck's constant: the number which gives, in human physics, the scale of quantum uncertainty.'

Five just stared. 'What are you *talking* about?'

Donn stared at her, remembering how she had been brought up. 'Planck's constant – a small number, very small, one of the fundamental constants of physics. It's to do with the Uncertainly Principle. But in real terms – suppose you measured an electron's position to within a billionth of a centimetre. Then the momentum uncertainty would be such that a second later you couldn't be sure where the damn thing was to within a hundred kilometres. The Principle is describing a fundamental fuzziness in reality—'

'So what?'

Donn frowned. 'Well, what if you could change that fuzziness? Make it more, or less . . . Everybody knows that Jack Raoul got himself involved in a situation where Ghosts messed with Planck's constant. They reduced it—'

'Yes,' said the Ambassador. 'We were endeavouring to produce an AI of arbitrarily large capacity.'

'It was a disaster.'

'Well, yes. But in the end a useful technology was derived – Ghost hide, as you call it.'

Five was struggling to follow all this. 'And is this what you've done here? You've decreased this Planck number again?'

'No. This time we have *increased* it, Sample.'

Donn saw it. 'You've increased the uncertainty in the universe – or a bit of it.' He thought fast. 'A particle has a quantum function, which describes the probability you'll find it in any given location. But the probability is non-zero *everywhere*, throughout the universe. And if you increase Planck then you increase all those probabilities.'

'You're beginning to see it,' the Ambassador said. 'It is hard to imagine a more elegant mode of transport, in theory: you simply make it more likely that you are at your destination than your starting point.'

Donn was stunned by this audacity. '*In theory.*'

'The engineering details are soluble.'

Donn laughed. 'Evidently. Or we wouldn't be standing here, would we?'

'"Soluble." "Evidently."' Five stared at Donn. 'You're talking to this Ghost as if all this is *normal*. As if you're discussing a new kind of stabbing sword.' She turned to the Ambassador. '*How* do you change the laws of physics?'

'Quagma,' said Donn immediately.

He understood some of this. The principle of the GUTdrive, which had powered ancient ships like his mother's own *Miriam Berg*, was related. Quagma was the state of matter that had emerged from the Big Bang, a magma of quarks. And at such temperatures the fundamental forces of physics unified into a single superforce. Quagma was bound together only by that superforce. When quagma was allowed to cool and expand, the superforce decomposed into the sub-forces of nature, nuclear, gravitational, electromagnetic. But by controlling the decomposition, you could select the ratios between those forces, ratios that governed the fundamental constants – including Planck's constant.

Humans knew the importance of quagma. In Donn's father's family legend, nearly two hundred years ago, Joens Wyman had been involved in a jaunt in some kind of impossible ship as humans had raced Ghosts across space to retrieve a lode of this primordial treasure.

Donn said, 'You scare us, with what you do, you Ghosts. You always have and always will.'

The Ghost rolled and bobbed. 'Sometimes we scare ourselves, believe it or not. Shall we proceed?' And it swept boldly into the open dodecahedral chamber. Doors dilated closed around it, and when they opened, only a second later, the Ghost had gone, a tonne of spinning flesh vanished.

Donn and Five were left alone, surrounded by anonymous shoals of Ghosts. Donn grabbed Five's hand again. 'Together?'

'Let's get on with it.'

The chamber was a blank-walled box, silvered like all Ghost architecture. When the doors closed behind them, they were suspended in the dark, just for a heartbeat.

And when the doors opened, they were not in the dark any more.

'Do not be afraid,' said the Sink Ambassador.

The Ghost hovered before them, bathed in dazzling light. Behind it Donn saw the silent figure of the Silverman, the stump of its severed arm a jarring asymmetry.

Five squeezed Donn's hand. 'Virgin—'

'It's all right. I mean, if they were going to kill us they'd have done it by now. And stop calling me "virgin". Come on.'

Deliberately he stepped forward, into the light. Keeping tight hold of his hand, Five followed.

Donn found himself standing on a silvered platform, three or four metres across. The Ghost hovered before him. He couldn't see any support for the platform, though gravity felt about normal. They were entirely bathed in pure white light, above, below, all around, an abstraction of a sky. The light was bright, not quite dazzling. And as Donn's eyes adjusted he gradually made out structure in the light – billows like clouds, all around, slowly evolving, vacuoles boiling.

When he glanced back, he saw the dodecahedral transit chamber had vanished, leaving just the platform they stood on. Somehow he wasn't surprised.

The Ambassador said, 'Where do you think you are?'

'In the heart of a star,' Five said. 'Where else?'

'But not just any star.'

'The Boss,' Donn said. 'But that's impossible. Isn't it, Ambassador?'

'How did you phrase it earlier? "Evidently not. Or we wouldn't be standing here, would we?"'

The Silverman said, 'I understand your reluctance, Donn Wyman. I am human enough to fear falling. Don't be afraid. Step to the edge. Look down.'

Five wouldn't move. She stood there, her hide suit still stained by Ghost blood, bathed in starlight. But Donn stepped to the rim of the floating disc.

And he looked down on a Ghost base in the heart of the star. It was a hollowed-out moon, a rock ball that must have been a thousand kilometres wide, riddled with passages and cavities.

The disc began to descend. The motion was smooth, but now Five lunged forward and grabbed at Donn's arm.

The moon turned into a complex machined landscape below them. Ghost ships and science platforms swept over the pocked terrain, tangles of shining net. And Ghosts themselves drifted up from the chambers and machine emplacements, bobbing like balloons, shining in the star's deep light. All over the moon's surface, vast cylindrical structures gleamed. The Ambassador said these were intra-System drives and hyperdrives, engines that had been used to fling this moon into the body of this star and to hold it here.

And there was quagma down there, the Ambassador said, little packets of the primordial stuff, buried in the pits of ancient planetesimal craters. I knew it, Donn thought.

Meanwhile, behind the moon, Donn saw, there were threads of a more intense brightness, just at the limit of visibility, dead straight.

'The work here is hard,' the Ambassador said. 'Often lethal. We have poured workers into this mine of light endlessly.' And Donn thought of the stream of Ghosts he had seen filing patiently into the transportation booth on Ghostworld. 'Not all come back, despite all our precautions. But now the work is nearly done.'

Five asked, 'So how come we aren't all burned up? We're in the middle of a *star*.'

'Perhaps you can see those illuminated threads, beyond the moon? Those are refrigeration lasers. By making ourselves hotter even than this star's core, we can dump our heat into it. Of course all that you are seeing is a representation, heavily processed. Starstuff is in fact very opaque . . .'

Donn said, 'You are messing with physics again, aren't you, Ambassador?' He thought back to the Coalition's recent observations of the Boss. 'We've been observing flares. Are you trying to mend the star, to stop the flares? No, not that. Sink Ambassador, *are you destabilising this star?*'

The Ambassador rolled. 'How would Jack Raoul have put it? "Guilty as charged." What do you understand of stellar physics?'

'A little . . .'

Every star was in equilibrium, said the Ghost, with the pressure of the radiation from its fusing core balancing the tendency of its outer layers to fall inwards under gravity. A giant star like the Boss, crushed by its own tremendous weight, needed a *lot* of radiation to keep from imploding. So it ran through its hydrogen fusion fuel quickly, and a detritus of helium ash collected in its core.

'But that "ash" can fuse too,' the Ambassador said. 'The fusion process produces such elements as carbon, oxygen, silicon, each of which fuses in turn . . . The chain ends in iron, which cannot fuse, for if it did so it would *absorb* energy, not release it. And so an inner core of iron builds up at the heart of a star like this. A core bigger than most worlds, Donn Wyman!'

Five asked, 'So how come it doesn't just collapse?'

'Its components are already crushed together as far as they will go. This is a property of atomic matter. Humans know it as the Pauli Exclusion Principle. Of course, in time, as the dead zone spreads through the heart of the star, the repulsion will finally be overcome. Electrons will be forced to merge with protons, producing neutrons – a neutron star will be born, smaller and denser than the iron core. And then there will be a collapse of the outer layers, a catastrophic one. But not yet, not for a long time; for now this star is stable.'

'Or it was before you came along,' Donn said. 'But now you're changing things, aren't you? Planck's constant again?'

'Jack Raoul would be proud of you, Donn. Like you, he was a good guesser.'

'If you were to use your moon-machine to reduce Planck in the star's core—'

'Then Pauli repulsion would be reduced. The iron core would collapse prematurely.'

The Ghost showed them a Virtual representation of what would happen next. The implosion would rapidly mutate into an explosion. Shock waves would form and rebound from the inner layers, and a vast pulse of neutrinos would power further expansion.

'The Boss will be blown apart,' said Donn, wondering.

'Yes. A detonation over in seconds, after years of preparation . . .

But the explosion will be asymmetrical, because that layer heated by the neutrinos is turbulent. This is the key to such explosions, and it is this turbulence we are hoping to control. For the asymmetry will blast the neutron star out of the debris of the Boss – it will leave with a significant velocity while releasing a pulse of gravitational wave energy which we would hope to tap and—'

'A supernova,' Five said. 'That's what you're talking about, isn't it? You're going to turn the Boss into a supernova.'

'We believe it will be the first *artificial* detonation of its kind in the evolution of the universe. A supernova used as a cannon to fire out a neutron star, directed as we please! History is watching us, Donn Wyman.'

The Silverman comically raised its stump of an arm. 'Magnificent!'

Donn paced around. 'You're insane.'

'Now you do sound like Jack Raoul,' said the Ambassador.

'You will devastate worlds—'

'Actually, stars too,' said the Ambassador. 'Nearby *stars* will be boiled away.'

'And the Reef,' Donn said grimly. 'Surely we're too close to survive.'

Five said, 'The Reef is a bunch of ships joined up together. Isn't it? Something like that. You could just fly away.'

'We don't have hyperdrive,' Donn said. 'Our units were confiscated by the Coalition for their Navy ships. I don't imagine they will be handing them back.' He turned on the Ambassador. 'This is mass murder. Why are you doing this?'

'Because of the Seer.' The new voice was a woman's: Eve Raoul's. Donn heard her words moments before a cloud of pixels popped into existence, and coalesced into her thin form.

She stepped to the edge of the platform. 'My. Quite a view. Quite a drop, too . . .' She reached out absently, but none of them had a Virtual hand to offer her, and she stepped back.

'I wasn't expecting to see you again,' Donn said.

'Well, I didn't expect to be revived again,' she said with a trace of bitterness. 'At least I'm not in any pain this time. I guess it's good to be useful.'

'Useful how?'

The Ambassador said, 'Eve is helping us understand an entity of our own creation. An entity whose wishes have brought us all here today.'

Donn's heart thumped. 'You mean the Seer.'

'Turn around, Five, Donn.'

They turned. The Silverman was holding, in his one hand, a box, a tetrahedron ten centimetres or so to an edge. It seemed to have clear walls, and its interior was black and full of stars, stars that swarmed – that, at any rate, was Donn's first impression. Five and Donn both stepped closer to look. Behind the box's triangular faces, the 'stars' were no more than dust motes, pushed to and fro by random currents in whatever air filled the box.

Donn said, 'It's like a toy. What is it?'

'The Seer,' Eve said.

The Ambassador said, 'The control of the core of a giant star during a catastrophic explosion is ferociously difficult. Even modelling it was beyond our processing resources. So we devised a new generation of AI.'

Five said, 'This box of dust?'

'This box of dust,' Eve said, 'is the most advanced AI we're aware of. For a machine like this, physically you need components that are small enough to be influenced by quantum effects, yet large enough to feel the effects of gravity. A swarm of smart microprobes – dust motes.'

'A machine like what?'

'A quantum gravity AI . . .'

'On the *Miriam* we have quantum AIs,' Donn said.

'Right,' Eve said, nodding. 'And that gives you an edge in processing speed. A simple switch can only be in one state at a time – on or off. A quantum switch holds information about *all* possible states of the switch at any one time. And so you can use it to do parallel processing. Many inputs, many outputs. You get a speed advantage, and a significant one.

'But a quantum *gravity* machine goes one step further. You abandon causality altogether . . .'

The blurring of position and velocity in quantum mechanics made traditional causality problematical. And in relativity, too, light-speed limits ensured that causality was more an aspiration than an iron law.

Donn started to see. 'And if you put quantum mechanics and relativity together—'

'In a quantum gravity computer, cause and effect are thoroughly mixed up. Time loops are commonplace . . . You can guess where this is going. You don't even need to have input before output, causally.'

'You get the answer before you've even asked the question.'

'That's it. In practice, I think, the Seer is able to glimpse the outline of a solution to a given problem *even before it has begun its calculation*, and so can guide its processing efficiently to that outcome. Its thinking must feel like guesswork, an unlikely series of inductive leaps. But it's always right, and very very fast.'

'The Seer really can see the future,' Five said. 'Just as the rumours say.'

'But its visions are limited, to the outcomes of computing algorithms a few microseconds ahead – or to the furthest future, millennia or more away.'

Five glared at the Ambassador. 'So why the tetrahedron, fatball? Why is this ultimate brain in a box the shape of the symbol of human freedom?'

'A tetrahedron was the most suitable shape for—'

'It's a totem, that's what I think,' Five snapped. 'Some of the Samples say Ghosts are starting to worship us humans, because we're becoming so good at killing you. So, the Silvermen, walking human statues. So, the tetrahedral box.'

The Ambassador said evenly, 'We Ghosts do have a propensity for worshipping that which destroys us, it is true. But you are not yet a goddess, Sample 5A43.'

Donn said sharply, 'Enough. Eve, you said how the Seer's thinking *feels*. How can you know that?'

'Ah. Good question. Because, not for the first time, the Ghosts created an artificial AI which ended up not performing *quite* as specified.'

'Like the Silverman.'

'Well, yes. And, not for the first time, I, or an avatar of myself, was asked to help interpret for it . . .' She looked at Donn, her grey hair shining in the light of the stellar core. 'The Seer sees the future, Donn. And it is afraid.'

Donn watched Eve. Her eyes were unfocused, and he thought her representation was degrading, her skin smoothing from lack of definition, a lock of her grey hair flickering. He wondered how it must be to *be* her, a representation every bit as sentient as he was, and yet having endured multiple lives already – and now bonded with a consciousness like no other.

She said, 'The Seer is sentient, born of dust into a baffling, acausal universe. But it is a Ghost artefact. And so it shares Ghost values, Ghost assumptions. The Ghosts survived the death of their world through symbiosis, dissimilar life forms gathering together as their sun failed. The Ghosts have faith that the life forms of this era of the universe, a transient age of light and water-based chemistry, will similarly use cooperation and symbiosis to survive the transition to the new cold age to come when the last star dies.'

Five shuddered. 'How can you *think* like that?'

'This has happened already, in the universe's history,' Eve said. 'There are life forms extant now, in this age of matter, which are survivors of earlier epochs, the age of radiation and of annihilation and of superforces. But when this age ends, when dark energy comes to predominate and the fabric of spacetime is torn apart – when this happens, and the Seer can *see* it – there will be no Ghost left alive to witness it, and no symbiotic descendant of the Ghosts.'

'Why not?'

'Because of us,' said Five savagely. 'Because of humans. *We win*. I don't need a quantum-gravity computer to tell me that. And we drive the Ghosts to extinction.'

'You must understand,' the Ambassador said. 'The detonation of this sun – we do this because we, this Ghost enclave, have been cut off from our home range by the forces of your Coalition. Billions of individuals, a whole world, trapped behind the lines. We were desperate. We looked for a way to change the parameters – the rules of the game. That is our way of resolving problems. We were looking for a way out. Now we see we must do more than that; we must take the Seer and its dreadful counsel to our home ranges. We need time to consider what must be done.'

'Such as what?' Five asked.

'Such as escape.'

Escape to where? Donn wondered. Where could the Ghosts go to escape a rampant, Coalition-led mankind? Out of the Galaxy? Out of the *cosmos* altogether?

He tried to focus on his own situation. 'Then why have you brought us here? Why tell us this?'

'Because of me,' said the Silverman. He stepped forward, still cradling the Seer. 'You made me smart in order to punish me. But I am human enough to guess how you would feel about an exploding star.'

The Ambassador said, 'We did not mean to engineer this star as an act of war, only as a means of escape. We understand now that humans might not see it that way.'

249

'You really don't get human psychology, do you?' Donn said.

'No,' said the Silverman cheerfully. 'Donn Wyman, you must warn your people. Make them believe, as we could not. Persuade them to flee. And make them believe the Ghosts did not mean war.'

'That's a tall order.'

'You are our only hope,' the Ghost said simply. 'You, who have shown empathy for our kind before, where others have turned away.'

Donn thought he ought to feel proud. He felt empty. Could it be true that so much was pivoting on this moment? Because if so, he thought, I am not strong enough to deal with it.

'You don't have much time,' said the Ambassador. It floated towards the lip of the platform.

Donn followed, and looked down at the engineered moon. Ghosts swarmed, pinpricks of dazzling light against the worked regolith. 'How long?'

'The mathematics is uncertain.'

'There are human colonies scattered through the Association,' Donn said, thinking. 'Many of them still have hyperdrive, I think. But the main human concentration is the Reef. And we no longer have hyperdrive—'

'Ask your father,' the Ambassador said.

'What?'

'I too approved of the Silverman's wish to contact you personally, Donn Wyman. Because *I* know that your family has resources. We will send you home now, Donn Wyman.'

They pulled back and stood in a row, the Silverman with the tetra-hedral box, the looming Ghost, and the Virtual of Eve, gradually disintegrating.

Eve raised her hand. 'There is more,' she said solemnly. 'Human and Ghosts must both join the great confluence of mind in the far future, join with the rest. That is the only way the next transition can be survived *by either of us*.'

Donn was shocked by this latest bit of bad news. 'And if humans destroy the Ghosts—'

'Then *neither* will survive. Remember,' she said, her voice scratchy. 'Remember . . .'

Five ran towards the Silverman, who stood stock-still, slow to react. She raised her fists and slammed them down on the Seer. Her hands passed through its substance, scattering pixels.

Donn pulled her away.

'Just an avatar,' she said, breathless. 'Worth a try. To strike such a blow . . . It would have been magnificent.'

The Ghost and its companions were surrounded by a cloud of pixels now. The star's light flickered.

And Donn was home.

His mother ran up to him and grabbed him. 'Oh, Lethe, Donn! I never thought I'd see you again.' He let her weep on his shoulder. 'Benj is back too,' she whispered. 'He's back!'

Here was Samm, his father, grinning hugely, grabbing onto Benj as hard as his mother was to Donn. The Commissary, Elah, was here too. She looked as shocked as any of them at Donn's sudden appearance, but she was looking up into the sky with some alarm and muttering into the air, evidently communicating with her Coalition colleagues. And Donn saw Five, still in her bloodstained Ghost-hide suit, looking even more scared and bewildered than in the centre of the star.

Donn found his brother. Benj was wearing a plain white bath robe; all his hair had been shaved off. 'Benj. What happened to you?'

'I've been a stark-naked lab rat for a day. If it really was you who got me out—'

'It was. You owe me.'

'I was afraid of that. Damn.'

There were twin concussions, soft explosions, and a breeze of displaced air, as Hama Belk and Kanda Fors returned, coalescing under the lifedome. Grubby, scrawny, they both staggered in the sudden change of gravity, and clung to each other in shock. Then they realised where they were, and their clinging turned to a hug of joy. Then Hama spotted Elah, standing apart in her black Commissary's robe, and he went over to her immediately.

And Kanda, recovering her composure quickly, came forward to Donn and Rima.

Donn gently disengaged his mother. 'Mother – you have guests.'

Rima turned. 'Do I know you?'

'Kanda Fors. Food tech, from the *Harry Poole*. We met a couple of times, I think . . . I've been lost for a number of years.'

'It's a day of shocks for us all.' Rima stepped forward, and the women clasped hands.

Amid more soft concussions, more of the ragged rats from Ghost-world started to appear, many naked, bewildered. One woman cradled a baby.

Five still stood alone, Donn saw, scared, resentful.

Donn went over, took Five by the hand, and led her to his mother. 'Mother, this one's called Five. Long story. I think she'd appreciate some help, her and her people. Some clothes for a start.' But Five flinched back. 'She's been living wild,' Donn murmured. 'It will take some time . . .'

'We've all the time in the world. Come, child. And, Kanda, you'll be wanting to tell your family you're back?'

'I feel nervous about it. Yes, of course . . .'

'And you – Five, was it? What about your family?'

'I don't remember.'

'I'm sure we can trace them. Come on, we'll sort it out.'

Now Donn approached Samm. 'Father. I need to talk to you. We're in trouble. The Boss—'

'I know. Look at this.' He showed Donn an image, returned by faster-than-light inseparability links from a Coalition drone observer close to the giant star. The Boss was spitting, flaring, ejecting knots of plasma large enough to swallow Earth's sun whole. 'It's becoming unstable.'

'It's worse than that . . .' As urgently as he could, Donn told his father all he had witnessed, of the Ghost experiments at the heart of the Boss – of the coming supernova. Samm listened gravely.

'You do believe me, Father?'

'Of course I believe you.'

'As do we,' Elah said, walking over.

Hama followed in her wake. Though he was just as grimy and under-fed, he didn't seem the same person he had been on the Ghostworld; he had immediately retreated into his Coalition role, like a shadow of the Commissary.

'What you say,' Elah went on, 'ties in with the projections we have been making of the star's instability.'

Samm folded his arms. 'You say you're here to protect us, you of the Coalition. What are you going to do about this?'

'We have already put out a warning to the other human colonies in the Association. Most of them have hyperdrive ships; they will be able to flee in time. Other Coalition centres are arranging refugee facilities—'

'Blankets and hot water. Great. But what about us? You know damn well the Reef contains the largest human population in the Association. You took away *our* hyperdrives.'

'In order to serve the greater needs of the Third Expansion—'

'That *star*'s going to expand before long and cook us all. Going to give us back our technology, are you?'

'That isn't practical,' Elah said simply. She listened absently to a voice only she could hear. 'Come,' she said to Hama. 'The flitters are lifting Coalition personnel from the Reef in fifteen minutes.'

'And us?' Samm tried to grab her arm, but she shook him off. 'What of us? You're leaving us to die!'

From nowhere Elah produced a handgun, a starbreaker. 'This conversation is over, regrettably.' Backing up, she and Hama made for the door cut into the lifedome.

Samm made to follow, but Donn stopped him. 'Father – let me. Wait, Commissary.' Cautiously he approached Elah and Hama. In a few, rushed words, he tried to tell them more of what the Ghost had told him within the star.

'The Ghosts don't want this to be seen as an act of war.'

'Then they shouldn't detonate supernovas in human space,' Elah said.

'They're only doing it to escape the cage we put them in.'

'*They* put humans in cages. Your friend Five, Hama here—'

'They fear we will drive them to extinction. That's what the Seer foresees. And if that's so, we may ultimately destroy ourselves in the process.'

Elah thought that over. 'Better a Galaxy in ruins,' she said, 'than a Galaxy that is not ruled by us. Good luck, Donn Wyman.' She backed to the door, and left. Hama looked back once, but it was as if he barely recognised Donn any more, and he followed his superior.

Donn went back to his father. 'I failed.'

'Well, what did you expect? You aren't going to overturn an ideology like the Coalition's with a couple of sentences. But the Commission for Historical Truth records everything that transpires – *everything*. Maybe they will figure all this out one day, after a couple of thousand years' study in some library on Earth – maybe you planted a few seeds for the future. In the meantime, we've a supernova to deal with.' Samm eyed his son. 'So did your new Ghost best buddy give you any advice?'

'It said I should ask you.'

Samm sighed. 'Smart of it. OK, son. I guess it's time you learned a little family history.' Carrying his data slate he walked off towards the copse at the centre of the dome, chlorophyll green leaves shining under the light of the bourgeoning supernova.

Donn hurried after him. 'Where are we going?'

'The engine room.'

The kilometre-long elevator descent along the ship's spine was slow, frustrating.

Donn knew his way around the control room at the heart of the *Miriam*'s GUTdrive pod. He had come down here as a kid, to play with his brother, and later as a young man to learn about his mother's family's technological legacy. There wasn't much to see – a couple of seats and couches, a water dispenser, an emergency pressurised locker. The instruments were blank, antique data slates tiling the walls. And, before the Coalition had taken them away, once in this space vast engines had brooded, engines capable of harnessing the energies of cosmic inflation to drive the ship forward.

Even though the engines were gone, Donn somehow expected his father to boot up the control slates. He didn't. Instead he took the small portable slate he had carried down from the lifedome, and pressed it against a wall. It lit up with a crowded panel of displays. 'There you go,' Samm said. 'Two hundred years old and it fires up like it was brand new.'

'What does?'

'This.' He tapped the slate and showed Donn an external view of the *Miriam*, seen from below, its lifedome embedded in the rough plane of the Reef, its spine and engine compartment dangling like a lantern. Samm zoomed in on the hull of the engine compartment, where a black slab clung like a parasite.

Donn leaned forward and stared. 'What is *that*?'

'The family secret.' Samm eyed his son. 'Look, Donn – you aren't the first Wyman to have run into the Sink Ambassador. Your grandfather a few times removed—'

Donn's heart sank as he realised that his father was falling back on the family legend. 'Joens Wyman.'

'That's it. Joens got involved in a kind of intergalactic race with the Ghosts. He was an entrepreneur. And he wanted to get his hands on—'

'A cache of quagma,' Donn said. 'You've been telling me about this since I was a little boy.'

'But it's the truth, son. Some of it, anyhow. Just listen. The trouble was the quagma cache was somewhere over twelve *billion* light years away – the figures are uncertain. Too far even for hyperdrive. But

Joens Wyman didn't use hyperdrive. He used an experimental human technology. It was called a Susy drive.'

'Susy? That's our flitter's name.'

'The flitter, and a secret space drive. It was kind of risky . . . It's not like hyperdrive. Look, they taught you at school that the universe has more dimensions than the macroscopic, the three spatial and one of time. Most of the extra dimensions are extremely small. When you hyperdrive you sort of twist smoothly through ninety degrees into an extra dimension, and go skimming over the surface of the universe like a pebble over a pond. Simple. Whereas with supersymmetry you're getting into the real guts of physics . . .'

There were two types of particles: fermions, the building blocks of matter, like quarks and electrons, and force carriers, like photons. The principle of supersymmetry had it that each building block could be translated into a force carrier, and vice versa.

'The supersymmetric twins, the s-particles, are inherently fascinating, if you're a physicist, which I'm not,' said Samm. 'But the magic comes when you do *two* supersymmetric transformations – say, electron to selectron and back again. You end up with an electron, of course – but an electron in a different place . . .'

'And that's the Susy drive.'

'Yep. A principle even the Ghosts have never explored, it seems. According to the Sink Ambassador anyhow. Well, Joens Wyman pumped his money into this thing, and got as far as a working prototype. But in those days nobody would invest in human research and development; it was always easier and cheaper to buy alien tech off the shelf. Joens hoped to cut his losses by sending his Susy-drive ship in search of treasure nobody else could get to.'

'The quagma. What happened?'

'Joens finished up with nothing but the Susy drive and the clothes he stood up in. He fled his creditors—'

'And he came here.'

'Yes. Good place to hide – anyhow, it was then. His son married into your mother's family, who owned the *Miriam*.'

'And he lodged the Susy drive on the hull of the ship.'

'Yeah. So it's come down the generations. My father told me about it, and gave me the data on this slate. I think Joens always thought this old monster might be useful as a last resort. Well, he was right.'

Donn stared at his father. This was a side of him Donn hadn't seen before, this decisive adventurer. But maybe no son saw that in his father. 'You're not serious. You're not planning to fire up this Susy drive, this two-hundred-year-old disaster?'

'You have a better idea?'

'When was it last tested?'

'When do you think? Look, according to these displays the field it generates will envelop the whole of the Reef. We'll get out of here, all of us. And then you and I will go down to Minda's Saviour, and drink free Poole's Blood for the rest of our lives.'

'If it works. And if it doesn't work?'

'Then what have we lost?' He tapped the screen. It switched to the external image. Panels blew out from the black casing fixed to the base of the pod; a zoomed-in view showed them the jewelled guts of the Susy drive.

Then the data slate chimed an alarm. The Susy-drive display cleared, to reveal an image broadcast from the Coalition monitor drone. An image of an exploding star.

'Damn,' said Samm. 'I didn't imagine it would be so quick.'

'Father, look.' The explosion was strongly asymmetrical, a flower of ugly light splashed across the slate. And there was a denser knot to one side of the supernova.

Samm tapped the screen, overlaying analyses of mass density and velocity vectors. 'That's the neutron star. The core of the Boss. It's been spat out of there like an apple seed – thousands of kilometres a second.' He brought up a Galactic display. 'Look at that. It's been fired straight out of the Association towards the Sagittarius Arm.'

'The Ghost home range.' Green asterisks began to appear around the fleeing neutron star. 'What's that?'

'Ghost technology . . . Ghost ships, popping up out of nowhere. Settling into orbit around that neutron star. And, wow, look at *that*.' A major green anomaly. 'It has to have the mass of a planet.'

'The Ghostworld.'

'Looks like it. How are they bringing all this to the neutron star?'

Donn said, 'Just by making it more *likely* that the planet should be in orbit around the neutron star than wherever it used to be . . .'

'What?'

'Never mind. Father, we need to get out of here.'

Samm brought back the Susy display and began to scroll through outputs. 'Let's just hope this damn Susy drive does what I tell it to.'

'Father – don't you *know*?'

'I told you. It's kind of unreliable, or so my father told me. We ought to end up just a little above the Galactic plane, however. OK, it's ready.'

'As quickly as that?'

'Well, that supernova shock wave is going to take a while to get here – years, as we're light years off from the Boss. But we can't expect rescue for years either, even if the Coalition is willing to try; the gravity waves from the detonation are going to churn up hyperspace for a long time. Best to get out of here now if we can – and if this doesn't work, we might have time to figure out something else. I've sent an alarm out through the Reef.'

'Shouldn't we ask Mother first?'

'She'd only say no. Hang onto that rail. Good luck, son!' He stabbed a finger at his data slate.

The Association stars turned to streaks and disappeared.

So, just as his father had tried to explain, Donn was leapfrogged through Susy-space. What he hadn't been told was what it would feel like.

Susy-space was another universe, laid over Donn's own. It had its own laws. He was transformed into a supersymmetric copy of himself – an s-ghost in Susy-space. And it was . . . different. Things were blurred. Susy-space cut through the distinction between Donn, here, and the stars, out there. Donn could *feel* the scale of the journey, as if the arch of the universe were part of his own being. Distance crushed him.

But at last it was done.

The Reef of ships popped out of Susy-space, sparkling with selectrons and neutralinos.

Samm and Donn stared at each other. 'Let's not do *that* again,' said Donn.

'Agreed.' Samm tapped his data slate to get an external view.

No stars. Just darkness, broken only by the faintest smudges of grey light.

'Are they galaxies?' asked Donn.

'Oops,' said Samm.

Humans spread across the stars, their capability increasing rapidly, their zone of influence expanding at many times light-speed.

A period known as the Assimilation followed, in which the wisdom and power of other species were absorbed, on an industrial scale. Those they conquered became mere resources: even the last traces of those pushed into extinction, like the Silver Ghosts, were exploited.

Soon, only the Xeelee stood between humans and dominance of the Galaxy, and beyond.

And all the time, as humans belatedly learned, the Xeelee were waging war on another front, against a cosmos-wide force that was wrecking the stars themselves.

The Xeelee war had its own terrible logic. Eventually the tide turned against humanity.

The conflict had lasted a million years. There were many casualties.

GRAVITY DREAMS
AD 978,225

1

'Massive sensor dysfunction!'

This time his own shout dragged Coton out of his dreams. He lay on his pallet, gasping, sweat coating his face.

'It's all right.' Here was his grandmother, Vala, in her night robe, her round, calm face shadowed in the glow cast by a single hovering light globe. Above him loomed the frame of Vala's house, a tetrahedron of metal bars and panels hung with musty tapestries, cosy and cluttered and mundane. 'You woke yourself up.'

'And you. I'm sorry.'

'Don't be.' She sat on his pallet and passed her hand over his brow. Her fingertip traced the tattoo there, an inverted black tetrahedron, like her own. 'It's why you came here, in a way. So I can help you cope with the nightmares.'

'But it wasn't like my other dreams.' He'd had plenty of nightmares of flight. It was only a month since the ships of the Second Coalition had appeared in the skies of Centre, and the officials and the troops had landed to impose their curfews and tithes and evacuations – and the population, enraged, had turned in on itself, and Weaponised families like Coton's had become targets of hate and frustration. Only a month since he'd had to abandon his parents, and his world, at the age of seventeen.

'But *this* was different.' He clenched his fists and huddled them into his chest. 'I couldn't move. As if my arms and legs had been cut off. I could see and hear, but there was something wrong with my head. I was floating in this big sky, a red sky that was full of glowing shapes, like light globes – or stars. But I hated it, for it was wrong.'

'Wrong?'

'I shouldn't have been there. It was my duty to get everyone out – to get them home. But *I couldn't move.*' He twisted, as if wrapped up.

She took his hands. 'There could be another cause. Your parents would have explained all this, one day . . . You know we're Adepts,

Coton, don't you? And young Adepts sometimes have dreams – we call them gravity dreams. It might be nothing to do with the pogroms back on Centre . . . But dreams of immobility are common even among normals, I think. These things are subtle, indirect. Your dream could be a sign that you're healing, in some way. The waking mind trying to reconnect with the body.'

'What did I say?'

'When you woke up? Not words I recognised. *Mas-eef* . . . Can you replay?'

Coton's own voice came echoing out of the air, the sound shaped by the smart systems that pervaded Vala's environment. *'Ma-seef senss-or dees-funx-eon.'*

'Doesn't mean anything,' Coton said.

'Perhaps not. The words sound archaic. It might be interesting to check.'

That was just like his grandmother, whose scholarship, according to his own mother, had made her a cold parent, and caused them to fall out. Her own world, this world, after all, had no name but a numbered label – Delta Seven – and Vala referred to it, not as home, but as 'the college'. Now he was stuck here with her, and she was studying his dream as if it was an academic puzzle.

He felt a surge of resentment. He needed to move, to blow away the last dark shreds of his nightmare. He pushed aside the sheets and rolled off his pallet, his bare feet on the cool floor.

'Are you all right?'

'I need some water.'

He shoved his way out through the thick woven flap that was the door of the house, and emerged into cavernous gloom. 'Lights.' A sprinkling of globes lit up and revealed the expanse of this Map Room, the shining floor, the complicated walls with their reefs of shelving, and the alcoves folding off into the dark like suppressed memories.

He made for a bathroom block, a neat cube a hundred paces away. Here there were spigots and low sinks. He bent, and the water, flowing without a command, poured into his mouth, cool and clean.

When he was quenched he stood back, and found himself staring at the spigot.

Vala walked to his side, wrapped in a black cloak, evidently uncertain of his mood. She saw what he was staring at. 'You know, that spigot was put here for the scholars who once worked in this chamber. Now the students are long gone. But the spigot itself, the tip of a vast self-maintaining system, doesn't care whose thirst it quenches; it just does its job, millennium after millennium. I'm sure there's a lesson for us all in that . . .'

He glanced back at her shack, sitting squat on the shining floor of this immense building. 'Long gone?'

'Oh, yes. It's obvious my house is much more recent than the Map Room itself. When I first moved in I could even see traces of a hearth. Somebody had been building fires, here on the floor of the Room. That's how badly things fell apart, when the last unified government collapsed. And *this* is what the worlds of mankind are like, all across the Galaxy – or at least the part of it we still inhabit. We are a lesser generation, squatting in the ruins of a greater past. Lighting fires on the marble floors of libraries.'

They walked together across the gleaming floor, their voices small in the huge hall. 'What did they study here?'

'You know, you've been here a month, and this is the first time you've shown any real curiosity about this place. I think that's a good sign, don't you?'

But he had no wish to be analysed, and he kept silent until she answered his question.

'The truth is, I'm not sure. The archives have been very damaged. The college probably served two main purposes. First it was a branch of the Library of Futures. The architecture is similar to the central Library on Earth.' She waved a hand. 'Once, you know, the air in here, those alcoves and shelves, would have been full of Virtual images of space battles, ships hurling themselves against the enemy in sheaves of unrealised possibilities!'

He barely understood this, but it was a thrilling vision. 'What enemy?'

'The Xeelee, of course. What other enemy is there? As for the second function – if I'm to show you that, you'll have to come outside, just briefly.'

She linked her arm in his, and led him to a walkway that jolted into motion, making Coton stagger. They were swept towards a blank wall at alarming speed. Coton tried not to show his nervousness. All this was grander than anything he was used to on Centre, and more ancient, and he couldn't help wondering what would happen if the power were to choose today to fail. Vala seemed quite unconcerned.

In the very last instant the wall puckered and opened, to reveal a gleaming corridor. The walkway swept them inside, and Coton tried not to flinch. They passed along the corridor, and emerged in the open air, on a parapet that rimmed this cubical building, under a star-filled sky. Coton's bare feet were cold.

He hadn't been outside since he'd been dumped here from the Coalition scow – he did recall it had been night then, always night here on this sunless world – and he only vaguely remembered the landscape, the city. Buildings stood proud as far as he could see, most of them intact, in rows and crescents and great overlapping circles. It was like a museum of architecture. But, under a sprinkling of light globes, most of the buildings were dark, and here and there fires flickered. And between the buildings, though some of the moving walkways evidently still ran, vegetation had broken through the ancient pavement and flourished green and black and purple.

Vala said, 'You must imagine this university-city as it was in its day, when these lanes were full of flitters and ground vehicles, and Commissaries crowded in their black robes. What a sight it must have been! The college was surely a strategic anchor of the Library of Futures, in this corner of the Sagittarius Arm. And the other purpose was – that!' She pointed into the sky.

There was nothing much to be seen just where Vala was pointing – but what a sky it was, Coton thought. Stars hung like crimson lanterns before a veil of wispy, glowing gas, where dense knots told of new stars struggling to shine. But behind all that lay a deeper darkness, a profound night that spanned half the sky. That was the signature of the Xeelee – of the Scourge.

'Do you recognise what you're seeing? Which way is Sol, for example?'

He jerked his thumb over his shoulder, away from the Scourge darkness. 'That way.'

'Yes. About nine thousand light years away, in fact. Sol is in the next spiral arm out from the centre of the Galaxy – and opposite the Scourge, the darkening of the stars. The Xeelee are only a few hundred light years out from us now, and they'll be here in a millennium or so. Before they pass on towards Sol itself.'

'Not if the Second Coalition can stop them. The Marshals have a plan. The crew told me on the freighter.'

She snorted. 'I'd like to hear it . . . As for the young stars, we're in the Carina nebula, one of the Galaxy's great stellar nurseries.'

'They won't last long—'

'No. Even the youngest star in the Galaxy is infested by photino birds. And it is the action of the photino birds that was, I believe, the second subject of the college's study . . .'

Photino birds: creatures of dark matter that swarmed in the hearts of stars, subtly manipulating their evolution. Subtly killing the light. Meanwhile the Xeelee, creatures of the light themselves, were opposing them, or trying to. Throughout human history, and for long ages before, a war in heaven had raged, all unobserved by mankind.

Vala pointed again. 'Up there is a neutron star. When it was discovered by astronomers on Earth, it was one of the brightest stars in the Galaxy – as massive as a hundred Sols, and a million times as luminous. Its catalogue number was HD93129A.'

'It must have imploded. A supernova—'

'Yes. But it popped too quickly. The photino birds had tinkered! And under the old Coalition, the college was established here to study how that supernova process differed from the usual, whatever might be strange about the remnant neutron star, and whatever could be learned of the birds themselves.' She smiled, and the coal-black tattoo on her forehead glinted in the red starlight. 'What a sky! I sometimes think you can see all of human history summarised from this spot – and our future.'

'So why are you here now? You and those you work with.'

'We're still studying the neutron star – but from a different point of view. We're looking for relics of a later age.'

'Relics?'

'*Weaponised.* In the course of the Xeelee war, a post-Coalition government called the Integrality threw a breed of Weaponised humans into neutron stars, so they could turn those stars themselves into engines of war. Direct their flight, so they became like huge cannonballs. There are some in *our* neutron star, we think.'

Weaponised people – as Coton was, and his grandmother. 'What will you do when you find them?'

'Try to save them.' She smiled. 'We Weaponised must stick together. There are many of us here – a few Adepts like us, and other kinds on this world – even a few exotic types around the neutron star—'

'*Around* it?'

267

'As knots in the magnetic field. When it came to creating human-analogues as weapons of war, the Integrality was nothing if not ingenious. We've organised ourselves for the rescue work; it is a project run by Weaponised for the benefit of Weaponised. No government supports us, and nor would we want it. We consult, trade, research, even farm, to support those who do the work of rescue; some local populations even pay us a tithe, for they recognise the worth of what we're doing. I'll show you what we're planning for the Starfolk – the inhabitants of the neutron star. We've even created a vivarium to hold them, when we retrieve them.'

'A vivarium?'

'A tank of neutron superfluid . . . The Starfolk are creatures of nuclear forces, Coton, and they scale accordingly. To them we're misty giants.'

He rubbed the inverted-tetrahedron tattoo on his own forehead. 'You know, I've grown up knowing I'm Weaponised. But I never knew what our special skill was supposed to be.'

'It was bred out of us – though some of us still have gravity dreams, when young. It's generally thought best if children don't know. They get into less trouble that way.'

She led him back into the building, along the corridor with its eerily dilating doors, and to the Map Room.

'I know you didn't want to leave home, Coton. You didn't want to come here. But you understand there was no choice.'

'My parents spent all they had keeping me out of the labour colonies.'

'Yes. But now you're here, and there's work to do. What do you think?'

His head whirled, full of new ideas and images and the lingering shadow of his nightmare. 'I think I'm tired.'

She laughed. 'Back to bed for both of us, then. We'll talk more in the morning.' She led him to their tetrahedral shack.

He lay down in his pallet. Soon his thoughts were dissolving into sleep.

But he was woken by Vala, outside the shack, murmuring questions. '*Ma-seef senss-or dees-funx-eon.* Seek possible translations and date the language. And keep the noise down . . .'

A solemn synthesised voice murmured a reply.

And Vala asked, '*How* old?'

*

He was next woken by the tumbling crash of supersonic flight, a noise too familiar from Centre. Without dressing, without looking for Vala, impatiently waiting for the walls to open, he rushed out of the building.

The sky was full of Second Coalition warships.

2

Massive sensor dysfunction!

Sometimes Lura thought that if she could only understand that strange complaint of the Mole, she would be able to make much more sense of the machine itself, her mother's strange bequest. On the other hand, if it just kept quiet she wouldn't have to fret so much about hiding it. Nothing was ever simple!

But right now she had other problems, for her tree wasn't happy. Lura could feel it, even hanging as she was in her fire pod, dangling from the central trunk of Tree Forty-Seven.

She had spent her shift as tree pilot artfully shaping the screen of grey smoke beneath the tree, and so she looked up at it now through billowing, sooty clouds. The tree was a wheel fifty paces across, its twelve radial branches fixed to the stout trunk at the centre. And that wheel turned, ponderously graceful like all of its kind, the light of the endlessly falling stars casting subtle shades and blood-red highlights, and she could feel the downwash created by its shaped branches as they bit into the air. Tree Forty-Seven was at the bottom of the great stack of the Forest, layer upon layer of straining trees all tethered by their long cables to the kernel far below her – the husk of a burned-out star, no wider than the tree, pocked and hollowed-out and rusted the colour of blood.

And she could sense her tree's unhappiness in the faint shudders that rustled those banks of leaves as it turned, and a groan of wood on wood as the massive bolus counterturned within the hollow trunk. She knew what was wrong, but there was nothing she could do about it, not for now.

It was a relief when she heard the whistles and rattles sound all across the Forest, calling the shift change.

Sweating, her bare arms covered in soot, her lungs full of smoke and her eyes gritty, she swarmed up the rope from the fire-pot through her smokescreen. Passing through the blade-like branches, with disturbed skitters spinning up around her, she picked up her pack of rope and food where she had left it hooked on a stubby branchlet.

She stroked the trunk's hard surface. 'Well, you've a right to be un-happy, Forty-Seven,' she said. 'Stuck down here as you are.' She didn't agree with the Brothers' policy of 'punishing' ill or poorly performing trees by marooning them at the base of the Forest stack – she'd argued over this with Brother Pesten, her own old tutor, many times. The tree had a subtle gravity sense and would be well aware of the pull of the kernel – very strong down on its surface, and still a perceptible drag here, two hundred paces or so up. Trees were creatures of the open air, and sought to flee deep gravity wells – which, of course, was the instinct their human masters exploited to put them to work. Lura, eighteen thousand shifts old, understood that to be unable to escape this deep well for shift after shift was torture for Forty-Seven. So she patted the tree's trunk, and put her cheek to its rugged surface and felt the mass of the bolus spinning in its confinement within. 'I'll see if those idiots in the pilots' conference will allow me to move you—'

'You still talking to the trees, Lura?' The coarse voice of Ord was loud in the branches above her. He came swinging down through the turning branches, and settled his webbed feet on a trunk gnarl near her. He was her replacement as tree pilot for the next shift. A thou-sand shifts older than Lura, he was a big man, strong, clumsy-looking, but graceful enough when he moved in the shifting gravity fields of the Forest.

'Oh, leave me alone, Ord.'

He swung closer, and she could feel the half-gee drag of his heavy body. He pulled his goad from his belt, a stabbing-spear of fire-hardened wood. 'This is all you need to make a tree do what you want it to do.'

She kicked away from the trunk and settled on a branch. 'You stink. You're so fat you trap your own foul air in your gee-well.'

'That's my manhood you're smelling, little girl,' he said, and he waggled his goad. 'Rumour is you've *still* never lain with a man. Maybe you should carve this tree a dick. Then you wouldn't have to bother with people at all.'

'Sooner that than lie with you.' She grabbed her pack and swarmed up through the tree's patiently turning branches, leaving Ord's coarse shouts behind her.

She climbed easily up through the stacked Forest, pulling herself through one turning tree after another or swinging on tether cables, and as she rose further out of the kernel's gravity well the climbing got easier still. She was making for Tree Twenty-Four, at the very apex of the stack, where she had hidden the Mole – and she was glad of an excuse to get as far as possible from Ord and his crude advances.

People lived in the Forest. Houses of wood and woven bark dangled in the air, fixed to tether cables that spanned the tiers of the turning trees, and the air was full of smoke from the fire-pots – the trees fled from shade as much as from gravity and could be controlled that way. Here folk lived and died, ate, slept and played, and worked with their trees, encouraging them in the generations-long task of feeding star kernels into the unfillable maw of the Core of Cores. Right now it was shift-change time, and people were in motion everywhere, the adults making their way to and from their assignments, the Brothers letting the children out of their classes.

She passed one party laden with baskets of food. You couldn't eat the substance of the trees themselves, neither the skitters, which were the trees' tiny spinning seeds, nor their round, pale leaves. But you could eat the fruit and berries and fungi that colonised the trunks and branch roots, and trap the various species of rat that fed off those growths in turn. Some said that the existence of the fruit and the rats proved that humans were part of this world, as much as flying trees and whales and the Core of Cores, and stars that fell through the air. Others clung to a legend that humans had come to this place from somewhere else – 'Humans don't belong here', went the slogan – and held that the rats and the fungi and the rest, everything people could eat, had come out of the Ship that had brought the people here, the Ship itself long since lost.

But all around her people swam in the air, their webbed feet kicking, and children played complicated aerial games of chase, dancing through each other's pinprick gravity wells with unconscious confidence. Lura felt a surge of joy as she watched the children – and envy for their carefree play. Wherever people had originally come from, *this* had been the reality of life for uncounted generations.

At last she'd climbed up through the forest to the highest tree in the stack: Twenty-Four, broad and handsome, its number etched into its bark. The pilot conference held that the trees were smart enough to respond to the lead of the strongest among them, and Lura wasn't about to say they were wrong. Clambering easily up Twenty-Four's tether, she swept with a smile past old Jorg, the tree's pilot this shift, with his battered fire-pot and grimy blankets. And, once up in the tree itself, she made her way to the trunk, scattering clouds of skitters that spun briefly before nestling back in their parent tree's leaves. For here, at the very crown of the trunk in a knot of immature branches, she had hidden the Mole.

She set down her rope and pack, anchored herself with her bare legs, dug her arms into the branches, and gingerly lifted out the Mole. It was a box about the size of her head, roughly square-edged. But it wasn't made of wood or whale cartilage or any substance she recognised, but of something pale and shiny, and the hide was punctured by holes within which some other substance glimmered, hard and transparent. You could see that the Mole had once been part of something else, for stubs of cut-off panels and bits of pipe stuck out of its sides, and scorch marks showed that great heat had been used to cut this remnant out.

Cautiously she whispered, *'Mole. Status.'*

'Massive sensor dysfunction. Massive sensor dysfunction—'

Its voice was blaring, grating, not like anything human at all. She always found it oddly upsetting. 'Hush, Mole.'

'Massive sensor dysfunction—'

'Stop it! Stop talking!' She found it hard to think, and to remember the phrases her mother had taught her. *'Mole. End report.'*

The voice cut off in mid-phrase. Lura heaved a sigh of relief, hugged the box to her chest, and settled back in the branches of Twenty-Four.

From up here, at the top of the Forest stack, her view of the sky she floated in was unimpeded. The air of the nebula was, as always, stained blood-red, and littered with clouds like handfuls of greyish cloth above and below her. Stars fell in a slow, endless rain that tumbled down to the nebula's misty core. Their light cast shifting shadows from the clouds, and the wild trees, and huge misty blurs that might be whales. Beyond this nearby detail she could see the greater expanse of the spaces beyond the sky: the knotty patches of light that marked other nebulae, and the brilliant pink pinpricks of the big-stars, all of them orbiting the Core of Cores, a sullen, dark mass.

She was relieved nobody had found the Mole. Her mother had told her it must be kept hidden, especially from the Brothers, for it was her family's oldest secret. For a time she had kept it tucked away inside the cabin she had shared with her parents. But when it had started squawking she could think of nowhere else to keep it but here, as far from the mass of people as she could find. Her mother's sole legacy was nothing but a hassle.

She thought about the playing children. How she had loved being little, and carefree, and cherished! But one day her father had been killed when he had descended to the kernel to fix a loose cable; in the powerful gravity field of the burned-out star a simple fall had broken his back. Then her mother, always weak, had fallen to a condition of the lungs. And Lura, burdened with care, was a child no more.

Sometimes, in fact, she thought she had grown up too quickly. She always seemed to see dark shadows in the Forest's daily bustle – the etiolated condition of some of the trees' leaves, and the pale faces and straining chests of the weaker children, unable to keep up with the others. The nebula air wasn't as rich as it used to be, the old folk said, it was smoky and made you gasp – and perhaps it had killed her mother. It was said that humans had come to this nebula from another that was dying. Well, it might be true, even if she had never heard anyone explain *how* people had hopped through the airless void from one nebula to another. But the trouble was, as she could see at a glance from here, even if that was possible, no nearby nebula was much healthier than this one – a healthy cloud being blue and full of bright yellow suns, and scattered with the greenery of trees. Every nebula she could see was a cramped red mass.

If *all* the nebulae were dying, then where were the people to go?

The Mole was certainly no help. She stared at its ugly hide, the stubby cut-offs. 'Mole, you are strange and useless and nothing but trouble. And if you hadn't meant so much to my mother I'd pitch you out of the tree—'

'I don't think that would be a good idea.'

Startled, she scrambled in the foliage, and nearly lost her hold.

Brother Pesten hovered before her.

Pesten wore the simple dyed-black shift of the Brotherhood of the Infrastructure, and soft sandals on his feet. Tall and stick-thin, he was bald, with a fringe of unruly greying hair. He held himself oddly rigid as he hung in the air, with one steadying hand on the tree trunk. He had always seemed old to Lura, even when he had been her tutor, and now, of course, he was older still – perhaps as much as fifty thousand shifts. The tree pilots resented the Brothers. Nobody grew as old as a Brother, they muttered, because everybody else had to work too hard. But when Pesten smiled at Lura, a little bit of her softened, as it always had.

She clutched the Mole. 'Who told on me?'

'How do you know I didn't just find the gadget for myself, shouting away in this treetop as it was?'

'I remember you, Brother, and you were never one for climbing any further than you had to. Who told? Ord, I bet, that fat rat's arse – no, if he'd found it he'd have blackmailed me for whatever he could get.'

'Ord isn't so bad. He's never actually harmed you, has he? He just doesn't know how to approach you.'

She couldn't have cared less about that. 'If not Ord then who?'

'Old Jorg. Chief pilot of the Forest's fulcrum tree.'

'Jorg! I trusted him.'

'You still can. He's our most senior and experienced pilot, and he's no fool. And when he saw you creeping around his tree with your gadget, he was concerned for you, for what you might be getting yourself into. So he came to me. Where did you get this thing?'

'From my mother,' she said ruefully. 'We call it a Mole. I don't know why. Handed down from her mother, and hers before her . . . I let them all down, didn't I? The Mole was kept secret by my family for generations, and now I've had it for a few dozen shifts and the whole Forest knows about it.'

'Don't blame yourself. Something about the Mole may have changed. I can't believe it can have been so noisy before and escaped detection. May I?' He reached out. Reluctantly she handed him the Mole. He hefted it, feeling its mass, turned it over in his hands, and rapped its hull. 'Do you know what it's made of? No? It's a kind of metal, I think. Like kernel iron, but processed . . . Do you know *what* it is?'

'I know what my mother said it is.'

'Tell me.'

She took a deep breath, for she was about to speak heresy to a Brother. 'Part of the Ship. Maybe the last surviving part. My mother said there was a big argument long ago. Some people wanted to forget about the Ship. Others wanted to remember. *Humans don't belong here* – that was their slogan. So when remembering the Ship was banned by the Brothers, and any remnants of it were destroyed, this Mole was saved, and hidden.'

'If it came from the Ship, do you know what it's for?'

She shrugged, reluctant to be drawn, unsure what kind of trouble she was in. She waited for the rebukes, the condemnation, the accusations of heresy.

But none of that came. Instead Pesten turned the Mole over in his

275

hands. He said, 'I can make an educated guess. It's probably a transport machine – or the clever part. All the working parts were cut away long ago.'

She was bewildered. 'The clever part?'

'Like a brain. A brain without a body – but perhaps these little holes are its eyes and ears. After all, it responds when you speak to it, doesn't it?'

'Brother – what are you saying? That this is actually from the Ship?'

He sighed. 'The Brotherhood doesn't believe in the Ship. But the Ship, nevertheless, existed.' He smiled. 'And, yes, you have a piece of it here, preserved through the generations.'

She was astonished by these admissions. 'You've been lying to us!'

'"Lie" is a hard word,' he said mildly. 'The Brothers only want what's best for everybody. I know we have our faults, Lura, but you have to believe that much.' He gestured at the tree, and the panorama of the Forest below. 'Look – you understand what we're doing here, with all these trees?'

She felt faintly insulted he'd asked. 'We pull at the star kernel. Eventually we'll make it fall out of the nebula, and all the way down into the Core of Cores.'

'And why would we want to do that?'

'Because in response the Core of Cores produces gushes of fresh air. You Brothers say it harbours gods that do that.'

'Yes. Air with oxygen, and other gases we need to breathe . . . Lura, a kernel is a massive object, and it takes a lot of pulling to deflect it from its trajectory, which, with the rest of the nebula, is a decaying orbit around the nearest big-star. And we only have the trees to pull it with. It takes whole generations to move a single kernel. But when this one falls we will cut the trees loose and move to another kernel, and we'll start all over again.

'This is what we do. This is *all* we can do, hauling kernels across the sky, trying to coax more air out of the Core of Cores. So what good is it for people to fill their heads with dreams of another world, and of a Ship that might have brought them here? Best for them to forget it all, and make do with what they have.' He lifted the Mole before his face. 'I'll regret destroying this, for it is a rarity – I have seen other fragments – I never heard of one that *spoke* before. Remarkable. But it must go, of course.'

'You have no right.'

'Of course I do,' he said gently.

'Will I be punished?'

'No. I think losing this will be punishment enough, won't it? I'll dispose of it, don't worry any more. Let's go down and have something to eat, and hope that the next shift turns out to be a bit more straightforward than this one.'

A shadow crossed the sky behind him.

She pointed. 'I think *they* might have something to say about that.'

He turned to see.

Out of the sky's crimson gloom a flock of whales came swimming, their massive tails beating at the air, human riders standing on their translucent backs. Humans with weapons.

Suddenly the Mole spoke again. *'Massive sensor dysfunction! Massive sensor dysfunction!'*

3

Vala received two contradictory summonses. They came two standard days after the arrival of the Second Coalition flotilla.

Grumbling, she showed the Virtual messages to Coton. One, heralded by a trumpet blast, was an order to attend a Marshal Sand, evidently the senior military figure on the planet and now the 'interim governor'. The second was an order to go to a 'processing' centre, along with all the Weaponised on Delta Seven. Vala snorted. 'Typical of this sort of strutting ninny – fanfares and petty cruelty, and sheer incompetence to boot. Which shall I attend, eh? Even if you try to do what these people want it's impossible to get it right. Curse them!'

As she ranted Coton stood back, rubbing the black tattoo on his forehead.

At last she noticed. 'Oh, child – I haven't been thinking of you. Don't be afraid.'

'This is how it started on Centre.'

'I know, I know.' Gently she pulled his hands away from his forehead. 'Look at this ludicrous mark – it's all out of shape. They apply them to babies, you know, and then when you grow . . . Look, they haven't even mentioned you in the summonses. They probably don't even know you're here.'

'Are we going to have to run again, grandmother?'

'We're not running anywhere. The work we're doing here is much too important.'

'The Starfolk?'

She squeezed his hands. 'Not just that. It's this business of your dreams – if that's what they are. I've been doing some research on those words you keep repeating . . . Oh, I'm sorry, I don't mean to be mysterious. We'll talk properly later. Well, we must obey one of our summonses, but which? We'll go see this Marshal character, shall we? At least she's the superior officer. Let's *both* go, and you can demonstrate your existence.'

*

The city was in chaos. The streets were crowded with Coalition soldiers and functionaries and their transports, and with citizens, some trying to go about their business, some laden with luggage and wandering anxiously. Many buildings had been requisitioned by the new authorities and displacing their inhabitants, so that heaps of furniture and other detritus were piled in doorways amid crowds of the evicted. One sector, an avenue lined by huge college buildings, had long been given over to a market. This morning the vendors were short of supplies, and the lines of would-be buyers were long and fractious, shabby people with bags and packs, holding unhappy children by the hand.

Vala snorted her contempt as she pushed her way along with Coton. 'The mighty hand of the Second Coalition at work! Refugees lining up to buy food that doesn't exist. This is what happens when a new authority tries to take control. They'll have carved up the region with new boundaries, cutting trading links, forcing people out of their homes to be relocated according to one grand scheme or another . . . Oh, I dare say it will sort itself out. But in the meantime we'll all go short.'

Coton didn't feel so judgemental. 'It's not just the Coalition's fault, grandmother. The Scourge is advancing, a curtain of darkness. Whole worlds are thrown into chaos. People abandon their homes, their planets, and fall as refugees onto those further out. We have to expect this over and over in the coming years as the Scourge looms ever closer, driving people ahead of it.'

Vala grimaced. 'A cold analysis, but probably an accurate one.'

They came to a pencil-slim building, its face adorned by light globes.

'This is it. Once the Chancellor's residence. Come on! If we follow the directions we've been given, we have to climb all the way to the roof.'

Much of the building was dark. The elevators were working, but patchily, and, comically, they had to break their journey around the middle of the ascent to cross corridors and climb three flights of stairs, transferring from one elevator shaft to another. At last they emerged through another dilating door, and Coton found himself on the roof of the building – and not a pace from the edge, which wasn't in any way fenced off.

Vala laughed. 'Oh, don't worry about that! Jump off and the inertial nets will trap you. It's quite impossible to come to any harm . . . It's rather obvious where we're supposed to go, isn't it?' She pointed at a space-going military flitter that sat square in the centre of the roof, adorned with flags bearing a bright green tetrahedral logo. She marched forward. 'Typical of such people to grasp at the symbols of a better past . . .'

Despite her sparky self-confidence, they were held up by armed guards before being allowed to enter the flitter. Vala had to give both their names, and the guards, in bright green uniforms, eyed their Weaponised identification tattoos suspiciously, and checked their identities against scrolling lists. It didn't help that Coton wasn't included in the summons, and they had to refer to an off-world database.

Then they were made to walk through a kind of open framework. When it was his turn Coton felt a kind of tingling, a heat that penetrated to his core.

The troopers puzzled over the resulting Virtual images of his head and Vala's – and Coton stared, astonished, at the sponge-like structures they had detected, meshed within the frontal lobes of both of their brains.

Vala had no patience with this procedure. She tapped the tattoo on her forehead. 'Don't you recognise this? We're Adepts. And Adepts are born with technology in their heads, just as you see here. Check your databases, man. We're known. We're harmless!'

While the man checked, Coton murmured to his grandmother, 'Technology? What technology?' Even though he had known he was an Adept, he'd had no idea that he had a head full of technology; his parents had told him nothing of this. It was another unwelcome surprise.

And Vala winked. 'Only the best. Alien expertise. *Silver Ghost technology . . .*'

The Ghosts: ancient enemies of mankind, long extinct. And he'd been born with their stuff inside his head? Coton, shocked, couldn't take it in.

It took a while longer, and another referral to the superior, before they were allowed to pass.

The flitter itself was expensive-looking, but heavily armoured. Once inside they were led down a short corridor to an expansive cabin. Here an officer sat behind a desk, with images flickering in the air around her head in response to her murmured commands. She wore a uniform of electric-blue fabric adorned with gold lacing, and a peaked cap sat on the desk beside her. This, evidently, was Marshal Sand. The cabin was functional; there was a cot folded up against one wall, and what looked like a small galley at the back behind the desk. An aide stood at Sand's side, a tough-looking soldier with a gun cradled in his arms.

While the guard didn't take his eyes off Vala and Coton, Sand didn't look up, or acknowledge them in any way. There were no seats, so they had to stand before the desk. Vala, irritable all morning, grew impatient quickly. Coton, aware of the guard's glare, longed for her to stay quiet.

At length the Marshal snapped her fingers, and her Virtual displays folded away and winked out of existence. She looked up at Vala. She had grey-blonde hair shaved short, and her features were strong, symmetrical. She might have been forty. 'I apologise for keeping you waiting—' She turned her head, and a Virtual copy of Vala's summons popped into the air before her. 'Academician Vala. Ah, yes, the Starfolk scholar.' She glanced at Coton. 'And this is your grandson.'

Vala snapped, 'Do you not have chairs for your guests?'

Sand seemed amused. 'You aren't guests. And meetings with me generally don't last long enough for chairs to be necessary.' She eyed their tattoos. 'I did not realise you were Weaponised, however.' She checked over the Virtual summary. 'Adepts. Both of you? Your talent is inactive—'

'We are born with the hardware in our heads, but not the ability. Not for generations.'

'Of course.'

'We had another summons that clashed with yours. To be "processed" with the other Weaponised.'

'You did?' Sand prodded the air, in the middle of the Virtual. 'There. I've rescheduled your processing, with a note that you're a special case, Academician.'

'Thank you,' Vala said acidly. 'And what does this "processing" entail?'

'These are times of turbulence,' the Marshal said. 'Of huge population movements – the coming of the Scourge sees to that. Times of fear and suspicion. We're taking steps to ensure the Weaponised and other minorities are protected. Useful roles will be found for them—'

'Ghettos? Forced labour?'

'The policy is not mine. I just implement it, as efficiently as I can. In any event, it will not affect you. Academician, let's get to the point. I need to discuss your work.'

'Do you indeed? You might find it's a short conversation.'

Sand held Vala's gaze, evidently weighing her up. 'You're not the first scholar I've spoken to, here on this world of universities and museums – in this bubble of privilege. Well, we of the Second Coalition, dealing with the issues of the real world, are only human. But you will learn that we are in fact mankind's last hope against the Scourge. Which is why I need to speak to you.'

Vala stood up straight, a small, frail woman in this military ship. 'You think a lot of yourself, don't you? Are you going to send me to the front against the Xeelee?'

'Not you,' Sand said, unfazed. 'Your Starfolk.' She snapped her fingers to summon up more Virtuals.

And they spoke of the Scourge.

It was a story that stretched back nearly half a million years.

From out of the dark aftermath of the Qax Occupation, the Interim Coalition of Governance had turned mankind into a colonising, appropriating force that had ultimately, in the form of the Exultant generation, driven the Xeelee themselves out of the heart of the Galaxy. That had taken twenty thousand years. And then the expansion had continued, deeper in time, beyond the Galaxy.

But the superhuman unity of the Transcendence, half a million years after the Qax terror, had proved the high water mark of humanity's achievement. When the Transcendence fell, man's ultimate enemies stirred.

Though they were always distracted by their cosmic war against a greater foe, the star-infesting photino birds, the Xeelee had not forgotten their defeats at the hands of humans. Their vengeance, the Scourge, was a simple strategy, but relentless. One by one the worlds of humanity fell dark, their stars cloaked in an impenetrable shell of the Xeelee's fabled construction material. And humanity was beaten back.

Sand said, a cold anger in her voice, 'Here they are, back in the Galaxy the Exultants won from them. Here they are, sweeping through the plane of the disc, and on the verge of crossing into the spiral arm containing Sol. It will take millennia more. But they will, in the end, take Earth itself – unless we make a stand.'

Coton found himself oddly stirred by her words. 'Make a stand? Where?'

'Have you ever heard of the Orion Line, lad? One of the most famous sites in human history – the inner edge of the Orion Arm, which contains Sol. Here the great human expansion across the Galaxy was held up for centuries by resistance from a species called the Silver Ghosts. Well, we won that war, and now nothing remains of the Ghosts.'

But Coton exchanged a glance with his grandmother, for now he knew that wasn't true, that the Ghosts, in some way, lived on in his own head, and in Vala's.

'After the collapse of unified government, mankind suffered hundreds of millennia of bifurcation. Even speciation, which the First Coalition would never have allowed. But now – in the coming centuries – a new unified government, the Second Coalition, intends to make its own stand on the Orion Line.'

'How?' Vala snapped. 'What bright new weapon do you have that could possibly stop the Xeelee?'

'Oh, nothing new,' Marshal Sand said. 'You know the nature of the age we live in better than most, I'm sure. A million years after mankind first left Earth, anything you can dream of has been invented before, and forgotten, a dozen times: archaeology is a better bet than innovation. And our own clever scholars have dug up a weapon we can use against the Xeelee.'

'The Weaponised?' Vala asked. 'The Starfolk? Are you going to start hurling neutron stars around the Galaxy again?'

'Not that, Academician. We have a much grander vision . . .'

And, with another Virtual display, she demonstrated the Coalition's dream.

The plan was simple and breathtaking: to turn back the Xeelee with supernovas, detonated in a wall thousands of light years long, right along the inner edge of the spiral arm.

'You're as insane as the Integrality.' Vala sounded stunned.

'Quite possibly,' Sand conceded.

'And it won't work. Only the most massive stars go supernova,' Coton put in. 'Everybody knows that. And besides, most of the Galaxy's stars have had their fusion processes tinkered with by the photino birds anyhow.'

Sand regarded him. 'But that's what we plan to do – tinker with the stars to suit ourselves. We'll send in the Starfolk through microscopic wormholes, just as in the past. They'll be equipped to adjust the fusion processes in a star's core. The physicists promise that a star of only one or two solar masses could be induced to deliver a good enough detonation for our purposes.'

'Many of those stars must have worlds. People.'

'Not by the time the stars are detonated,' Sand said. 'Remember, lad, the Scourge will be closing.'

Vala asked, 'And will you abandon the Starfolk to their fate?'

'Of course not,' Sand said evenly. 'They'll be retrieved in each case. There will inevitably be losses—'

'She won't do it,' Coton burst out.

Sand looked at him in surprise.

Vala said, 'Coton, hush—'

'My mother taught me that what was done to us Weaponised was wrong, and it's been a wrong that's lasted generations. Vala's here to help the Starfolk, not exploit them. She won't help you. Tell her, Vala.'

Sand glanced at Vala. 'Academician?'

And, to Coton's horror, Vala hesitated.

4

As the whale flotilla closed in on the Forest, alarm whistles blasted and wooden rattles were spun. Lura crouched down in the lead tree's foliage with the Mole tucked under her belly. Pesten was beside her, and old Jorg came scrambling up the tether from his fire-pots. But Lura felt very exposed up here.

Twenty-Four gave a great wooden groan, and shuddered and strained. It was a standard tactic to cut a few trees loose when a raid came, to provide platforms for counter-attacks, and Twenty-Four, with the rest, was adjusting its spin and angle to take up the greater burden that was left.

And now the whales were here, sooner than Lura had expected, looming out of the crimson sky.

One slid by her position, only the diameter of the tree away. It was a rough sphere as much as fifty paces across, with tremendous paddle-like flukes turning at the back, and three misty eyes in the 'face' at its front, the whole swathed in ropes and ragged nets for its riders to cling to. Its skin, cartilage covered by a soft foamy layer, was translucent, and inside she could see the shadows of internal organs. The riders on the whale's flanks, clinging to the nets, leaned over, whooping and shaking spears – naked, pumped up and exhilarated, and ready for the fight. One man saw Lura and grinned, showing sharpened teeth. She yelled obscenities back, until the tree's rotation took her away.

Further down the flank of the Forest, the whale riders were making their attacks. Looking down through the foliage Lura saw spears being thrown from whales into the Forest, and in response arrows shimmered in clouds from the trees. But the whale riders were already leaping across the void to take on the Forest folk, and the cries of battle rose up – and the screaming began. Twenty-Four's shuddering worsened as the ongoing battle interfered with the work of the tree pilots, and the trees began to grow as confused as their occupants. All this evoked deep primal fears in Lura; the

285

Forest hadn't been raided like this since she was a child.

'You need to get down from here,' Jorg said to Lura. 'We're vulnerable – the lead tree always is.'

'I agree,' said Brother Pesten sternly.

'All right. But I'm not leaving the Mole behind.'

'Here.' Pesten took his rope belt from his waist. 'Make a harness out of this. Be quick.'

But even as she started fumbling with knots, Jorg cried, 'Here they come!'

That whale came in again, much closer now, rising up over the rim of the tree. Lura found herself looking directly into its huge, misty face, those three great eyes swivelling to fix on her as the whale rolled on its axis, its body counter-turning to the rotation of the flukes. The face was vast, each eye alone as big as a person. There was nothing remotely human about the whale – it wasn't even as much like a human as a rat, say. *Humans don't belong here.* But she thought she read something in those eyes – pain, perhaps, or pity.

And now the whale's roll brought a party of riders up above the tree rim, half a dozen of them, all armed, all naked and smeared with some kind of oil. Their faces were twisted into masks of bloody anticipation and there was the man with the sharpened teeth, now sporting an erection.

'By the Bones!' Jorg cried. With startling strength he ripped a slice of wood from the leading edge of the nearest branch, threw it as an improvised spear, and put his other gnarled hand on Lura's head and tried to push her deeper into the foliage. But the riders dodged the splinter easily, laughing; it stuck harmlessly in the hide of the whale. Two of them let fly with their own spears at Jorg, one after the other. He dodged the first – but the second skewered his chest. Jorg clutched the spear, trying to speak, and a hissing gurgle came from the wound. Lura reached for him. But he went limp and fell back, floating down through the turning branches of his tree. Lura was horrified by the skill and efficiency with which his long life had been ended.

And, unopposed, the whale riders sailed easily across the gap.

Lura, still holding her Mole, scrambled to find something to fight with, anything. She felt she was moving as slowly as an old woman; the riders were so much faster, so much more determined.

They came plummeting down out of the sky.

One landed on Lura's back, pushing her over, flattening her face down against the branch. Pinned by huge strength, she managed to twist her head. She saw that Pesten was on his back, trying to fight. But he had no weapons, and when he tried to grab one of the riders his hands slid over slick, oily skin.

Already it was over.

5

Vala had requested an hour's break to gather more data, and her thoughts, before she made any decision. She rushed off, leaving Coton in a small cabin aboard the Marshal's flitter – so small it was like a cell, he thought, and sparsely furnished.

When she returned to collect him, they had to wait once more, outside the Marshal's cabin, while Sand completed yet another meeting.

Vala looked at Coton, agonised. 'I came here with no idea what this Marshal wanted of me. Now I see I have some leverage with our new overlords. And I have a chance to save you – and, perhaps, for us to achieve much more together. Later we'll discuss it properly—'

'You always say that. You never do. You haven't discussed any of this with me. Nobody told me I had this alien thing in my head—'

'I'm sorry,' she said. 'Sincerely. But events press, Coton. You have to take opportunities when they come.'

A guard beckoned them back into Sand's cabin.

Marshal Sand still sat behind her desk. As Vala entered she looked up, faintly amused. 'You again.'

Vala marched up to her desk. 'Marshal, I'll not waste time. I've come to a decision. I'll work with you—'

'Grandmother!'

'On one condition,' Vala said, facing Sand. 'Let him go. The boy. Spare him your "processing".'

Coton cried, 'No!'

Marshal Sand said evenly, 'How can I bargain with you, woman? If I make an exception for him it's going to be rather visible, isn't it? I do have a duty to maintain order.'

Vala sounded desperate. 'It's not just that he's family. It's more than that. I think he could turn out to be important – very important.'

Coton was frightened and bewildered. 'What are you saying?'

Vala turned to him. 'I hoped it wouldn't come to this. We haven't even had time to discuss it ourselves . . . It can't be helped, and here we are. Coton – tell the Marshal about your dreams.'

'Dreams?' The Marshal glanced at her Virtual displays again. 'You mean visions? Your kind of Weaponised are precognitive, aren't you? Or were. Has that somehow switched itself back on in this boy's head?' She eyed Coton, interested. 'Are you seeing the future, child?'

'The future?' He looked at his grandmother, still more bewildered.

Vala took his hand in hers. 'I told you,' she said. 'They bred it out of us. Coton, you were born hamstrung but the modifications are still in your head, the technological relic. They feared us, child, and hate us still. Because we could see what is to come . . .'

The Adepts' precognitive ability had always been limited. They could see only a few minutes, or less, into the future, and only aspects of it that concerned their own surroundings – their own destiny. Beyond that, quantum uncertainty led to a blurring of competing possibilities.

'But that few minutes' edge made our ancestors formidable soldiers,' Vala said. 'Just enough to let us get out of the way of the next bullet.'

'The Adepts were among the more effective of the Integrality's Weaponised types, in fact,' Sand said, checking her archives as they spoke. 'But they were more useful in policing activities than against the Xeelee.'

'We were used against humans,' Vala said. 'No wonder we were feared, and hated. When the Integrality fell we were rounded up, though we were as hard to catch as we were to kill. And those who survived were genetically modified.'

Sand regarded Coton analytically. 'You never knew this, did you, boy? Never knew what your Weaponisation entailed.'

'He would have been told, if his parents had lived. It's our way to keep it from the children, for if they blurt it out to normals the fear starts up again. Coton, I would have told you,' Vala insisted.

Sand watched them, judgemental. 'I've always found truth the best policy myself. So is this stunted precog now seeing the future after all?'

'Not that,' Vala said. 'I think he's seeing another universe entirely.'

The Marshal just stared. Then she rubbed her eyes. 'Is that supposed to make sense, Academician?'

'It's the way our talent was engineered into us,' Vala said. 'May I use your display facilities?'

Access to the future depended on paths in spacetime called closed timelike curves – faster-than-light transitions. Humanity's hyperdrive warships had routinely travelled faster than light, and, at the height of the Exultant war, had just as routinely shown up scarred by battles *that hadn't yet been fought*. The First Coalition's Commissaries had learned to harvest such information, and, in suites like Vala's own Map Room, they had charted the outlines of the war's future progress.

'But there are other sorts of closed timelike curves,' Vala said. 'Marshal, our universe of three space dimensions floats in a greater space, which the physicists call the Bulk, of many extra dimensions. There are many universes' – and she held her palms together – 'floating parallel to each other in the Bulk, like pages in a book. You can reach these other universes through engineering, like wormholes—'

'Like Bolder's Ring.' The most titanic Xeelee construct of all, at the heart of the galactic supercluster.

'Yes – and I'll come back to the Ring. But there are also certain sorts of leakages between the universes. Most particles are bound to space-time, but some wash out into the Bulk – especially gravitons, which mediate gravity. Now, if our universe is folded in the Bulk – or if the Bulk itself is distorted – these particles can take shortcuts through the Bulk from one point in our spacetime to another.'

'Thus creating closed timelike curves.'

'Exactly.' Vala turned to her grandson. 'Coton, in your head there is a sort of transmitter-receiver of gravitons. You can sense gravitons coming via the Bulk from events a few seconds or minutes ahead of us in time, and your brain processes them into sound or vision.'

'But,' Sand said, 'you said this facility has been bred out.'

'No,' Vala said with strange patience. 'The mechanism is still there, growing in each child's head; it's the faculty to process the data that's been turned off. As if Coton had healthy eyes but lacked the cortical equipment for his brain to process the information from those eyes.

'But you're dealing with biology, Marshal, and a very ancient modification. Things drift with the generations. Many of our young have always had *gravity dreams*, as we call them, dreams of other places and times – even of the future. Residual perception. They usually grow out of it. And we don't announce it to the world. Would you? In Coton's case it may be something to do with the proximity of the neutron star – spacetime is grossly distorted hereabouts, and the graviton flux—'

'Get to the point, Academician.'

'Marshal, I believe my grandson is receiving a graviton signal, not from any future event in our own universe, but from *another universe entirely* – a universe where the descendants of the crew of a warship, which sailed there through Bolder's Ring, have been stranded for several hundred thousand years. Coton, you're picking up a distress call! And the first thing you must do is respond . . .'

6

The man with the sharpened teeth anchored his feet in the tree's foliage and stood straight. His short hair was shaved into elaborate patterns, Lura saw, and a crude zigzag tattoo had been carved into his belly. He leered in triumph. 'Take the girl,' he said, his language coarse and heavily accented but recognisable. 'She looks worth a hump.'

'You'll have to kill me first,' Lura spat.

The rider kneeling on her back, a woman, laughed. 'Oh, I wouldn't give old Otho ideas like that, little girl. It only makes him hornier.'

Otho laughed in turn, showing those gruesome teeth. 'She'll keep. Just sit on her, Anka. Kill the old man, he's no use.'

Pesten roared his defiance, and struggled with his captors, but he couldn't get a fist free. A rider held his spear over his chest.

'No!' Lura yelled. 'Don't kill him.'

The leader, Otho, bent down so his face was close to hers. His breath stank of blood. 'And why not? Will you be nice to me if we let him live, little girl?'

'He's a Brother,' she snapped. 'Look at his robe. The Brotherhood of the Infrastructure will pay you ransom to get him back.'

'She's right,' said the woman Anka, still on Lura's back. 'Might save a bit of fighting, Otho.'

'But I like fighting . . . Oh, very well, bring him. Tie him first.'

They got Pesten up on his knees and stripped him of his robe, leaving him naked, and tore lengths off the robe to truss him up. Pesten kept struggling throughout. 'You'll get no ransom for me!' He was silenced by a punch in the mouth by Otho, a sickening impact that cracked teeth. They got Lura up too, and tied some of the strips from Pesten's robe around her body. She still had hold of the Mole, which Anka, a red-haired woman with a body like a whip, eyed curiously. But the riders were rushing too much to do anything about it for now.

Hurriedly, they ransacked the tree for anything they could steal – the dead pilot's scraps of food, a water skin, spare clothing, even the tipped-out fire-pot.

Then they lined up with their trussed-up prisoners at the tree's rim. The whale, its huge eyes mournful, beat its flukes and approached the tree again. Timing their jumps to match the spin of tree and whale, the riders started to cross, leaping confidently through the air.

And, Lura realised with mounting horror, she was going to have to make that leap herself.

Otho and Anka got hold of Lura's arms, one to either side. Lura could feel the tide-like tug of their bodies' gravity fields, and Otho's free hand roamed over her buttocks and thighs, though she squirmed to get away.

And they leapt with her, still holding her, with the whale seeming very far away.

In the air, she looked down at the expanse of the aerial Forest, and she saw the fighting everywhere, the whales skirting the turning trees, the riders dwarfed by their rolling animals. One tree came wheeling out of its formation, foliage ablaze, and as she watched its rim and branches began to disintegrate, and flaming chunks spun off into the air.

And, just before she landed on the whale, another tree rose up in the air above her, and she heard a man roar – Ord! She'd know that voice anywhere. He ran around the rim of his turning tree, throwing spears down at the riders. One spike caught Otho in the leg. He let Lura go, yelling his anger and agony, and without hesitation ripped the spear out of his flesh and muscle, braced and threw it back at Ord, who ducked. All this in mid-air, before Otho completed his leap and landed on his back on the whale's flank.

Lura and the woman followed him down, hitting hard.

Soon all the riders were down, clinging to ropes to keep from being thrown off by the whale's spin. Lura, beside Pesten, had ended up on her back in the whale's dry, foamy outer flesh, and was held down by Otho's massive arm.

But Ord, in his tree, wasn't done yet. He held up his fire-pot, a wooden bowl from which flames still licked. The riders scrambled away, around the whale's hull.

Lura yelled, 'Do it, Ord! Burn these bastards!'

With a mighty throw Ord hurled down the pot, and he disappeared backwards, shoved away by the recoil. The pot splashed against the whale's flank, spilling fire. Swathes of outer flesh caught fire and burned off in sheets, and the whale rolled and spasmed, its agony obvious. The riders clung to their ropes.

'We need to get inside,' Anka yelled at Otho. 'We'll be thrown off.'

He nodded. 'Hold this she-rat.' Leaving Anka with Lura, he wrapped his feet in the netting, blood still streaming down his leg from his wound. He took a wooden knife from his belt, braced himself, and slashed down through the whale's skin and into the layer of tougher cartilage beneath. Then he backed up, dragging his blade through one pace, two, and foul, hot, moist air spilled out of the lengthening wound. He tucked away the knife and forced his arms into the slit he'd created, pushing the flanges apart. 'In. Fast.'

One by one the riders piled through the orifice and into the whale's body cavity. It got easier as the first of them made it inside, and were able to help hold the breach open.

Lura was shoved through, head first and bound up. The air within was foul and hot and stank of sweat.

Once inside she was rolled over away from the hole, onto a slick, moist surface. Pesten was dragged through the orifice as unceremoniously as she had been, and dumped beside her. Now the whale's spin, instead of threatening to throw them off the outer skin, kept them pinned in place.

And Lura lay on her back, exhausted, shocked, breathing hard. She was *inside the whale*, and its translucent skin was a great shell all around her, with the riders' clothing and blankets and weapons and spoil from the raid heaped up on its floor of flesh. The beast's internal organs were massed around a digestive tract that spanned its diameter, from the face at the front to an anus at the back end, where lumps of muscle worked the great flukes, dimly seen from within the body. And at the front Lura found herself looking *out* through the whale's huge face, an inverted mask that dwarfed the rider who worked there, held in place with a harness, jabbing goads into a tissue mass.

Otho stood over her, tying a strip of cloth around his wounded leg. 'You caused us a lot of trouble, little girl. Took a spear for you. Time for Otho's reward.' He ran his tongue across his sharpened teeth. The others laughed, even the woman, Anka. He reached down.

She struggled against her bonds. 'Leave me alone, you savage.'

'Savage is right,' he said. He rummaged at the strips of cloth that held her and pulled out the Mole. 'So what's this?' He turned it around and spun it in the air, and he licked its casing. 'Can't eat it, that's for sure.'

'Leave that alone!'

Anka approached him, curious. 'Never saw anything like it.' She rapped the box with her knuckles. 'Maybe we could smash it up. Make knives.'

'No.' Otho grinned down at Lura, who struggled against her bonds. 'It's driving her crazy. Let's just throw it out of the whale. I like them wild.'

Pesten, bound and naked, glared at him. 'You don't know what you're dealing with.'

'Don't I?' Otho casually kicked Pesten in the kidney.

The Brother groaned and rolled, but he twisted his head and spoke again. 'I mean it—'

Lura called clearly, 'Status!'

'Massive sensor dysfunction.'

Otho yelled and dropped the box; it fell and bounced on the resilient floor. 'What did you do?'

'Untie me or I'll have my magic box kill you,' Lura snarled, as confidently as she could. When they didn't move, she called again, 'Mole! Status!'

And, to her astonishment, the Mole replied with a phrase she'd never heard before. *'Incoming signal received.'*

7

'My name is Coton. Can you hear me?'

'Yes! You're talking out of the Mole. But all the Mole ever said before was "Massive Sensor Dysfunction". You're not in the Mole, are you?'

'No. I am speaking through the – what did you call it? The Mole? I am human, like you.'

'Are you a man or a woman?'

'I am a boy. Coton. What is your name?'

'Lura! My name is Lura! I was born about eighteen thousand shifts ago.'

'Shifts? . . . Please wait. Lura, we think a shift is about a third of a standard day. An old Integrality navy term. Very ancient! So that makes you . . . about sixteen years old.'

'Years?'

'You're a bit younger than me.'

'Are you talking to other people there? Are you asking them questions?'

'Yes, there are people here. My grandmother, Vala. And we have other machines that help us understand what you say. Actually there are lots of machines, talking to each other in a kind of chain. Your language and mine were once the same, but that was a long time ago.'

'Am I talking to you out of a machine too?'

'No. Yes . . . In a way. Lura, the machine is in my head.'

'How strange. Does it hurt?'

'No. Well, I don't think so. I don't like it much.'

'You said your grandmother is there. Where are your parents?'

'Not here. We were moved. My father spent all he had sending me to safety. Not that I feel very safe where I am now . . . An enemy was coming. Well, it still is coming. Everybody had to move. What about your parents, Lura?'

'They both died.'

'Are you with friends? At home?'

'It's difficult. I can't talk about it.'

'We're in such different places. But we don't have easy lives, do we?'

'Different places? Coton, I don't understand any of this. I know you're speaking to me through the Mole. I don't know where you are.'

'Where do you think I could be?'

'In another of the nebulae that are orbiting the big-star. But there are lots of big-stars orbiting the Core of Cores. Perhaps you're closer to one of them. Are you on a tree, or in a whale?'

'I don't understand much of that. No, Lura, I'm not in any of those places.'

'Are you further away, then?'

'Lura, I'm in another universe.'

'A what? Another everything? What does that mean?'

'I think sometimes the translation isn't very good. Maybe you don't have the word in your language. I'm in the place people originally came from. Your people. Your ancestors went through a kind of gate, and ended up where you are. They couldn't get back. Everything is different here. The stars, the stars are bigger than you can imagine—'

'Humans don't belong here.'

'What?'

'My parents taught me that when I was small. They said it's the most important thing people should remember. The Brothers would punish you if they caught you saying it. But you can't do that now, can you, Pesten? Humans don't belong here! It's true! Here's the proof!'

'You haven't forgotten, then. After all this time. In a way, your Mole never forgot either. It must have been a component of the original ship—'

'The Ship! We have stories about the Ship – some of us. People lived on it for a while, and then they made the Raft out of it, but they had to give that up too.'

'And in the end the Mole called. I managed to hear it . . . It's complicated.'

'Why did it call?'

'Because it thinks you need help, Lura. All of you, in that universe.'

'I like talking to you, Coton.'

'And I like talking to you. Tell me what you see.'

'The air is red and filled with stars, all falling down . . .'

8

Coton lay on his pallet, propped up on pillows, outside Vala's tetra-hedral house. His talks with Lura were draining, and after a half-hour session he always felt as if he hadn't slept for days.

Meanwhile Sand and Vala argued over their data, their interpret-ations, their Virtual reconstructions. They were using facilities loaned by the local Second Coalition authority and imported into this ancient Map Room – and, remarkably, the Marshal herself had invested the time to come here in person.

What they were discovering was remarkable, inspiring, haunt-ing. Vala had actually found a scrap of a log fired back by the crew of the *Integrality's Constancy of Purpose* as the warship, its engine blazing, had fallen through Bolder's Ring, an immense Xeelee artefact under assault from human fleets – fallen into a new universe . . .

The ship imploded, and fell into a compact, glowing nebula. Crew members hurried through the corridors of their failing vessel. Smoke filled the passage-ways as lurid flames singed the air. And then the hull was breached. The raw air of the nebula scoured through the cabins, and through rents in the silver walls the crew saw flying trees and huge, cloudy whales, all utterly unlike any-thing in their experience . . .

'It's a miracle anything survives at all,' Vala said. 'It's nearly nine hundred thousand years since this ship was lost! A date, incidentally, we confirmed from the linguistic drift between Lura's tongue and our own.'

'Perhaps you could skip the self-congratulation, Academician—'

'Gravity!' Vala said forcefully. 'That's the key to universe Beta – which is what the Integrality archivists of the time called it.'

'Our own universe being Alpha, I suppose,' said Sand drily.

Vala smiled. 'Gravity in Beta is a billion times stronger than in Alpha – you understand I mean the fundamental force, the magnitude of the constant of gravity. Other physical constants, the speed of light for instance, are the same.'

'Then everything is different there,' Sand said, pondering. 'If Earth was projected into universe Beta—'

'It would have a surface gravity of a billion gees – but it would implode in an instant. Even a mass as small as a human body would have a perceptible gravity field. In Beta, you could make a "star" with the mass of a small comet, say; that would give enough pressure to initiate fusion in the core. Stellar masses scale inversely as the gravity constant raised to the power of three over two . . . Other cosmic objects scale similarly – neutron stars, black holes.

'The cosmology in Beta, reconstructed from what Lura has been able to tell us, is quite unlike our own. Well, you'd expect that.'

She conjured up a Virtual that looked to Coton like a false-colour sketch of a Solar System, with a dark, brooding sun at the centre, around which orbited bright pinprick 'planets', and around these in turn circled glowing clouds of crimson gas, speckled with sparks. A strange orrery, Coton thought. He saw how the light of the Virtual stars reflected from the sheen of the Marshal's electric-blue jacket.

Vala said, 'We don't think Beta has galaxies of the kind we have here. Primitive gas clouds would implode violently and fragment, and you would quickly end up with massive black holes and an undergrowth of miniature stars. So you get a different sort of clustering, different hierarchies.

'The centre of the system Lura sees is this mass they call the Core of Cores. We suspect this is an extremal black hole – a black hole of the largest possible mass.'

'I didn't know there was a limit,' said Sand.

'The larger a hole the more eagerly it consumes infalling matter, crushing it in the process. You reach a point where the resulting radiation blasts away any more infall. That limit's pretty high, at around fifty billion solar masses in our universe – a good fraction of a galaxy's mass. In universe Beta you'd expect to find many holes pushing at that limit. Here such a hole would span the Solar System, out to the comets. In Beta, an extremal hole is only a few hundred kilometres across. Lura is pretty far out, on the fringe of the gravity well.

'Star formation probably starts with interstellar birth clouds of the same sort of mass and density as here – like the Carina nebula. But instead of Sol-sized stars spaced a few light years apart, such a cloud will collapse into many more comet-mass stars, as close to each other as the planets in the Solar System. We think these are the "big-stars" Lura sees orbiting the Core of Cores.

'Such stars don't have planetary systems like ours. Instead you have these quite dense gas clouds – nebulae, Lura calls them – orbiting each star, and centred on their own smaller black holes.

'The nebulae are held together by gravity balanced by internal heat, generated by lesser stars *inside* the nebulae – the ones Lura sees falling through the air. We call them "flare stars". They seem to be mountain-mass splinters, but with stellar fusion going on in their cores. The flares form at the edge of a nebula and then fall inward, as you see. Whereas the big-stars and the Core are analogues of objects in our universe, scaled according to the gravity constant, the flare stars aren't like anything we have. Well, you'd expect some exotic objects.

'The nebulae themselves can be full of heavy elements. In Beta, stellar evolution proceeded fast, and churned the primordial hydrogen and helium through fusion processes much more rapidly than here. And the flare stars do more processing in turn. Marshal, those nebulae contain oxygen. You could breathe the air!'

Marshal Sand seemed unimpressed. 'Well, of course. Otherwise the crew of the *Constancy* could not have survived.'

'No indeed. They fell through Bolder's Ring into air they could breathe, and adapted, and survived, and spread through the nebula . . .

'Marshal, I believe that because of its ferociously strong gravity, Beta's cosmogony must be accelerated. If the initial Big Bang singularity was like ours, a great spewing of hot hydrogen and helium, gravity would have started to compete with the universal expansion much earlier. Massive stars and huge black holes must have formed quickly, and churned through the raw material of the interstellar medium. And the cosmos itself is ageing much more rapidly too. In Alpha the smallest stars, with a mass of perhaps a tenth of Sol – red dwarfs – are the longest-lived. They may last a hundred *trillion* years, perhaps ten thousand times longer than a medium mass star like Sol.'

'The photino birds may have something to say about that picture.'

'Oh, the photino birds seem to like red dwarfs . . . The point, Marshal, is that in universe Beta a Sol-mass star's lifetime would not span five billion years but a mere *five years*.'

Sand stared. 'It's barely believable.'

'Yes. But it's simply a matter of proportion. A star's lifetime scales inversely as the gravitational constant. And even the most parsimonious red dwarf would last only perhaps a million years – which is thus, I believe, roughly the span of Beta's stelliferous age.'

'A million years, and then the stars die,' the Marshal pondered. 'But Lura's people have already been in there about that expanse of time.'

'Quite. They were lucky, Marshal; their ancestors stumbled into Beta when that universe was very young.'

'You'd think people would know they didn't belong there,' Coton blurted. 'They wouldn't have to *remember* by repeating nursery rhymes.'

'How so?' Sand asked.

'Because they can't eat the native life, for one thing. Lura told me. And then there's evolution.' He glanced at Vala, uncertain, but she nodded encouragement. 'It took billions of years for complex life to evolve on Earth. But if universe Beta is only a million years old, there hasn't been enough time for humans to evolve.' Another thought struck him. 'Or the trees, or the whales. Where did *they* come from?'

Vala smiled. 'Good thinking, grandson! Of course you're right. I can only conclude that the whales and the trees and whatnot are refugees like the humans – not from our universe, but from others linked by wormholes to Beta, from universes Gamma and Delta and Epsilon! Beta is a particularly porous place, I suspect. Gravity has surely twisted it up on a cosmological scale, and torn holes in it everywhere . . . Perhaps it's no surprise that it was Beta that the *Constancy* crew fell into; in the greater Bulk of universes this sponge-like cosmos must be something of a sink. That's not to say Beta couldn't host native life of its own,' she mused. 'Fast-living creatures of exotic physics, perhaps, down in the highly stressed spacetime around those big black holes. Lura says there have been observations of something like that. But not biochemical like our own.'

'And still the castaways linger on,' Sand said. 'A minor, but remarkable, story of human endurance. Perhaps after all this time we should leave them be. Beta is, by now, their home . . . Ah, but it is dying.'

'I'm afraid so. They have surely had to flee before, within Beta – Lura has told us fragmentary tales of stars dying and nebulae becoming exhausted. But when the last stars go out there will be nowhere left to run.

'And things may get worse yet, and quite quickly. Unlike our universe, which seems destined to endless expansion, Beta, dominated by gravity, will collapse back to a Big Crunch. I don't know when this will be – we need better data and subtler modelling – but not long! Not compared to our own cosmological timescales.'

'So is it a coincidence that we have made contact with Lura just as her universe is failing?'

'No,' Vala said. 'Remember, *it was the Mole* that called us. A component of the starship. Despite its own "massive sensor dysfunction" it seems to have perceived the problems ahead.'

'And it sent a distress message *out of its own universe*? That seems quite a conceptual leap.'

'Actually it seems to have sent its messages inwards towards the Core of Cores. That's where local spacetime is most distorted, and the machine's message had the best chance of leaking out into the wider Bulk.' She coughed. 'There are more speculative possibilities. As I said there may be concentrations of complex matter there, around the Core of Cores. Maybe there is life there – even intelligence—'

Sand dismissed that. 'Idle guesswork. The point is this Mole did manage to get its message out, to be picked up by the alien thing in your grandson's head.'

Coton thought he felt that phantom ache deep in the core of his brain.

'The question now is how we proceed,' Vala said.

Sand frowned. 'Proceed to do what?'

'Why, to help them, of course. They are humans, Marshal Sand, whose ancestors became castaways following their duty!'

'Their "duty" was to a government that has long vanished, in a long-forgotten war—'

'Against the same enemy,' Vala said quietly.

The Marshal stared at her. Then she paced, impatient, one hand slapping her hip. 'All this is a . . . curiosity. I can see your motivation, Academician. You have spent your life trying to save other relics of dead wars, such as the Starfolk. But what, in the end, can you actually do for these people? *They* are in another universe – and *I* have other priorities. I'm under pressure to tidy up here—'

'"Tidy up"?'

'I'm aware of the cultural and historical sensitivities,' Sand said wearily. 'But the military priority is to fall back to the Orion-line Wall zone, before the pressure of the Scourge in this region becomes overwhelming. And at the Wall itself, where the demarcation lines are being drawn, there is already some trouble among the displaced, the refugees . . .' She took off her elaborate peaked cap and rubbed her stubbly hair. 'Yet I am not without compassion, Academician. And curiosity. You may continue with this, for now. But whatever you intend to do, get it done quickly.' And she placed her cap back on her head and walked out.

*

Vala sighed. She came to sit beside Coton. 'Well, we're going to have to get on with it – and so are Lura and her people.'

'Get on with what?'

Vala smiled and stroked his cheek. 'To retrace their steps through Bolder's Ring is out of the question . . . I suppose teleportation is a possibility. I'll have to look into it. Go poking around the museums again . . . Do you feel up to talking to the castaways some more? Whatever we do is going to depend on having some kind of anchor at their end. They need to get hold of more high technology, more relics of the ship. There must be *some*. Perhaps they can find this "Raft" Lura spoke of—'

He cut through the torrent of words. 'Grandmother, I don't understand. Are you going to save the people in Beta?'

She smiled. 'Of course I am. What else?' She stood up. 'I've a lot to do. You rest, and when you feel up to it try to contact Lura again.' She patted his shoulder and walked off across the floor of the Map Room.

Wild ideas whirled in his head.

9

As the shifts had worn away the whale riders hadn't disturbed Lura's lengthy conversations with her machine, and the eerie figures it seemed to speak for. Lura supposed they were kept back by superstition or fear – as she felt only a little less, she suspected. But the riders were becoming increasingly disturbed by the Mole's pronouncements. They went off towards the whale's vast inverted face, so they could talk away from their captives.

But Lura was confused too. In the course of his latest conversation, Coton had told them they needed to find the Raft. It was as if they had been told to chase a fantasy from a child's bedtime story!

Lura and Brother Pesten sat side by side, somewhere near the whale's midriff. They had been left unbound for a few shifts now, and Pesten had been given a coarse, ill-smelling blanket to cover his nakedness. They drank water from sacks made of the skin of sky wolves. The Mole sat on the slippery skin-floor between them, silent for now, its transparent 'eyes' gazing out at what they had learned to call universe Beta.

The whale itself appeared to be feeding. Lura could see a series of ill-defined lumps passing down the huge digestive tract that spanned its diameter, from face to anus, passing above their heads.

And Lura watched the whale riders. The effective gravity imparted by the whale's spin was weakest near its axis, and as Anka and Otho and the other half-dozen riders argued, they drifted in the air and spun around, clustering together under their mutual gravity and pushing each other away. They were like squabbling children, she thought.

In the shifts since they'd been taken she had seen something of how the riders lived. All she'd known of them before was their ferocity during raids. Now she had watched them eat, sleep, laugh, squabble, shit – they respected the whale, and kept their waste in containers that they dumped out through hull lesions. They lived naked, for the whale's body cavity was too hot for them to need clothes. Their life seemed shabby, featureless, unfulfilled between bouts of raiding one

Forest or another, and when they weren't attacking somebody else, it seemed, they'd fight each other. Otho, who seemed a deeper-thinking individual than she'd imagined, sometimes broke this up, but not always; maybe he liked to keep his riders combat-ready.

And they rutted, coupling randomly, in shadowed corners of the whale's body cavity. There seemed little tenderness in the sex. Lura wondered what became of their children.

Now Coton's mention of this 'Raft' had sent the whale riders into a spin.

Pesten said, 'I wonder if they regret taking us in the first place. We've brought them nothing but trouble.'

Lura murmured, 'Do you believe all it says? The Mole. About the other "everything", and all the people there—'

'Well, I have no idea *how* it is saying these things to us – how your friend Coton can use it to speak to us at all – but, given all that, I don't see why anyone would go to all that trouble to lie to us. And it does fit what we know of our history. *Humans don't belong here.*'

'A history you Brothers have been beating out of us for generations. You know, my uncle used to argue with my father. He used to say that we *know* mankind evolved here because our gods are here, living in the Core of Cores.'

He winked at her. 'That was a particularly good lie, wasn't it? Silenced a lot of doubters, such as your uncle . . .'

Thinking of her father and uncle reminded her how far she was from home. She glanced around, at the smoky sky that rotated grandly around the spinning carcass of the whale. 'I wonder if I'll ever see the Forest again.'

The Brother took her hand. 'You will. If only because the riders will have to go back there if they're to ransom me. I'll make sure you get off when I do—'

The blunt end of a spear slammed down between them, and they flinched away. Anka loomed over them. 'Making promises you can't keep, Brother, to add to a lifetime of lies?'

'Oh, leave them alone, Anka.' Otho and some of the others came towards them, moving with big low-gravity footsteps.

Anka ground her spear butt into the floor. 'Maybe we should truss them up again. What could your boyfriend Coton do about that, Lura? Oh, come on, Otho, enough of this. It's all just some kind of trick. A voice in a box!'

'It's more than that,' said one of the other riders – a woman who looked away from Lura and Pesten as she spoke. Most of the riders kept their distance from them, evidently spooked by the Mole. Even after so many shifts since her capture, Lura didn't know their names. The woman said now, 'If it's just some trick, *why would it tell us to go to the Raft*? No tree pilot or kernel-grubber has ever seen the Raft. It's just a story to them.'

Pesten frowned. 'Wait – no one from the Forest has ever seen the Raft. Are you saying *you've* seen the Raft for yourself?'

'*I* saw it,' Otho said. 'Long ago – as a kid.' He waved a hand vaguely. 'In a dead nebula, choked up, a few whale hops away from here.'

Lura tried to take this in. She really had always imagined the Raft was just another legend, a detail in the half-mythic saga of the Ship and its crew. 'So when Coton said we should go there – you could take us?'

Anka loomed again. 'What right have you got to make demands? What do you woodentops know about riders, and how we live?'

It all swirled inside Lura, her anger and fear, the strangeness of the words that had come out of the Mole – the extraordinary suggestion that the whole universe was dying. And on top of all that she had to deal with this ridiculous woman. She snapped back, 'Oh, we know all we need to know about you and your kind.'

Pesten murmured, 'Lura—'

'Enough, Brother! Let her kill us if she wants – it can't be worse than hearing her droning voice. While we work to feed the Core of Cores, *you* prey on us like rats, or fleas that bite the skin. That's all you are – rats and fleas.'

'Why, you—' Anka raised her hand. 'Otho, is she to speak of us like that?'

'Oh, shut *up*, Anka, and let me think,' Otho said, and he jammed his fists against his temples.

'Of course you're right, Lura,' Pesten murmured smoothly. 'The riders do prey on the Forest folk. And so they need us. But here's another unwelcome truth. We need them.'

'Rubbish.'

'It's true. When this nebula dies we'll have to abandon it for another, as we have many times before. The only way we know to do that is to ride the whales, for the whales can pass through the airless spaces between the nebulae, as we can't. *Then* we'll need the whale riders' skills, as we did before – and forgot!' He shook his head. 'Maybe it's always like this. Riders and Forest folk fighting out the generations, until it's time to move again, and they remember how to cooperate. What a depressing picture of humanity. But *we* don't forget – we Brothers. And I think you haven't forgotten either – have you, Otho?'

'Perhaps it will be different this time,' snarled Otho. 'Perhaps we'll leave you behind, to choke.'

'No, you won't. What will you eat? How will you live? And *who will take your babies*?'

Otho turned away, and Lura saw, at last, what became of the children of whale riders. This place, this violent arena, was no nursery, no place for children. They must drop them off in communities like the Forest – and they made up their numbers through abductions, from those same communities. No wonder they were so savage, she thought, with a stab of pity.

Pesten shifted so he was kneeling with his blanket around his shoulders, and he gazed at Otho, intent. 'And there's more. Think about what Coton has told us, about the end of the universe. *You must have seen it.* You must have travelled to the edge of the nebula, and maybe beyond. I know you riders take your whales between the star clouds, once or twice a generation – else you would forget how it's done, when it's needed. I think you have seen that Coton is right.'

'The stars are going out,' Otho said bitterly. 'The nebulae are all choked. You hardly ever see the yellow spark of a new star . . . Even in Atma's day it was different. Atma was boss before me. So he said before I killed him. It's true enough.'

'Coton is right,' Pesten repeated. 'And we have to do what he says. We have to go to the Raft – for in the end it's our only hope. And you could do it, couldn't you? Oh, come on,' he said, grinning. 'I've spent my life watching you people control these beasts – and envying you, if you want to know.'

Lura said, 'Pesten!'

'I wasn't always a dried-up old scholar, you know. And there is a certain romance about the whale riders.'

'You don't know what you're asking, Brother,' Otho said. 'You're talking about a dive deep into the nebula – to the very core, where we'll scoot around the black hole. It's dark and hot and thick down there. Half the whale's flesh burns off, and it shits away a chunk of its mass to drive itself out of the gravity well, and it doesn't care if we live or die in its gut or not. And then we'll have to plunge into another nebula, and do it all over again.'

Anka said, her anger nearly choking her, 'I can't believe I'm listening to this. Otho, you only brought these two in for a quick shag of *her*, and a fat ransom for *him*. And now it's all *this*.'

Pesten sat back on his heels. 'Well, I've said all I can. What's it to be, Otho? Steep yourself in blood and die with the rest of us – or live on, a hero?'

Otho growled, 'I'd shut up if I were you, Brother, before you go too far.' But he hesitated, his face twisted, and Lura could see Pesten's persuasion was working. At last he snapped, 'Let's do this, and get it over, and we can get back to what we're good at – riding and robbing. Start the singing, Anka.'

'You can't be serious.'

He held her gaze for long heartbeats. Lura wondered if Anka was deciding whether to challenge him, as he had once challenged Atma. Then she broke away.

And she began to sing, a wordless melody, and walked back towards the whale's face. One by one the others walked with her and joined in, repeating the melody in an overlapping round. By the time they had reached the inside-out face of the whale the song was eerie, discordant, but it pulsed with a compelling rhythm.

'Some say this is how the riders really control their whales,' the Brother said, fascinated. 'With song – not with goads. Once there were no riders, just hunters who learned to call the whales down from the sky. Some say the whales can read our minds . . .'

The riders gathered behind the whale's eyes, and sang on and on. Lura and the Brother could do nothing but sit and listen.

And the whale turned. Lura could feel the shifting acceleration, and the shuddering of its skin as the great flukes beat at the air.

10

Croq, a small, plump, confident man, was Vala's contact at the Palace of the Assimilation.

'Welcome to our Palace, Academician, Marshal! I regard myself as something of a scholar though I have no formal qualification, but I could hardly do my job without acquiring a little learning . . . Come, come, follow me.'

Coton, Vala, Sand and a single Coalition guard followed him into the grounds of the ruined complex. The Palace of the Assimilation had been built on a massive tetrahedral frame, as had many of mankind's greatest buildings. Though the frame survived, much of the facing, a kind of foam-concrete with a golden patina, had crumbled to leave huge gaps open to the sky, and where the weather had got in the internal partition walls and floors had rotted away. The ground floor was littered with chunks of debris and choked with weeds, and Coton could see people inhabiting lean-tos and shacks in the lee of the surviving walls. Some even had fires burning on the remnants of the polished floor. Vala, picking her way through the rubble, looked faintly embarrassed.

Croq had his own staff here, younger men and women in purple robes similar to his own, with weapons at their waists and antique-looking data slates under their arms. They nodded to Croq as he passed.

'You can see we have taken in our share of the dispossessed, just as the rest of the planet,' Croq said. 'Well, they do no harm here, for little has survived of the Palace's treasures above ground level. Let them stay, as long as they don't disturb the customers!' And he smiled, showing gappy teeth.

Marshal Sand strode impatiently, her head swathed in a Virtual bubble with update reports scrolling in the air. Coton was surprised to find Sand spending so much time on Vala's projects, which were surely peripheral to her main objectives, yet here she was. Her guard kept a heavy rifle cradled in his arms – or hers; it was impossible to tell the sex under the gleaming green body armour.

Coton, meanwhile, was fascinated by Croq. He was bald with a thick black beard, and his sweeping purple robe, ancient and much patched, was a kind of imitation of Vala's Academician robe – which was itself a homage to the learning of the past, especially the famous Commission for Historical Truth of the First Coalition. But Croq's purpose was not scholarship but selling. Coton thought he had seen his type in the markets of Centre, smiling, hustling, dealing. But those vendors of bread and second-hand shoes would have looked crude beside this man, who clearly had expensive wares to sell to a much more discerning set of customers.

They came to a small cylindrical chamber that stood directly under the pinnacle of the main tetrahedral frame, Coton saw, looking up. A couple of Croq's assistants waited here, weapons visible, evidently keeping the refugees out. Croq waved his party inside the chamber. They filed in, the door closed, and a single light globe lit up the space.

Coton heard the hum of ancient engines, felt a subtle acceleration. Sand grunted her annoyance as her Virtuals flickered.

'An elevator,' Vala murmured. 'Evidently.'

Croq said, 'Since the Palace was first built, whole civilisations have washed over it like breaking waves. I'm afraid that it's only in the deepest basements, tucked away in caches, hidden purposefully or simply lost, that you'll find much of value nowadays. Of course it gives you some idea of just *how much* was piled up here that there is still something left, even after all this time.'

Sand banged her gloved fist on the wall. 'And this still works.'

'Oh, yes. They built their infrastructure well, the ancients.'

Still the descent went on, smooth, its speed undetectable, and Coton, who in his short life had learned to be suspicious of elderly technology, wondered just how far they were falling. He tried to mask his gnawing anxiety.

At last the doors slid open, and Croq led them out into a long, sweeping corridor, illuminated by sparse light globes and curving in the far distance. Coton saw that the walls were shelved, and doors and side branches led off into more shadowy spaces. Croq let them pause as they passed shelves crowded with artefacts – gadgets, what looked like biological samples in specimen jars, even shimmering Virtuals. Coton stared at one beautiful image of another tetrahedral form with a densely structured surface that appeared to have been constructed around a star. He understood nothing of what he saw.

'It would take me a day to explain the provenance of any one of

these wonders,' Croq said smoothly. 'And of course the physical artefacts stored here are only a small percentage of the Palace's holdings;
far more is stored as data in the archives – what survives of them,
anyhow.'

'This is the fruit of the Assimilation,' Marshal Sand said. 'I studied
the period at military school. It was an age that has some similarities
with our modern times, this era of the Scourge – save then it was not
the Xeelee burning their way across the Galaxy, but humanity.'

Vala looked up at her. 'You're certainly a more complex character
than I once thought, Marshal. You're a soldier who sounds as if she
regrets the Assimilation.'

Sand shrugged. 'What's done is done. It would have been fascinating
to travel the Galaxy *before* humans consumed its diversity, however.'

'Do you believe in guilt, Marshal Sand? Do you believe that humanity is now being punished for our actions in the past? Whole religions
have been built upon the premise.'

'I know. Even in the military there are sects who worship the Xeelee
as cleansing gods. I'm not a Transcendent, Academician. I don't believe in the guilt of mankind – or in the possibility of the redemption
of the species, as they did. But I do believe that if you waste any more
time on analysing my personality—'

'Quite, quite,' Croq said nervously. 'Let's get to the point, shall we?'

He hurried them along a side corridor, and then into a room
equipped with modern-looking Virtuals and data desks. This room,
long and narrow, was dominated by two pieces of equipment, rather
like upright coffins, Coton thought, made of some featureless grey
material, and facing each other along the length of the floor. A couple
of assistants, young, bright-looking, but nervous and subservient,
huddled in the room's corners.

Croq watched his party keenly, constantly aware of shifting moods
and changing expressions. He really was a salesman, Coton thought.
'I can see you're impressed by the equipment we've assembled here.
We've worked hard to get this right for you, Academician, and I believe we've found exactly what you required.'

Vala grunted, and flicked one of the coffin-boxes with a dismissive
fingernail. 'This, I presume?'

'Academician, this is a teleport.'

Marshal Sand seemed intrigued, if unimpressed. She shut down her
Virtual displays and stalked around the coffin-boxes, pacing out the

distance between them. 'A teleport, eh? And dug up out of the past – what did I tell you, Academician? No doubt teleports of one kind or another have been invented over and over.'

'Indeed,' said Croq. 'And many alien variants were retrieved during the Assimilation.'

'But it's not a technology humans ever used much,' Vala said. 'Essentially you convert any object you're sending – even human beings – into a stream of data to be transmitted. But that stream can be blocked or corrupted or illicitly intercepted. And the process is always expensive, as usually you have to destroy the rest mass of the object you wish to send.'

Sand nodded. 'Because quantum information laws forbid the making of true replicas.'

Croq said, 'Nevertheless, Academician Vala, I'm convinced this is your solution. As long as you have a communications link of some kind to your parallel universe out in the Bulk, you can use it to send a teleport signal. In fact I found a variety of suitable technologies in the archives – but I chose this, as I thought there was a certain poetic logic to it.'

Sand arched an eyebrow. 'Poetic?'

'This is Silver Ghost technology! And you Adepts are crucial to this process, aren't you?' He stepped up to Coton and gazed into his eyes, as if they were windows into Coton's skull. 'You actually have Silver Ghost material growing inside your heads. Remarkable! As if you are Ghost-human hybrids.'

Vala looked furious. 'So you have known this of us all along.'

Coton felt like punching him.

But he said smoothly, 'Of course we have, madam. There are no secrets to be kept from archivists such as ourselves.'

Sand said, 'Get to the point, salesman. How does this work?'

And Croq described how the Silver Ghosts, notorious tinkerers at the fringe of physics, had meddled with the values of fundamental constants. 'An object's quantum wave function describes the probability of finding it at any particular location. But that function is given its scale by a number called the Planck constant. And if you increase the value of that constant, if only locally, then the probability of the object being found over *there* rather than *here* is increased. Then all you have to do is pluck the apple from the tree on which you wish to find it, so to speak: *there* rather than *here*. The engineering details are a little complex—'

Sand held up her hand. 'I don't *care* how the thing works. No more words. Show us.'

'If I may have a test object – perhaps your hat, Marshal?'

Sand's glare was incendiary.

Coton hastily slipped off his jacket. 'Here. Use this.'

Croq opened up one of the boxes. Featureless inside, it was easily large enough to accommodate a standing human. Carefully Croq folded the jacket and set it down on the floor of the box, and closed up the door. He nodded to his assistants, who murmured to each other and manipulated Virtual displays. Coton thought he heard the hum of some engine gathering its energies, and an ozone, electric smell in the air.

'It will take a few minutes to prepare . . .' Croq looked at Vala. 'This is a proof of concept. We will have to consider the specific details of your project. For instance, the senders in your universe Beta will need access to some kind of technology capable of quantum-level scanning.'

Vala nodded. 'The ship that stumbled into Beta was equipped with devices to fabricate food and air – even human skin for grafts. They were clearly capable of quantum-level manipulation. We're hoping that if the folk in Beta can find one of those machines, and if it's still working, we can download instructions to adjust its function to our purposes.'

'But then there's bandwidth. As I understand it the intercosmic signal is transmitted by a stream of gravitons and neutrinos. The greater the flux the faster and more reliable the transmission.'

'I'm thinking about that,' Vala said. 'We should set up a receiving station deep in the gravity well of the neutron star, where spacetime stress is greatest.'

'And whose ships will you use to do that?' Sand asked. 'Ours, I suppose?'

Vala waved that away. 'You will need access to the gravity well anyhow if we are to help you use the Starfolk. Our projects complement each other, Marshal.'

'And of course,' Croq said, 'you will also need to consider the capacity of the receiver.'

Coton was aware that the salesman was deliberately *not* looking at him. Vala said nothing. And Coton felt a deep dread. For, of course, that 'receiver' was embedded inside Coton's own head: indeed, it was part of him.

The machine's low humming continued, and the assistants fussed at their controls.

'Not much longer,' Croq said, soothing. 'Would you like to sit? Something to eat or drink? Of course, Marshal, there may be other facilities we could offer that might be of interest to you as you embark on separate projects—'

Marshal Sand looked down on him. 'Your manner doesn't impress me. You'd be surprised how often I come across people like you, salesman – petty and avaricious, grubbing for profit in the misery and ruin the Scourge brings, as humanity flees in a great wave.'

Croq laughed, and Coton grudgingly admired his defiance. 'What refreshing honesty! Well, I note your contempt, Marshal, but it will not prejudice me against accepting payments in the new Coalition scrip. You disapprove of me selling off bits of the past, do you? But look in the sky. *The Scourge is coming*, despite your schemes and your strutting and your rather magnificent uniform. So you see, Marshal, I may as well sell off our past, for we humans have no future – eh?' And he laughed again.

There was a soft chime. One of the assistants hurried to the second coffin-box, opened it, and drew out a jacket. This was unfolded and brought to Coton to inspect. It was undoubtedly his; it fitted when he put it on, and he recognised tears and other minor flaws. Yet it stank slightly of ozone, and was warm to the touch.

The teleport was ready. They were, it seemed, committed.

And now Vala and Sand, together, quite gently, began to tell Coton what they needed of him. Or, more specifically, the alien thing in his head.

11

The Raft was an oval shadow against dull crimson.

The whale plummeted blind, through dead air. Since crossing the void between the nebulae the animal had become a slender missile, its deflated flesh a smooth casing around its internal organs. Even the great eyes had closed. At times Lura had thought it was asleep, or dead, but it continued to respond to the handling of its master – Otho himself worked the goads. Now the whale's great flukes were beating at the air, and its body was counter-turning, so that the Raft rotated in her view as they approached, close enough now for Lura to see detail, how the light shone through rents in that great floor in the sky.

'Not long now,' said Pesten.

Otho snapped, 'Then hope we find what we came here for, and that it makes this jaunt worthwhile.' He hauled on his harness. The whale shuddered, and a deep bass groan filled its cavernous interior.

Pesten gave Lura a small smile. They had spoken of how Otho seemed to care for his whale more than he cared for his riders, or himself, and now he demonstrated that. He was a bandit, a killer and a rapist, yet he was a competent leader and capable of sentiment – complicated, like all humans.

As the whale spun closer, the Raft grew until it blocked out half the sky. In the light of a big-star somewhere beyond, it cast a diffusing shadow far down through the dusty air. Otho stopped the whale's spin, and let it drift in slowly for its final approach. Now, as they floated up towards the rim, the Raft foreshortened into an elliptical patchwork of battered deck plates. Lura could see the sooty scars of welding around the edges of the nearer plates, but as her eye tracked across the ceiling-like surface, the plates crowded with distance into a blur.

At last the whale rose up above the rim, and the upper surface of the Raft opened out below them, an enormous dish, full of complexity. The deck, which itself looked knife-thin, was studded with buildings, constructed of wood panels or metal and jumbled together like toys.

The surface was damaged everywhere, tears and holes ripped through it, and at the very heart of the Raft a long rectangular gash lay open like an unhealed wound. And on the farside rim tall machines hulked, silent guardians.

They were all silent before this tremendous unfolding spectacle.

Pesten murmured to Lura, 'Just remember it's worse for these whale riders than for us. They live in a world of animals, where nothing humans make is much bigger than those goads Otho is sticking into his poor beast's nerve stumps. *We* couldn't make anything like this, but it isn't so strange to us. Look, that floor is made of iron that probably came from some star kernel or other – although it looks to have a different texture towards the centre. It's big – what, a thousand paces across? – but it isn't *so* big, our Forest wouldn't be dwarfed. And this is *ours*, remember – made by our ancestors, and inhabited for generations, and only abandoned when this nebula ran out of air to breathe.'

The whale continued to rise up over the Raft. Otho looked back at Lura and Pesten. 'What now?'

Pesten said, 'Coton told us to look for something big, bigger than a human. And obvious.' He pointed. 'What about those structures on the far rim?'

Lura peered that way. 'They look like a row of broken teeth. But they're big enough, aren't they?' She drifted up to the whale's translucent skin. 'Mole—'

'*Massive sensor dysfunction!*'

'Shut up.' She held it up to the skin, with the small apertures facing out. 'Are those machines over there what you're looking for?'

The Mole hesitated, and not for the first time Lura wondered what strange parodies of thought went on inside its cool shell. Then: '*Confirmed.*'

'Let's get it done,' Otho grunted. He braced in the harness, and pressed the goads hard.

The whale's flukes beat, its collapsed skin rippled, and it groaned. Even Lura could sense the animal's unhappiness as it was forced to swim down towards the vast, strange surface. Apparently unconsciously the riders held each other's hands and murmured one of their strange, rhythmic, cyclical songs, trying to reassure the beast.

The Raft became a floor that fled beneath them. Pesten lay down on his belly, peering through translucent flesh at the panorama passing below, and Lura joined him, face down, her elbows tucked under her. As they moved in from the rim they passed over an area of big blocky structures, clean-edged. Lura made out cones set in the surface, evidently firmly anchored, some of which had cables trailing from their upper points. But whatever those cables had once been attached to was long gone.

'It's extraordinary,' Pesten said. He pointed excitedly. 'Look at that! See the way the buildings are tipped over, away from the centre? And those rows of terraces?'

She frowned. 'No, I don't see.'

'Well, think about the Raft's gravity – how the mass of this vast, thin dish would tug at you if you stood on it. At the edge, you'd feel as if you were being pulled towards the centre of mass, as you walked in it would feel as if you were standing on a tipped-up plate. But at the centre you'd be pulled straight down, as if that big plate was level. So they've built their houses here on a slant, to make it feel as if they are locally vertical. And the terraces, I suppose, are to stop you rolling all the way down to the centre if you fell over.'

She hadn't had a Brother's education, but she sensed the ingenuity of the design. It was somehow reassuring to think that the builders of the Raft really had been human, thinking about the needs of the people who would inhabit it.

As they headed to the centre they crossed a different zone, of smaller, more open buildings with doors and windows.

'Houses,' Pesten said. 'This is where people lived. Look at all those houses, stuck to the plate in rows . . .'

Lura said, 'Coton told me this is how people live in his universe. On surfaces, the surfaces of *planets*.' Another Coton-word. 'Not floating around in the air, as we do.'

'We're designed to live that way, after all. Walking around on the ground of planets, I mean.' Pesten slapped his thin thighs. 'That's why we have legs. But it's a long time since anybody lived *here*. And it doesn't look like they finished their time peacefully.'

He was right. Lura saw the evidence of fires, in burned-out buildings and scorched deck plates. And – 'Oh, Pesten, look.'

The bodies were human, one large, one small, huddled up on the floor, spooned together with the adult sheltering the child. They were still clothed, and scraps of skin clung to their bones, withered and dried.

Pesten reached out and took her hand. 'Long dead. Perhaps these were among the last – when there was nobody left to take care of the bodies.'

And, she thought grimly, in this lethal air there were not even any rats left to consume the flesh, or worms or bugs.

The whale groaned again, and shuddered under them.

Braced in his harness, Otho called, 'We're being drawn into the Raft's own gravity well. In the middle it's going to be a good fraction of a gravity, I guess, and she doesn't like it . . .'

Pesten, peering down, ignored him. 'We're approaching the centre of the Raft. It's different again here.'

These buildings were grander, Lura thought, bigger and more elaborate, with fancy colours and decorations, carved doorways and window frames.

'But if anything, the evidence of burning is even worse,' Pesten said. 'Maybe this is where the bosses lived. They'll have taken the blame when people got angry and frightened. And look at the floor, the texture. That's different too . . .'

Where the deck further out seemed to have been assembled from sheets of rusted iron, here the material shone, gleaming and rust-free, though it was still a patchwork, and in places was marked with a kind of decoration, markings of black and green on a white surface.

'Look, the plates curve,' Pesten said, growing excited. 'There, and there . . . And *that* plate looks like it's been beaten flat. I think this was once some curved surface that's been cut up and put back together to make this floor.'

'The hull of the Ship,' Lura breathed. 'The stories say it was a great cylinder. Is it possible? And those markings—'

'I think I recognise numbers,' the Brother said. 'Look – that's a four, I think, and that's part of a seven. But if the Ship's name is written here, it must be cut up and fragmented.'

And Lura, who could read nothing but the numbers pilots etched on their flying trees, could not have recognised the letters of the name anyhow.

Now they reached the very centre of the Raft, where a jagged hole perhaps a hundred paces long had been cut into the floor. Pesten said, 'It looks as if something was fixed here, and was just ripped out. But how, or why?' He sighed. 'There's so much we'll never know.'

Lura spotted another body. It was small and naked, its withered skin bare – it must have been another child. It was suspended in the centre of the hole, bobbing up and down through the plane of the Raft, held there, she supposed, by the great artefact's own gravity field.

To the whale riders, passing the rent in the deck marked the halfway point in this strange journey across the Raft. Encouraged, they sang louder, and Otho worked his goads.

Once past the centre, the whale crossed over the Raft's concentric zones again, the rich central area, the cruder living spaces beyond, the more functional outer rim. They saw more burning and destruction, and a few more bodies. But Lura saw no movement, nothing that looked fresh – no sign that anybody or anything had lived here for a very long time.

At last the whale hovered before one of the big structures at the very edge of the deck. The machine was an irregular block as tall as two humans. Outlets pierced its broad face, and on the far side a nozzle like a huge mouth strained outwards at the atmosphere of the nebula.

'Coton said it might be like this, remember,' Pesten said. 'He said the Raft must have had machines that drew in stuff from the air and turned it into food and water for the people. Doesn't that look right?'

Yes, Lura thought; it wasn't hard to imagine the machine taking giant breaths through those metal lips. On a whim she held up the Mole so it could see. 'Can you identify that?'

Without hesitation it called loudly, 'Supply Machine, Deck Seven, Sector Twelve, Model 4-X-7-B, *Integrality's Constancy of Purpose*. Report status!'

To Lura's astonishment a panel on the front of the Raft machine lit up, and she heard a voice, carried through the thick dead air, muffled by the whale's skin: '*Operational.*'

The riders quailed back in superstitious awe.

Otho looked back at Lura. 'Well, here we are. What now?'

Pesten said, 'Coton said we have to work on the machine. How can we get to it?'

Lura said, 'If we go outside—'

'You'll be dead in heartbeats,' Otho said. Lura saw a kind of resentment cloud his face. 'I'll have the whale swallow the machine. Then, when it's sealed up in her gut, we'll cut it out. This is going to hurt her. You'd better hope it's worth it, tree girl, because if it's not, I'll cut you. Come on, baby. It won't be so bad.'

He worked his goads, and the whale groaned and shuddered as its face was driven towards the strange old machine.

12

'We're in the Marshal's flitter, deep in the system of the neutron star, Lura. There isn't much to see. The neutron star is a dull ember, but its huge density twists space. Vala said that if you tried to measure pi by dividing the star's circumference by its diameter, you'd be out by about ten per cent. I'm not sure what that means . . . We've already done some close passes around the star. I thought I could feel the tides, and the hull groaned—'

'That's gravity, Coton!'

'Yes. Which shapes your world. It's all so strange. When I look at the neutron star I can't believe that there are people down there, inside it – or anyhow, Vala says, they *feel* like they're people, even though they are made of nuclear material and you could fit thousands of them on your thumbnail.

'But there's more, Lura. There is life *outside* the star too, in knots in the magnetic field, blobs of plasma with internal structure. You can barely see them with the naked eye, but they're very clear in Vala's instruments. They're yet another kind of Weaponised people. Nobody knows *why* they were spun out of magnetism. Vala says maybe they came here as a refuge. When we make our approaches they cluster close to the ship, and they send signals – a kind of screech, which Vala hasn't managed to decipher yet. They're trying to talk to us.'

'Can you help them?'

'I don't know. Not today.'

'And how are you, Coton? Are you sleeping well?'

'The gravity dreams are too vivid for that. Spacetime is stretched here, and my brain is bathed in gravitons and sterile neutrinos . . . It's better to stay awake, if I can. And when I do, I can hear you so clearly now.'

'Coton – are you afraid? After all, it's your head they're going to use, if I understand you, to save me. And then those who will follow me. The thing in your head, the only machine they have that's powerful enough to bring me across . . .'

'I try not to be afraid. I trust my grandmother.'

'If all this fails – or if you decide you don't want to do this after all, Coton, and I'll understand – it will still have been worth it. Even if we can't come home, at least you'll know our story.'

'Yes.'

'And we'll still be able to talk, won't we?'

'Until I grow out of my dreaming faculty – yes. I'll try as long as I can. Vala is waving at me. I think she wants me to rest.'

'We'll talk later. One way or another.'

'Yes. One way or another. Goodbye, Lura . . .'

13

Coton at last drifted to sleep.

Vala returned to the Marshal's cabin. Fold-out seats had been set up by the main observation window, and Sand sat there, cradling a cup of hot tea, Virtual status displays hovering around her head.

Behind a partition Sand's crew controlled the flitter with military competence. And in another cabin Croq the antiquarian was adjusting his ancient Ghost teleport equipment, complaining about the challenge of interfacing systems from technological traditions separated by hundreds of thousands of years. But in this lounge the atmosphere was calm.

Vala sat down with Sand and picked up her own cup – which, when it sensed her presence, began to fill up with tea, a minor miracle bequeathed by some long-dead engineer of the deep past.

Sand asked, 'Is the boy sleeping?'

'Badly. The dreams—'

'How sweet it is to hear their conversation,' Sand said. Vala had arranged a pickup so that Coton's sub-vocalising of Lura's speech could be heard. 'Boy chatting to girl, an eternal story. They aren't so far removed in age, are they, Academician? Maybe if this girl is successfully retrieved through your lashed-up teleport, they'll fall in love! How fitting that would be. If she isn't turned into some grotesque protoplasmic mass, or if a million years in Beta's super-gravity hasn't turned her kind into monsters. And if the process doesn't burn out *his* frontal lobe. Does Coton fully understand the risks for himself, by the way? I imagine not – I imagine you haven't fully informed him – for Coton might have refused, and then you might have had to face the inconvenience of *forcing* him to obey your will. That wouldn't fit your image of yourself at all, would it, Vala, as an Academician or a grandmother?'

Guilt swirled in Vala, under a crust of denial. But she had lived a long time and was in control of her emotions, she believed; and she clung to the principle that higher purposes sometimes required sacrifices. Yes, she thought. If she'd had to force her grandson into this, she would have done it. 'Does it give you pleasure to jab at me in this way, Marshal?'

'I am interested in people. I could hardly fulfil my role otherwise. And you are quite an extraordinary specimen, Academician. So much conflict! You seethe with ambition and resentment.'

'Resentment? I am a Weaponised, Marshal Sand. And I am highly educated. The more a Weaponised learns of her own past and the past of her kind, the more resentment deepens, I would say. A natural reaction.' She savoured her anger, as she savoured the tea's exotic flavour on her tongue. 'Why, we Weaponised don't need the Xeelee Scourge. We have you normals, and that's enough.'

'Oh, don't be ridiculous, Vala. *You* have hardly been persecuted, have you? You make an inappropriate martyr! And besides – what is "normal"? Humanity has been engaged in interstellar war for a million years. After such a history perhaps we are all Weaponised. It's just that with some of us it isn't so obvious—'

A faint alarm chimed, and Sand pointed to one of the Virtuals fluttering around her head. It expanded to show a schematic of the ship, with lenticular forms sweeping around it.

'The mag-field creatures again,' Vala said.

'Yes. They don't seem able to keep away. They beat against the hull like butterflies battering against a window.'

Vala wondered what this stern Marshal knew of butterflies. 'Military goals were rarely achieved with these projects, you know. The Weaponising. When you read the records of that period, you sometimes think the Integrality scientists created such beings simply because they *could* . . . And certainly little thought was given to those abandoned when the military projects were over.'

'How do we look to them, do you imagine, the mag-field butterflies?'

Vala shrugged. 'Cages of electromagnetic and molecular forces. Perhaps like themselves, but made of clumsy, dense stuff, rather than their own graceful plasma wisps. That's if they perceive such different creatures as ourselves as intelligent entities in the first place. It's interesting – there may be forms in universe Beta that don't exist here, that perhaps *we* would have trouble recognising as sentient, or even alive. Like the "beasts of gravitic chemistry" that supposedly swarm in accretion surfaces surrounding their great black holes . . .'

'All that complexity. And all implicit, I suppose, in the knotted-up strangeness that was the universe Beta Big Bang – as our own

323

existence was implicit in our own singularity.' Sand studied her own hand, and the Virtual displays' green and red light reflected in her clear eyes. 'How strange it all is.'

Vala realised she knew nothing of Sand's background. Did she have children of her own, for example? 'You are in a reflective mood today, Marshal. I'll admit that you are not the person I took you for, when we first met in this very flitter down on Delta Seven.'

'Well, there you are. How can we expect to make sense of the universe if we can't understand each other – eh, Academician?'

'I haven't wished to push the issue, for fear it would drive you off. But I'm not sure I understand *why*, in the end, you've diverted resources to support this project of mine. Unlike the Starfolk, I can't see that the Beta castaways will be of any use to you as a weapon.'

'I wouldn't be so sure.' Sand gestured, conjured another Virtual, and with a wave sent it spinning through the air to Vala. 'Here's a conceptual study on how we might use Beta itself as a source of gravitons, perhaps of gravity waves . . . After all, the ancient starbreaker weapon is essentially a gravity wave cannon. Could Beta work as a universal energy source for such weapons? Or, as you said yourself, Beta is a messy, porous spacetime. Perhaps it could be used as some kind of cosmic interchange, a wormhole junction. The Xeelee might use it that way already. Maybe we could even tap into the energies of Beta's Big Crunch, which is coming soon.'

Vala smiled. 'You would weaponise an entire cosmos? You think big, for a soldier.'

'We are fighting a big war.'

'But I don't buy any of that as a personal motive for attempting this rescue, of Lura and her people. What is it, Marshal? Humanitarianism?'

Sand shrugged, unperturbed. 'Call it that if you want. We are a species who once won a Galaxy. I believe that even now we should aspire to do more than simply retreat – that even as the darkness closes in, at least we can help each other.' She was looking steadily at Vala, with a hint of that cold humour in her eyes. 'And what about you, Academician? I hardly think *you're* here for reasons of warmth and kindness. Oh, it might have started out that way, when you first heard of the plight of these Beta castaways through the mouth of Coton. But it's gone beyond that now, hasn't it? The risk you're prepared to take with Coton has convinced me of that.

'You scientists are all the same. You don't want to make this transfer to save the castaways. *You want to do it because you think you can.* And the cost is irrelevant. Why, you're as bad as the Weaponeers of the Integrality, who made your ancestors and whom you affect to despise. You're nothing but a crucible of ambition. And into this crucible your own grandson, young and smiling, is to be thrust.'

Vala glared at her. But she was the first to turn away, her face hot. The Marshal laughed.

Another alarm sounded, a gentle chime.

Croq rapped on the door and opened it. 'The Beta castaways have powered up their booth. We're ready to attempt the transfer.'

Sand looked Vala in the eye, and the Academician knew what she was thinking. *Last chance to back out.*

Vala stood. 'Let's do this.'

14

The whale ploughed steadily towards the Core of Cores. The crew huddled behind the whale's face, singing their eerie repetitive chants.

Lura sat looking out through the whale's scarred hide. Her Mole was in her arms, and the great Supply Machine that the whale had literally bitten off from the perimeter of the Raft was lying on its back beside her. On its far side Brother Pesten sat, long since awed into silence.

The whale shuddered and shook, and let out another deep, agonised groan. Well might it groan, Lura thought, for it had been many shifts since Otho and his crew had forced it to leave the last rich nebula where it had been able to feed, and it had begun this appalling dive deep into the heart of the tremendous gravitational system in which they were all embedded. Otho had said his whale would never recover from this ordeal – and Lura sensed that he would never forgive *her* for that, whatever the outcome of this strange adventure.

Yet here they were, plunging into the Core of Cores, at the behest of a boy from another universe.

For some shifts the whale had ploughed through layers of the thick black debris cloud that surrounded the Core itself. But now things were changing. Sombre clouds parted before them, and the debris began to show depth and structure. A pale, pinkish light shone upwards, and veils of the stuff of shattered stars and nebulae arched over the whale, dwarfing it.

Then, abruptly, the clouds cleared, and they were sailing over the Core of Cores itself.

'By the Bones,' Pesten muttered, an ancient, un-Brother-like curse. '*It's like a planet.*'

The Core of Cores was a compact surface clustered about the massive black hole at its heart, a flattened sphere that would have taken hundreds of shifts to walk across – if you could have withstood the gravity. It was by far the largest organised object any of them had ever seen or heard of.

And it was indeed like the 'planets' Coton had described in his own universe, a planet rendered in shades of red and pink against charcoal grey and black. There were 'oceans' of some quasi-liquid material, thick and red as blood; they lapped at 'lands' that thrust above the general spherical surface. There were even small 'mountain ranges', like wrinkles in the skin of a soured fruit, and clouds like smoke that sped across the face of the seas. There was continual motion: huge waves crossed the seas, and the mountain sheets seemed to evolve endlessly, and the coasts of the strange continents writhed.

Pesten was ecstatic. He peered through the whale skin as if he wished he could climb through it. 'It is more like an Alpha world, as Coton described them, than anything we've seen before. More like Earth itself than anything we've ever seen! Perhaps it's the largest-scale structure to be found in Beta. Yet even this is much smaller than a trivial Alpha world.

'You understand that we're seeing a kind of shell containing the black hole itself. It represents a balance between the influx of material from the debris cloud, and the radiation from the accretion around the black hole itself. It is not as Coton described the environment of Alpha black holes; this has much more structure, and apparently a greater density. And it is held together by something else unique to Beta – gravitic chemistry!'

'You sound as if you're proud of it.'

'Well, why shouldn't I be? There is no spectacle like this in Alpha.'

'But it has nothing to do with us,' Lura murmured.

'Yes, yes . . . You have your Mole? We must send images of what we're seeing through to Alpha.'

The crew muttered. Lura saw that they were silhouetted against a new, paler glow, and they were pointing. Lura turned to see. At the centre of one of the strange continents was a grid of pink-white light, etched into the surface like a vast game board.

'Look,' Pesten breathed. 'Look!'

Ideas crowded into Lura's mind. 'Life,' she whispered.

'And intelligence. Two staggering discoveries in a single glance.'

'How is this possible?'

'Well, why should it not be so? Life feeds on sharp energy gradients, places where structure emerges out of chaos and organisation arises.'

Not for the first time Lura wondered how much of the ancient learning he repeated he really understood.

And now she saw more gridworks. Some covered whole continents, and lines of light arrowed around the globe, and embedded in the lattice Lura thought she saw individual structures: pyramids, tetra-hedrons and cubes.

'But we knew they were here,' she said. 'Didn't we, Brother? That was the whole point of our endless labour to shift the star kernels, and drop them into the Core of Cores. *These were our gods*, the inhabitants of the Core. And they rewarded us with oxygen, pumped out into the veil of nebulae . . .'

The Mole murmured, 'This is Coton, speaking for Academician Vala. She says she's surprised to find evidence of intelligence here, despite your beliefs. She thought you were just being superstitious about gods in the Core of Cores.'

Pesten flared. 'Primitive we may be compared to you – we have forgotten much in this hostile place – but we are not fools!'

'No, no . . . She apologises . . . That's not the point she was trying to make. She imagined the oxygen venting was unrelated to your kernel-dropping. Like praying for rain, she says. Now she's not so sure. However, she says it's unlikely that whatever intelligence res-ides here *needs* your lumps of iron. Look at the scale of this Core; think of the masses involved. She thinks that the intelligences of the Core most likely took the infall of your star kernels as a signal that life persisted in the clouds of nebulae surrounding the Core – chemical life, like yours. And as long as it did, the Core beings have tried to support you. As if your kernels were messages, cries for help hurled into the Core. You were right that there were mighty minds in the Core, protecting life in your cosmos. It's just that they weren't gods . . .'

Lura was stunned by these ideas.

Pesten said, 'To think of it – that creatures of this scale, and so different in every way, should take any notice of *us*.'

'Empathy seems to be universal,' said Coton, through the Mole. But Lura wasn't sure what that word meant. 'In the end, however, Vala says, this experiment in symbiosis will end. *Symbiosis*, grandmother, what does that mean? For the nebulae, all of them, are dying, as your stars go out.'

Lura knew this was true. But long after the trees and whales and sky-wolves were extinct, and all the stars and nebulae were dark, and the people were all gone, the gravitic entities would still swarm over their roiling black hole world. These creatures were the true denizens of this Beta cosmos; humans, soft, wet, dirty and flabby, were mere transient interlopers.

Of course when the 'Big Crunch' Coton had described came to this universe, even the gravitic gods of the Core of Cores would not survive.

There was a soft chime. Coton called through the Mole, 'The space-time stresses – the graviton flux—'

Pesten said, 'Just tell us!'

'My grandmother says we're ready to try the transfer.'

Lura quailed from the metal box that lay beside her.

The engineers in universe Alpha had found a way to modify the Raft Supply Machine.

They had had Pesten connect it to the Mole with bits of wire pulled out of the stumps of one machine and thrust into orifices in the other. This had been enough, it seemed, for information to be sent chattering from universe Alpha via the Mole into the Supply Machine.

And then, under instruction from Alpha, the Supply Machine had rebuilt itself. Lura had seen waves of sparking light pass through its carcass, and a ripple of tiny adjustments, like muscles flexing under skin. Coton had told her that the machine had smaller machines inside, most too small even to see, that were intended to repair minor flaws – as the body of a human or a tree could heal its own petty injuries. Now, via the Mole, the engineers had subverted these little mechanisms and had ordered them, not to fix the Supply Machine, but to turn it into something else entirely.

Of all the changes made, Lura had understood very few – but the most obvious had been the growth of a seam along the side of the Supply Machine's carcass, complete with thick metal hinges. Now Pesten and Otho got their fingers under the lip of this seam and lifted. The lid of the great box rose slowly, for it was very massive, but at last it flipped back and fell away. And in the interior you could clearly see a space hollowed out from the nest of components that had been crammed in there – a nest the size and shape of a human body.

Lura felt Pesten's hand slide into hers; his palm was clammy, as if he was more afraid than she was.

Otho glared at her. 'So you're going to climb into this thing, and the

Brother and I will close the lid on you, and some kind of little knives are going to come out and chop you up—'

'Not knives,' Pesten said.

'Then what? There won't be anything left of her. That's what they said.'

'It's been turned into a quantum-level scanner . . .' But Pesten fell silent.

Lura knew he understood little. It may as well be knives, she thought.

'You're afraid,' Otho said, watching her.

'Of course, I'm afraid,' she snapped. 'Wouldn't you be? But there will be somebody on the other side of this door who knows me, and will help me.'

'You really believe that?'

'If it was all fake, why would Coton and his people go to all this trouble?' She looked at him closely, the sharp, intelligent eyes, the brutalised features. 'You helped us get this far. You could have just killed us, as Anka always seemed to want you to do. But you didn't. You believe in what we're doing.'

'This machine's *old*. And now it's been fooled around with. Suppose it breaks down before the rest of us can get through?'

'So what are you saying? That you want to go first? If so, help yourself.'

His eyes narrowed. 'I'd rather be second, after I see it work, and I hear you call back through that Mole box.' He moved closer, and she could feel the gravitational tug of his body, still massive and powerful despite the rationing they had all endured during the whale's strange odyssey. 'Or, I'll tell you a little idea I dreamed up. Suppose I knocked you up, and *then* sent you through? If you made it, and even if nobody else got through, at least a little piece of me would survive in universe Alpha.'

Lura faced him. 'You try it and I'll rip your seed out of my body with my bare hands – in this universe or any other.'

He grinned. 'Just a thought, tree lady. Just don't make me regret letting you go.'

'It's time, it's time,' wheezed the Mole. 'Lura? This is Coton. Can you hear me? It's time . . .'

Regretfully she handed the Mole to Pesten. 'You'd better take this.'

Pesten cradled it. 'This little box has worked hard.'

'Yes. *Massive sensor dysfunction.* Do you think it's been suffering – cut up, and unable to do its job – for all this time, since the Ship crashed?'

'Maybe when you're gone, it can rest at last. I'll take care of it.'

'Oh, Pesten—' Something broke, and she threw herself at him, and they embraced. 'I'll see you in Alpha,' she said.

He pulled back. 'But will I still be *me*, after such a strange passage? Will you be you?' He drew back and eyed the Supply Machine, and Lura saw how terrified he was of it, for all sorts of deep reasons other than the obvious danger.

The Mole murmured, 'Lura, please . . .'

No more time. She jumped, lifted her legs, and let herself drift down into the body-shaped cavity, where she lay with arms at her side and legs out straight. Immediately, machine components bristled over her bare flesh.

Pesten loomed over her. 'How does it feel?'

'Like I'm lying on rough bark. Not so bad.'

'Lura, I—'

'Close the lid, Brother. It's all right.'

The lid descended. Pesten's face and Otho's, illuminated by the pinkish light of the Core of Cores, were the last she saw of universe Beta.

She was alone in the dark and silence.

Now the machine's components closed in on her from above and below and to either side, rough, scratching, some jabbing hard enough to hurt. She was uncomfortably reminded of Otho's jibe about knives. But she sensed a gathering energy, and she could smell a sharp electric scent, and the hairs on her skin stood on end.

Coton had tried to describe the process to her. This Supply Machine, designed to manufacture food and drink, was scanning her body, quantum function by quantum function. She understood little beyond the Alpha-language phrases, but she knew that before she saw the light again, the numbers that defined *her* would be stripped out and read off and sent through the space between the universes – and, in the end, lodged safely in the head of her friend. When she thought of that, and conjured up Coton's face as she imagined it, she relaxed and smiled . . .

Her awareness sparkled and subsided.

And she was beyond time and space. The great quantum functions that encompassed all the universes slid past her like stars streaming from the edge of an unseen nebula, and her eyes were filled with the grey light that shone beneath reality, the light against which all phenomena are shadows.

Time wore away, unmarked.

And then—

15

Marshal Sand stood before the coffin-box, set on end in the flitter cabin, which would serve as the terminal of the transfer. An armed guard stood by.

And Coton writhed on his couch, trying to scream around the gag in his mouth. His head was swathed in a silvery helmet, and the air sparkled with Virtual read-outs. Two crew members hovered over him, evidently anxious, and they tucked a med blanket over his slight body.

Vala stood back, helpless, trying not to tremble. 'How much longer, Croq?'

But Croq, studying Virtuals that scrolled and danced in the air before his face, had no answer.

'I wouldn't worry, Academician,' Sand said calmly. 'The alien thing in his head can be used for more transfers, even if this first experiment kills him.'

'Have some pity, Marshal—'

Now Croq gasped. 'It's working! But it shouldn't be. In the end the graviton flux just isn't sufficient. Or it wasn't. Something is *boosting* it, like an amplification. Otherwise we'd be losing the data, too much of it . . .'

'*Something*,' Sand said. 'What something?'

'I think I can guess,' Vala said. 'The gravitic creatures in the Core. What else could do this? They saw what we were trying to do. They helped! They amplified the flow—'

'Why should they?'

'As you may open a window to release a butterfly, Marshal. A trivial kindness.'

The door of the coffin-box creaked open, just a crack in the seal. There was a smell of smoke, Vala thought – of meat, of sweat. Croq gasped and stepped back.

But Sand held her ground. 'Well, let us see what it is they have been kind to.' She stepped forward, and her guard followed, weapon ready.

Sand faced the coffin-box, dug the fingers of one gloved hand into the seal of the opened door, and pulled it back.

A girl fell out.

The Marshal caught her in her uniformed arms. Limp, the girl wore a dirty tunic of what looked like plaited tree bark, and her grimy hair was tied back. She was too tall, too spindly, her stick-thin legs didn't look as if they would support her, Vala thought, and her head lolled on a skinny neck. It was a paradox that the creatures of a high-gravity universe spent most of their lives in effective freefall. And she had distinct webbing on her toes – an adaptation for swimming in the air?

Sand lowered her to the deck. But the girl struggled, and tried to raise her head, and spoke in a scratchy voice. *'Ma-seef senss-or dees-funx-eon . . .'*

Sand stared at her. 'By Bolder's ghost. I think she made a joke!'

The girl tried to speak again, and the flitter's Virtual suite translated for her. 'Coton? Where is he?'

Vala had not thought of her grandson since the coffin-box had cracked open. She whirled.

Coton lay immobile on his couch. The crew members worked on him frantically. But, one by one, the Virtual lights hovering around his head were turning red.

One by one, the human worlds fell dark before the Xeelee Scourge. At last, a million years after Poole's time, the streams of refugees became visible in the skies of Earth itself.

Since the time of Michael Poole there had been immortals among the ranks of mankind. The descendants of Jasoft Parz were among them. They emerged, lived, and sometimes died through accident or malice, in their own slow generations, hidden within humanity. They had been called many names. 'Ascendant' was one of the more acceptable. Yet they endured.

The Ascendants had come to believe that as long as Earth survived, mankind would survive.

And so they took steps to make that happen.

PERIANDRY'S QUEST
AD c.3.8 BILLION YEARS

The funerary procession drew up in the courtyard of the great House. Through a screen of bubbling clouds the blueshifted light of Old Earth's sky washed coldly down over the shuffling people, and the stars spun through their crisp two-minute cycles.

Peri took his place at the side of his older brother MacoFeri. His mother CuluAndry, supported by her two daughters, stood behind him. ButaFeri's hearse would be drawn by two tamed spindlings. Peri's father had been a big man in every sense, a fleshy, loud, corpulent man, and now his coffin was a great box whose weight made the axles of his hearse creak.

Despite his bulk, or perhaps because of it, Buta had always been an efficient man, and he had trained his wife, sons and daughters in similar habits of mind. So it was that the family was ready at the head of the cortege long before the procession's untidy body, assembled from other leading citizens of Foro, had gathered in place. Their coughs and grumbles in the chill semi-dark were a counterpoint to the steady wash of the river Foo, from which the town had taken its name, as it passed through its channelled banks across the Shelf.

'It's that buffoon of a mayor who's holding everybody up,' MacoFeri complained.

Culu's face closed up in distress. BoFeri, Peri's eldest sister, snapped, 'Hold your tongue, Maco. It's not the time.'

Maco snorted. 'I have better things to do than stand around waiting for a fat oaf like that – even today.' But he subsided.

As the family continued to wait in the cold, servants from the Attic moved silently among them, bearing trays of hot drinks and pastries. The servants were dressed in drab garments that seemed to blend into the muddy light, and they kept their faces averted; the servants tried to be invisible, as if their trays floated through the air by themselves.

The delay gave PeriAndry, seventeen years old, an unwelcome opportunity to sort through his confused emotions. This broad circular

339

plaza was the courtyard of ButaFeri's grand town House. The lesser lights of the town were scattered before the cliff face beneath which Foro nestled, dissipating in the enigmatic ruins at the town's edge. In this setting the House glowed like a jewel – but ButaFeri had always counselled humility. Foro had been a much prouder place before the last Formidable Caress, he said. The 'town' as it was presently constituted seemed to have been carved out of the remains of a palace, a single mighty building within a greater city. And once, ButaFeri would say, even this wide courtyard had been enclosed by a vast, vanished dome, and over this ancient floor, now crossed by the hooves of spindlings, the richer citizens of a more fortunate time had strolled in heated comfort. Buta had been a wise man, but he had shared such perspectives all too infrequently with his younger son.

Just at that moment, as PeriAndry's sense of loss was deepest, he first saw the girl.

Suddenly she was standing before him, offering him pastries baked in the shape of birds. This Attic girl was taller than most of her kind; that was the first thing that struck him. Though she wore as shapeless a garment as the others, where the cloth draped conveniently he made out the curve of her hips. She was slim; she must be no more than sixteen. Her face, turned respectfully away, was an oval, with prominent cheekbones under flawless skin. Her mouth was small, her lips full. Her colouring was dark, rather like his own family's – but this was a girl from the Attic, a place where time ran rapidly, and he wondered if her heart beat faster than his.

As his inspection continued she looked up, uncertain. Her eyes were a complex grey-blue. When she met his gaze she seemed startled, and looked away quickly.

BoFeri, his elder sister, hissed at him, 'Lethe, Peri, take a pastry or let her go. You're making an exhibition of us all.'

He came back to himself. Bo was right, of course; a funeral was no place to be ogling serving girls. Clumsily he grabbed at a pastry. The girl, released, hurried away, back to the Elevator that would return her to her Attic above the House.

MacoFeri had seen all this, of course. Buta's eldest son sneered, 'You really are a spindling's arse, Peri. She's an Attic girl. She'll burn out ten times as fast as you. She'll be an old woman before you've started shaving . . .'

Maco's taunting was particularly hard for Peri to take today. After the ceremony MacoFeri and BoFeri, as eldest son and daughter the co-heirs of ButaFeri's estate and the only recipients of his lineage name, would sit down and work out the disposition of Buta's wealth. While Bo had shown no great interest in this responsibility, Maco had made the most of his position. 'You love to lord it over me, don't you?' Peri said bitterly. 'Well, it won't last for ever, Maco, and then we'll see.'

Maco blew air through finely chiselled nostrils. 'Your pastry's going cold.' He turned away.

Peri broke open the little confection. A living bird, encased in the pastry, was released. As it fluttered up into faster time the beating of its wings became a blur, and it shot out of sight. Peri tried to eat a little of the pastry, but he wasn't hungry, and he was forced to cram the remnants of it into his pocket, to more glares from his siblings.

At last the cortege was ready. Even the Mayor of Foro, a wheezing man as large as ButaFeri, was in his place. Maco and Bo shouted out their father's name and began to pace out of the courtyard. The procession followed in rough order. The spindlings, goaded by their drivers, dipped their long necks and submitted to the labour of hauling the hearse; each animal's six iron-shod hooves clattered on the worn tiles.

The road they took traced the managed banks of the river Foo. Rutted and worn, it ran for no more than a kilometre from the little township at the base of the cliff and across the Shelf, and even at a respectfully funereal pace the walk would take less than half an hour. As they proceeded, the roar of falling water slowly gathered.

The Shelf was a plateau, narrow here but in places kilometres wide, that stretched into the mist to left and right as far as Peri could see. Behind the Shelf the land rose in cliffs and banks, up towards mistier heights lost in a blueshifted glare; and before it the ground fell away towards the Lowland. Foro was just one of a number of towns scattered along the Shelf, whose rich soil, irrigated by ancient canals, was dense with farms. Peri knew that representatives of towns several days' ride away had come to see off Buta today.

At last the hearse was drawn up to the very edge of the Shelf. The family took their places beside the carriage. Peri's mother had always had a fear of falling, and her daughters clustered around her to re-assure her. There was another delay as the priest tried to light her ceremonial torch in the damp air.

341

The edge was a sheer drop where, with a shuddering roar, the river erupted into a waterfall. Reddening as it fell, the water spread out into a great fan that dissipated into crimson mist long before it reached the remote plain far below. The Lowland itself, stretching to a redshifted horizon, was a mass of deep red, deeper than blood, the light of slow time. But here and there Peri saw flashes of a greater brilliance, a pooling of daylight. There was no sun in the sky of Old Earth; it was the glow of these evanescent ponds of pink-white light, each kilometres wide, reflecting from high, fast-moving clouds, which gave people day and night, and inspired their crops to grow.

Standing here amid this tremendous spectacle of water and light, Peri was suddenly exhilarated. He felt as if he was cupped in the palm of mighty but benevolent forces – forces that made his life and concerns seem trivial, and yet which cherished him even so. This perspective eased the pain of his father's loss.

At last the priest had her torch alight. With a murmuring of respectful words, she touched her fire to the faggots piled in the carriage around the coffin. Soon flame nuzzled at the box that confined ButaFeri.

Among the faggots were samples of Buta's papers – diaries, correspondence, other records – the bulk of which was being torched simultaneously at Buta's home. This erasure was the custom, and a comfort. In four thousand years, according to tradition, when the next Formidable Caress came and civilisation fell once more, everything would be lost anyhow – all painfully accumulated learning dissipated, all buildings reduced to ruin – and it was thought better to destroy these hard-won monuments now rather than leave them to the relentless workings of fate.

For long minutes family, priest and crowd watched the fire hopefully. They were waiting for an Effigy to appear, a glimpse of a miracle. The spindlings grazed, indifferent to human sentiment.

And in that difficult moment Peri saw the Attic girl again. Once more she moved through the crowd bearing a tray of steaming drinks, restoratives after the march from Foro. Now she was wearing a dress of some black material that clung languidly to her curves, and her dark hair was tied up so that the sweep of her neck was revealed. Peri couldn't take his eyes off her.

Maco nudged him. 'She's changed, hasn't she? It's – what, an hour? – since you last saw her. But in that time she's been to the Attic and back; perhaps half a day has passed for her. And perhaps it's not just her clothes she's changed.' He grinned and licked his lips. 'At that age these colts can grow rapidly, their little bodies flowing like hot metal. I should know. There was a girl I had, oh, three years ago – an old crone by now, no doubt – but—'

'Leave me alone, Maco.'

'I happen to know her name,' Maco whispered. 'Not that it's any concern of yours – not while our father burns in his box.'

Peri couldn't help but give him his petty victory. 'Tell me.'

'Lora. Much good it will do you.' Maco laughed and turned away.

There was a gasp from the crowd. A cloud of pale mist burst sound-lessly from the burning coffin. It hovered, tendrils and billows pulsing – and then, just for a heartbeat, it gathered itself into a form that was recognisably human, a misty shell with arms and legs, torso and head. It was ButaFeri, no doubt about that; his bulk, reproduced faithfully, was enough to confirm it.

Buta's widow was crying. 'He's smiling. Can you see? Oh, how won-derful . . .' It was a marvellous moment. Only perhaps one in ten were granted the visitation of an Effigy at death, and nobody doubted that ButaFeri was worthy of such an envoi.

The sketch of Buta lengthened, his neck stretching like a spindling's, becoming impossibly long. Then the distorted Effigy shot up into the blueshifted sky and arced down over the edge of the cliff, hurling itself after the misty water into the flickering crimson of the plain below. It was seeking its final lodging deep in the slow-beating heart of Old Earth, where, so it was believed, something of Buta would survive even the Formidable Caresses.

The watching dignitaries broke into applause, and, the tension released, the party began to break up. Peri did his best within the bounds of propriety to search for the girl Lora, but he didn't glimpse her again that day.

MacoFeri and BoFeri, brother and sister armed with the name of their dead father, went into conclave for two days. They emerged smiling, clearly having decided the fates of their siblings, their mother and the cast of servants in the House and its Attic. But they stayed silent, to PeriAndry's fury; they would take their own sweet time about re-vealing their decisions to those grateful recipients. Though his own uncertainty was thereby prolonged, there was nothing Peri could do about it.

Maco's first independent decision was to organise a wild spindling hunt. He proclaimed the hunt would be a final celebration of his father's life. Despite his own turmoil Peri could hardly refuse to take part.

A party of a dozen formed up on laden spindlings and galloped off along the Shelf. It was a young group; Maco, at twenty-three, was the oldest of them. He carried a bundle of goodwill letters to hand to the mayors of the towns they would pass through. And he prevailed upon his youngest sister KelaAndry to keep a chart of their travels; the world wasn't yet so well known that there wasn't more to be mapped.

As they rode, the roar of the Foo diminished behind them, and Foro was soon lost in the mist. It would likely take them many days before they even glimpsed their first wild spindling. After the Formidable Caress, it was said, the spindlings had come to graze in the very ruins of the ancient, abandoned towns, and to kill or capture them had been easy; but as the settlements at the foot of the cliff had grown again, the wild spindling herds were harder to find. But the journey itself was pleasant. The party settled into a comfortable monotony of riding, making camp, cooking, sleeping.

Of the dozen who travelled, five were men, seven women, and there was a good deal of badinage and flirting. As early as the second night, three couples had formed.

Peri had always been a vigorous, athletic type, and he had hoped that the hunt would take his mind off his own troubles. But he kept himself to himself, by day and by night.

It was not that he was inexperienced. Since the age of fifteen his father had programmed for him a series of liaisons with local girls. The first had been pretty, compliant, experienced, Buta's intention being to tutor his son and to build his confidence and prowess. After that had come brighter, tough-minded girls, and subtler pleasures followed as Peri learned to explore relationships with women who were his peers. Though he had formed some lasting friendships, nothing permanent had yet coalesced for him. That was only a matter of time, of course.

The trouble was that now it would not be his father selecting potential mates for him: no, from now on it would be his brother Maco, with perhaps a little advice from Bo. Maybe the women on this very trip had been invited with that in mind – although Peri was sure Maco would sample the wares before allowing his inferior brother anywhere near them.

All this, and the lingering uncertainty over his destiny, was hard to bear. He seemed to lose confidence. He had no desire to mix with the others, had nothing to add to their bantering conversations. And as he lay in his skin sleeping bag, with the warm presence of his favourite spindling close by, Peri found his thoughts returning to Lora.

He hadn't forgotten the surge of helpless longing he had felt as he studied her demure face, her carelessly glimpsed figure. She hadn't said a word to him, or he to her – and yet, though she was just a servant, he sensed there had been something between them, as elusive yet as real as an Effigy, there to be explored if only he had the chance. And how he longed for that chance!

In his obsessive imagining, Peri constructed a fantasy future in which he would seek out the girl. He would show her his life, perhaps fill the inevitable gaps in her learning – though not too quickly; he rather liked the idea of impressing her with his worldliness. They would grow together, but not through any seduction or displays of wealth: their Effigies would call to each other, as the saying had it. At last they would cement their love, and much of his detailed imagining centred on *that*.

After all that, well, he would present their liaison to his family as an accomplished fact. He would ride out their predictable objections, claim his inheritance, and begin his life with Lora . . . At that point things got a bit vague.

It was all impossible, of course. There were few hard and fast laws in Foro; the community was too young for that, but it went against all custom for a Shelf man to consort with an Attic servant, save for pure pleasure. But for Peri, a romance with Lora would bring none of the complication of his liaisons with women from the town, none of the unwelcome overlay of inheritance and familial alliance – and none of his brother's gleeful manipulation, for this would be Peri's own choice.

Elaborating this comforting fantasy made the days and nights of the hunt easier to bear. Or at least that was so before Maco, with almost preternatural acuity, figured out what Peri was thinking.

It was a bright morning, a couple of weeks after the hunters had set off. They were running down a small herd of wild spindlings, perhaps a score of the animals including foals. Here the Shelf was heavily water-carved, riddled with gullies and banks, and the southern cliffs were broken into round-shouldered hills. The party was galloping at top speed, their spare mounts galumphing after them, and they raised a curtain of dust that stretched across the Shelf.

The spindlings' six-legged running looked clumsy but was surprisingly effective, a mixture of a loping run with leaps forward powered by the back pair of legs. The spindlings' six-limbed body plan was unlike those of most of Old Earth's land animals, including humans. But then, so it was said, the spindlings' ancestors had not come from Old Earth. Unladen, the wild spindlings were naturally faster than their hunters' mounts, but, panicking, they would soon run themselves out.

Maco rode alongside Peri. He yelled across, 'So how's my little brother this morning?'

'What do you want, Maco?'

Maco was very like his father when he had been young – dark, handsome, forceful – but already he showed traces of Buta's corpulence in his fleshy jowls. 'We've been talking about you. You're keeping yourself to yourself, aren't you? Head full of dreams as usual – not that there's room in there for much else. The thing is, I think I know what you've been dreaming about. That serving girl: *Lora*. Your tongue has been hanging out ever since the funeral . . .' He clenched his fist and made obscene pumping motions. 'Is the thought of her keeping you warm in your sack?'

'You're disgusting,' Peri said.

'Oh, don't be a hypocrite. You know, you're a good hunter, Peri-Andry, but you've a lot to learn. I think you will learn, though. You're certainly going to have plenty of opportunity.'

Peri hauled on his reins to bring his spindling to a clattering halt. Maco, startled, rode on a few metres before pulling up and trotting back. Their two panting beasts dipped their long dusty heads and nuzzled each other.

Peri, furious now, said, 'If you're talking of my inheritance then tell me straight. I'm tired of your games.'

Maco laughed. 'You're not a very good sport, little brother.'

Peri clenched his fists. 'I'll drag you off that nag and show you what a good sport I am.'

Maco held up his hands. 'All right, all right. Your inheritance, then: in fact it's one reason I organised this hunt – to show you what I'm giving you.'

'What do you mean?'

Maco swept his arm wide. 'All the land you see here, across the width of the Shelf – all this belonged to Buta. Our father bought the land as a speculation from a landowner in Puul, the last town, half a day back. Right now it's got nothing much to offer but wild spindlings and scrub grass . . .'

'And this will be mine,' Peri said slowly.

'It's a good opportunity,' Maco said earnestly. 'There's plenty of water in the area. Some of these gullies may actually be irrigation channels, silted up and abandoned. Good farming land – perhaps not for our generation, but certainly our children. You could establish a House, set up an Attic in those hills. You could make your mark here, Peri.'

'This is a dismal place. My life will be hauling rocks and breaking dirt. And we're fourteen days' ride from home.'

'*This* will be your home,' Maco said. As he spoke of Peri's inheritance, Maco had seemed to grow into his role, sounding masterful, even wise. But now a brother's taunting tone returned, sly, digging under Peri's skin. 'Perhaps you could bring your little serving girl. She can make you pastries all day and let you hump her all night . . .'

Peri blurted out, 'It is only custom that keeps me from her.'

Maco let his jaw drop. 'Hey – you aren't serious about this foal, are you?'

'Why should I not be?'

Maco said harshly, 'Kid, she lives in the Attic. Up there, for every day that passes for you, ten or twelve pass for her. Already months have gone by for her . . . I know from experience: those Attic girls are sweet but they turn to dust in your hands, until you can't bear to look at them. Already your Lora must be ageing, that firm body sagging . . .'

If it had gone on a minute longer Peri might have lost control, even struck his brother, and the consequences would have been grave. But there were cries from across the plain. Peri saw that the party had backed the family of spindlings into a dry gully. Grateful for an excuse to get away, Peri spurred his mount into motion.

The spindlings, cornered, clustered together. There were more than a dozen adults, perhaps half as many colts. They seemed helpless as the hunters closed their circle; old and young, in their panic, they puked lumps of faeces from their mouths in the spindlings' unique manner.

But then four of the adults craned their necks high in the air, and their heads, three metres above their bodies, turned rapidly. With a whinny the four broke together, clattering up the gully's dusty wall. The movement was so sudden and coordinated they cut through the hunters' line and escaped.

The spindlings' long necks were an evolutionary response. On Old Earth, time passed more rapidly the higher you went, a few hundredths for each metre. The spindlings were not native to Old Earth, but they had been here long enough for natural selection to work. That selection had favoured tall animals: with their heads held high, the longer-necked were able to think just a little faster and, over time, that margin of hundredths offered a survival advantage. Now these accelerated adults had abandoned the young, old and feeble, but they would live to breed again.

The young hunters didn't care about evolutionary strategies. The aged adults made easy meat, and the captured youngsters could be broken and tamed. The hunters closed in, stabbing spears and ropes at the ready. Already they sang of the feast they would enjoy tonight.

But PeriAndry did not sing. He had made up his mind. Before the night came he would leave the party. Perhaps this desolate stretch of remote scrubland was his destiny, but he was determined to explore his dreams first – and to achieve that he had to return home.

It took Peri just ten days to ride back to Foro. Each day he drove on as long as he could, until exhaustion overtook him or his mounts.

When he got home he spoke to his mother briefly, only to reassure her of the safety of the rest of the hunting party, then retired to his room for the night.

His sister BoFeri insisted on seeing him, though, and she briskly extracted the truth of what he intended.

'Listen to me,' she said. 'We're different stock, we folk of the Shelf, from the brutes of the Attic, and similar lofty slums. Time moves at a stately pace here – and that means it has had less opportunity to work on us.' She prodded his chest. '*We* are the ones who are truest to our past – we are the closest to the original stock of Old Earth. The Attic folk have been warped, mutated by too much time. Think about it – those rattling hearts, the flickering of their purposeless generations! The Attic folk aren't human as we are. Not even the pretty ones like Lora. Good for tupping, yes, but nothing more . . .'

'I don't care what you say, Bo, or Maco.'

Her face was a mixture of his mother's kindness and Maco's hard mockery. 'It is adolescent to have crushes on Attic serving girls. You are evading your responsibilities, Peri; you are escaping into fantasy. You are so immature!'

'Then let me grow up in my own way.'

'You don't know what you will find up there,' she said, more enigmatically. 'I'm afraid you will be hurt.'

But he turned away, and would not respond further.

He longed to sleep, but could not. He didn't know what the next day would bring. None of his family, to his knowledge, had ever climbed the cliff before, but that was what he must do. He spent the night in a fever of anticipation, clutching at shards of the elaborate fantasy he had inflated, which Maco had so easily seen and punctured.

In the morning, with the first light, he set out in search of Lora – if not yet his lover, then the recipient of his dreams.

There were two ways up the cliff: the Elevator, and the carved stairways. The Elevator was a wooden box suspended from a mighty arrangement of ropes and pulleys, hauled up a near-vertical groove in the cliff face by a wheel system at the top. This mechanism was used to bring down the servants and the food, clean clothes and everything else the Attic folk prepared for the people of the House; and it carried up the dole of bread and meat that kept the Attic folk alive.

The servants who handled the Elevator were stocky, powerful men, their faces greasy with the animal fat they applied to their wooden pulleys and their rope. When they realised what Peri intended they were startled and hostile. This dismayed Peri; he had anticipated resistance from his family, but somehow he hadn't considered the reaction of the Attic dwellers, though he had heard that among them there was a taboo about folk from the House visiting their aerial village – not that anybody had wanted to for a long time, it seemed.

But anyhow, he had already decided to take the stairs. He imagined the simple exertion would calm him. Ignoring the handlers, without hesitation he placed his foot on the first step and began to climb, counting as he went. 'One, two, three . . .'

These linked staircases, zigzagging off into the blue-tinged mist over his head, had been carved out of the face of the cliff itself; they were themselves a monumental piece of stonework. But the steps were very ancient and worn hollow by the passage of countless feet. The first change of direction came at fifty steps, as the staircase ducked beneath a protruding granite bluff. 'Fifty-four, fifty-five, fifty-six . . .'

The staircase was not excessively steep, but each step was tall. By the time he had reached a hundred and fifty steps he was out of breath, and he paused. He had already climbed above Foro. The little town, unfamiliar from this angle, was tinged by a pinkish redshift mist. He could see people coming and going, a team of spindlings hauling a cart across the courtyard before his House. He imagined he could already see the world below moving subtly slower, as if people and animals swam through some heavy, gelatinous fluid. Perhaps it wasn't the simple physical effort of these steps that tired him out, he mused, but the labour of hauling himself from slow time to fast, up into a new realm where his heart clattered like a bird's.

But he could see much more than the town. The Shelf on which he had spent his whole life seemed thin and shallow, a mere ledge on a greater terraced wall that stretched up from the Lowland to far above his head. And on the Lowland plain those pools of daylight, kilometres wide, came and went. The light seemed to leap from one transient pool to another, so that clusters and strings of them would flare and glow together. It was like watching lightning spark between storm clouds. There were rhythms to the sparkings, though they were unfathomable to Peri's casual glance, compound waves of bright and dark that chased like dreams across the cortex of a planetary mind. These waves gave Old Earth not just its sequence of day and night, but even a kind of seasonality.

He continued his climb. 'One hundred and seventy-one, one hundred and seventy-two . . .'

He imagined what he would say to Lora. Gasping a little, he even rehearsed small snippets of speech. 'Once – or so it is said – all of Old Earth enjoyed the same flow of time, no matter how high you climbed. Some disaster has disordered things. Or perhaps our stratified time was given to us long ago for a purpose. What do you think?' Of course his quest was foolish. He didn't even know this girl. Even if he found her, could he really love her? And would his family ever allow him to attain even a fragment of his dreams? But if he didn't try he could only imagine her, up here in the Attic, ageing so terribly fast, until after just a few years he could be sure she would be dead, and lost for ever. 'Ah, but the origin of things hardly matters. Isn't it wonderful to know that the slow rivers of the Lowlands will still flow sluggishly long after we are dead, and that in the wheeling sky above worlds shiver and die with every breath you take?' And so on.

At the Shelf's lip, where his father's pyre still smouldered, he saw the Foo waterfall tumble into space, spreading into a crimson fan as it fell. Buta had once tried to explain to him *why* the water should spread out instead of simply falling straight down. The water, trying to force its way into the plain's glutinous deep time, was pushed out of the way by the continual tumble from behind, and so the fan formed. It was the way of things, Buta had said. The stratification of time was the key to everything on Old Earth, from the simple fall of water to the breaking of human hearts.

At last the staircase gave onto a rocky ledge. He rested, bent forward, hands on his knees, panting hard. He had counted nine hundred steps; he had surely climbed more than two hundred metres up from the Shelf. He straightened up and inspected his surroundings.

There was a kind of village here, a jumble of crude buildings of piled stone and wood. So narrow was the available strip of land that some of these dwellings, or store-rooms or manufactories, had been built into crevices in the cliff itself, connected by ladders and short staircases. This was the Attic, then, the unregarded home and workplace of the generations of servants who served the House of Feri.

He walked along the Attic's single muddy street. It was a grim, silent place. There were a few people about – some adults trudging wearily between the rough shanties, a couple of kids who watched him wide-eyed, fingers picking at noses or navels. Everybody else was at work, it seemed. If the children were at least curious, the adults were no friendlier than the Elevator workers. But there was something lacking in their stares, he thought: they were sullen rather than defiant.

At the head of the Elevator the pale necks of tethered spindlings rose like flowers above weeds. They were here to turn the wheel that hauled the Elevator cage up and down. One weary animal eyed him; none of its time-enhanced smartness was any use to it here.

Near some of the huts cooking smells assailed him. Though it was only morning, the servants must be working on courses for that evening's dinner. The hour that separated two courses on the ground corresponded to no less than ten hours here, time enough to produce dishes of almost magical perfection, regardless of the unpromising conditions of these kitchens.

A woman emerged from a doorway, wiping a cauldron with a filthy rag. She glared at Peri. She was short, squat, with arms and hands made powerful by a lifetime's labour, and her tunic was a colourless rag. He had no idea how old she was: at least fifty, judging from the leathery crumples of her face. But her eyes were a startling grey-blue – startling for they were beautiful despite their setting, and startling for their familiarity.

He stood before her, hands open. He said, 'Please—'

'You don't belong in blueshift.'

'I have to find somebody.'

'Go back to the red, you fool.'

'Lora,' he said. He drew himself up and tried to inject some command into his voice. 'A girl, about sixteen. Do you know her?' He fumbled in his pocket for money. 'Look, I'll make it worth your while.'

The woman considered his handful of coins. She pinched one nostril and blew a gout of snot into the mud at his feet. But, ignoring the coins, wiping her hands on her filthy smock, she turned and led him further into the little settlement.

They came to the doorway of one more unremarkable shack. He heard singing, a high, soft lilt. The song seemed familiar. His breath caught in his throat at its beauty, and, unbidden, fragments of his elaborate fantasy came back to him.

He stepped to the doorway and paused, letting his eyes adapt to the gloom. The hut's single room contained a couple of sleeping pallets, a hole in the ground for a privy, a surface for preparing food. The place was hot; a fire burned in a stone-lined grate.

A woman stood in one shadowed corner. She was ironing a shirt, he saw, shoving at tough creases with a flat-iron; more irons were suspended over the fire. The work was obviously hard, physical. The woman stopped singing when he came in, but she kept labouring at the iron. Her eyes, when they met his, were unmistakable, unforgettable: a subtle grey-blue.

For a moment, watching her, he couldn't speak, so complex and intense were his emotions.

That could be my shirt she's ironing: that was his first thought. All his life he had been used to having his soiled clothes taken and returned as soon as he wanted, washed and folded, ironed and scented. But here was the cost, he saw now, a woman labouring for ten hours for every hour lived out by the slow-moving aristocrats below, burning up her life for his comfort. And if he lived as long as his father, he might see out *ten generations* of such ephemeral servants before he died, he realised with a shock: perhaps even more, for he could not believe that people lived terribly long here.

But she was still beautiful, he saw with relief. A year had passed for her in the month since he had seen her last, and that year showed in her; the clean profile of a woman was emerging from the softness of youth. But her face retained that quality of sculpted calm he had so prized on first glimpsing it. Now, though, there was none of the delicious startle he had seen when he had first caught her eye; in her expression he saw nothing but suspicion.

He stepped into the hut. 'Lora – I know your name, but you don't know mine . . . Do you remember me? I saw you at my father's funeral – you served me pastries – I thought then, though we didn't speak, that something deeper than words passed between us . . . Ah, I babble.' So he did, all his carefully prepared speeches having flown from his head. He stammered, 'Please – I've come to find you.'

Something stirred on one of the beds: a rustling of blankets, a sleepy gurgle. It was a baby, he realised dimly, as if his brain was working at the sluggish pace of the ground. Lora carefully set down her iron, walked to the bed and picked up the child. No wonder her song had seemed familiar: it was a lullaby.

She had a baby. Already his dreams of her purity were shattered. The child was only a few months old. In the year of her life that he had already lost, she must have conceived, come to term, delivered her child. But the conception must have happened soon after the funeral . . .

Or at the funeral itself.

She held out the child to him. 'Your brother's,' she said. They were the first words she had ever spoken to him.

He recoiled. Without thinking about it he stumbled out of the hut. For a moment he was disoriented, uncertain which way he had come. The dreadful facts slowly worked into his awareness. *Maco*: had he really wanted her – or had he taken her simply because he could, because he could steal her from his romantic fool of a younger brother?

The old woman was here, the woman with Lora's eyes – her mother, he realised suddenly. 'You mustn't be here,' she growled. 'You'll bring harm.'

In his befuddled state, this was difficult to decode. 'Look, I'm a human being as you are. You've no reason to be frightened of me . . . This is just superstition.' But perhaps that superstition was useful for the House folk to maintain, if it kept these labouring servants trapped in their Attic. And this mother's anger was surely motivated by more than a mere taboo. He didn't understand anything, he realised with dismay.

The woman grabbed his arm and began to drag him away. Still dazed, his emotions wracked, he allowed himself to be led through the mud. There seemed to be more people about now. They all glared at him. He had the odd idea that the only thing that kept them from harming him was that it hadn't occurred to them.

He reached the Elevator. The boxy cage was laden with cereals, fruit, platters of cold meat, pressed tablecloths. It was the stuff of a breakfast, he thought dully; no matter how much time had elapsed up here, on the ground the House had yet to wake up. He took his place in the cage and waited for the descent to begin, with as much dignity as he could muster.

'. . . And you can go too, you with your red-tinged bastard!'

He turned. The scowling woman had dragged Lora out of her hut and had hauled her by main force to the Elevator. For a second Lora resisted; holding her child, she met Peri's eyes. Perhaps if he had acted then, perhaps if he had found the right words, he could have saved her from this dreadful rejection. But there was nothing inside him, nothing left of the foolish dream he had constructed around this stranger. Shamed, he looked away. With a final shove the hard-faced woman deposited Lora inside the cage.

As they waited for the captive spindlings to start marching in their pen, Peri and Lora avoided each other's gaze, as if the other didn't even exist.

The Elevator descended. Peri imagined slow time flowing through him once more, dulling his wits. His mood became sour, claustrophobic, resentful. But even as he cowered within himself, he reflected how wrong BoFeri had been. These Attic folk couldn't be so different from the people of the Shelf after all, not if a son of the House could sire a baby by an Attic woman.

At last the Elevator cage thumped hard against the ground. The heaps of cold meat and tablecloths slumped and shifted.

Peri threw open the gate, but it was Lora who pushed out of the cage first. She ran from the Elevator, away from the House, and made for the cobbled road that led to Buta's pyre by the edge of the Shelf. Peri, moved by shame, wanted nothing more to do with her. But he followed.

At the edge of the Shelf he came on his eldest sister BoFeri. She was feeding more papers into the pyre, kept smouldering a month after the funeral. This was a morning job; again he was reminded that for all the time he had spent in the Attic, here on the Shelf it was still early in the day.

The girl Lora was only a few metres away. Clutching her baby, she stood right on the edge of the Shelf and peered down at the waterfall as it poured into the red mist below. The wind pushed back her hair, and her beautiful face glistened with spray.

Bo eyed Peri. 'So you went up into the Attic.' She had to shout over the roar of the Foo. 'And I suppose that's the girl Maco tupped so brazenly at Buta's funeral.'

Peri felt as if his world was spinning off its axis. 'You knew about that? Was I the only one who didn't see?'

Bo laughed, not unkindly. 'Perhaps you were the one who least wanted to see. I said you would be hurt if you went up there.'

'Do you think she's going to jump?'

'Of course.' Bo seemed quite unconcerned.

'It's my fault she's standing there. If I hadn't gone up, they might have let her be. I have to stop her.'

'No.' Bo held his arm. 'She has no place in the Attic now. And what will she do here, with her half-breed runt? No, it's best for all of us that it ends here. And besides, she believes she has hope.'

It was a lot to take in. 'Best for all of us? How? And hope? Hope of what?'

'*Look down*, Peri. The Lowland is deep beneath us here, for the waterfall has worn a great pit. Lora believes that if she hurls herself down, she and her baby will sink deeper and deeper into slow time. She won't even reach the bottom of the pit. Her heart will stop beating, and she and her baby will be preserved for ever, like flies in amber. There have been jumpers before, you know. No doubt they are there still, arms flung out, their last despairing thoughts frozen into their brains, trapped in space and time – as dead as if they had slit their throats. Let her join that absurd flock.'

Lora still hesitated at the edge, and Peri wondered if she was listening to this conversation. 'And how is her death supposed to benefit us?'

BoFeri sighed. 'You have to think in the long term, Peri. Maco and I enjoyed long conversations with Buta; our father was a deep thinker, you know ... Have you never thought how vulnerable we are? The

Attic folk live ten times as fast as we do. If they got it into their heads to defy us, they could surround us, manufacture weapons, bombard us with rocks – destroy us before we even knew what was happening. And yet that obvious revolution fails to occur. Why? Because, generation by generation, we siphon off the rebels: the defiant ones, the leaders. We allow them to destroy themselves on the points of our swords, on our guillotines or scaffolds – or simply by hurling themselves into oblivion.'

Again Peri had the sense that Lora was listening to all this. 'So each generation we cull the smart ones. We are selectively breeding our servants.'

'It's simple husbandry,' Bo said. 'Remember, ten of their generations pass for each one of ours . . .' She studied him, her face, a broader feminine version of his own, filled with an exasperated kindness. 'You're thinking this is inhuman. But it isn't – not if you look at it from the correct point of view. While the Attic folk waste their fluttering lives above, they buy us the leisure we need to think, to develop, to invent – and to make the world a better place for those who will follow us, who will build a greater civilisation than we can imagine, before the next Caress comes to erase it all again.

'My poor baby brother, you have too much romance in your soul for this world! You'll learn, as I've had to. One day things will change for the better. But not yet, not yet.'

Lora was watching the two of them. Deliberately she stepped back from the edge of the Shelf and approached them. 'You think blueshift folk are fools.'

Bo seemed shocked to silence by Lora's boldness. Even now, Peri was entranced by the blaze of light in the girl's face, the liquid quality of her voice.

'Addled by taboo, that's what you think. But *you* can't see what's in front of your nose. Look at me. Look at my colouring, my hair, my height.' Her pale eyes blazed. 'Three of your seasons ago my mother was as I am now. MacoFeri took what he wanted from her. He left her to grow old, while he stayed young – but he left her *me*.'

For Peri the world seemed to swivel about her suddenly familiar face. 'You're Maco's daughter? *You're my niece?*'

'And,' she went on doggedly, 'despite our shared blood, now MacoFeri has taken what he wanted of me in turn.'

Peri clenched his fists. 'His own daughter – I will kill him.'

Bo murmured, 'It's only the Attic. It doesn't matter what we do

356

up there. Perhaps it's better Maco has such an outlet for his strange lusts . . .'

Lora clutched her baby. 'You think we are too stupid to hate. But we do. We hate. Perhaps things will change sooner than you think.' She wiped the mist from her baby's face, and walked away from the cliff.

Around her, the flickering light of day strengthened.

CLIMBING THE BLUE
AD c.4 BILLION YEARS

'Everything about our world is *made*,' said the Natural Philosopher. 'Made by intelligence, perhaps even built by human hands! Tonight I will prove it to you – prove it, at least, to those with minds flexible enough to understand . . .'

To Celi, to any Foron, such thoughts were radical, shocking. But Celi was electrified.

Celi had only taken Qaia to the lecture that night because he had heard rumours that the Philosopher was going to cut up a body. A *human* body, sliced apart in Foro's own town hall! It was a sight no self-respecting sixteen-year-old could miss.

Celi's father, Sool, had given his permission in his usual absent way. After all, he was going too. But his mother had seen right through him, as always. Pili was kneading bread, her powerful forearms coated in flour. 'You're going because you think it will be some kind of circus. Blood and bone and guts.'

Immersed in rich kitchen smells, Celi squirmed, ashamed. 'Mother, it's not like that—'

'She's a bad influence, you know.'

'Who?'

'Qaia. Her Effigy has yours by the throat, doesn't it? And she has you climbing the blue at a snap of her fingers.'

Climbing the blue. On Old Earth, time was layered: the higher you climbed, up towards the blueshifted sky, the faster time passed. So, said the more serious citizens of Foro, if you burned up your life on nonsense, you were climbing the blue.

Celi didn't know what to say.

Pili sighed, and cuffed his head gently. 'Go, go. But if you only have eyes for Qaia, at least keep your ears open. You might learn something, and then the evening won't be a total waste. But get the flour out of your hair first.'

So off he had set, at a run, to Qaia's house.

And as it happened, he did learn something that night: something about the world he lived in, and about himself.

HuroEldon, Natural Philosopher, stalked back and forth over the stage in his richly woven robe, casting flickering shadows by the light of the torches on the walls.

The setting was magnificent. The town hall was a domed chamber, big enough to hold all Foro's adult citizens. It was actually a wing of a palace, ruined in the last Formidable Caress. Now it had been rebuilt, and not as the home of a ruler, but as a meeting place for all Forons, rich and poor.

But even here HuroEldon's voice resounded like Lowland thunder, Celi thought, a voice too large to be contained by mere stone. The Philosopher had about him a rich whiff of antiquity: it was a strange thought that, though Huro looked no older than fifty, he might have been born centuries ago.

And as he made his prefatory remarks, on the stage beside Huro were two bodies, corpses strapped to tables, covered by dust sheets and attended by assistants. Celi felt deeply queasy.

'The world is a made thing,' Huro said again. 'An extraordinary claim that requires extraordinary evidence – and I have it!' With a showman's flourish he drew a long knife from his sleeve, and his assistants pulled the cover sheets from the tables.

The audience gasped. One revealed corpse was of a young spindling, its six legs splayed, its long neck limp as string. And the other corpse was of a little girl.

Celi felt Qaia's hand creep into his own. He had actually known the child; she had been called Bera, and she had died of the Blight aged only eight. Celi could see the disfiguring burn-like stains on her skin. Celi was ashamed at his earlier grisly curiosity: it made a big difference when you knew *who* was to be cut up.

HuroEldon held up his knife, inspecting the blade. Then with a butcher's casual expertise he slit the girl's pale body from throat to pelvis and emptied the chest cavity of organs. There was a smell of sour chemistry; the body's blood seemed to have been dried to a powder, and the organs were shrivelled, like blackened fruit. But still people groaned, and a few stumbled out of the hall, their hands pressed to their mouths.

Huro displayed the essentials of Bera's bone structure, the long spine, the ribs, the limbs attached by ball-and-socket joints. 'Thus the architecture of a human,' he said. 'And if you were to dissect a rat or a bird you would find much the same body plan – adjusted for the purpose of running or flying, of course, but with an essential unity of design.' Despite his revulsion, Celi was fascinated by this brisk lesson in skeletal anatomy.

Huro turned his back on the girl and stalked to the other table. 'A spindling, though, is quite different. Why, you can see it even before I open it up. Look at it! *Six legs.* Six limbs, not four! And if we look deeper, we will find more divergences . . .'

Efficiently he peeled back skin and prised out bones from the spindling's once-elegant long neck – except that these greyish objects weren't actually bones. 'The spindling has an inner skeletal structure. That much we have in common with it. But look – can you see?' He stalked around the front rows of the audience, who flinched back from his gory specimens. 'This isn't bone. It's a kind of cartilage, quite unlike the human design.'

He tore apart the spindling, displaying more features of the animal. For instance, a human's digestive system was essentially a duct that passed through the body: food in one end, waste out of the other. In contrast a spindling had a closed digestive loop, so that it used its mouth as its anus, for food and for waste. Celi was struck by this observation. Everybody knew to keep out of the way of a spindling when it prepared to vomit up its shit, but it had never occurred to him before how different it was to the human way of doing things. He felt curiosity stir; he wondered how many other strange features of the world were waiting for him to notice them, if only he could learn how to look.

'What does all this mean?' Huro demanded. 'It means that the spindling does not come from the same tree of life as humans and rats and birds. The spindling has been *brought* here, to this world of ours, from somewhere else – or else we have been brought to *its* world, although that seems less likely as there are more creatures like us here than like it. And the spindling is not the only example of an alien among us, among the plants and the animals.

'Like most primitive cultures on the Shelf, you Forons cling to a naive naturalism! You believe that the world as we experience it emerged from the blind operation of natural laws, that intelligence had no hand in it. But *that cannot be true.* The spindling is *proof* that the world could not have developed organically; one counter-example is enough to demonstrate that nature lacks the necessary unity for that to be so. The simplest hypothesis is in fact that it has *all* been made, all shaped by intelligence, from blueshifted sky to redshifted Lowland.' He held up spindling cartilage, and a hip joint from poor Bera. 'Here is the proof!' And he threw the bones to the floor.

There was a long silence. Then one man rose to his feet. Celi was moved to see that it was his own father. Sool was a proud Foron who clearly bristled over Huro's comments about primitivism and naivety. He demanded to know if this 'radical creationism' was the only philosophical choice. Must Forons now accept gods and devils? Must they cower from storms like their ancestors, and worship the light that flared across the Lowland? Was not Huro's presumption of a higher intelligence actually the more intellectually primitive point of view? He spoke well, a dignified anger deepening his voice, and his neighbours applauded.

But Huro was able to counter him point by point. Despite himself, Celi found himself accepting the Philosopher's arguments. But he felt deeply disturbed at the way this arrogant man dismissed his father, and had so easily upset his own world view.

On impulse Celi stood up himself.

His father, surprised, yielded the floor. As he became the focus of the packed hall – the Mayor herself was here – Celi quailed. But he held his nerve, and dramatically pointed at Bera's corpse. 'Philosopher, if you can tell us the design of the whole world, why could you not save *her* from the Blight?'

Huro smiled. 'If you ask such a question, young man, perhaps you have it in you to become a doctor, so you can answer it yourself. Talk to me later.' He turned away to take more questions.

As Celi sat down, stunned, Qaia tugged his sleeve. 'You won't go to that awful man, will you?'

'No,' said Celi immediately. 'No, of course not.' But as he stared into Qaia's wide blue eyes, he knew he was lying.

Foro was situated on the side of a cliff, on the broad plain of the Shelf. The Forons were proud of their town, for they had built it with their own hands. But it was cupped in the mighty ruins of a much older city, devastated generations ago by the Formidable Caress.

And if you climbed the rocky walls above and below the Shelf, you climbed into stratified time. You could ascend into a rarefied air where time raced like a pumping heart, or go down into the grave torpor of redshift.

In practice nobody from Foro ever did climb the rocks. It just wasn't practical to run your life with time's cogwheels slipping constantly. And the Forons' reluctance was cultural too. Celi's people were proudly descended from a group who had once been kept in an up-cliff community called the Attic, where their lives had been burned up in the service of slower-living rich folk on the Shelf below. Celi was the great-grandson of rebels against that strange enslavement.

But if the folk of Foro ignored the stratification of time, the Philosophers, like HuroEldon, exploited it.

The Philosophers marketed knowledge. In their own community far down the slope, their lives, slowed by time, were stretched out. The Philosophers devoted their extended existences to recovering some of the wisdom that had been lost during the Caress, through study and patient archaeology. And they made their living by selling that learning back to those who had lost it. Thus HuroEldon had ascended grandly from his redshifted keep to instruct the people of Foro on how to turn their growing town from a heaped-up clutter into a functioning city with common services like water supplies and sewage, how to reclaim the ancient canal system to irrigate their fields, and so on; he could then step forward across time to advise on such projects as they were carried out.

Celi came to realise that this gift of knowledge was essential. It was only a few generations since the Forons had begun to grope their way out of the fog of fearful superstition that had been the enduring legacy of civilisation's fall in the Formidable Caress. And it was even less time since the deeper psychological shock of that fall had begun to fade: the edge of the Shelf was still lined by the remains of funeral pyres, where the citizens of Foro, despairing of a future in which another Caress must inevitably shatter all they had built, had burned all their learning with them when they died.

But however useful his advice, for Forons, who prided themselves on their egalitarian instincts, it was hard to stomach Huro's arrogance. That lecture on creationism had been a gift by Huro, rich with too much knowledge, a bauble tossed carelessly away by a man come to advise on sewage. His manner had been infuriating, let alone the content of his lecture.

And Huro had deflected Celi's young life just as casually.

In the end, Celi did speak to the Natural Philosopher after the lecture. And within days he was assigned to Dela, the town's physician, to begin his apprenticeship as a doctor. It all happened so quickly, his whole life upset. When he thought this over, Celi found he resented it, but he knew he would not step off the path he had chosen – or rather, that the Philosopher had chosen for him.

But when HuroEldon called on him again, long after that fateful night in the town hall, Celi found it hard to hide his nervousness.

HuroEldon walked grandly through Celi's study. In his Philosopher's cloak Huro was magnificent in this shabby background. He inspected Celi's notes, carefully scraped onto spindling-skin parchment, and pored over an area he called Celi's 'laboratory', an array of herbs, fluids and minerals labelled and annotated.

Five years had worn away. Celi, now twenty-one, was growing into his role in the town, as a practising physician – and as husband to Qaia, and expectant father of her first baby. But for HuroEldon, who had returned to his redshifted community of Philosophers, less than a year had passed.

'I'm grateful that you called on me,' Celi said stiffly.

'I wanted to see how the town's bright-eyed young doctor was progressing. It is always amusing to skip forward in time, so to speak, and see how such stories as yours have played out.'

'I'm not a doctor yet,' Celi said. 'I'm still learning.'

'That will never cease, I hope.'

'And Dela is still working—'

'That old witch! Oh, Dela has the charm, she knows the right words to murmur when Effigies go spiralling up from the dying. But *you* have something far more important than that.' Huro tapped Celi's temple. 'A mind, my boy. That and your spirit, your doggedness. I saw it in you even during that night in the town hall.'

'I'm surprised you remember it . . .' But for Huro it wasn't long ago at all. 'Your lecture made a great impression on me.'

'Obviously,' Huro said dismissively.

'It wasn't you showing off your knowledge that intrigued me,' Celi said, irritated. 'It was Bera.'

'Who? Oh, the little girl on the butcher's slab. What use is all the knowledge in the world, you asked, if it can't save a child from the Blight?' He waved a hand at Celi's home-made laboratory. 'I can see you've devoted yourself to the cause. But the Blight won't be wrestled into submission, will it?'

No, it wouldn't. That was why Celi had asked to see HuroEldon.

Celi was already a competent physician. He could deliver babies, stitch up wounds, set broken limbs and comfort the dying, and he had acquired basic knowledge of the vectors of infection, of antisepsis and antibiotics. Much of this learning, preserved and sold by the Philosophers, was rumoured to be very old.

But Celi had also learned that there was nothing anybody could do about the Blight.

It showed up as a skin discolouration first, like a burn. This stage could last a year, even more. But eventually it got into your lungs, and within three days you were dead. None of Dela's medicines could fight it; it was only rigid quarantine procedures that kept it from overwhelming the community altogether.

What frustrated Celi was that he was sure a cure for the Blight was achievable. As he had visited case after case, Celi had made notes of the folk medicines he encountered, concocted from animal blood, plant roots and seeds, mineral salts – potions and salves born out of desperation. The surprising thing was that some of these remedies showed signs of slowing the disease. Somewhere in all these ingredients was a cure, he became convinced.

But finding that cure was a tremendous challenge. There were no full-time scientists here; Foro wasn't rich enough to afford them. And a little systematic thought demonstrated that there were simply too many combinations of ingredients and relative concentrations to be tested, even if Celi were to dedicate himself to the project full time – which, as one of Foro's two doctors, was quite impossible.

And now HuroEldon, who he had hoped would be a source of old wisdom on the Blight, dismissively told him it was all futile anyhow. 'We live in a world in which time is stratified, remember. Time flows faster the higher you go—'

'I understand that,' Celi said testily.

'Do you? That's impressive. *I* don't. And you must also understand, my boy, that organisms change – especially the pesky little brutes that bring us diseases. The Blight can transmit itself through blood, or spittle, or through the air. Whatever we do, a subset of the Blight's disease vectors can always waft up into the blue where, accelerated in time, they can mutate, faster than we can hope to match them with our remedies. You see? It's thus a fundamental feature of our world that disease is always beyond our control.' He shrugged massive shoulders. 'One must simply accept the losses.'

Celi could not fault the Philosopher's logic. But on some level, he saw, Huro simply did not *care* that it was impossible to defeat the

Blight. Perhaps this was a legacy of the past. HuroEldon's very name was a relic of the complicated compound nomenclature once adopted by the aristocracy of Foro, while Celi's was a blunt Attic name. Even generations after the rebellion, in Huro's heart he still thought he was better than Celi, better than the swarming townspeople Celi tended. Celi kept such thoughts to himself.

Huro seemed to be growing bored. 'You're wasting your time here, you know. There are much more intriguing questions for a mind like yours to address.'

'Such as?'

'Such as the subject of that lecture of mine: the indisputable fact that the whole of our world is a made thing, or at least assembled from disparate components, from blue to red, top to bottom. We've plenty of evidence beyond spindling skeletons. Why, we believe that the very stratification of time is an artefact.'

Celi walked to the window and peered up at the sky. The light of Old Earth came from the shifting glow of the Lowland, reflected from the clouds. 'Why would anybody *make* all this?'

'Think it through,' Huro said. 'If you could climb down from the sky, down into this redshifted pit we call our world, you would be preserved, locked in time.'

'Preserved?'

'We believe that once Old Earth was a world *without* this layering of time, a world like many others, perhaps, hanging in the sky. And its people were more or less like us. But Old Earth came under some kind of threat. And so, to protect their children, the elders of Old Earth pulled a blanket of time over their world and packed it off to the future. You must understand this is a rather flimsy hypothesis, and as I always say myself, extraordinary claims require extraordinary proof, and we don't have it yet! But it's the best justification we've come up with so far: Old Earth is a jar of time, stopped up to preserve its children.'

Celi frowned. 'But then, what about the Effigies?' The ghostly forms released by the dying represented the biggest single mystery he had encountered as a doctor. 'Are they *us* – are they human souls, leaving a dying body? And if so, why do so few of us release them on death? And why should the world periodically shake itself to pieces in the Formidable Caresses?'

'Good questions. I wish I had good answers! Perhaps you will find out for yourself – when you come down into the red and join us.'

So here was the invitation, bluntly stated. Celi said, 'I am a doctor. I have patients here in Foro.'

'They will die in the end, whatever you do. *While you could live on.*'

'I have a wife. Qaia. She is carrying our first child—'

'The blue-eyes who was with you the night of the lecture? How cute. Bring her with you. Or, better still, leave her behind.' He leaned closer, and Celi smelled gin on his breath. 'Stride into the future with me, five years, ten, twenty. There will always be more girls, not even conceived yet, fresh fruit waiting to be plucked. How do you think I keep myself entertained during these visits to your dismal little town? It isn't all sewage systems and creationism, you know.'

The curiosity Huro had woken in Celi that night five years ago would never leave him. But everything else about Huro and his proposal repelled Celi, everything but the allure of knowledge. It was easy for him to turn down Huro's invitation.

As it turned out, however, Celi's future was after all decided that day. When he returned home, he found Qaia sitting alone, stroking her belly, her face streaked by desolate tears. A pale-pink stain, like a burn, was spreading across her neck: it was the Blight.

Her life and his had been destroyed, he thought, by a vector of infection he couldn't even see, and which he would never have the time to defeat. He couldn't bear it.

It took a sleepless night of calculation for Celi to decide what he must do. He would not follow HuroEldon, down into the red. He must climb up into the blue, alone.

In the morning he packed quickly: a few clothes, some dried food, bags of seeds and roots, a set of his medicinal samples. Then, with his pack on his back and a cage of mice dangling awkwardly from his belt, Celi walked out of Foro.

He made for the cliff face, and began to climb. Once there had been an elevator system here, worked by tethered spindlings. Now you had to walk. But a whole series of staircases had long ago been cut into the face of the rock, heavily eroded by usage and weathering, but still usable.

He was winded by the time he had climbed the nine hundred steps to what remained of the Attic, where once his ancestors had toiled.

He walked around curiously; he had never been up here before. There was nothing left of his people's village but post-holes in the ground, the scorch-marks of abandoned hearths, and gaunt caves in

369

the cliff walls that had once been used as kitchens and dormitories. It all looked much older than the two or three generations since its abandonment, but that was in Foro time; up here in the blue this place had grown much older than the Forons' memories of it.

He dangled his legs over the edge of the cliff, sipped water from a spring, and looked down into the depths of the Lowland, an ocean of misty redshift. From here, Foro too was bathed in a crimson glow; he could see the people and their spindling-drawn vehicles crawling as if through syrup. Already he was cut off from his family, from his patients, from Qaia, by the streaming of time. He wondered how many of them he would see again.

Once he had made his decision to leave he had been determined to keep his plan secret from everybody – even from Qaia. Perhaps it had been the kindest thing to do; or perhaps he had feared his own determination might waver if he hesitated.

But Dela, the doctor who had tutored him, had seemed to have an idea what he was up to. 'It's the white mice,' she told him. 'You're taking white mice.'

'What about them?'

'Mice can catch the Blight, like humans. Spindlings, for instance, can't. And that's important to you, isn't it?'

'I don't know what you're talking about.'

Unexpectedly she hugged him. Old enough to be his mother, she was a nurturing doctor, but not given to physical displays of affection. 'I will miss you. You're a good colleague.'

'I'll be back in a few days.'

'Of course you will.'

His father had accepted his bland assurances that he would return. He had a more strained encounter with his mother, who, with her usual acuity, guessed he was up to something. 'I always did say that girl would have you climbing the blue.'

'Look after her, mother.'

'I will.' He embraced her; she smelled of warm bread.

And then had come his parting from Qaia. He had left her, and his unborn child, with lies. Now, as he looked down into the layers of time that trapped her, he couldn't bear even to think about it. Wearily he collected his kit and continued the climb.

Above the Attic he plodded steadily along the trails of migrant animals, and when the trails petered out, scrambled over rocks. There were no more people or animals now, but he saw the flash of wings, and occasionally heard an echoing caw. He was not alone, not while the birds flew with him.

After a time he noticed a change in the rock. Shattered by frost or heat, its surfaces scarred by lichen, it seemed much more sharply eroded than the cliff faces down by Foro. The stratification of time must be having a profound effect on the very fabric of the world, with higher rock sections eroding away much more rapidly than lower. When he paused to sleep, wrapped in a skin blanket on a narrow ledge, he scratched a note about this in his spindling-skin journal, the first note he had made there.

On the third day he climbed a narrow pinnacle, heading up to a summit. By now it seemed that only he existed in a normal stream of time; he was alone in the clean, thin air, sandwiched between the stars over his head and the crimson glow beneath.

The slope levelled out, and he stood on a smooth, worn plateau. There was life here: tufts of grass, low trees that clung to the rock face, even a couple of abandoned birds' nests. Food and water: he could live here, then. But Foro and the Shelf, far beneath him, were lost with the Lowland in a dank sea of redshift. Perhaps there were higher mountains to climb. But surely he had come high enough to achieve the temporal advantage he sought, high enough to defeat the evolutionary enthusiasm of the Blight vectors – high enough to give him the time he needed to save Qaia. This would do.

But now that he had stopped moving, doubt plagued him. Could he really bear to lose himself in time like this?

Better not to think about it. Better to begin work; once his patient methodology gathered momentum, his soul would be filled with the work and his purpose. Grimly he began to unload his kit.

Celi stood in the doorway of the home he had built with Qaia. He looked round at the walls of mud and plaster, the furniture they had made and bought, the carving with their names over the door. For him, all of it was a lifetime old, yet as fresh as a morning. And there was no place for him, he knew.

He felt an odd stab of nostalgia for his mountaintop refuge, the hut he had built, the cages for the mice. But even if he could climb back up there it would already all be gone, weathered away by accelerated time. The core of his life had been hollowed out; he felt as if he had been away only a moment, that he had been aged in a heartbeat.

371

Qaia walked into the room, humming, a towel around her hair. For a moment she did not see him, and he watched her, his breath catching in his throat. It hurt him to see what the Blight had done to her: the crimson stain had spread up from her neck across her once-pretty face. Yet he was relieved that he had, after all, returned in time to save her.

Then she saw him. She recognised him immediately, and her blue eyes widened. It was unbearable to have her look at what he had become, with his white hair, his stooped back.

He longed to hold her, but time stood between them like stone. Only a year had passed for her, while more than forty had worn away for him.

'You said you would be gone a few days,' she said. 'Some "few days".'

'I'm sorry,' he said. 'Qaia, the baby—'

'You have a son, Celi. A son. Four months old.'

He tried to take that in. His leathery old heart beat faster. He held up his precious vial. 'Take this. It is—'

'I know what it is. Your mother guessed what you must be doing. So did Dela. Oh, you fool! What use is saving me if I had to lose you in the process?'

He pressed the vial into her hand. 'Take it to Dela,' he whispered. 'She will know what to do. Hurry now. It's what all this has been about, after all.'

She bit her lip, and ran out of the door.

And HuroEldon walked in, his robe sweeping. 'Well, well. Somebody told me they saw you come staggering back down out of the blue.'

Celi straightened. 'Philosopher.'

Huro leaned closer. 'You smell like a spindling's breath. And what is this you're wearing, mouse fur? I take it you found your cure. I knew you would do it,' Huro said grudgingly. 'But I never thought you would reduce yourself to this in the process. And you ran out on your patients, despite the vows you doctors take.'

'I came back—'

'But what use are you now, like this?' He inspected Celi, as if he were a curious specimen. 'Your wife can't love you again, you know. We humans don't seem to have evolved to handle such differential shifts in time. That's another point that convinces me this is a made world, by the way, that we are designed for a different environment . . .' He idly picked up Celi's notebook, and paused at the very first observational note Celi had made so long ago, about the effects of differential weathering rates at altitude. 'An acute bit of geology. I told you, you would have made a good Philosopher. But you've thrown your life away.'

Celi had no reply. Huro was articulating doubts that had plagued him during his vigil on the mountain – in all those years alone, how could he not have had doubts? As he had worked through his monumental combinatorial challenge with his vials of infected blood and trial remedies, slaughtering generation after generation of white mice, his intellectual curiosity, even his basic impulse to save his wife, had worn away, leaving nothing but a grim determination to keep on to the end. He had even stopped counting the years as they had piled up. Of course he had been lonely, up there on his plateau, looking out over uncounted layers of time! But what choice had there been?

Well, he had succeeded, and he must not let Huro stir ancient doubts in his soul. 'You Philosophers exploit the time strata selfishly—'

'While you have burned up your own life to save others. Yes, yes. You aren't the first, you know; your heroism isn't even original.' Huro peered into Celi's eyes, his mouth. 'You might have found your Blight treatment up there, Celi, but you sacrificed your own health in the process. I'd give you a year. Two at the most.'

'It doesn't matter.'

'No, I don't suppose it does to you, does it?' Huro's expression softened, just a little. 'My offer still stands.'

'What offer?'

'To come with me, down below. You may only have a year, but spin it out! Some of us are planning to go on, you know.'

'Go where?'

'*Down into the red*. Nobody knows how deep we can go, how much we can stretch time before it snaps like an overextended sinew. Some of us dream of pushing on into the future, all the way to the next Formidable Caress. And if we can do that, who knows what's possible? Come with me, Celi. You've given up almost all of your life. Surely you owe yourself that much.'

But Celi heard a sound from a neighbouring room. It was a soft gurgle, the cry of a waking baby. 'I have all I need here,' he said.

HuroEldon snorted. 'Well, we won't meet again. The time streams will see to that.' The Philosopher walked out of the house.

And Celi, broken and old, went to comfort his infant son.

THE TIME PIT
AD c.4.5 BILLION YEARS

The Mechanist balloons, fast and grey, drifted over the ruins of Old Foro. Belo couldn't even see the crude bombs they dropped until they came streaking down out of the blueshifted air to splash fire. But the Mechanists' advance was driving Belo and the last of his troopers towards the Shelf's edge, where the river Foo, running with blood, plunged into the abyss.

And all across the battlefield, Creationist soldiers were dying. Belo could see their Effigies rising up like smoke, spectral distortions of the human form that twisted and spun away.

All this for the sake of an idea, Belo thought. No, not an idea – the truth. He must cling to that, even as the blueshifted fire from the sky blossomed around him.

'Captain?'

Tira, his most trusted lieutenant, was shaking his shoulder. In his exhaustion he had drifted into abstraction, as he so often did. He was after all trained as a Natural Philosopher, and his senior officers had never let him forget that intellectuals, with their long perspective, didn't necessarily make for good soldiers. But if not for intellectuals like him, there would have been no war anyhow.

'I'm sorry, Tira. It's just that you have to admire them.'

'Sir?' Her small face, smeared with blood and dirt, was creased with concern.

'The Mechs. We think of them as stupid, you know, backward. After all, the reason we fight is because they cling to their absurd, primitive idea that the world is a product of natural forces, acting blindly, in the absence of mind. But now they have come up with *this*.'

For a soldier of Old Earth, gaining the high ground was *everything*. If you were higher than your enemy you had the benefit of acceler-ated time; you could think faster, prepare your strategy and aim your weapons, while your opponents tumbled, slow-moving, trapped in glutinous, red-shifted slow time.

So, in this campaign, the Creationists of Puul had taken the Attic, the long-abandoned community on the cliff face above the town of Foro itself, where once rich Forons had kept time-accelerated slaves. The campaign had gone well, and Belo had started to believe that the Forons and their hated Mechanist notions might soon be purged from the world.

But then the Forons had produced their hot-air balloons, which wafted even higher than the Attic, and the Creationists' advantage was lost.

'A stunning idea,' Belo said. 'So simple! Nothing but bags of hot air. But look at that formation. You've got to give them credit.' Belo had a flask of gin in his coat pocket, meant to comfort battlefield wounded. Perhaps he should crack it now, and spend his last moments watching the wondrous spectacle of fighting soldiers and flying machines working in tandem to snuff out his life.

But Tira was almost screaming in his face. 'Sir! We have to get out of here. Dane has found a way.'

'Dane?'

Stumbling towards them through the rubble came a trooper, blood-soaked, a small, squat man. Dane's bayonet had been snapped in two, and he was dragging one leg: both weapon and man damaged, Belo thought bleakly. Grimacing with pain, Dane showed Belo what he had found: a shaft in the ground, no wider than Belo's own shoulders, covered by a heavy stone slab. 'I think it's a well,' he said.

'Or a larder,' Tira said. A place where you could store meat, preserved in the slower time of depth.

'No,' Belo said grimly. 'See the lock on this hatch, broken now? This is a time pit. A place you would throw down thieves and murderers and forget about them.'

'So where does it come out?'

'Who knows? But *where* scarcely matters. It just needs to be deep enough, deep into slow time. A neat way to dispose of your criminals – to hurl them one-way into the future!'

Tira peered into the time pit, her face twisted with fear. 'It's this or nothing,' she said.

Belo said, 'Do you love your Effigy so much, Tira? Shall we not stand and fight?'

Dane said, 'Dying like this won't do any good.' His accent was coarse; he had been a farm worker before the war. He was wheezing, exhausted. 'I say we live to fight another day.'

'Even if that day is far in the future?'

'Even so,' Dane said.

Fire-bombs bloomed ever closer. Looking around, Belo saw that the three of them were alone, beyond help.

Belo grinned. 'Another day.'

'Another day,' they mumbled.

Belo lifted his legs into the shaft, raised himself over a tunnel of darkness, and fell into time.

'I'll have your boots.'

Belo was reluctant to wake. Even half-asleep he remembered the endless fall down the tight, filthy shaft, as if he was being swallowed into some terrible stomach. And now here was this ugly voice, dragging him back into the world.

'I said, I'll have your boots. I know you can hear me, soldier boy.'

Reluctantly he opened his eyes. He was dazzled by a glaring blue sky, by stars that wheeled above his head. And a face loomed over him, a man's face, broad, dead-eyed, roughly shaven, surrounded by a mass of dirty black hair.

Belo tried to speak. His throat was bone dry. 'What's your name?'

'I am Teeg. And you're in my world now.'

'Really?' Belo had no idea where he was, and he wondered where Dane and Tira were – if they were still alive. All that would have to wait. First he had to deal with this grubby buffoon. 'You want my boots?'

The face cracked in a grin, showing blackened teeth. 'That's right, soldier boy.'

'Try taking them.'

The grin disappeared. Then Teeg's face twisted, and he roared and raised two huge scarred hands. Belo aimed a kick at where he guessed the man's crotch would be, but his legs felt feeble, heavy, as if the muscles had drained of energy. Besides, this Teeg was so massively built, a hulk of muscle and bone dressed in filthy rags, that the kick only enraged him. Teeg got his hands around Belo's throat, and pressed him back into the dirt. Belo flailed and struggled, but he was like a child battling an adult.

He had been conscious here only a few heartbeats, yet already he had given his life away. Quite a miscalculation, he thought, weakening.

'Get off him!' A squat mass came hurtling from Belo's left side and slammed into Teeg.

Belo, the pressure on his throat gone, coughed for breath. He struggled upright, clinging to consciousness. He was sitting on a dirt plain. Beside him a cliff face rose up into the blue. He was close to a ragged cave, perhaps the chute down which he had tumbled. People huddled a few paces away. Four women, five kids – no men. Scrawny, filthy, dressed in rags, they stared at him fearfully.

He couldn't see an end to this scrubby plain. Perhaps it was another Shelf – or perhaps he had fallen all the way into the Lowland itself, he thought with a stab of despair.

And beyond the people he glimpsed something moving over the ground – not on it, *over* it, at about waist height, almost like a Mechanist balloon. It was a rough sphere of some silvery metal that gleamed in the blueshifted light of the sky. Was it a machine? But it was like no machine he had ever seen, no pump or elevator or cannon. And what could possibly support such a mass of metal in the air? He longed to see more, but details were blurred by heat haze—

'Soldier boy.'

Teeg's ugly voice snapped him back to the here and now.

Teeg had hold of Dane, by an arm locked around his throat. It was obviously Dane who had knocked Teeg away and saved Belo's life. Dane wasn't struggling. His injured leg was twisted back at an impossible angle. But his eyes were locked on his commanding officer, and he made no sound.

'Let him go,' Belo said.

Teeg looked mock-puzzled. 'How did you put it? . . . Try taking him.'

Belo tried to stand. The world greyed.

'No.' It was Tira. She was sitting on the ground, the remnants of her blood-stained uniform in disarray. 'Don't fight him,' she said. 'Not now. He's too strong. *Not yet.*'

Belo knew she was right. But still Teeg was squeezing the life out of Dane. 'Let him go,' he said again. 'We didn't come here to do you harm.'

'I don't care why you came here,' Teeg said. 'I told you. You're in my world now. And you will do what I say. You know why? Because of the Weapon.' He held Dane at arm's length, with one mighty fist locked on his collar, as if he was holding up a doll. Dane bit his lip, and his leg trailed beneath him, but still he made no sound.

And then Teeg grabbed Dane by neck and belt, and hurled him bodily at the floating machine.

A window clicked opened in the side of the machine. Fire, purple and bright, snaked into Dane's belly and simply blew him apart, into fragments of flesh and bone amid a mist of blood – all this before the body could hit the ground. Then the window closed, like an eyelid shutting, and the machine continued its serene patrol around the huddling people.

Teeg grinned, cocksure in his ragged robes. He stood over Tira, who was still sprawled on the ground. 'Now, where were we before soldier boy woke up?'

Despite everything he had seen, Belo stepped forward again. 'Touch her and I will kill you, I swear.'

Tira said grimly, 'I already made the same promise.'

Even in this moment of power Teeg looked from one to the other, and something in their determined stare seemed to put him off. 'You'll keep. But you,' he said, stabbing a finger at Belo. 'Your boots.'

Belo sat down and began to work at his laces.

Teeg walked over to the group of huddled women. 'You.' The woman he had selected cowered from him, but he grabbed her by the shoulder, threw her to the ground, and began to fumble at her rags. She lay passively; the children watched empty-eyed.

'You're right to give him a victory,' Tira whispered. 'There's nothing to be done as long as he controls that machine. We must play for time. Wait for an opportunity . . .' She was staring at a charred fragment of Dane's corpse, and her composure cracked. 'Oh, Belo, what horror have we fallen into?'

He said grimly, 'We are soldiers. We have been trained to survive. We will survive this, together.'

'But how long has this monster kept these women as his slaves? Can you see the faces of the children? *They look like him.*'

'It won't happen to you.'

'Oh, you can be sure of that,' said Tira, her voice full of hate.

Life in Teeg's nasty little kingdom turned out to be simple.

They lived outdoors, on the arid plain. For the first couple of days they stayed close to the cliff where the time chute had decanted, huddling at night in caves or under rocky overhangs.

But then they were led away by Teeg and the enigmatic hovering machine, the 'Weapon'. So, by default, Belo was exploring the Lowland, the greatest mystery of all to Shelf Philosophers of all persuasions. If it hadn't been so brutally hard it would almost have been interesting.

They slept out in the open. They ate berries they gathered from the sparse bushes, or they chewed on strips of dried meat – Belo wasn't sure yet where the meat came from. Their clothes were rags, replaced if they came across a handy corpse, like poor Dane's. But it appeared Teeg always got the best pick, like Belo's own boots.

And, while they walked, they carried fragments of Dane's corpse with them. The women of Teeg's grim harem seemed used to this. Even the blank-eyed children stumbled along with grisly butchered remnants. Belo had no clear idea why they did this.

Indeed, Belo's own continued existence puzzled him. It was obvious what Teeg wanted of Tira – but why keep Belo alive? Another man could only be competition, a threat; why tolerate him taking another breath?

And towering over all these personal issues was the deeper mystery of the Weapon: where it had come from, how and why it had been made – and what its true purpose was, for Belo was beginning to suspect that it had nothing to do with Teeg and his petty lording. Belo couldn't even see how Teeg communicated with it; he never spoke to it directly, never touched it. Sometimes, Belo thought, it was almost as if Teeg was following the Weapon, rather than the other way around. Belo longed to examine the Weapon, but he dared not approach it, not until he understood more.

Belo tried to talk to Teeg as they walked. In his military service he had learned that any knowledge could be a lever. But he had to bury his resentment as Teeg marched along in his own spindling-leather boots, while Belo's feet bled on the rough ground.

'You are a victim of the time pit,' Belo essayed.

'As are you,' Teeg snapped, as if Belo had tried to insult him.

'We are soldiers. We fled a lost battlefield.'

Teeg listened, his massive face closed up. For all his brutish behaviour, Belo sensed that this man was no fool. But Belo's talk of his war clearly meant nothing to Teeg.

Belo tried again. 'You were cast in the pit by your enemies. Perhaps it was unjust—'

'Unjust? More than that. I was born in the Attic, over Foro.'

'I know it.'

'I was a bastard, sired by some red-tinged Foron who raped a servant, my mother. Nobody accepted me, neither the Forons nor their slaves. In the end they stuck me down the pit and stranded me in the future. But not before I got to my father.' Teeg grinned, remembering; Belo could see that this moment of patricide had been the peak of his life.

'Teeg, the Forons are my enemies. But they no longer keep time-accelerated servants.'

Teeg twisted his face. 'How long?'

'I'm not sure.' It was history to Belo. 'Many generations.'

Teeg shrugged. 'Then that's how long I've been down here, isn't it?'

And here was the cruel reality of the time pit. Even if you survived, to be cast down here was to be sent into the future, to live out a futile life adrift from family, friends, cut off even from the context of your crime.

It was this that distressed Tira more than anything. After all, she and Belo were not criminals; had devoted their very lives to a cause.

Foro had long been a centre of the traditional 'Mechanistic' philosophy, an argument that the world was a product of blind natural processes, while the community of Puul, further along the Shelf, had become a haven for heretics, 'Creationists', who clung to the idea that everything about the world had been shaped by mind – perhaps human mind. The sharp intellectual content of these ideas had burned away the last of the old animist religions to have emerged after the last Formidable Caress, among the tribes that huddled in the ruins of a fallen civilisation. But these contrasting world systems, sharpened by incompatibility, had become a banner of identity, as such theologies often would, and hostility had deepened.

At last, border friction between the growing trading empires of Foro and Puul had provided the excuse everybody wanted for a cathartic war. It was a war that Belo had eagerly signed up for – a war that the Creationists of Puul had managed to carry all the way into the heart of Old Foro itself – but which, at the last, the Mechs had turned, thanks to their stunning bit of inventiveness with the balloons.

And now he and Tira had been ripped out of their time, out of the very context of their war.

As they discussed this, Tira said grimly, 'We don't even know how slowly time passes here, compared to home. We are surely already stranded far from our time. Everybody we knew must be dead. The war must be over, one way or another – perhaps even forgotten. And every day we are stuck here we are further removed from home.'

Belo took her hand. 'As long as we are alive the war is not over, for the truth burns in our hearts.'

'As long as we are alive,' Tira echoed.

They held each other's hands in a silent pact.

*

Some of Belo's questions were answered perhaps a week after their stranding on this doleful plain, when Teeg's group of captives, shepherded by the patrolling Weapon, encountered others.

It was a convocation of several groups, eight or ten of them, coming together across the emptiness of the plain. There were no more than a dozen people in each subdued little flock – and each was patrolled by a circling Weapon. These machines seemed more or less similar to the one associated with Teeg, but some showed wear, their carapaces patched with dull materials.

Belo was surprised to see a herd of spindlings, six-legged, nervous and skittish, briskly controlled by a Weapon. While most of the machines were content to patrol, this Weapon regularly spat fire into the dirt; perhaps the spindlings needed reminding how to behave.

And Belo spied another class of machines altogether: squat, ugly carts that ran along the ground. These devices gathered together heaps of dirt, which they circled jealously. Belo had no idea what their purpose could be.

As the groups converged, Belo expected Teeg to call out to the other slave-keepers and Weapon-masters, perhaps even to socialise with them. But he stayed as silent and sullen as the rest, following the machines as they swept busily over the dusty ground.

Their group was brought to a central place, marked out by the Weapons' patrols. And here a very strange trade began to take place.

Under Teeg's direction, Belo, Tira and the others began to hurl the rotting scraps of Dane's corpse into the rough arena marked out by the toiling wheel-based machines. Belo saw that similar body parts, and even corpses, some heartbreakingly tiny, were thrown out by other groups.

Meanwhile one Weapon peremptorily isolated a spindling and sliced it up with brisk slashes of its sword of fire. The other animals bucked and mewled, their long necks twisting. The people took their chance to grab slices of meat, bloody, still warm.

But the other Weapons were circulating. Some of them settled on the mounds of rusty dirt that had been gathered by the wheeled machines. Others took chunks of meat, spindling or human, charred it black with their belly-fires, and absorbed it within their metal carapaces.

'It is a kind of market,' Belo whispered to Tira. 'Meat is exchanged for meat, or for the heaped-up dirt.'

'And this is how Teeg keeps his people alive,' Tira said grimly, 'by trading with other slave runners.'

But Belo, watching closely, suspected this strange process had little to do with Teeg. After all, it was the machines who took the dirt, and absorbed much of the meat into their bodies. 'Perhaps these Weapons need meat as we do, for fuel,' he mused.

Tira said, 'But why the dirt?'

Belo had an idea about that too. He knew a little of the lore of iron-smelting; his mind was bright and acquisitive, and he knew a little about a great many things. Perhaps the Weapons needed this rusty dirt for its iron, or other minerals, to repair their gleaming bodies. And so these toiling wheeled carts gathered iron-rich dirt, or dug it out of the ground as ore, and exchanged it for the organic material, the meat delivered here by their hovering cousins.

There was a kind of economy operating here, Belo saw. But the trade wasn't really about the people and their needs. It was about the Weapons.

When the strange trade was done, the various groups moved apart, shepherded by the Weapons. The toiling wheel-machines scurried away over the ground, no doubt in search of more iron-rich soil.

That night Teeg's group ate comparatively well. Spindling flesh was tough and unsatisfying, but better than nothing. Belo believed that was because spindlings weren't even native to the Old Earth, as humans were. Teeg muttered that sometimes the Weapons brought more palatable meat, rodents or birds.

As he ate, Belo looked out upon the dismal plain, which flickered with light storms, distant, irregular, silent. Day and night on Old Earth were controlled by the rhythmic cycling of these light storms across the face of this, the deepest Lowland. In the midst of a landscape of mysteries, even this simple pattern baffled Belo. For if time was stratified, how could the days and nights down here on the Lowland itself have the same duration as up on the Shelf? For so it felt to him, now that he was here.

But he had no answer to such questions. Belo was now a slave who ate roots and raw meat and slept in the dirt, a situation hardly conducive to theorising, and with time his thinking would surely grow stagnant. But for now he kept his wits.

And as he watched Teeg and his machine, he thought he began to see certain truths about their situation.

That night, in the dark, Tira came to Belo. 'I think things are coming to a head,' she whispered.

'Teeg?'

'He's been looking at me . . . I think my grace period is up.'

'And mine,' said Belo.

'What do you mean?'

'He doesn't need another male around. But as long as he had Dane's flesh to trade, it was in his interests to keep me alive.'

Tira grimaced. 'As a walking larder.'

'Yes. Easier for me to walk than for my flesh to be carried. But now he needs my meat.'

Tira said, 'As for me, I'll fight to the last. But while he has that machine of his—'

'Oh, I don't think the Weapon is "his" at all.'

'You don't?' She turned to him, her face grimy and drawn. 'What's going on here, Belo?'

'I'll explain it all,' he whispered. 'But first we need to deal with Teeg. This is what you must do . . .'

As the light of day began to gather, Belo sought out Teeg. The big man sat at the edge of the rough perimeter patrolled by the hovering Weapon, peering out at the other groups scattered over the plain. He watched Belo suspiciously.

Belo was careful to keep his hands in sight at all times. 'I have something for you. Two things, actually. Gifts.'

Teeg pointed. 'The Weapon is just over there.'

Belo held his hands up. 'I won't try anything; I know it's pointless. And I know what you intend to do to me.'

'Oh, yes?'

'I won't fight. What's the point? I'm sick of fighting. I'm sick of it all. I was sick of it before I fell down that chute to this hellhole. Just make it quick, all right?'

'So what do you want?'

'I told you. I have gifts for you. Can I reach inside my jacket?'

Teeg hesitated. 'Slow as you like.'

Belo reached into his jacket pocket and retrieved his military-issue flask of gin. 'It's meant for the battlefield, to comfort the dying. An anaesthetic, you know?' He unscrewed the cap and smelled the liquor. 'Ah, the memories—'

'Give me that.' Teeg swiped the flask out of his hand and raised it to his lips. His small eyes closed; it was the nearest Belo had seen him come to showing pleasure.

'When was the last time you had a real drink?'

Teeg grunted. 'When my father's blood was still wet under my fingernails.'

'Lovely memory. Well, have it all. You'd have taken it anyhow once I was dead.'

'That and your boots.' Teeg laughed, an ugly noise, and he wiped his watering eyes with the back of a filthy hand.

The powerful drink was having the effect on a long-abstinent Teeg Belo had hoped for.

Teeg raised the bottle again. 'So what's your other gift?'

'What? Oh – Tira. The woman. Take her.'

Teeg eyed him blearily. 'You serious?'

'She turned me down once too often.'

'She turned *you* down?'

'I mean, I got her out of the battle, and protected her from *you*, and she still won't open her legs. I've had enough of her.' Belo forced a smile. 'Take her now, if you want. Have a party.'

'Where is she?'

'When I tried it on she got away.'

'What?' Teeg, hot with the drink, got to his feet, swaying.

Belo pointed into the dark. 'Somewhere over there. I couldn't see. You can get her back. You're the boss here, aren't you?'

'Damn right.' Teeg took a step forward, two.

And the Weapon came drifting up with an almost-silent whisper of displaced air.

'Wait.' Teeg tried to get back inside the perimeter of its patrol. Belo braced himself to push him back – but compact bundles of rags hurtled past him and slammed into Teeg, knocking him to the ground, right in the path of the Weapon. Cold eyes gleamed in small, begrimed faces; Teeg's slaves had rebelled at last, shoving him out of the Weapon's cordon.

And the Weapon spat fire.

The wounds didn't kill Teeg, not straight away. But Belo saw from the way he tried to hold closed his belly that the end wouldn't be far away. Teeg's eyes were full of pain and hatred.

Tira stood over him. She had been hiding among Teeg's women. 'An appropriate way for you to die.'

'She's right,' Belo said. 'After all, you lied, didn't you? That Weapon was never under your control. *You have been farmed by it*, farmed by a machine, just as much as these others, your hapless slaves. The only difference was that you had the cunning to turn the situation to your advantage. But now it's over for you. Well, I'll have my boots back. Don't trouble to take them off. I can wait.'

And he sat on the dirt while the flickering light of day gathered in the sky, and Teeg's life blood spilled on the ground.

For the first time the women talked, and even laughed. The children, hesitantly, began to play.

And still the Weapon continued its deadly circling.

'It is all about the Weapons,' Belo said to Tira. 'It always was.' He smiled. 'I call myself a Creationist. I should be ashamed of myself for not seeing it sooner.'

The Creationists believed that everything about Old Earth had been made for a conscious purpose. But they also believed that the world was very ancient, and that time, too, had shaped the world and its contents – even here, where time ran like syrup.

'The Weapons are made things,' he said. 'And made for one thing—'

'To fight in battle.'

'Yes. Imagine going to war with such gleaming beasts at your command! But when those who had made them had finished their war, they forgot the Weapons, discarded them. And the Weapons, intelligent, purposeful in their own way, sought a new reason to exist.'

The abandoned Weapons, programmed to survive, must have fought among themselves, cannibalising each other for raw materials. But with time a more stable 'food chain' emerged, with the toiling ore-extractors at the bottom, and the most aggressive battlefield machines at the top. The Weapons needed organic material too, which they took from animals like the spindlings – and, later, humans.

So a kind of ecology had emerged, involving humans and Weapons and spindlings: an ecology composed of people, and the technology they had made, and animals, which, Creationists believed, had been brought to this world from somewhere else entirely. It was an ecology that could not have existed without the actions of space-spanning humans, far in the past. But it was the Weapons that had emerged as top predator, machines that learned to farm the remote descendants of those who first made them.

'It is a very fable of Creationism,' Belo breathed, marvelling. 'Wait until I tell them about this back at the seminary in Puul!'

'Except,' Tira said dolefully, 'the seminary, and Puul itself, probably don't even exist any more.'

'True, true.' For a brief moment, exhilarated by new understanding, he had forgotten where they were.

'And anyhow,' Tira said, 'I don't see how any of this helps *us*. We are just as much slaves of the Weapon as these women ever were.'

'Ah, but we are not like Teeg,' he said. 'Whatever his crime, he was a survivor of an age deep in the past, a pretechnological age. We, though, come from an age used to machines, though not so advanced as these. I am confident we will find a way to convince our Weapon to serve *us*, rather than the other way around.'

One of Teeg's women tapped his arm. 'We help you. We watch machine. Long, long time. Know its ways.' Her accent was stronger than Teeg's; he wondered from what era she had come. She smiled at him. She looked very young.

'There you are,' Belo told Tira. 'We can't fail!'

'And then what?'

'And then we will go home, and finish the war.'

So they did.

By the time they stormed back up the time chute, so many years had passed on the Shelf that the war itself was a matter of history, the theological dispute over the nature of the world had been transformed by new evidence, and conquerors and conquered had interbred so much that nobody could untangle the whole mess anyhow. But none of that mattered as Belo and Tira, free and vengeful, with a Weapon of untold potential at their command, began to make their own history.

THE LOWLAND
EXPEDITION
AD c.4.8 BILLION YEARS

Enna relished her flights in the spotting balloon.

She loved to see the Expedition train strung out across the Lowland's arid plain, with its spindling-drawn wagons, the chains of servants and bearers, the gleaming coach that transported her father and his precious books, even the small flock of runner-birds. If the weather was fine the Philosophers themselves would walk alongside the wagons, marching into the Lowland's mysteries, arguing endlessly. The Lowland Expedition was a grand gesture of the civilisation of the Shelf that had spawned it.

And it was brave too, for all the explorers knew that they could never go home again, whatever they discovered. Already the communities they had left had been whisked by stratified time into the deep past; the explorers would bring home their treasure of knowledge to their own remote descendants in an unknowable future.

Down there on the ground was Tomm, one of the junior cartographers. Whenever Enna flew, Tomm always wore a special red cap so she could pick him out, a bright-red dot in the dusty line of Philosophers. At twenty-one he was just a year older than Enna herself – and he was her lover, though that was a secret to all but her closest friends, and certainly to her father, or so she hoped. When he saw her, he waved.

But his waving was sluggish, like an old man's. When she rode her balloon up into the air, Enna was ascending into quicker time. If Tomm's ears had been sensitive enough he would have heard her heart fluttering like a bird's, and conversely when she looked down at him she saw him slowed, trapped in glutinous, redshifted time.

The balloon flights were invaluable aids to navigation, but Bayle, Enna's father, had strictly ordered that flights should be short, and that his party should take it in turns to man them, so that no one fell too far out of synchronisation with the rest. 'This trip is challenging enough for us all,' he insisted, 'without the cogs of time slipping too.' Enna accepted this wisdom. Even now, despite the joy of the flight, she longed to break through the barriers of streamed time that separated her from her love.

But when she spied the city on the horizon she forgot even Tomm.

The light of the Lowland was strange, shifting. Storms of light constantly swept across its surface, silent and flaring white. These founts of brightness were in fact the major source of daylight on Old Earth, but they made the seeing uncertain. Enna thought at first that the bright white line she spied on the horizon must be weather: a low cloud, a dust devil, even a minor light storm. But in a rare instant of clear seeing, the bright band resolved into a cluster of geometrical shapes, unmistakably artificial. It must be a city, stranded in the middle of the Lowland, where nobody had expected to find any signs of humanity but the meanest degradation. And Enna had discovered it.

She turned immediately to the pilot. 'Do you see it? There, the city, can you see? Oh, take us down! Take us down!'

The expedition's chief pilot was a bluff good-humoured fellow called Momo. A long-time military-service companion of her father, he was one of the few people to whom Bayle would entrust his daughter's life. As he had lost one eye in the wars he 'couldn't see a blessed thing', he told her. But he believed her, and began to tug on the ropes that controlled the hot-air balloon's burner.

Enna leaned over the descending gondola, yelling out news of her discovery. As the time differentials melted away, faces turned slowly up towards her.

The Philosophers entered the city in wonder. Enna walked hand in hand with Tomm.

The city was a jumble of cubes and rhomboids, pyramids and tetrahedrons – even one handsome dodecahedron. The buildings towered over the explorers, immense blocks of a geometric perfection that would have shamed even the grand civic centre of New Foro, Enna thought.

There were no doors, though, and the windows weren't glazed. And there were plenty of other peculiarities. Without inner partitions, each building was like 'one big room', as Tomm put it. Between the buildings the ground was just dirt, not paved or cobbled as were the streets of New Foro, back on the Shelf. It was more *abstract* than any city Enna had seen before, more like an art installation perhaps. And yet these great structures were clearly habitable.

'And there's nobody here,' Enna whispered. 'Not a soul! It's so strange.'

'But wonderful,' Tomm said. He was tall, strong but sparsely built, with a languid grace that disturbed her dreams. 'This must be a terribly ancient place. Look at the finish of these walls – what is this stuff, stone, ceramic, glass? Far beyond anything we are capable of. Perhaps the builders were Weapon-makers.'

'Maybe, but don't you think it's all rather eerie? And the layout is such a jumble—'

'A cartographer's nightmare.' Tomm laughed.

'And why are there no windows or doors?'

'We can make windows,' he said. 'We can hang doors.' He took her hands. 'Questions, questions, Enna! You're worse than all these grumpy old Philosophers. This is your discovery. Relish the moment!'

There was a deep *harrumph*. Bayle, Enna's father, came walking towards them, trailed by acolytes, lesser men but Philosophers themselves. Tomm hastily released Enna's hands.

'But Enna is right,' Bayle said. 'There is some familiarity about the place, and yet perhaps that merely blinds us to how much is strange . . .'

Bayle wore his dress uniform, topped off by his cap of spindling fur and feathers. Though he had devoted the last three decades of his life to science, Bayle had retained an honorary rank in the army of New Foro, and 'for the sake of general morale', as he put it, he donned his uniform to mark moments of particular significance during their long journey. But Enna knew that no matter how extravagant his appearance, her father's mind was sharper than any of those around him.

He tapped the walls of the nearest building with his stick. 'Certainly the layout follows no obvious rational design, as does the centre of New Foro, say. But there are patterns here.' He walked them briskly through the narrow alleys between the buildings. 'Can you see how the largest buildings are clustered on the outside, and the smaller huts are in their shade?'

'It almost looks organic,' Enna said impulsively. 'Like a forest, dominated by its tallest trees.'

Bayle eyed her appreciatively. '*I* was going to compare it to a bank of salt crystals.' Salt had become something of an obsession of Bayle's during their journey. There was salt everywhere in the Lowlands; there were even plains covered with the stuff, the relics of dried-up lakes.

Bayle was gathering evidence for his contention that the Lowland had once been the bed of a mighty body of water. 'But I admit, daughter, that your analogy may be more apt. This city is not planned as we think of it. It is almost as if it has *grown* here.'

Tomm seemed confused. 'But that's just an analogy. I mean, this is a city, built by human hands – though maybe long ago. That much is obvious, isn't it?'

Bayle snapped, 'If everything were obvious we would not have needed to come out here to study it.' He gave Enna a look that spoke volumes. *The boy has a pretty face but a shallow mind*, said that withering expression. *You can do better*.

But Tomm was Enna's choice, and she returned his glare defiantly.

They were interrupted by a raucous hail. 'Sir, sir! Look what I've found!' It was Momo. The burly, one-eyed pilot came stumbling around the corner of a building.

And walking with him was a woman. Dressed in some kind of scraped animal skin, she was tall, aged perhaps fifty, in her way elegant despite her ragged costume. She eyed the Philosophers, detached. In that first moment Enna thought she seemed as cold, strange and hard-edged as her city.

Bayle stepped forward, his gloved hand extended. 'Madam,' he said, 'if you can understand me, we have a great deal to discuss.' The woman took Bayle's hand and shook it. The subordinate Philosophers applauded enthusiastically.

It was yet another remarkable moment in this unprecedented trek of discovery. This was Bayle's first contact with any of the 'lost souls' believed to inhabit the Lowland, stranded here from ages past; to find such people and 'rehabilitate' them had been one of his stated goals from the beginning.

But Enna caught a strange whiff about the woman, an iron stink that at first she couldn't place. It was only later that she realised it was the smell of raw meat – of blood.

As night fell, the explorers and their attendants and servants dispersed gladly into the city's bare buildings. After the dirt of the plain, it was going to be a relief to spend a night within solid walls.

Bayle himself established his base in one of the grander buildings on the edge of the city, bathed in light even at the end of the day. It seemed he planned to spend most of the night in conversation with the woman who was, as far as anybody could tell, the city's sole inhabitant; he said they had much to learn from each other. He kissed his daughter goodnight, trusting her safety to his companions, and to her own common sense.

So it was a betrayal of him, of a sort, when in the darkest night Enna sought out Tomm's warm arms. It wasn't hard for her to put her guilt aside; at twenty she had a healthy awareness of how far her father's opinions should govern her life.

But she dreamed. She dreamed that the building itself gathered her up and lifted her into the sky, just as she was cradled by Tomm's arms – and she thought she smelled that iron tang again, the scent of blood.

The dream became disturbing, a dream of confinement.

Bayle had formulated many objectives for his Expedition.

Always visible from Foro, Puul and the other towns of the Shelf, the Lowland, stretching away below in redshifted ambiguity, had been a mystery throughout history. Now that mystery would be dispelled. Cartographers would map the Lowland. Historians, anthropologists and moralists hoped to make contact with the lost people of the Lowland plains, if any survived. Clerics, mystics, doctors and other Philosophers hoped to learn something about Effigies, those spectral apparitions that rose from dying human bodies, or some of them, and fled to the redshifted mysteries of the Lowland. Perhaps some insight would be gained into the cause of the Formidable Caresses, the tremendous rattlings that regularly shook human civilisation to pieces. There were even a few soldiers and armourers, hoping to track down Weapons, ancient technology gone wild, too wily to have been captured so far.

There had already been many successes. Take the light storms, for instance.

Old Earth's blueshifted sky was a dome of stars that spun around the world. Day and night, and the seasons of the year, were governed not by the sky but by the flickering uncertainties of the light that emanated from the Lowland. Now Bayle's physicists had discovered that these waves of light pulsed at many frequencies, 'like the harmonics of a plucked string,' as one mathematician had described it. Not only that, because of the redshifting of the light that struggled up to higher altitudes, the harmonic peaks that governed the daily cycles here were different from those to be observed from Foro, up on the Shelf, where time ran faster.

Enna was walked through the logic by her father. The effects of time stratification, redshifting and light cycling subtly intermeshed, so that whether you were up on the Shelf or down in the Lowland the length of day and night you *perceived* was roughly similar. This surely couldn't be a coincidence. As Bayle said, 'It adds up to a remarkable mathematical argument for the whole world having been *designed* to be habitable by people and their creatures.'

That, of course, had provoked a lively debate.

Forons were traditionally Mechanists, adhering to a strand of natural philosophy that held that there was no governing mind behind the world, that everything about it had emerged from the blind working-out of natural laws – like the growth of a salt crystal, say, rather than the purposeful construction of a machine. However, there were hard-line Creationists who argued that *everything* on Old Earth required a purposeful explanation.

After centuries of debate a certain compromise view had emerged, it seemed to Enna, a melding of extreme viewpoints based on the evidence. Even the most ardent Mechanists had been forced to accept that the world contained overwhelming evidence that it had been manufactured, or at least heavily engineered. But if Old Earth was a machine, it was a very old machine, and in the ages since its formation, natural processes of the kind argued for by the Mechanists had surely operated to modify the world. Old Earth was a machine that had evolved.

At the heart of Bayle's expedition was a deep ambition to reconcile the two great poles of human thought, the Mechanist versus the Creationist – and to end centuries of theological conflict over which too much blood had been spilled. He and his companions would see through this goal, even though they could only return to a distant future.

In the morning Enna and Tomm were among the first to stir. They emerged from their respective buildings, and greeted each other with a jolly innocence that probably fooled nobody.

Cartographer Tomm had been detailed to take up the balloon for a rapid aerial survey, to provide context for the more painstaking work on the ground. Enna, free of specific chores, decided to ride up with him.

But there was a problem. They couldn't find Momo. The pilot was a habitual early riser, like Bayle himself – a relic from his military days, it seemed. He was *always* up for Enna.

Tomm was unconcerned. 'So old One-eye treated himself to a party last night. He won't be the only one—'

'That isn't like Momo!' Enna snapped, growing impatient. When Tomm treated her like a foolish child, Enna had some sympathy for her father's view of him. 'Look, this is a strange city, which we barely explored before splitting up. You can help me find Momo, or use the hot air you're spouting to go blow up the balloon yourself.'

He was crestfallen, but when she stalked off to search, Tomm, embarrassed, hurried after her.

She thought she remembered the building Momo had chosen as his shelter. She headed that way now.

But something was wrong. As she followed the unpaved alleys, the layout of the buildings didn't quite match her memory of the night before. Of course, she had only had a quick glimpse of the city, and the light of morning, playing over these crisp creamy walls, was quite different. But even so, she wouldn't have expected to get as lost as this.

And when she came to the place where she thought Momo's building should have been, there was only a blank space. She walked back and forth over the bare ground, disoriented, dread gathering in her soul.

'You must be mistaken,' Tomm insisted.

'I'm good at direction-finding, Tomm. You know that.'

Playfully he said, 'You found your way to my bed well enough—'

'Oh, shut up. This is serious. This is where Momo's shelter was, I'm sure of it. Something has changed. I can feel it.'

Tomm said defensively, 'That doesn't sound very scientific.'

'Then help me, o great cartographer. Did any of you make a map last night?'

'Of course not. The light was poor. We knew there would be time enough today.'

She glared at him. But she was being unfair; it was a perfectly reasonable assumption that a city like this wouldn't change overnight.

But the fact of the matter was, Momo was still missing.

Growing increasingly disturbed, she went to her father's room. That at least was just where it had been last night. But her father wouldn't see her; a busybody junior Philosopher barred her from even entering the door. Bayle was still deep in discussion with Sila, the ragged city woman, and he had left strict instructions to be disturbed by nobody – not even Enna, his daughter.

Tomm, apologetically, said he had to get on with his flight, Momo or no Momo. Distracted, Enna kissed him goodbye, and continued her search.

In the hours that followed, she walked the length and breadth of the city. She didn't find Momo. But she did learn that he wasn't the only missing person; two others had vanished, both servants. Though a few people were troubled, most seemed sure it was just a case of getting lost in a strange city. And as for the uncertain layout, she saw doubt in a few eyes. But the Philosophers, far better educated than she was, had no room in their heads for such strange and confusing notions as an indeterminate geography.

When Tomm went sailing over the city in his balloon, a junior pilot at his side, she dutifully wore the red cap so he could see her, down here on the ground. Time-accelerated, he waved like a jerky puppet. But still she couldn't find Momo, or dispel her feeling of disquiet.

That evening, to her astonishment, her father let it be known that he was hosting a dinner – and Sila, the ragged city woman, was to be guest of honour.

Enna couldn't remember her father showing such crass misjudgement before, and she wondered if he had somehow been seduced by this exotic city of the Lowland, or, worse, by the woman, Sila, of whom Enna knew nothing at all. But still Bayle's entourage would not let Enna near her father; he was much too busy for mere family.

Enna made the best of it. She put on the finest dress in her luggage, and decorated her hair with her best jewellery, including the pretty piece her mother had given her when they bade their tearful goodbyes. But as she brushed her hair by the light of her spindling-fat lamp, the blank walls of the city building she was using seemed to close in around her.

She met Tomm outside the building. He was still in his travelling clothes; he had not been invited to the dinner.

'You look wonderful,' he said.

She knew he meant it, and her heart softened. 'Thank you.' She let him kiss her.

'Do you suppose I'm allowed to walk you over?'

'I'd like that. But, Tomm—' She glanced back at the building, the gaping unglazed windows like eye sockets. 'Put my luggage back in one of our wagons. I don't care which one. I'm not spending another night in one of these boxes.'

'Ah. Not even with me?'

'Not even with you. I'm sorry, Tomm.'

'Don't be. As long as you let me share your wagon.'

When they got to her father's building she was stunned by the sight. Inside, three long trestle-tables had been set up and laid with cloths and the best cutlery and china. Candles glowed on the tables, and finely dressed guests had already taken their seats. At the head table sat Bayle himself, with his closest confidantes – and his guest of honour, Sila, dressed now in a fine flowing black robe, sat beside him. From a smaller building co-opted as a kitchen, a steamy smell of vegetables emanated, while five fat runner-chicks slowly roasted on spits. Enna had grown up in a world shaped by her father's organisational skills, of which the Expedition was perhaps the crowning glory. But even she was impressed by the speed and skill with which this event had been assembled. After all, the party had only reached this mysterious Lowland city a day before.

When he saw Enna, Bayle stood up and waved her forward. Led by Nool, Bayle's sleek manservant, Enna took her place at her father's right-hand side. Sila sat on his left.

Enna leaned close to her father. 'I've got to talk to you. I've been trying all day.'

'I know you have. Priorities, my dear.'

That was a word she had heard all her life. But she insisted, 'Something isn't right here. People are missing. The geography—'

He cut her off with a wave of his hand. 'I know you're no fool, my daughter, and I will hear you out. But not now. We'll make time at the end of the dinner.'

She wasn't going to get any more from him. But as her father sat back, she caught the eye of the city woman, Sila. She imagined there was a calculation in Sila's deep gaze as it met her own. She wondered what Sila truly wanted – and what it would cost them all if she achieved it.

The food was good, of course; her father would have allowed nothing less, and the wine flowed voluminously, though Enna refused to touch a drop. She longed for the meal to be over, so she could talk to Bayle before another night fell. At last the final dish was cleared away, the glasses refilled for the final time.

And, to Enna's intense frustration, Bayle got to his feet and began to make a speech.

He had spent the night and much of the day in conversation with Sila, he said, and a remarkable experience it had been.

Everybody had expected to find people down here on the Lowland. For generations the judges of Foro had used 'time pits' as a punishment measure. The logic was simple. The deeper you fell, the slower time passed for you, so by being hurled into the time pits you were banished to the future. Only a handful had ever climbed back up, bewilderingly displaced in time. But as time had gone by, rumours wafted up to the Shelf that some, at least, of the criminals of the past had survived, down there in their redshifted prison.

'The time pits have long been stopped up,' Bayle said now, 'and we look back on such methods with shame. Now we long to discover what had become of our exiled citizens, and their offspring – and we long to reach out to them a hand of reason and hope. Our consciences would permit nothing less.

'And now we have found those lost souls, in the person of Sila. She is the daughter of an exile, whose crime was political. Sila grew up almost in isolation with her mother, her only society a drifting, transient collection of refugees from many ages. And yet she is educated and articulate, with a sound moral compass; it would take very little grooming indeed for her to pass as a citizen of Foro.

'There may be no society as we know it here, no government, no community. But the inhabitants of the Lowland are not animals but people, as we are. In her person Sila demonstrates the fundamental goodness of human nature, whatever its environment – and I for one applaud her for that.'

This was greeted by murmured appreciation and bangs of the tables. Sila looked out at the Philosophers, a small smile barely dissipating the coldness of her expression.

Now Bayle came to the emotional climax of his speech. 'We all knew when we embarked from Foro that this would not just be an Expedition to the Lowland, but into time. We are all of us lost in the future, and with every day that passes here, the further that awful distance from home grows.' He glanced at Enna, and she knew he was thinking of her mother, his wife, who had been too ill to travel with them on this journey – and who, as a consequence, Enna would never see again. 'All of you made a sacrifice for knowledge, a sacrifice without precedent in the history of our civilisation.

'But,' Bayle said, 'if this is a journey of no return, it need not be a journey without an end.

'Look around you! We do not yet know who built this place, and why – I have no doubt we will discover all this in the future. But we do know that *it is empty*. The sparse population of the Lowland has never found the collective will to inhabit this place. But we can turn this shell into a true city – and with our industry and communal spirit, we will serve as a beacon for those who wander across the Lowland's plains. All this I have discussed at length with Sila.

'Our long journey ends here. Oh, we will send emissaries back to our home on the Shelf – or the daughter civilisations of those we remember. But this city, bequeathed to us by an unimaginable past, will host *our* future.' He raised his hands; Enna had never seen him look more evangelical. 'We have come home!'

He won a storm of applause. Sila surveyed the crowded room, that cold assessment dominating her expression – and again Enna was sure she could smell the cold iron stench of raw meat.

At the end of the dinner, despite her anxiety and determination, Enna still couldn't get to talk to her father. Bayle apologised, but with silent admonishments, warned her about spoiling the mood he had so carefully built; she knew that as Expedition leader he believed that morale, ever fragile, was the most precious resource of all. It will keep until the morning, his expression told her.

Frustrated, deeply uneasy, she left the building, walked out of the city to her wagon, and threw herself into Tomm's arms. He seemed surprised by her passion.

Wait until the morning, Bayle had said.

But when the morning came the city was in chaos.

They were woken by babbling voices. They hastily pulled on their clothes, and hurried out of the wagon.

Servants and Philosophers alike milled about, some only half-dressed. Enna found Nool, her father's manservant; dishevelled, unshaven, he was nothing like the sleek major-domo of the dinner last night. 'I'm not going back in there again,' he said. 'You can pay me what you like.'

Enna grabbed his shoulders. 'Nool! Calm down, man. Is it my father? Is something wrong?'

'The sooner we get loaded up and out of here the better, I say . . .'

Enna abandoned him and turned to Tomm. 'We'll have to find him, Tomm! My father—'

But Tomm was staring up at the sky. 'By all that's created,' he said. 'Look at that.'

At first she thought the shape drifting in the sky was the Expedition's balloon. But this angular, sharp-edged, white-walled object was no balloon. *It was a building*, a parallelepiped, like a slanted cube.

With no sign of doors or windows, it had come loose from the ground, and drifted away on the wind like a soap bubble.

'I don't believe it,' Tomm murmured.

Enna said grimly, 'Believe it or not, we have to find my father even so. Come *on*.' She grabbed his hand and dragged him into the city.

The unmade streets were crowded today, and people swarmed; it was difficult to find a way through. Again she had that strange, dreamlike feeling that the layout of the city was different. 'Tell me you see it too, cartographer,' she demanded of Tomm. 'It has changed, again.'

'Yes, it has changed.'

She was relieved to see her father's building was still where it had been. But Philosophers were wandering outside, helpless, wringing their hands.

The doors and windows, all of them, had sealed up. There was no way into the building, or out.

She shoved her way through the crowd, grabbing Philosophers. 'Where is he? Is he in there?' But none of them had an answer. She reached the building itself. She ran her hands over the wall where the doorway had been last night, but it was seamless, as if the doorway had never existed. She slammed on the wall. 'Father? Bayle! Can you hear me? It's Enna!' But there was no reply.

And then the wall lurched before her. Tomm snatched her back. The whole building was shifting, she saw, as if restless to leave the ground. Still she called, 'Father! Father!'

'He can't hear you.' The woman, Sila, stood in the fine robes Bayle had given her. She seemed aloof, untouched.

Enna grabbed Sila by the shoulders and pushed her against the wall of the building. 'What have you done?'

'Me? I haven't done anything.' Sila was unperturbed by Enna's violence, though she was breathing hard. 'But you know that, don't you?' Her voice was deep, exotic – ancient as Lowland dust.

Desperate as Enna was to find her father, the pieces of the puzzle were sliding around in her head. '*This is all about the buildings*, isn't it?'

'You're a clever girl. Your father will be proud – or would have been. He's probably already dead. Don't fret; he won't have suffered, much.'

Tomm stood before them, uncertain. 'I don't understand any of this. Has this woman harmed Bayle?'

'No,' Enna hissed. 'You just lured him here – didn't you, you witch?

It's the building, Tomm. That's what's important here, not this woman.'

'The building?'

'The buildings take meat,' Sila said.

Tomm looked bewildered. 'Meat?'

'Somehow they use it to maintain their fabric. Don't ask me how.'

'And light,' Enna said. 'That's why they stack up into this strange reef, isn't it? It isn't a human architecture at all, is it? They *are* more like a forest. *The buildings are competing for the light.*'

Sila smiled. 'You see, I said you were clever.'

'Light?'

'Oh, Tomm, don't just repeat everything we say! He's in there. My father. And we've got to get him out.'

Tomm was obviously bewildered. 'If you say so. How?'

She thought fast. Buildings that take meat. Buildings that need light . . . 'The balloon,' she said. 'Get some servants.'

'It will take an age for the heaters—'

'Just bring the envelope. Hurry, Tomm!'

Tomm rushed off.

Enna went back to the building and continued to slam her hand against the wall. 'I'll get you out of there, Father. Hold on!' But there was no reply. And again the building shifted ominously, its base scraping over the ground. She glanced into the sky, where that flying building had already become a speck against the blueshifted stars. If they fed, if they had the light they needed, did the buildings simply float away in search of new prey? Was that what had become of poor Momo?

Tomm returned with the balloon envelope, manhandled by a dozen bearers.

'Get it over the building,' Enna ordered. 'Block out the light. Hurry. Oh, please . . .'

All of them hauled at the balloon envelope, dragging it over the building. The envelope ripped on the sharp corners of the structure, but Enna ignored wails of protest from the watching Philosophers. At last the thick hide envelope covered the building from top to bottom; it was like a wrapped-up present. She stood back, breathing hard, her hands stinking of leather. She had no idea what to do next if this didn't work.

And a door dilated open in the side of the building.

Fumes billowed out, hot and yellow, and people recoiled, coughing

405

and pressing their eyes. Then Bayle came staggering out, and collapsed to the ground.

'Father!' Enna knelt, and took his head on her lap.

His clothes were shredded, his hands were folded up like claws, and the skin of his face was crimson. But he was alive. 'It was an acid bath in there,' he wheezed. 'Another few moments and I would have succumbed. It was like being swallowed. Digested.'

'I know,' she said.

He looked up; his eyes had been spared the acid. 'You understand?'

'I think so. Father, we have to let the doctors see to you.'

'Yes, yes . . . But first, get everybody out of this cursed place.'

Enna glanced up at Tomm, who turned away and began to shout commands.

'And,' wheezed Bayle, 'where is that woman, Sila?'

There was a waft of acid-laden air, a ripping noise. Philosophers scrambled back out of the way. Cradling her father, Enna saw that the building had shaken off the balloon envelope and was lifting grandly into the air. And Sila sat in an open doorway, looking down impassively, as the building lifted her into the time-accelerated sky.

Bayle was taken to his wagon, where his wounds were treated. He allowed in nobody but his daughter, the doctors, Nool – and Tomm, who, Bayle admitted grudgingly, had acquitted himself well.

Even in this straitened circumstance Bayle held forth, his voice reduced to a whisper, his face swathed in unguent cream. 'I blame myself,' he said. 'I let myself see what I wanted to see about this city – just as I pompously warned you, Tomm, against the self-same flaw. And I refused to listen to you, Enna. I wanted to see a haven for the people I have led out into the wilderness. I saw what did not exist.'

'You saw what Sila wanted you to see,' Enna said.

'Ah, Sila . . . What an enigma! But the fault is mine, Enna; you won't talk me out of that.'

'And the buildings—'

'I should have seen the pattern before you did! After all, we have a precedent. The Weapons are technology gone wild, made things modified by time, grown into a kind of ecology – and so are the buildings of this "city".'

Once, surely, the buildings had been intended to house people. But they were advanced technology: mobile, self-maintaining habitats. They fuelled themselves with light, and with organic traces

– perhaps they had been designed to process their occupants' waste.

Things changed. People abandoned the buildings, and forgot about them. But the buildings, self-maintaining, perhaps even self-aware in some rudimentary sense, sought a new way to live – and that new way diverged ever more greatly from the purposes their human inventors had imagined.

'They came together for protection,' Bayle whispered. 'They huddled together in reefs that looked like towns, cities, jostling for light. And then they discovered a new strategy, when the first ragged human beings innocently entered their doorways.

'The buildings apparently offered shelter. And whenever a human was foolish enough to accept that mute offer—'

'They feed,' said Tomm with horror.

Bayle said, 'It is just as the Weapons of the plain once learned to farm humans for meat. We share a world with technology that has gone wild and undergone its own evolution. I should have known!'

Enna said, 'And Sila?'

'Now she is more interesting,' Bayle whispered. 'She told me exactly what I wanted to hear – fool as I was to listen! She cooperates with the city, you see; in return for shelter – perhaps even for some grisly form of food – she helps it lure in unwitting travellers, like us. Her presence makes it seem safer than a city empty altogether.'

'A symbiosis,' Tomm said, wondering. 'Of humans with wild technology.'

Enna shuddered. 'We have had a narrow escape.'

Bayle covered her hand with his own bandaged fingers. 'But others, like poor Momo, have died for my foolishness.'

'We must go on,' Tomm said. 'There is nothing for us here.'

'Nothing but a warning. Yes, we will go on. The Expedition continues! But not for ever. Someday we will find a home—'

'Or we will build one,' Tomm said firmly.

Bayle nodded stiffly. 'Yes. But that's for you youngsters, not for the likes of me.'

Enna was moved to take Tomm's hand in hers.

Bayle watched them. 'He may not have a first-class mind,' he said to Enna. 'But he has an air of command, and that's worth cultivating.'

'Oh, father—'

Outside the wagon there came shouting, and a rushing sound, like great breaths being drawn.

'Go and see,' Bayle whispered.

Enna and Tomm hurried out of the wagon.

Displacing air that washed over the people, the sentient buildings of the city were lifting off the ground, all of them now, massive, mobile. Already the first was high in the blueshifted sky, and the others followed in a stream of silent geometry, a city blowing away like a handful of seeds on the breeze.

FORMIDABLE CARESS
AD c.5 BILLION YEARS

As the women tried to pull her away, Ama hammered with her fist on the blank wall of the Building. 'Let me inside! Oh, let me inside!'

But the Building had sealed itself against her. If the Weapon that ruled the people decreed that you were to bear your child in the open air, that was how it was going to be, and no mere human being could do anything about it.

And she could not fight the logic of her body. The contractions came in pulses now, in waves of pain that washed through the core of her being. In the end it was her father, Telni, who put his bony arm around her shoulders, murmuring small endearments. Exhausted, she allowed herself to be led away.

Telni's sister Jurg and the other women had set up a pallet for her not far from the rim of the Platform. They laid her down there and fussed with their blankets and buckets of warmed water, and pre-pared ancient knives for the cutting. Her aunt massaged her swollen belly with oils brought up from the Lowland. Telni propped Ama's head on his arm, and held her hand tightly, but she could feel the weariness in her father's grip.

So it began. She breathed and screamed and pushed.

And through it all, here at the lip of the Platform, this floating island in the sky, she was surrounded by the apparatus of her world, the Buildings clustered around her – floating buildings that supported the Platform itself – the red mist of the Lowland far below, above her the gaunt cliff on which glittered the blue-tinged lights of the Shelf cities, the sky over her head where chains of stars curled like wind-blown hair . . . When she looked up she was peering into accelerated time, into places where a human heart fluttered like a songbird's. But there was a personal dimension to time too, so her father had always taught her, and these hours of her labour were the longest of her life, as if her body had been dragged all the way down into the glutinous, redshifted slowness of the Lowland.

When it was done Jurg handed her the baby. It was a boy, a scrap of

411

flesh born a little early, his weight negligible inside the spindling-skin blankets. She immediately loved him unconditionally, whatever alien thing lay within. 'I call him Telni like his grandfather,' she managed to whisper.

Old Telni, exhausted himself, wiped tears from his crumpled cheeks.

She slept for a while, out in the open.

When she opened her eyes, the Weapon was floating above her. As always, a small boy stood at its side.

The Weapon was a box as wide as a human was tall, reflective as a mirror, hovering at waist height above the smooth surface of the Platform. Ama could see herself in the thing's silver panels, on her back on the heap of blankets, her baby asleep in the cot beside her. Her aunt, her father, the other women hung back, nervous of this massive presence that dominated all their lives.

Then a small hatch opened in the Weapon's flank, an opening with lobed lips, like a mouth. From this hatch a silvery tongue, metres long, reached out and snaked into the back of the neck of the small boy who stood alongside it. Now the boy took a step towards Ama's cot, trailing his tongue-umbilical.

Telni blocked his way. 'Stay back, Powpy, you little monster. You were once a boy as I was. Now I am old and you are still young. Stay away from my grandson.'

Powpy halted. Ama saw that his eyes flickered nervously, glancing at Telni, the cot, the Weapon. This showed the extent of the Weapon's control of its human creature; somewhere in there was a frightened child.

Ama struggled to sit up. 'What do you want?'

The boy Powpy turned to her. 'We wish to know why you wanted to give birth within a Building.'

'You know why,' she snapped back. 'No child born inside a Building has ever harboured an Effigy.'

The child's voice was flat, neutral – his accent was like her father's, she thought, a little boy with the intonation of an older generation. 'A child without an Effigy is less than a child with an Effigy. Human tradition concurs with that, even without understanding—'

'I didn't want *you* to be interested in him.' The words came in a rush. 'You control us. You keep us here, floating on this island in the sky. All for the Effigies we harbour, or not. That's what you're interested in, isn't it?' Her father laid a trembling hand on her arm, but she

412

shook it away. 'My husband believed his life was pointless, that his only purpose was to nurture the Effigy inside him, and grow old and die for you. In the end he destroyed himself—'

'Addled by the drink,' murmured Telni.

'He didn't want *you* to benefit from his death. He never even saw this baby, his son. He wanted more than this!'

The Weapon seemed to consider this. 'We intend no harm. On the contrary, a proper study of the symbiotic relationship between humans and Effigies—'

'Go away,' she said. She found she was choking back tears. 'Go away!' And she flung a blanket at its impassive hide, for that was all she had to throw.

The Weapon returned to visit Telni when he was six years old. Ama chased it away again.

The machine next came to see Telni after the death of Ama and her father. Telni was ten years old. There was no one to chase it away.

The double funeral was almost done, at last.

Telni had had to endure a long vigil beside the bodies, where they had been laid out close to the rim of the Platform. He slept a lot, huddled against his kind but severe great-aunt Jurg, his last surviving relative.

At the dawn of the third day, as the light storms down on the Lowland glimmered and shifted and filled the air with their pearly glow, Jurg prodded him awake.

And, he saw, his mother's Effigy was ascending. A cloud of pale mist burst soundlessly from the body on its pallet. It hovered, tendrils and billows pulsing – and then, just for a heartbeat, it gathered itself into a form that was recognisably human, a misty shell with arms and legs, torso and head.

Jurg, Ama's aunt, was crying. 'She's smiling. Can you see? Oh, how wonderful . . .'

The sketch of Ama lengthened, her neck stretching like a spindling's, becoming impossibly long. Then the distorted Effigy shot up into the blueshifted sky and arced down over the lip of the Platform, hurling itself into the flickering crimson of the plain below. Jurg told Telni that Ama's Effigy was seeking its final lodging deep in the slow-beating heart of Old Earth, where, so it was believed, something of Ama would survive even the Formidable Caresses. But Telni knew that Ama had despised the Effigies, even the one that turned out to have resided in her.

They waited another day, but no Effigy emerged from old Telni.

The bodies were taken across the Platform, to the centre of the cluster of box-shaped, blank-walled Buildings that supported this aerial colony, and placed reverently inside one of the smaller structures. A week later, when Jurg took Telni to see, the bodies were entirely vanished, their substance subsumed by the Building, which might have become a fraction larger after its ingestion.

So Telni, orphaned, was left in the care of his great-aunt.

Jurg tried to get him to return to his schooling. A thousand people lived on the Platform, of which a few hundred were children; the schools were efficient and well organised.

But Telni, driven by feelings too complicated to face, was restless. He roamed alone through the forest of Buildings. Or he would stand at the edge of the Platform, before the gulf that surrounded his floating home, and look up to watch the Shelf war unfold, accelerated by its altitude, the pale-blue explosions and whizzing aircraft making an endless spectacle. He was aware that his great-aunt and teachers and the other adults were watching him, concerned, but for now they gave him his head.

On the third day, he made for one of his favourite places, which was the big wheel at the very centre of the Platform, turned endlessly by harnessed spindlings. Here you could look down through a hatch in the Platform, a hole in the floor of the world, and follow the tethers that attached the Platform like a huge kite to the Lowland ground half a kilometre below, and watch the bucket chains rising and falling. The Loading Hub was down on the ground directly beneath the Platform, the convergence of a dozen roads that were crowded with supply carts day and night. Standing here it was as if you could see the machinery of the world working. Telni liked to think about such things, to work them out, as a distraction from thinking about other things. And it pleased him in other ways he didn't really understand, as if he had a deep, sunken memory of much bigger, more complicated machinery than this.

Best of all you could visit the spindling pens and help the cargo jockeys muck out one of the tall beasts, and brush the fur on its six powerful legs, and feed it the strange purple-coloured straw it preferred. The spindlings saw him cry a few times, but nobody else, not even his great-aunt.

And so the Weapon came to see him.

Telni was alone in one of the smaller Buildings, near the centre of the cluster on the Platform. He was watching the slow crawl of lightmoss across the wall, the glow it cast subtly shifting. It was as if the Weapon just appeared at the door. Its little boy stood at its side, Powpy, with the cable dangling from the back of his neck.

Telni stared at the boy. 'He used to be bigger than me. The boy. Now he's smaller.'

'We believe you understand why,' said Powpy.

'The last time I saw you was four years ago. I was six. I've grown since then. But you live down on the Lowland, mostly. Did you come up in one of the freight buckets?'

'No.'

'You live slower down there.'

'Do you know how much slower?'

'No,' Telni said.

The boy nodded stiffly, as if somebody was pushing the back of his head. 'A straightforward, honest answer. The Lowland here is deep, about half a kilometre below the Platform, which is itself over three hundred metres below the Shelf. Locally the stratification of time has a gradient of, approximately, five parts in one hundred per metre. So a year on the Platform is—'

'Only a couple of weeks on the Lowland. But, umm, three hundred times five, a year here is fifteen years on the Shelf.'

'Actually closer to seventeen. Do you know *why* time is stratified?'

'I don't know that word.'

Powpy's little mouth had stumbled on it too, and other hard words. 'Layered.'

'No.'

'Good. Nor do we. Do you know why your mother died?'

That blunt question made him gasp. Since Ama had gone, nobody had even mentioned her name. 'It was the refugees' plague. She died of that. And my grandfather died soon after. My great-aunt Jurg says it was of a broken heart.'

'Why did the plague come here?'

'The refugees brought it. Refugees from the war on the Shelf. The war's gone on for years, Shelf years. My grandfather says – said – it is as if they are trying to bring down a Formidable Caress of their own, on their families. The refugees came in a balloon. Families with kids. Grandfather says it happens every so often. They don't know what the

Platform is but they see it hanging in the air below them, at peace. So they try to escape from the war.'

'Were they sick when they arrived?'

'No. But they carried the plague bugs. People started dying. They weren't im—'

'Immune.'

'Immune like the refugees were.'

'Why not?'

'Time goes faster up on the Shelf. Bugs change quickly. You get used to one, but then another comes along.'

'Your understanding is clear.'

'My mother hated you. She was unhappy when you visited me that time, when I was six. She says you meddle in our lives.'

'"Meddle." We created the Platform, gathered the sentient Buildings to support it in the air. We designed this community. Your life, and the lives of many generations of your ancestors, have been shaped by what we built. We "meddled" in many ways long before you were born.'

'Why?'

Silence again. 'That's too big a question. Ask smaller questions.'

'Why are there so many roads coming in across the Lowland to the Loading Hub?'

'I think you know the answer to that.'

'Time goes twenty-five times slower down there. It's as if they're trying to feed a city twenty-five times the size of the Platform. As if we eat twenty-five times as fast as they do!'

'That's right. Now ask about something you don't know.'

He pointed to the lightmoss. 'You put this stuff in the Buildings to give us light. Like living, glowing paint.'

'That's correct.'

'Is this the same stuff that makes the light storms, down on the Lowland?'

'Yes, it is. Later you may learn that lightmoss is gathered on the Lowland and shipped up to the Platform in the supply lifts. That's a good observation. To connect two such apparently disparate phenomena—'

'I tried to eat the lightmoss. I threw it up. You can't eat the spindlings' straw either. Why?'

'Because they come from other places. Other worlds than this. Whole other systems of life.'

Telni understood some of this. 'People brought them here, and mixed everything up.' A thought struck him. 'Can spindlings eat lightmoss?'

'Why is that relevant?'

'Because if they can it must mean they both came from the same other place.'

'You can find that out for yourself.'

He itched to try the experiment, right now. But he sought another question to ask, while he had the chance. 'Did people make you?'

'They made our grandfathers, if you like.'

'Were you really Weapons?'

'Not all of us. Such labels are irrelevant now. When human civilisations fell, sentient machines were left to roam, to interact. There was selection, of a brutal sort, as we competed for resources and spare parts. Thus we enjoyed our own long evolution. A man called Bayle mounted an expedition to the Lowland, and found us.'

'You were farming humans. That's what my mother said.'

'It wasn't as simple as that. The interaction with Bayle's scholars led to a new generation of machines with enhanced faculties.'

'What kind of faculties?'

'Curiosity.'

Telni considered that. 'What's special about me? That I might have an Effigy inside me?'

'Not just that. Your mother rebelled when you were born. That's very rare. The human community here was founded from a pool of scholars, but that was many generations ago. We fear that by caring for you we may have bred out a certain initiative. That was how you came to our attention, Telni. Your mother rebelled, and *you* seek to answer questions. There may be questions you can answer that we can't. There may be questions you can *ask* that we can't.'

'Like what?'

'You have to ask. That's the point.'

He thought. 'What are the Formidable Caresses?'

'The ends of the world. Or at least, of civilisation. In the past, and in the future.'

'How does time work?'

'That's another question you can answer yourself.'

He was mystified. 'How?'

A seam opened up on the Weapon's sleek side, like a wound, revealing a dark interior. Powpy had to push his little hand inside and grope around for something. Despite the Weapon's control, Telni could see

417

the boy's revulsion. He drew out something that gleamed, complex, a mechanism. He handed it to Telni.

Telni turned it over in his hands, fascinated. It was warm. 'What is it?'

'A clock. A precise one. You'll work out what to do with it.' The Weapon moved, gliding up another metre into the air. 'One more question.'

'Why do I feel . . . sometimes . . .' It was hard to put into words. 'Like I should be somewhere else? My mother said everybody feels like that, when they're young. But . . . Is it a stupid question?'

'No. It is a very important question. But it is one you will have to answer for yourself. We will see you again.' It drifted away, two metres up in the air, with the little boy running beneath, like a dog on a long lead. But it paused once more, and the boy turned and spoke again. 'What will you do now?'

Telni grinned. 'Go feed moss to a spindling.'

That was the start of Telni's scholarship, in retrospect, much of it self-discovered, self-taught. And as his understanding increased, he grew in wisdom, strength, and stature in his community.

In Telni's twenty-fifth year, a group of Natural Philosophers from the Shelf visited the Platform. Telni was the youngest of the party selected to greet the Shelf scholars.

And MinaAndry, a year or two younger, was the most junior of the visitors from Foro. It was natural they would end up together.

The formal welcomes were made at the lip of the Platform, under the vast, astonishing bulk of a tethered airship. The Shelf folk, used to solid ground under their feet, looked as if they longed to be far away from the Platform's edge, and the long drop to the Lowland below.

Then the parties broke up for informal discussions and demonstrations. The two groups, of fifty or so on each side, were to reassemble for a formal dinner that night in the Hall, the largest and grandest of the Platform's sentient Buildings. Thus the month-long expedition by the Shelf Philosophers would begin to address its goals, the start of a cultural and philosophical exchange between Shelf and Platform. It was a fitting project. The inhabitants of the Platform, their ancestors drawn long ago from Foro, were after all distant cousins of the Shelf folk.

And Telni found himself partnered in his work with MinaAndry.

There was much good-natured ribbing at this, and not a little jealousy in the glances of the older men. All the folk from the Shelf were handsome in their way, tall and elegant – not quite of the same stock as the Platform folk, who, shorter and heavier-built, were themselves different from the darker folk of the Lowland. They were three human groups swimming through time at different rates; of course they would diverge. But whatever the strange physics, MinaAndry was striking, tall yet athletic-looking with a loose physical grace, and blonde hair tied tightly back from a spindling-slim neck.

They walked across the Platform, through the city of living Buildings. The walls were gleaming white surfaces, neither hot nor cold, and pierced by sharp-edged doorways and windows.

Mina ran her hand across one smooth wall. Through an open door, inside the building, could be glimpsed signs of humanity: a bunk bed made of wood hauled up from the plain, a hearth, a cooking pot, cupboards and heaps of blankets and clothes, and outside a bucket to catch the rain. 'This place is so strange. We build things of stone, of concrete, or wood. But *this*—'

'We didn't build these structures at all. The Buildings grew here. We don't even know what they are made of – we call it Construction Material. That may not even be a human invention. They bud from units we call Flowers, and soak up the light from the storms. Like the Weapons, the Buildings are technology gone wild, made things modified by time.'

'It all feels new, although I suppose it's actually very old. Whereas Foro *feels* old. All that lichen-encrusted stone! It's like a vast tomb . . .'

But Telni knew that the town she called Foro was built on the ruins of a city itself called *New* Foro, devastated during the wars he remembered watching as a boy. He had naively expected the Shelf folk to be full of stories of that war when they came here. But the war was fifteen Platform years over, more than two hundred and fifty Shelf years, and what was a childhood memory to Telni was long-dead history to Mina.

'Is it true you feed your dead to the Buildings?' She asked this with a kind of frisson of horror.

'We wouldn't put it like that . . . They do need organic material. In the wild, you know, down on the Lowland, they preyed on humans. We do let them take our corpses. Why not?' He stroked a wall himself. 'It means the Buildings are made of *us*, our ancestors. Sometimes people have to die inside a Building. The Weapon that rules the Platform decrees it.'

'Why?'

'It seems to be studying Effigies. It thinks that the Construction Material of which Buildings are made excludes Effigies. Some of us are born inside Buildings, so no Effigy can enter us then. Others die within a Building, a special one we call the Morgue, in an attempt to trap the Effigies when they are driven out of their bodies. My own great-aunt died recently, and had to be taken inside the Morgue, but no Effigy was released.'

'It seems very strange to us,' Mina said cautiously. 'To Shelf folk, I mean. That here you are living out your lives on a machine, made by another machine.'

'It's not as if we have a choice,' Telni said, feeling defensive. 'We aren't allowed to leave.'

She looked down at her feet, which were clad in sensible leather shoes – not spindling hide like Telni's. 'I could tell that a machine built this place. It lacks a certain humanity.' She glanced at him uncertainly. 'Look, I'm speaking as a Philosopher. I myself am studying geology. The way time stratification affects erosion, with higher levels wearing away faster than the low, and the sluggish way rivers flow as they head down into the red . . . All this is a manifestation of depth, you see, depth that pivots into time. On the Shelf we all grew up on a cliff-top, over all that depth. But here we are suspended in the air on a paper-thin sheet! Whatever the intentions of the Weapon that governs you, it doesn't *feel* safe. A human designer would never have done it like this.'

'We live as best we can.'

'I'm sure.'

'I'll show you,' he said with a dash of defiance.

He took her to the very centre of the Platform, and the wheel that turned as always, drawn by teams of patient spindlings as they laboured to draw up supplies from the plain below.

MinaAndry patted the necks of the plodding beasts. The cargo jockeys, unloading buckets and pallets of supplies drawn up from the Lowland, stared at her curiously.

She said, 'How charming these beasts are! You know that on the Shelf they were driven to extinction during the Creationist-Mechanist Wars. We are slowly restocking with animals drawn up from the Lowland herds, but it's ferociously expensive . . .'

Something about the way she patted and stroked the tall, elegant creatures moved Telni deep inside. But he had to pull her aside when he saw a spindling was ready to cough up its faeces. Mina was aston-ished at the sight.

He took Mina's hand and led her to the centre of the Hub, close to the great hatch in the floor of the Platform, which revealed the goods-laden cables that dangled down to the Lowland far below.

Mina squealed and drew back. 'Oh! I'm sorry. Vertigo – what a foolish reaction that is! Although it proves my point about the uncom-fortable design.'

He pointed down through the hole. 'I brought you here to see my own work. I earn my living through my studies with an apothecary. But *this* is my passion . . .'

Holding tight to the rail, pushing a stray strand of hair back from her face, she peered down through the floor. From here, Telni's cradles of pendulums, of bobs and weights and simple control mechanisms, were clearly visible, attached in a train along one of the guide ropes that tethered the Platform to the Lowland plain.

'Pendulums?'

'Pendulums. I time their swing. From here I can vary the length and amplitude . . .' He showed her a rigging-up of levers he had fixed above the tether's anchor. 'Sometimes there's a snag, and I go down in a harness, or send one of the cargo jockeys.'

'How do you time them?'

'I have a clock the Weapon gave me. I don't understand how it works,' he said, and that admission embarrassed him. 'But it's clearly more accurate than any clock we can make. I have the pendulums spread out over more than a quarter of a kilometre. There's no record of anybody attempting to make such measurements over such a height difference. And by seeing how the period of the pendulums vary with height, what I'm trying to measure is—'

'The stratification of time. The higher up you raise your pendulums, the faster they will swing.' She smiled. 'Even a geologist understands that much. Isn't it about five per cent per metre?'

'Yes. But that's only a linear approximation. With more accurate measurements I've detected an underlying curved function . . .' The rate at which time flowed faster, Telni believed, was actually inversely proportional to the distance from the centre of Old Earth. 'It only *looks* linear, simply proportional to height, if you pick points close enough together that you can't detect the curve. And an inverse relationship makes sense, because that's the same mathematical form as the planet's gravitational potential, and time stratification is surely some kind of gravitational effect . . .' He hoped this didn't sound naive. His physics, based on philosophies imported from Foro centuries ago with the Platform's first inhabitants, was no doubt primitive compared to the teachings Mina had been exposed to.

Mina peered up at a sky where a flock of stars, brightly blueshifted, wheeled continually around an empty pole. 'I think I understand,' she said. 'My mathematics is rustier than it should be. That means that the time distortion doesn't keep rising on and on. It comes to some limit.'

'Yes! And that asymptotic limit is a distortion factor of around three hundred and twenty thousand – compared to the Shelf level, which we've always taken as our benchmark. So one year here corresponds to nearly a third of a million years, up there in the sky.'

She looked up in wonder. 'It is said that nearly ten thousand years have elapsed since the last Formidable Caress. An interval that spans all the history we know. But ten thousand years *here*—'

'Corresponds to about three billion years *there*. In the sky. We are falling into the future, Mina! And if you study the sky, as some do, you can see the working-out of time on a huge scale. A year up there passes in a mere hundred seconds down here, and we see the starscape march to that pace. And even as the sky turns, the stars in their flight spark and die, they swim towards and away from each other . . . We live in a great system of stars, which we see as a band across the sky. Some say there are other such systems, and that they too evolve and change.

'And some believe that once Old Earth was a world *without* this layering of time, a world like many others, perhaps, hanging among the stars. Its people were more or less like us. But Old Earth came under some kind of threat. And so the elders pulled a blanket of time over their world and packed it off to the future: "Old Earth is a jar of time, stopped up to preserve its children" – that's how it has been written.'

'That's all speculation.'

'Yes. But it would explain such a high differential of perceived time. I'm always trying to improve my accuracy. The pendulums need to be long enough to give a decent period, but not too long or else the time stratification becomes significant *even over the length of the pendulum itself*, and the physics gets very complicated—'

She slipped her hand into his. 'It's a wonderful discovery. Nobody before, maybe not since the last Caress, has worked this out before.'

He flushed, pleased. But something made him confess, 'I did need the Weapon's clock to measure the effects sufficiently accurately. And the Weapon set me asking questions about time in the first place.'

'It doesn't matter what the Weapon did. This is your work. You should be happy.'

'I don't feel happy,' he blurted.

She frowned. 'Why do you say that?'

Suddenly he was opening up to her in ways he'd never spoken to anybody else. 'Because I don't always feel as if I *fit*. As if I'm not like other people.' He looked at her doubtfully, wondering if she would conclude he was crazy. 'Maybe that's why the Machine has been drawn to me since the day I was born. And maybe that's why I'm turning out to be a good Philosopher. I can look at the world from outside, and see patterns others can't. Do you ever feel like that?'

Still holding his hand, she walked him back to the wheel and stroked a spindling's stubby mane, evidently drawing comfort from the simple physical contact. 'Sometimes,' she said. 'Maybe everybody does. But the world is as it is, and you just have to make the best of it. Do you get many birds on this island?'

The question surprised him. 'Not many. Just caged songbirds. Hard for them to find anywhere to nest.'

'I ask because I used to watch birds as a child. I'd climb up to a place we call the Attic . . . The birds use the time layers. The parents will nest at some low level, then go gathering food higher up. They've worked out they can take as long as they like, while the babies, stuck in slow time, don't get too hungry and are safe from the predators. Of course, the parents grow old faster, sacrificing their lives for their chicks.'

'I never saw anything like that. I never got the chance.' He shook his head, suddenly angry, resentful. 'Not on this island in the sky, as a servant of some machine. Sometimes I hope the next Caress comes soon and smashes everything up.'

She took both his hands and smiled at him. 'I have a feeling you're going to be a challenge. But I like challenges.'

'You do?'

'Sure. Or I wouldn't be here, spending a month with a bunch of old folk while *seventeen* months pass at home. Think of the parties I'm missing!'

His heart hammered, as if he had been lifted up into the blue. 'I've only known you hours,' he said. 'Yet I feel—'

'You should return to your work.' The familiar child's voice was strange, cold, jarring.

Telni turned. The Weapon was here, hovering effortlessly over the hole in the floor. His tethered boy stood some metres away, tense, obviously nervous of the long drop. The spindlings still turned their wheel, but the cargo jockeys stood back, staring at the sudden arrival of the Weapon, the maker and ruler of their world.

Telni's anger flared. He stepped forward towards the child, fists clenched. 'What do you want?'

'We have come to observe the formal congress this evening. The Philosophers from Shelf and Platform. There are many questions humans can address that we—'

'Then go scare all those old men and women. Leave me alone.' Suddenly, with Mina at his side, he could not bear to have the Weapon in his life once more, with its strange ageless boy on his umbilical. 'Leave me alone, I say!'

Powpy turned to look at Mina. 'She will not stay here. This girl, MinaAndry. Her home is on the Shelf. Her family, the Andry-Feri, is an ancient dynasty, with a lineage reaching back almost to the last Caress. She has responsibilities, to bear sons and daughters. *That* is her destiny. Not here.'

'I will stay if I wish,' Mina said. She was trembling, Telni saw, evidently terrified of the Weapon, this strange, ancient, wild machine from the dark Lowland. Yet she was facing it, answering it back.

Telni found himself snarling, 'Maybe she'll bear *my* sons and daughters.'

'No,' said the boy.

'What do you mean, no?'

'She is not suitable for you.'

'She's a scholar from Foro! She's from the stock you brought here to populate the Platform in the first place!'

'It is highly unlikely that she has an Effigy. Few in her family do. *Your* partner should have an Effigy. That is why—'

'Selective breeding,' Mina gasped. 'It's true. This machine really is breeding humans like cattle . . .'

'I don't care about Effigies!' Telni yelled. 'I don't care about you and your stupid projects.' He stalked over to the boy, who stood trembling, clearly afraid, yet unable to move from the spot.

'Telni, don't,' Mina called.

The boy said tremulously, 'Already you have done good and insight-ful work, which—'

Telni struck, a hard clap with his open hand to the side of the boy's head. Powpy went down squealing.

Mina rushed forward and pushed herself between Telni and the boy. 'What have you done?'

'He, it – all my life—'

'Is that this boy's fault? Oh, get away, you fool.' She knelt down and cradled the child's head on her lap. With the umbilical still dangling from the back of his neck, Powpy was crying, in a strange, contained way. 'He's going to bruise. I think you may have damaged his ear. And his jaw – no, child, don't try to talk.' She turned to the Weapon, which hovered impassively. 'Don't make him speak for you again. He's hurt.'

Telni opened his hands. 'Mina, please—'

'Are you still here?' she snarled. 'Go get help. Or if you can't do that, just go away. Go!'

And he knew he had lost her, in that one moment, with that one foolish blow. He turned away and headed towards the Platform's hospital to find a nurse.

He would not see the Weapon again for two decades.

The little boy walked into Telni's cell, trailing a silvery rope from the back of his neck.

Telni was huddled up in his bunk, a spindling-skin blanket over his body. Though feverish, Telni was shivering: drying out from the drink, and not for the first time. He scowled at the boy. 'You again.'

'Be fair,' the boy said. 'We have not troubled you for twenty years.'

'Not twenty for you.' His figuring was cloudy. 'Down on Lowland, less than a year—'

'This boy is not yet healed.'

Telni saw the boy's face was distorted on the right-hand side. 'I apologise.' He sat up. 'I apologise to *you* – what in the blue was your name?'

'Powpy.'

'I apologise to you, Powpy. Not to the thing that controls you. Where is it, by the way?'

'It would not fit through the door.'

Telni lay back and laughed.

'We did not expect to find you here.'

'In the drunk tank? Well, I got fired by the apothecary for emptying her drugs cabinet once too often. So it was the drink for me.' He patted his belly. 'At least it's putting fat on my bones.'

'Why this slow self-destruction?'

'Call it an experiment. I'm following in my father's footsteps, aren't I? After all, thanks to you, I have no more chance of happiness, of finding meaning in my life, than he did. And besides, it's all going to finish in a big smash soon, isn't it? As you smart machines no doubt know already.'

It didn't respond to that immediately. 'You never had a wife. Children.'

'Sooner no kids at all than to breed at your behest.'

'You have long lost contact with MinaAndry.'

'You could say that.' When the month-long tour of the Shelf Philosophers was concluded, she had gone home with them to continue her interrupted life on Foro. Since then, the accelerated time of the Shelf had whisked her away from him for ever. 'After – what, three hundred years up there, more? – she's dust, her descendants won't remember her, even the language she spoke will be half-forgotten. The dead get deader, you know, as every trace of their existence is expunged. That's one thing life on Old Earth has taught us. What do you want, anyway?'

'Your research into the Formidable Caress.'

'If you can call it research.'

'Your work is good, from what we have seen of that portion you have shared with other scholars. You cannot help but do good work, Telni. The curiosity I saw burning in that ten-year-old boy, long ago, is still bright.'

'Don't try to analyse me, you – *thing*.'

'Tell me what you have discovered . . .'

He could not hold back what he had learned, he found. At least the telling distracted him from his craving for drink.

After his discovery of the huge rate at which the inhabitants of Old Earth were plummeting into the future of the universe, Telni had become interested in spans of history. On the Shelf, written records went back some four thousand years of local time. These records had been compiled by a new civilisation rising from the rubble of an older culture, itself wrecked by a disaster known as the Formidable Caress, thought to have occurred some six thousand years before *that*.

'But in the external universe,' Telni said, 'ten thousand Shelf years corresponds to over three *billion* years. So much I deduced from my pendulums, swinging away beneath the Platform amid streams of spindling shit and cargo jockey piss . . . Everybody has always thought that the Caresses come about from local events. Something to do with the planet itself. But three billion years is long enough for events to unfold on a wider scale, a universal one. Time enough, according to what Shelf scholars have reconstructed, for stars to be born and to die, for whole galaxies to swim and jostle . . . "Galaxy", by the way, is a very old term for a system of stars. I found that out for myself. So, you see, I wondered if the Caresses could have some cosmic cause.'

'You started to correspond with scholars on the Shelf.'

'Yes. After that first visit by Mina's party we kept up a regular link, with visits from them – once every couple of years for us, once a generation for them . . . I spoke to the astronomers over there, about what they saw in the sky. And their archaeologists, about what had been seen in the past. There was always snobbishness, you know. Those of us down in the red think we are better because we are closer to the original stock of Old Earth; those up in the blue, who have produced more generations, believe they are superior products of evolution. None of that bothered *me*. And as their decades ticked by, I think I helped shape whole agendas of research by my sheer persistence.'

'It must have been rewarding for you.'

'Academically, yes. I've never had any problem, academically. It's the rest of my life that's a piece of shit.'

'Tell us what you discovered.'

'I don't have my notes, my books—'

'Just tell us.'

He sat up and stared into the face of the eerily unchanged boy – who, to his credit, did not flinch. 'The first Caress destroyed almost everything of what went before, on the Shelf and presumably elsewhere. Almost, but not all. Some trace inscriptions, particularly carvings on stone, have survived. Images, fragmentary, and bits of text. Records of something in the sky.'

'What something?'

'The Galaxy is a disc of stars, a spiral. We, on a planet embedded in the disc, see this in cross section, as a band of light in the sky. Much of it obscured by dust.'

'And?'

'The ancients' last records show *two* bands, at an angle to each other. There is evidence that the second band grew brighter, more prominent. The chronological sequence is difficult to establish – the best of these pieces were robbed and used as hearths or altar stones by the fallen generations that followed . . .'

'Nevertheless,' the boy prompted.

'Nevertheless, there is evidence that something came from out of the sky. Something huge. Another galaxy, so some believe – so *I* believe. And then there are crude, scrawled images – cartoons, really – of explosions. All over the sky. A million suns, suddenly appearing.' He imagined survivors, huddled in the ruins of their cities, scratching what they saw into fallen stones. 'After that – nothing, for generations. People were too busy reinventing agriculture to do much astronomy. That was ten thousand years ago.

'The next bit of evidence comes from around three thousand years back, when a Natural Philosopher called HuroEldon established new centres of scholarship, at Foro and down on the Lowland . . . Once again we started keeping good astronomical records. And not long after Huro's time, the astronomers observed in the sky—'

'Another band of stars.'

'No. *A spiral* – a spiral of stars, ragged, the stars burning and dying, a wheel turning around a point of intense brightness. This object swam towards us, so it seemed, and at its closest approach there was another flare of dazzling new stars, speckled over the sky – but there was no Caress, not this time. The spiral receded into the dark.'

'Tell us what you believe this means.'

'I think it's clear. This other spiral is a galaxy like our own. The two orbit each other.' He mimed this with his fists, but his hands were shaking; shamed before the boy's steady gaze, he lowered his arms. 'As twin stars may orbit one another. But unlike stars galaxies are big, diffuse structures. They must tear at each other, ripping open those lacy spirals. Perhaps when they brush, they create bursts of starbirth. A Formidable Caress indeed.

'The last Caress was a first pass, when the second galaxy came close enough to *our* part of our spiral to cause a great flaring of stars – and that flaring, a rain of light falling from the blue, was what shattered our world. Then after HuroEldon's time, two billion years later externally, there was another approach – this one not so close, not a true Caress; it was spectacular but did no damage, not to us. And then . . .'

'Yes?'

He shrugged, peering up at the Construction-Material roof of the cell. 'The sky is ragged, full of ripped-apart spiral arms. The two galaxies continue to circle each other, perhaps heading for a full merger, a final smash. And that, perhaps, will cause a new starburst flare, a new Caress.'

The boy stood silently, considering this, though one leg quivered, as if itchy. He asked: 'When?'

'That I couldn't calculate. I tried to do some mathematics on the orbit. Long time since I stayed sober enough to see *that* through. But there's one more scrap of information in the archaeology. There was always a tradition that the second Caress would follow ten thousand years after the first, Shelf time. Maybe that's a memory of what the smart folk who lived before the first Caress were able to calculate. They *knew*, not only about the Caress that threatened them, but also what would follow. Remarkable, really.'

'Ten thousand years,' the boy said. 'Which is—'

'About now.' Telni grinned. 'If the world ends, do you think they will let me out of here to see the show?'

'You have done remarkable work, Telni. This is a body of evidence extracted from human culture that we could not have assembled for ourselves.' Even as he spoke these calm words, the boy trembled, and Telni saw piss drip down his bare leg.

Telni snorted. 'You really aren't too good at running the people you herd, are you, machine?'

Ignoring the dribble on his leg, Powpy spoke on. 'Regarding the work, however. *We* are adept at calculation. Perhaps we can take these hints and reconstruct the ancients' computations, or even improve on them.'

'So you'll know the precise date of the end of the world? That will help. Come back and tell me what you figure out.'

'We will.' The boy turned and walked away, leaving piss-footprints on the smooth floor.

Telni laughed at him, lay back on his bunk, and tried to sleep.

It was to be a very long time before Telni saw the Weapon and its human attendant again.

'He refuses to die. It's as simple as that. There's nothing but his own stubbornness keeping him alive . . .'

His hearing was so bad now that it was as if his ears were stuffed full of wool. But, lying there on his pallet, he could hear every word they said.

And, though he needed a lot of sleep these days, he was aware when they moved him into the Morgue, ready for him to die, ready to capture his Effigy-spirit when it was released from his seventy-seven-year-old body.

'Leave me in here if you like, you bastards.' He tried to laugh, but it just made him cough. 'I'm just going to lie here as long as necessary.'

'As long as necessary for what?'

'For it to come back again.'

But, more than thirty years since the last visitation, only a handful of the medical staff knew what he was talking about.

In the end, of course, it came.

He woke from another drugged sleep to find a little boy standing beside his bed.

He struggled to sit up. 'Hey, Powpy. How's it going with you? You've grown, a little. You're not afraid of me, are you? Look, I'm old and disgusting, but at least I can't slap you around the head any more, can I?'

He thought he saw a flicker of something in the boy's eyes. Forgiveness? Pity? Fear? Contempt? Well, he deserved the latter. But then Powpy spoke in that odd monotone, so familiar even after all these years. 'We were here at the beginning of your life. Now here we are at the end.'

'Yes.' He tried to snap his fingers, failed. 'Just another spark in the flames for you, right? And now you've come to see me give up my Effigy so you can trap it in this box of yours.'

'We would not describe it as—'

He grabbed the boy's arm, trying to grip hard. 'Listen, Weapon. You can have my Effigy. What do I care? But I'm not going to die like this. Not here, not now.'

'Then where, and when?'

'*Fifty years*,' he whispered. He glanced at the medical staff, who hovered at the edges of the Building. 'I did my own calculations. Took me ten years. Well, I had nothing better to do . . . Fifty years, right? That's all the time we've got left, until the fireworks.'

The boy said gravely, 'We imagine our model of the galaxies' interaction is somewhat more sophisticated than yours. But your answer is substantially correct. You understand that this Caress will be different. *Those on the Platform will survive.* The Construction Material of the Buildings will shelter them. That was always one long-term purpose of the Platform project, to provide refuge. And from this seed, the recovery of civilisation after the Caress should be much more rapid.'

Telni cackled weakly. 'You built us a shelter from a Formidable

430

Caress? Well, well, you do care. But the cities of the Shelf – Foro, Puul—'

'People will survive in caves, underground. But the vast loss of life, the destruction of the ecology, of their agriculture—'

'Serves those bastards right. They lost interest in talking to me decades ago.' Which was true. But since the Creationist-Mechanist Wars, there had been centuries of peace on the Shelf – and they had built something beautiful and splendid up there, a chain of cities like jewels in the night, cities that sparkled in the time-accelerated view of witnesses on the Platform. In his head Telni imagined a race of blueshifted Minas, beautiful, clear-eyed, laughing. 'Well. There's nothing I can do for them.' He struggled to sit straighter. 'But there's something I want you to do for me. You owe me, artefact. Now you're going to take away my soul. Well, you can have it. But you can give me something back in return. I want to see the Caress.'

'You have only weeks to live. Days, perhaps.'

'*Then take me down into the red.* No matter how little time I have left, you can find a pit deep enough on this time-shifted world to squeeze in fifty Platform years.' Exhausted, he fell back coughing; a nurse hurried over to lower him gently to his blankets. 'And one more thing.'

'More demands?'

'Let this boy go.'

When Telni woke again, he found himself staring up at a sky of swirling blue stars. 'Made it, by my own redshifted arse.'

A face hovered over him, a woman's. 'Don't try to move.'

'You're in the way.' He tried to sit up, failed, but kept struggling until she helped him up and he could see.

He was on a plain – *on the ground*, his pallet set on red, rusty dirt, down on the true ground of Old Earth for the first time in his life. Something like a rail track curled across his view. Buildings of Construction Material were scattered around like a giant's toys. He got the immediate sense this was a kind of camp, not permanent.

And figures moved in the distance. At first sight they looked human. But then something startled them, and they bucked and fled, on six legs.

'What are *those*?'

'They are called Centaurs.' Powpy was standing beside him, his neck umbilical connecting him to the Weapon, which hovered as impassive

431

as ever, though rusty dirt clung to its sleek hide. 'Human-spindling hybrids.'

He stared, astonished. But he had no time left for wonder. 'You were going to let this kid go.'

'He will be released,' said the woman sternly. 'My name's Ama, by the way.'

Which had been his mother's name. He felt a stab of obscure guilt. 'Glad to meet you.'

'You should be. I'm a nurse. I volunteered to stay with you, to keep you alive when they brought you down here.'

'No family, I take it.'

'Not any more. And when this business is done, I'll be taking Powpy here back up top, to the Platform. You did ask for him to be released, didn't you?'

'His mother and father—'

'Long dead,' she whispered.

'We're all orphans here, then.'

Powpy said solemnly, 'We will have to shelter in a Construction-Material Building to ride out the Caress. We are deep enough that it should be brief—'

'How deep?'

'We are in the Abyss. Once the bed of a deep ocean, far below the offshore plains you call the Lowland . . . Deep enough.'

'Nice sky.'

'Most of the stars' radiation is blueshifted far beyond your capacity to see it.'

'And how long – ow!' There was a sharp pain in his chest.

Ama grabbed him and lowered him back against a heap of pillows. 'Just take it easy. That was another heart attack.'

'*Another* . . .'

'They've been coming thick and fast.'

'That Weapon won't want me dying out in the open. Not after all this.'

'We have a Morgue designated just over there,' Ama said. 'Your bed's on wheels.'

'Good planning.'

'Not long now,' murmured Powpy.

But he, the boy, wasn't looking at the sky. Telni touched Powpy's chin, and lifted his face. 'He should see this for himself.'

'Very well,' the Weapon said through the boy's mouth.

'Why, Weapon? Why the grand experiment? Why the Platform? *Why are you so fascinated by the Effigies?'*

'We believe the Effigies are not native to the Old Earth, any more than the spindlings or the lightmoss or—'

'But they're pretty closely bound up to humans. They live and die with us.'

'They do not die. So we believe. We have mapped disturbances, deep in the Old Earth . . . We believe there is a kind of nest of them, a colony of Effigies that dwells deep in the core of the planet. They emerge to combine with humans, with infants at birth. *Some* infants – we don't know how they choose. And we don't know how they bond either. But after the human carrier's death, the Effigy symbiote is released, and returns to the core colony. Something of the human is taken with it. We believe.'

'Memories.'

'Perhaps.'

'And are these memories brought back up from this core pit the next time an Effigy surfaces?'

'Perhaps. Everything about this world is designed, or modified. Perhaps the purpose is to preserve something of the memory of humanity across epochal intervals.'

'Maybe this is why I always felt like something in me really doesn't belong in this time or place.'

'We Machines can study this only at second-hand. It is something about humanity that no Machine shares.'

'I think you're jealous. Aren't you, Machine? You can farm us, keep us as lab animals. But you can't have *this*.'

'There is no reliable mapping between human emotions and the qualia of our own sensorium . . .'

But he didn't hear the rest. Another stabbing in his chest, a pain that knifed down his left arm. The nurse leaned over him.

And the sky exploded.

These weren't just new stars. They were stars that detonated, each flaring brighter than the rest of the sky put together, then vanishing as quickly, blown-out matches.

'Supernovas,' said the boy, Powpy. 'That is the ancient word. A wave of supernovas, triggered by the galaxy collision, giant exploding stars flooding nearby space with lethal radiation, a particle sleet . . .'

But Telni couldn't talk, couldn't breathe.

'He's going,' the nurse said. 'Get him to the Morgue.'

He glimpsed people running up – no, not people, they were six-legged, Centaurs – and his bed was shoved forward, across the rusty dirt towards the enclosure of a Building. He tried to protest, to cling to his view of that astounding sky as long as he could. But he couldn't even breathe, and it felt as if a sword were being twisted in his chest.

They got him indoors. He lay back, rigid with pain, staring at a Construction-Material roof that seemed to recede from him.

And a glow, like the glow of the sky outside, suffused the inside of his head, his very eyes.

'It's happening,' he heard the nurse say, wonder in her voice. 'Look, it's rising from his limbs . . . His heart has stopped.' She straddled him and pounded at his chest, even as a glow lit up her face, the bare flesh of her arms – a glow coming from *him*.

He remembered – a glimmering tetrahedron, looming, an electric-blue framework swallowing him up – memories that had nothing to do with *this* world . . .

He heard Powpy call, 'Do you know who you are? Or who you *were*?'

And suddenly *he knew*, as if his eyes had suddenly focused, after years of myopia. With the last of the air in his lungs he struggled to speak. 'Not again. Not again!'

The nurse peered into his eyes. 'Stay with me, Telni!'

'Who are you? *Who are you?*'

The light detonated from deep inside him. Suddenly he *filled* this box of Construction-Material, he was contained within it, and he rattled, anguished. But there was the door, a way out. Somehow he fled that way, seeking the redshift . . .

Even after the Xeelee had finally won their war against humanity, the stars continued to age, too rapidly. The Xeelee completed their great Projects and fled the cosmos.

Time unravelled. Dying galaxies collided like clapping hands. But even now the story was not yet done. The universe itself prepared for another convulsion, greater than any it had suffered before.

And then—

'Who are you?'

'My name is Michael Poole.'

THE XEELEE SEQUENCE – TIMELINE

Singularity: Big Bang

ERA: Earth
AD 476–2005: Events of **Coalescent**.
AD 2047: Events of **Transcendent** (see also *c*.AD 500,000).

ERA: Expansion
AD 3000+: Opening up of the Solar System.
AD 3685: 'Return to Titan'.
AD 3717: Launch of GUTship *Cauchy*. Events of **Timelike Infinity** begin.
AD 3829: The Emergency: time-travel invasion by Occupation-Era Qax (**Timelike Infinity**).
AD 3951: Events of **Ring** begin (see also *c*. AD 5,000,000).
AD 4820: 'Starfall'. Collapse of Empire of Sol.

ERA: Squeem Occupation
AD 4874: Conquest of human planets by Squeem.
AD 4925: Overthrow of Squeem.
AD 5071: 'Remembrance'.

ERA: Qax Occupation
AD 5088: Conquest of human planets by Qax.
AD 5274: 'Endurance'. Return to Solar System of GUTship *Cauchy*. Launch of backward time-travel invasion by Qax (**Timelike Infinity**).
AD 5407: Overthrow of Qax. Third Expansion begins under Coalition.

ERA: The War with the Ghosts
AD 5810: 'The Seer and the Silverman'.

ERA: The War to End Wars
AD 24973: Events of **Exultant**.

AD 104,858+: Events of **Raft**.

c.AD 193,700: Events of **Flux**.

c. AD 500,000: Events of **Transcendent** (see also AD 2047). The retreat of mankind begins.

AD 978,225: 'Gravity Dreams'.

c.AD 1,000,000: Final siege of the Solar System by Xeelee. The Saving of Old Earth.

ERA: Photino Victory

c.AD 5,000,000+: Events of **Ring** (see also AD 3951).

ERA: Old Earth

c. AD 3.8 billion years: 'PeriAndry's Quest'.

c. AD 4 billion years: 'Climbing the Blue'.

c. AD 4.5 billion years: 'The Time Pit'.

c. AD 4.8 billion years: 'The Lowland Expedition'.

c. AD 5 billion years: 'Formidable Caress'.

Singularity: Timelike Infinity

This outline timescale provides the context for the stories in this collection, as well as the novels published in the Xeelee Sequence so far. Other short fiction has been collected in *Vacuum Diagrams* (Harper-Collins, 1997) and *Resplendent* (Gollancz, 2006). For a full timeline of the 'Xeelee Sequence' of novels and stories, please visit:

www.stephen-baxter.com